To my dear friend ♡ —

With best wishes,

Ron / Roméo

April, 2006

1- 718-317-7328

Let Us Be True

A Novel

By

Roméo Mannarino

authorHOUSE™

1663 LIBERTY DRIVE, SUITE 200
BLOOMINGTON, INDIANA 47403
(800) 839-8640
WWW.AUTHORHOUSE.COM

First published by AuthorHouse 11/30/04

ISBN: 1-4208-0385-9 (sc)
ISBN: 1-4208-0386-7 (dj)

Library of Congress Control Number: 2004097509

Printed in the United States of America
Bloomington, Indiana

This book is printed on acid-free paper.

This novel is dedicated to the memory of my parents, Andrea and Fortunata Mannarino.
It is also dedicated to my beloved wife, Rita, whose support, devotion and encouragement made the writing of this novel possible.

Ah, love, let us be true
To one another! For the world, which seems
To lie before us like a land of dreams,
So various, so beautiful, so new,
Hath really neither joy, nor love, nor light,
Nor certitude, nor peace, nor help for pain . . . ."

Matthew Arnold,
From *Dover Beach*

One

The house lights dimmed. The audience buzz stopped suddenly as the conductor walked onto the stage. Enthusiastic applause broke out and Maestro Lorelli bowed twice and faced the orchestra. The silence was again palpable. Lorelli lifted his baton and the dramatic opening of the *Resurrection Symphony* began to transfix his listeners. This was one musical work that Lorelli had become associated with both in Europe and in America. He had made it a specialty of his and he always conducted it without a score, for the music was embedded in his subconscious and needed only to be called up at will. It was a composition that Lorelli identified with on a number of levels, both musical and philosophic.

As his eyes surveyed the orchestra, faces he had become familiar with over the past few years, Lorelli could feel good about himself. He had come a long way, had accomplished much in his chosen profession. He stood on the podium in Symphony Hall, conducting a world-class orchestra. As the music swelled to its first great climax, Lorelli pondered the composer's own feeling that this movement represents a search for the meaning of life. Lorelli's connection to the music started here, for hadn't he been searching for that same meaning all of his life? Lorelli loved his work. He loved everything about the music he studied and played and conducted. He was passionate about everything connected with this world—the instruments, the musicians who gave all of themselves in the service of music. Each and every one of the great composers were personal friends of his. He knew them, knew their lives, their compositions, how they came to write them, how they struggled for recognition. Daniel Lorelli was immersed in this world, and he was happy. Just then, inexplicably, a thought flashed across his mind, something about a man gaining the whole world and losing his soul. Where is that from he wondered. Biblical, certainly.

1

"I must put these thoughts aside for now," Lorelli mused as his arms swung about and his facial expressions and body language transmitted all he needed to convey to the musicians. He would return to these reflections after the concert.

On the drive home, Daniel Lorelli realized why that phrase had popped into his mind. A few days earlier he had received a note of congratulations from his brother Stephen, a Roman Catholic priest. Stephen had read an article about his brother in the *New York Times* and sent him a congratulatory note.

"You have certainly come a long way and achieved a great deal," it read. "My best wishes and love always. Stephen." That was really nice, but at the bottom of the note Stephen had added: "*For what does it profit a man to gain the whole world and lose his soul.*" *(Mark, 8).* Daniel had been so annoyed, even angry on reading that phrase. It wasn't as if he and Stephen had never discussed his apostasy. They had had meetings for months, at Stephen's request, and had gone over all the reasons, all the beliefs they could no longer agree on. No, Daniel had no concern at all about losing his soul. And what about gaining the whole world? In a sense he *had* gained everything in the world that meant anything to him, but not in the material way that Stephen was implying. Yes, his life was a rich one, a life of success and love, and for the first time he was spiritually fulfilled. It had not been an easy thing to do. His family and others refused to understand his position, but Daniel knew it could not be otherwise. For them, he had transgressed, gone beyond the limit. One could commit evil acts and still be accepted, for it was the very nature of their faith to forgive, and this was commendable. But a non-believer, particularly one who had been brought up to *believe*, this could not be tolerated. Daniel would never try to change their beliefs, even if he came to feel that so many of them were ultimately without real meaning, false, dishonest. Nevertheless, he retained a certain fondness—was it a kind of nostalgia?—for some of the religious practices that had informed his childhood and youth. Certain aspects of the liturgy, the rituals, the emotions that could be kindled by prayers had become a part of his very inner being. They no longer had the power over him they had once had. That could never happen again, but there was an emotional tug similar to how one feels when recalling a cherished moment from an earlier part of one's life. It was like the memory of a neighborhood one grew up in, the sounds and smells and various shades of colors, or the very special sensation that comes on recalling falling in love for the first time.

As the sleek Lexus approached the Boston suburb where Daniel would spend the night, his mind drifted back, recalling in swift succession, from the present to the distant past, key persons and events that had come

2

together to make him the man he was today. When it came to faith, there was no one like his dear mother. She had had her faith instilled from earliest childhood, growing up in a small village in Southern Italy. He remembered her enthusiasm whenever she spoke to him about the wonders of her religion. He had seen ample evidence of this kind of devotion when he had visited her place of birth himself. Such good people, he thought. They had had hard lives and sacrificed much to move to a new country so very far away. Daniel smiled to himself and an aura of warmth and, yes, pride, engulfed him as he recalled that one hundred years had passed since his grandfather, his mother's father had first arrived in America.

Two

On a crisp clear day the residents of Longobardi can see the island of Stromboli. Looking out from the foothills, from their modest if well made homes, the view could be quite fine or even spectacular. When visible, the island appears as an irregularly shaped mass. When the volcano becomes even moderately active, smoke can be seen rising above it into the clear blue sky. In centuries past, many of the more ignorant inhabitants of the village believed it to be an island inhabited by demons, and the smoke a manifestation of the certain burning of innocent souls—mariners who had had the misfortune to sail too close to its magnetic periphery, or perhaps even an extension of that fiery place below where damned evildoers spent their eternities. Others saw it as a miraculous apparition, with the smoke symbolic of a liturgical ceremony, as of a magnificent offering of incense to the Almighty.

Longobardi, called *Lunguvardu* by its native citizens in the Calabrese dialect peculiar to this town and also to the largest nearby city, Cosenza, capital of the province, was founded according to the best available scholarship sometime between 650 and 715 A.D. Long bearded (*lunga barba*) Germanic conquerors swept through the area and settled there, mating with the women and producing offspring whose descendents centuries later would acknowledge that their blond hair and blue eyes most probably originated in the genes of these sometimes benevolent warriors. The town boasted some 6,000 inhabitants during the middle eighteen hundreds and would maintain that population level through the early years of the 20th century, decreasing to some 4,000 inhabitants by the 1940's. Later, with increased emigration both abroad and within Italy, that figure would dwindle down to between 2500 and 3000 inhabitants.

Such was its natural beauty that all who had been born in Longobardi would speak of it with pride and emotion throughout their lives. Those who made their homes there would boast to others that they were from *Lunguvardu*, always displaying an air of superiority, especially when confronted with claims of the merits of nearby towns such as Amantea, Belmonte-Calabro, Sambiase, Falconara-Albanese, or Fiummefreddo-Bruzio. The emigrants, whether they settled in New York, Cleveland, Pittsburgh, Buenos Aires, Caracas or dozens of other cities would recall with nostalgia their very special *paese*, the home town that they loved but had to leave.

The homes had been built of stones and lime that had been worked into a kind of cement, beginning some 200 meters above sea level and continuing on upwards for another 130 meters where the center of the town burgeoned with houses one after another, one on top of another, sometimes built so close together that the surrounding streets were defined by their width, streets that were not designed for the automobiles that would squeeze their way through them centuries later. Each house has a roof composed of red or reddish brown *tegole*, known in the Calabrese dialect as *ceramili*. These curved tiles, composed of terracotta, provided a fail-proof system for keeping the rain out, for one tile fit into another and any water would flow down easily into a drain. Above the heat of the town, going high into the upper hills, more homes had been built and these were inhabited by that particular group of citizens referred to somewhat condescendingly by their neighbors, those who lived *nel paese*, in the village, as *campagnoli*. No matter where one lives in this magnificent accretion of rustic native architecture, the view is spectacular. To the west the vast expanse of the *Mare Tirreno* provides a panorama of azure in a sky that meets the deep blue of the water in a communion of sweeping grandeur. To the east the hills rise up as if in supplication to the majestic mountains high above, reaching their zenith at the peak that became known as *Monte Cocuzzo* from *cocuzzolo*, the crown or highest point.

In the spring and autumn, the air is cool and refreshing, blowing strongly through the vast expanse of the dense saturation of trees and other greenery, planted or dispersed throughout the hills and on up to the mountain peaks. Summer brings days of torrid heat that sends many to the *marina* to dip themselves into the sparkling waters. Winters are mild compared with many other parts of the world and snow is almost never seen except in the high mountains.

In the early morning light, as the wind sweeps in from the sea, an inhabitant standing in this village will invariably experience emotions and stirrings of the soul that evoke a sense of eternity. A feeling of immortality engulfs one gazing out over the waters, knowing assuredly that one's ancestors stood here and saw and felt all that he or she sees and feels. A villager's identification with the past, with those whose names and lives are recalled lovingly in highly detailed and joyfully retold stories by the older *paesani*, provides him or her with the certainty of truly belonging to a place. The sea and the world beyond beckon, but the home exerts its own pressure. Finally, the decision must be made to remain or to depart.

The morning that Francesco Nardi , was preparing to leave for Naples, with New York his ultimate port of disembarkation, he looked out of his bedroom window and saw the outline of Stromboli in the far distance across the Tyrrehenian Sea. He took this as a good omen for his trip to America, since it had been some time since he was last able to glimpse this natural wonder. He had only to eat his breakfast, *prima collazione* of moistened bread, left over from the previous day's dinner, along with some milk—goat's milk from goats raised by nearby *contadini*—and prepare to take his leave of his mother, father, two brothers and two sisters before joining the three other men from his village who were also making the four day journey by horse and wagon to Naples to embark on a ship that hosted two classes of passengers, 60 in first class and another 2,500 in third class. No second class cabins were provided for. Francesco, called *Ciccio* by his family and friends, would, of course, find himself among those in the lowest class, called at that time "*Passeggeri Generale.*" His trip had been paid for by a *paesano*, a successful emigrant to America from Paola, a town about 35 kilometers from Longobardi, who had developed a construction company in New York and needed cheap labor to work on the many projects his company undertook. Every year or two, he or his brother would return to Calabria to recruit workers, strong young men who could be relied on to work 14 hour days of grueling intensity. Each week they would get very little money until the cost of their trip was paid back to their benefactor.

Francesco had been recruited for this purpose and he was excited about the prospect of seeing the "new world." His father Gaetano was born in Longobardi in 1855 and married his mother, Rosina Pucci in 1875. Rosina had her first baby at the age of nineteen when she delivered her first son, Francesco in 1876. Francesca was born next in 1877, Emilio in 1878, Claudio in 1880 and Patrizia in 1881. Gaetano managed to provide for his family by making excellent shoes and boots that were highly valued by the shoemaker's clientele. His shop was in a small room next to his home that faced one of the smaller *vie*. Gaetano was against Ciccio's going so far away, but being a man of some vision, he knew that there was not very much in their village to ensure anything but a dull future for his first-born son. Perhaps Francesco would make the way for his brothers and sisters so that they too could eventually settle in America and, who knew, even he and Rosina could possibly follow their children to a better life for the entire family. Others had gone and settled there, and tales came back of undreamed of riches and well-being.

Rosina had a sister, Laura, who had gone to America with her husband, Amadeo Goffreddo, some ten years earlier. They had settled in Pittsburgh and Rosina had never heard from her sister since she left. She heard stories from returning friends and relatives that her sister had become very well-to-do. Rosina had suggested to her son that he try to look up his aunt after he arrived in America. Francesco tried to explain to his mother that he had been told that the place where his aunt lived was quite far from New York, where he was going to live.

"How far can it be?" Rosina asked. "After all, America is America."

Francesco sighed, "Oh, Mamma, Italy is Italy too, but how long does it take to get to Rome? To Milan? In America the distances are even greater, and I will be working, with very little free time." His mother was placated.

"All right," she said. "But see if you can find out anything about your aunt, anything at all."

At the age of nineteen, Francesco still had no idea of anything to do with women. Of course, he knew that men and women had to have sexual intercourse to have children and he also knew—there were enough discussions among the young men of the town about the various pleasures that could be experienced by discovering and uncovering that wondrous place between the legs of a desirable woman, but he had never left his village without his parents and had never even gotten close enough to any of the lovely young girls he saw in the *paese* to stir his blood and allow him to have any fantasies, whether they could come to fruition or not. At the age of fourteen he was apprenticed to his own father and learned to make shoes, if without the skill or beauty of execution that marked the work of Gaetano. He was not happy making shoes, and the prospect of going to work in construction, in another environment, in another country with all kinds of fascinating things happening all around him excited him so much that he could not wait for his chance. The stories that others had brought back about life in America were so exotic and yes, even fantastic, that any young man who heard them could not fail to be impressed and to wish for an opening that would allow him to become a part of that splendid panorama. Francesco, then, had never really thought about finding someone to share his life with. He knew from observing everything around him that this would come about at some point in the future. Once the possibility of leaving became a reality, however, he wondered how long he would be away. Would he make enough money to return home for a visit and then go back to America? He pondered the likelihood that he would work for a few years after paying off his debt for the passage to America. Then he would see if he could pay for his brother's trip, and then his sister's— although it was likely that his sister would marry before that time and would have to remain behind with her husband, even if his mother and father were to make the journey themselves. As for his other sister and brother, he could not think far enough ahead. He liked to imagine that he would do well enough to come back and marry one of the girls from his town and take her back with him to the United States. But who would he choose? Who would accept him and agree to leave her own family to go abroad? The more he thought about this, the more one particular face appeared in his mind's eye, a young woman then barely sixteen years old, Maria Saggio. He had seen her in church and as she made her way through the village carrying fruits and vegetables that her parents grew and sold to those they referred to as *i nobili* (nobles). They had never spoken, but twice they had exchanged a glance, a practice that was absolutely unheard of as far as young women were concerned. Maria had heard her mother talking to her aunt once while walking out of church about what a fine young man Francesco was. She said that Rosina had raised a son with true religious piety, since there was never a time when Emilia Saggio went to church that she did not see him taking Communion. Maria passed Francesco with her mother one Sunday as they exited the church and that was their first look at one another. Their second brief encounter came some months later when Maria went to Gaetano's *bottega* to pick up a pair of shoes that had been repaired, a pair that belonged to an old aunt who had died—in actuality Maria's first pair of shoes since she went barefooted most of the time, as did most of the girls and women of the town.

Both the Nardi and the Saggio families, truly like most of the families that inhabited Longobardi then, were extremely religious and their homes were filled with images of *Gesu Cristo, il cuore sacro di Jesù* (a vivid image of the sacred heart of Jesus, bright red and wounded by the sins of the world), *La Madonna*, saints—local saints like Santa Domenica, San Francesco di Paola, Santa Innocenza, as well as others like San Giuseppe, San Antonio and more. In some families the men did not go to church, but in all the families the women went all the time, except for those who lived far from the town, on the other side of the river that ran down from the mountain (perhaps not a real river, indeed a swiftly running brook, but it was referred to as *fiume* by everyone) and those too in the higher hills who would only come to town on Sunday mornings. From the earliest age children would be taught about Jesus and his Virgin mother Maria, about how all one had to do was to call on them in time of need or whenever there was any kind of problem and how their prayers would certainly be heard. And one did not have to bother Jesus or Mary if it was a little matter. Then one could pray to the saints. Francesco thought about Maria and how pious she looked when she walked back from Holy Communion and he thought that he could some day be happy with such a woman. There was also the matter of her beauty, for she was without a doubt the most beautiful unmarried young woman in Longobardi, or for that matter, most likely in the entire Province of Cosenza.

Emilio and Claudio were still asleep in their bed as Francesco made his final preparations. He had one wooden box which contained all his personal items, clothing, hairbrush, and a few other things he did not want to leave behind such as a book he had read when he was fourteen about the lives of some Italian saints and a small hammer his father had given him when he first started to make shoes. The wooden container had been made for him by the local cabinet maker and a handle was securely fastened to one side of it. His mother was already up and preparing the *orzo* and milk. Soon all were awake and ready to take care of the day's first principal activities, disposing of the waste and gathering the day's water supply into buckets and bottles. Even though Francesco was leaving for who knew how long, it was natural that he should join his brothers in supplying the household. In those days running water within a house was unheard of. *Paesani* would get their water from one fountain or another, depending on which was closest to their homes. The Nardi's went to the fountain *davant'u Cumunu*, in front of the town hall and waited their turn. One the buckets and bottles were filled, they would take them all back to the house and distribute the water according to the day's needs. The water in bottles was saved for cooking; that in the buckets was needed for washing themselves. Once a week, usually on a Saturday night, more water was needed so that each family member could bathe in preparation for Sunday Mass, when cleanliness of body was deemed akin to Godliness, but the bathing never involved total immersion. That would be possible only in warm weather when one went down to the ocean.

Before the water was even gathered, the emptying of the buckets of human waste that accumulated during the previous day and night had to be dealt with. Some families used an area below the house for these purposes while others used the attic. Those less enterprising *paesani* would crouch down or stand over their buckets. But there were those who already made makeshift toilets for themselves, setting off an area that somewhat resembled a toilet, like those that would be common later in the new century. A bench with a round opening that one could sit upon was devised and the bucket fit neatly beneath it. Wealthier *Longobardesi* made use of the services of poorer women, widows, spinsters, to come in and take out the *merda*, but usually the parents emptied the buckets until their children were old enough to share in this unpleasant and, for some, humiliating activity. There were always those who made jokes about the carrying of waste to a field that was set aside for the purpose. In Spring and Summer small tomatoes could be seen growing in these fields of human waste. Tomato seeds in the feces grew into tomato plants that had natural fertilization, plenty of it in fact. These tomatoes were similar to what would become known as "cherry" tomatoes at a future time. (Years later, transplanted Longobardesi would see these tomatoes in stores or find them in salads in restaurants, and there were those who could never bring themselves to partake of these cultivated vegetables, recalling how they appeared in a field of dung.) This activity of carrying the waste to the field was especially trying for young girls who would return home crying, *"Non voglio farlo più."* Often when a young woman reached the age of sixteen, her mother would see to it that she no longer had to share in this activity, since among some it was considered unattractive, and they even assumed it could spoil the maiden's chances of making a good marriage, but this was just nonsense.

After the chores were completed, the Nardi family sat together around the small table, each one downcast knowing they would soon be missing a member of their family, their oldest brother and son without whom they had never been. The thought was painful and soon the tears would flow uncontrollably for all of them. A call from below the window from Francesco's good friend Paolo Morrone indicated that it was time to leave.

Rosina grasped her son's neck with both hands and pulled him to her.

"God protect you my son. May our blessed Mother keep you in her care and drive all evil away from you. Don't stay in the company of any bad people. Stay with your *paesani* and save your money. St. Francis protect you now and for always."

Her voice was cracking and her tears were flowing profusely. Her words brought the emotional temperature to the breaking point and Gaetano, trying to maintain his composure as the head of the family, as a man who should be strong, could no longer contain the pressure welling up inside him, and he began to sob and threw his head down on the table. When he embraced his son, he needed to reassure him.

"Our Lord will certainly protect you until we are together again. St. Francis [the saint from Paola] will be at your side."

His two brothers and two sisters encircled him and beseeched him to write to them as soon as possible. As they all held on to him Francesco made his way out of the small house and joined Paolo Morrone, Pietro Rogano, two young men the same age as Francesco, and also Domenico Saiardi who was 24 years of age and married. His wife was expecting their first baby and she cried as she walked behind him as they began to descend to the *marina* to board the covered wagon that would take them to the ship in Naples.

Three

In the 1800's and continuing into the early twentieth century, Longobardi was dominated by a few families of "nobles", *nobili*, that perpetuated a type of feudal system. In 1806-07, French invaders conquered the town and brought with them the ideals of the French Revolution, wiping out in principle the rampant feudalism that had become institutionalized during the previous centuries. However, the system continued de facto. Most of the lands and the most extravagant *palazzi* were owned or controlled by these families, *famiglie nobili*. Even though the word *palazzo* sounds like the English word "palace" and it can mean this, whenever the reference was made by the Longobardesi to *palazzo*, they meant a building. But there was a distinction between a modest house and a *palazzo*. The "nobili" lived in large buildings with spacious rooms, decorated with the finest furnishings possible in those times, including ceilings that were hand painted by talented local artists who had been hired specifically for that purpose. The theme of the painting was left up to the artist, with some of the more learned men from these rich families sometimes offering indefinite suggestions such as, "I would like a scene from mythology, perhaps one of the Roman goddesses like Diana or one of the Greek gods like Zeus." Then the artist would do as he saw fit and the result would be accepted with gratitude and appreciation. Some of the more enterprising artists would manage to paint the face of their benefactors someplace in the painting and when the work was completed point this out, even though one would never take note of it if it had not been pointed out. In the corner of the ceiling of the Minarchi family's *salotto* (the Minarchis were one of the town's first families), a young artist named Lorenzo Capitelli painted a scene of a woman copulating with a horse. Capitelli had lived and studied in Rome and had become aware of a similar "secret" inclusion on the painted ceiling of one of the rooms in the Castel Sant'Angelo. When Matteo Minarchi asked Capitelli to paint something special, the artist, over a period of six months, created an amazing fresco that covered some thirty square meters. There were allusions to stories from Greek mythology, battles connected with the expansion of the Roman Republic, Biblical themes from the Old and New Testaments, and then, buried in a corner of the painting between some horses and chariots, the lustful artist had painted in the woman whose depraved libido required a horse to satisfy her needs. After the work on the ceiling had been completed, Capitelli, smiled and told Minarchi that he had done something extra special for him. Minarchi smiled approvingly and corroborated the artist's self praise.

"But no, you do not understand," Capitelli insisted.

"No, I agree, I love what you have done. No one here has such a beautiful ceiling."

"Ah," persisted the artist, "But there is a secret that only you and anyone else you care to tell can see in this painting."

Lorenzo took Matteo directly under the "secret" area and pointed upwards.

"Look up there," and enjoining his patron to direct his eyes to the corner of the ceiling that depicted a group of riders in chariots circling their prey, a grand lion, Lorenzo prompted Matteo to look carefully and he would surely see a horse, and . . . a woman! At first Matteo was dumbfounded, then angry.

"What is the meaning of this?" he demanded. "How dare you paint such a scene in my home?"

Matteo Minarchi was open to discussions of lewd stories with his male friends, and when he had sex with any woman besides his wife, he demanded that they use foul language when he was penetrating them. He was not a man one would call a prude. But this was unprecedented. Lorenzo was calm.

"It's not a problem," he offered, "I can easily paint over it. But I thought that you would be proud to have something on your ceiling that can only be found elsewhere on the ceiling of the Camera Dilettante of the Castel Sant' Angelo in Rome."

When Matteo heard this, he quickly reconsidered, asked for more information about the Roman castle's unique attribute, and told Lorenzo to leave it there.

"After all," Matteo said, "No one will ever notice it unless I point it out to them." And this he did, proudly and often, whenever he had a male visitor he felt comfortable enough with to divulge his secret to.

Society in Southern Italy in the late 1800's and early 1900's, as indeed it had been for many, many years before, was founded on a class system, and there were three basic classes: the nobles, addressed as Don or Donna, who controlled the wealth and amassed all the power and influenced most aspects of daily life for all the town's citizens; the artisans, addressed as *Maestro* ("*Mastro*" in their dialect), cabinet makers, tailors, shoemakers, carpenters, house builders and others who had been apprenticed to other *Mastri* to learn a particular skill; and finally, the lowest rung on the social ladder, the *campagnuoli*, those who tended to the land and did not live in the *paese* proper.

In order to keep the riches confined to the smallest family unit, and to insure that the family controlling the wealth would be able to contain and retain their wealth and power, without it being diluted though a series of marriages that would weaken the prime family's position, only one of the male offspring would marry and any others would remain bachelors who, however, had access to any woman they desired for whatever sexual inclinations their normal needs or, in some instances, depraved fancies could envision. Paolo Morrone, one of the young men who accompanied Francesco Nardi to America was the son of Antonio Pellini, a noble whose actions belied completely the title conferred on him by force of habit on the part of the populace. He had two brothers, Giovanni and Nicola. Antonio was married to Stefania Mirelli, the daughter of another wealthy family from Fiumefreddo, the next town to the north. The couple had a son and daughter. Giovanni, another bachelor, had taken holy orders and was assigned to the church in the village of Amantea, another nearby town south of Longobardi, where he wielded considerable power, not only there but in towns up and down the coast. In his case, since he seemed to have the most religious fervor of all the male members of the family, the family "council," made up of the older brothers and uncles, chose the life of a priest for Giovanni. He was known to everyone as Don Giovanni–all priests and nobles were given the title "Don," a sign of respect and an acknowledgement that they were superiors—and his resemblance to Don Juan or Mozart's Don Giovanni was not lost on the more learned, not to say cultured, members of this contrived nobility. Despite his vows of celibacy, he rarely failed to act on an opportunity to break these vows, and such opportunities were sought by him with greater fervor than that he devoted to gaining indulgences for his immortal soul. His value to the family was in paving the way for all the produce that the tenant farmers grew and cultivated to be sold to the many church affiliated convents, monasteries, orphanages, and hospitals throughout Calabria and beyond.

14

Don Gio, as he was known to his intimates, exacted the best possible prices for all transactions.

Nicola Pellini was probably the most despicable and villainous of all the *nobili*. His lust was insatiable and if he saw a woman he wanted, he would stop at nothing to have her, including having her husband dispatched by his heinous handymen if the man tried to protect his wife's honor. For this reason, whenever it was known that he was about, husbands and fathers would keep their wives and daughters well hidden. Nicola used devious methods to satisfy his wanton desires. He befriended some of the more impressionable older women who had connections with young damsels he sought to deflower, and would invite them into his *salotto*, offering them cheap, but to the women desirable trinkets, even placing currency in amounts they did not usually come across into their greedy hands. The young women were either their nieces or daughters of friends. Don Nicola would instruct them to bring the maidens to a particular house under false pretences and leave them there alone. Soon after, Don Nicola would arrive and unravel the particular fantasy he had prepared for that day, and the innocent young woman would be unable to refuse.

One day as he was out riding among the groves of olive trees, he saw a young woman bending over and he was immediately taken by her ample female form which could be gleaned beneath the light clothing she was wearing. He instructed one of his henchmen to direct her to come to his *palazzo* that evening. When the young woman, Saveria Saporito was so instructed, her husband would not allow her to go, nor did she wish to since her heart was already filled with fear. Gregorio Saporito decided to go in her place. When he appeared at the door of Don Nicola and the servant who opened for him went to tell Don Nicola who was there, the Don told the servant to tell the man that his wife was the one sent for, not he. The man told the servant his wife had nothing to do with anything concerning the Don. At that point, the Don called his burly bodyguard, Achille Scaravaglione to his drawing room and gave him instructions. Gregorio Saporito was never seen by his wife or children after that day. Saveria was fetched the same evening and despite her fervent pleas and protestations, she became the toy of Don Nicola until he tired of her and found a new woman that could satisfy his insatiable inclinations. She continued to work the land along with her two children as they grew up, and was not even ever given any special consideration when it came to allowing the *contadini* to keep some of the provisions for their own family's use. Saveria attributed her husband's disappearance and her own violation to "*la volonta di Dio*," the will of God, and her faith was so deeply rooted in her psyche, so embedded in her daily routines, that she truly believed that there was a Divine purpose to everything that happened. The only thing that she could not do was to forgive Don Nicola, even though in Confession, her confessor told her that we must always forgive those who trespassed against us just as Christ forgives our trespasses without qualification.

Don Gio was very good at involving the family in all the liturgical manifestations of the Roman Catholic religion. Anyone speaking to any of them would think immediately that here were truly devout practitioners of the faith. The many feast days were celebrated, self denial was practiced during Lent—save for denial of the flesh, of course—and pilgrimages were made to Rome from time to time. Don Gio was a good priest in many ways. He visited the sick, consoled the grieving and preached with fire and conviction. Nevertheless, his loyalty was more to his family than to God, and to the practices that made his family so contemptible in the eyes of all the righteous men and women who suffered the indignities that they bestowed with such gratuitous contempt and self-righteous hypocrisy. Don Gio was also the father of a child. One day while a nineteen year old woman who worked for the church was cleaning the priest's bedroom, he walked in and began to question her about her knowledge of contact with men. Caterina Viteritti was an orphan and she had grown up in various convents in Calabria. The sisters who raised her wanted her to become a nun, but although she was very religious, she was certain that she was unworthy and not intelligent enough to join one of the orders of nuns that were willing to accept her. She felt that her intelligence was limited for she could never achieve the points that other girls her age won so easily whenever she had been involved in any kind of studies. And although she loved the saints, she could not even remember all their names, or even the important ones as the other girls could. She was determined, then, to devote herself to working in a lowly if not, she felt, a demeaning way for her Lord. She would clean the church, dress the altar—all of these things she did quite well. But she would not go beyond that.

"Caterina," Don Gio asked, "have you ever been with a man?" Caterina looked puzzled.

"Don Gio, you know I have always been with the priests and in some places with the brothers."

"No," Don Gio insisted, "I mean have you ever touched a man, seen a man without his clothes on?"

"Don Gio," replied Caterina, now showing signs of alarm, "You know I would have told you this in confession if I did anything wrong like that." She began to weep softly.

"No, no, my child," the priest persisted, "I don't mean that you have sinned. I just want to know what you have seen or not seen of men."

16

"I have seen nothing," the young woman pleaded. Her reaction made her even more attractive to the priest and his desire now began to burn inside him, for even if he had not always lived up to his vows of chastity, he had not been with a woman for some time.

"Caterina, you are a woman now, no longer a little girl. You have to know something about the world, about men and women."

The priest spoke softly and conveyed a sense of true concern for the young woman's welfare.

"What do I need to know Don Gio?" Caterina entreated. "I know about how our Lord was born of a Virgin, how Saint Joseph never slept with her and how Jesus was born. I know how babies are born. I have assisted women in delivering them. I know I must be good and humble and obey the commandments."

Don Gio persisted.

"Caterina, but do you know how these babies get into their mothers' wombs?"

"When two people are married, they lie together and a baby results," Caterina answered, somewhat hesitantly.

The priest thought to himself that this young woman was really so innocent and so naive that he began to feel shame for his intentions. On the other hand, he convinced himself that it really was his duty to educate her in the ways of the world. But all this paled beside the force of the desire that had taken hold of him, that fire inside him that needed to be quenched.

"Caterina, do you know what a man and woman do when they lie together?"

"They just go to sleep?" she offered, now blushing and tentative in her reply.

"No, no, my dear," said Don Gio. "Look, it is my duty as your spiritual counselor to teach you things you must know now. Now answer me truthfully: do you ever touch yourself down there?" He pointed towards her pelvic area. Caterina looked back at him with a look of anguished incredulity.

"Of course I do. But why do you ask me this. Do not all of us touch ourselves when we pass water and other things too?" She was blushing and turned her head aside, away from Don Gio's demanding eyes.

"No, no, no, that is not what I mean," Don Gio continued.

"Do you touch yourself just for the good feeling it provides?" Caterina now was beside herself and did not know what to say.

"It is only natural," said Don Gio. "I must show you. It is my sacred duty." With the word "sacred," Caterina suddenly thought that she was not conforming to an obligation of her faith and she quickly beseeched Don Gio to forgive her if she did not do anything that the Church demanded of her. With this, the priest seized on his opening and instructed the timid Caterina to lie down on his bed. As she did, he began to slowly pull up her long skirt and to push her legs apart.

"I must show you what needs to happen if you will be ready when a man comes to ask for your hand in marriage."

As unlearned and pure of heart as she was, Caterina knew that there was something inappropriate to the priest's actions, but he had imposed on her a vow of secrecy to what transpired between them, and then, too, to whom could she confide and disclose the details of what had occurred between them. After many more such episodes when each time Don Gio assured her that her instructions had to continue, Caterina became pregnant. As soon as this was evident, Don Gio never touched her again. She delivered a baby girl and named her Domenica because she was born on Sunday and because Santa Domenica, virgin and martyr, was the saint Caterina was particularly devoted to. Many of the gullible townspeople believed the baby was most likely fathered by the church gardener or by one of the men who came to bring milk and vegetables to the priest's house. Others had no doubts about what truly had transpired there.

Antonio Pellini was somewhat soft hearted, a characteristic that his two brothers criticized at every opportunity. One day, for example, as he was riding down to the *marina* on his mule, he saw a poor decrepit *campagnuolo*, Giacinto Scrugli walking back to the hills where he lived with his wife and five children in a hut that could barely contain them all. In his arms, he was carrying a large fish.

"Where did you get that fish?" demanded Antonio.

"*Vussuria*," replied Giacinto deferentially, addressing him according to the local traditions and acknowledging the master's superiority,

"I have been fishing all week. This is the first fish I have caught."

"Bring it to my wife!" Antonio ordered.

"But, I, I . . ." Giacinto tried to interject.

Antonio raised his voice and shouted,

"Bring it to my wife, now! I will ride ahead and tell her to prepare to cook it." With that, the landowner did not wait for any further discussion of the matter. He rode past his house and shouted out to his wife that a good fish was about to be delivered and that she should see to it that the servants prepare it the way he liked. Giacinto was a poor man, but he was not a fool; at least he did not want anyone to make a fool of him. Furthermore, he had these seven mouths to feed, including his own and he had not had anything besides bread for days, and that he had taken on credit. He considered the matter. If I give this fish to Don Antonio, what will I have to feed my children today? No, I will cut it into pieces, sell some, keep some, and with the money I get I can buy some other food. This is what he did. For the next three months, Giacinto avoided Don Antonio and went out of his way to make sure he was nowhere near any of the paths the landowner usually took. One day, however, after three months had passed, Giacinto was walking down to the *marina* and suddenly Don Antonio was there around a bend in the dirt path high on his horse.

"I don't like that trick you played on me, you pig!" Antonio growled.

"But *vussuria*, I had no food for my children and I needed to feed them," stammered Giacinto.

"That is not my interest," Antonio asserted with a complete lack of any sympathy for the poor man.

"If that ever happens again, you can be sure you will never be around to worry about your children." With that declaration, Antonio rode off and Giacinto was left trembling at the very real possibility that his fate could be sealed thusly. When Antonio mentioned the occurrence to his brother Nicola, Nicola scoffed at him and said,

"I always told you that you are too soft. You should have given him a proper lesson that very day!"

Antonio Pellini was also quite different from his brother when it came to women too. He certainly was not faithful to his wife, but he would not abuse the wife or daughter of another man. He sought unmarried women who for whatever reason were still young and unmarried and who would consent to Antonio's entreaties, knowing that he would make life easier for them. Truthfully, too, whether they were virgins or had already tasted the pleasures of the flesh, most of them consented and enjoyed themselves, while some bore a measure of guilt as they succumbed, which continued to haunt them for some time thereafter. Three bore children as a result of their unions with Antonio, children that he would never publicly acknowledge, but whom he enjoyed meeting from time to time and ascertaining any possible resemblance to either himself or any member of his immediate family. Uncannily, some thought, but in reality not so strange at all, one of Antonio's daughters bore a striking resemblance to a daughter who had been born to Amelia Caimi, a woman who was a servant in Antonio's home and with whom he had had some brief encounters when his wife had gone to Fiumefreddo to care for her ailing mother. Amelia's daughter lived with her in the servants' quarters and the townspeople whispered about how obvious it was that this was the daughter of Antonio Pellini, but Stefania refused to even listen to any allusion to the kinship, not even from her sister with whom she was very close whenever her sister tried to broach the subject. As Amelia's daughter grew up and began to assist her mother with the chores around the house, Stefania would belittle her and insult her intelligence at every possible opportunity. Ironically, although she could be mistaken for the legitimate daughter's twin—fraternal if not identical—all who saw her were immediately struck, noting her even more beautiful face and body than that of her half sister. And her demeanor added to the overall impression she made. She had an inner beauty that Stefania's daughter lacked.

The one offspring that Antonio had developed a real liking for was Paolo Morrone, the young man who was on his way to America with Francesco Nardi. At the town hall registry, Paolo was given his mother's family name since Giuseppina Morrone would not identify the baby's father. Giuseppina and Antonio met when she was working in a *taverna* in Paola, the largest nearby city to Longobardi. The *taverna* was prized by local residents for its fine wine, but good hearty food was also served. Antonio used to stop in when he visited Paola on business and was attracted to Giuseppina so much that he could think of nothing else but his lust for her. She was a strikingly beautiful woman whose husband had died by drowning 6 months after they were married. She was only 20 at the time. When Antonio met her she was 24 and a headstrong woman who would not easily be won over by any man. She worked for her husband's family's friends who looked after her and would ward off any flirtatious attempts by men who fancied themselves conquerors of the female heart. One evening after a late *cena*, Antonio waited outside the *taverna* for Giuseppina and offered to walk with her to her home, in actuality a single room that she rented from the same people who employed her. Giuseppina was impressed by the gentle way in which Antonio always spoke to her, a mixture of appreciation for her beauty and respect for her strength of character. She told him it was not necessary, but that it would be all right. As they walked, they passed close by to where Antonio slept whenever he came to Paola, a house owned by his family that was not being used then, except when a family member needed a place for the night. Giuseppina asked Antonio where he lived and he told her he was from Longobardi. When she asked where he stayed in Paola, he pointed to the house which they were walking beside. He asked her if she would like to see it, but she refused even if she really would have liked to go in. She had passed that house hundreds of times and was always impressed and wondered who lived in it. It took four more such walks before Giuseppina agreed to see the inside of the house and three more visits inside before Antonio was able to induce her to sleep with him therein. Within a few months Giuseppina was pregnant with Paolo (Antonio's trips to Paola had become more frequent). With her son, Giuseppina settled in Longobardi. She worked for another of the noble families where the principal agents of power were women, unmarried and widowed, and Antonio called upon an old debt to get this "safe" place for his beautiful Giuseppina. As the boy grew, all remarked at how good looking he was and Antonio listened proudly to all the compliments and blessings that were directed at the young man. Paolo never knew that Antonio was his father until the day he left for America, when his mother decided that he should know. Paolo heard the news with a mixture of annoyance and pride. In his young and impressionable mind, he now believed himself to be of noble birth, but he was angry at his father, for the man had always treated him well and had gone out of his way to help him at times, but he sensed that Antonio was aloof and would never allow the younger man to express some minor acknowledgment of feelings for him, even when it was in the form of gratitude. When Antonio learned that Paolo was leaving for America, he offered his assistance in acquiring traveling apparatus, transit to Naples, or anything else, but Paolo thanked him and declined his offer. Now as he made his way to Naples and afterwards on the ship, he wondered about this man who had joined with his mother to bring him into the world.

Four

New York was a thriving city in 1896 when the four *Longobardesi* arrived on November 15th with hundreds of other immigrants who had come to seek, if not the better life—for a life of unrelenting work and no enjoyment can hardly be said to be better than the life they already lived— but a life that promised much more if one worked hard and exercised thrift, a promise of a better future. The voyage over had been difficult for many, especially those who became seasick and experienced a nausea that tore at their heads and stomachs. Indeed, during the nine day journey some feared they would die before the arrival. Francesco, fortunately, was able to withstand the turbulence of the ocean even though he had never had such an experience before.

They were met at the port by one of the brothers from Paola who had assured them they would find work on their arrival. He brought them to a tenement a few blocks from the Bowery in Manhattan and they walked up three flights of stairs to meet their new "family," three other men from Southern Italy who had been living there for some time and sub-letting rooms to new immigrants who eventually left for better quarters. Until the arrival of the four *Longobardesi*, they never housed more than five men in the three rooms. Now they would have seven, four in one bedroom, three in another. The apartment also boasted a small kitchen, and a very small room with a couch that they could sit on if they did not go directly to bed on returning from work. The bathroom was in the hallway and was also used by two other families on the floor. There was no shower. When one wanted to bathe, it was necessary to walk a few blocks to the public baths where a bath could be negotiated for 5 cents.

Within a day after arriving in New York, the four *paesani* were escorted to the construction site for the new Williamsburg Bridge. The company owned by the Italians from Paola did sub-contracting work for a much larger company. Construction had begun on November 7th and much work remained before the bridge could open in 1903. Francesco and Paolo were assigned to carry materials to various parts of the construction zone. From 6:00 A.M. in the morning until 8:00 P.M. in the evening, the friends worked along with dozens of other laborers, loading materials, carrying them, sometimes with weights of over one hundred pounds, emptying and returning for more. The foreman, a big burly German who had been living in the United States for 15 years, looked upon the Italians with a mixture of revulsion and contempt. He saw them as dirty, ignorant fools who were not even as worthy of respect as some of the dogs that had been adopted as mascots, and would remain in the work camp for the seven years it would take to complete the work.

Gunther Mueller had very little patience for any mistakes, so that one day when Paolo dropped a pail filled with sand, one of six he was carrying on a metal bar placed across his shoulders, Gunther shouted with fury,

"You stupid wop! Now you get down on your knees and pick up every last grain of sand!"

Paolo understood so little English that he had no idea what the German was saying. He knew what he had done, but he didn't think it merited such rage. Mueller kept shouting over and over,

"Dumb wop! Stupid greenhorn!!"

One of the Italians who had been in America for some years and who spoke English, if with a very thick accent, was later approached by Paolo. When Paolo learned that these terms were coined to discredit Italians, he became enraged and wanted to exact revenge against Mueller. His friends told him to forget any such ideas and Paolo calmed down, but he always regarded Mueller with his own contempt, feeling superior because he now knew that his heritage was one of nobility.

The only day the laborers had any relief from their toils was on Sunday. On Saturdays their work ended at 6:00 P.M. Then, and the day following they could move around the electrically charged city and discover the many amazing sights they had never even imagined back in their *paese*. Pietro, Paolo and Francesco would first go to the public baths and then set out to see what they could uncover of interest. Domenico, married man that he was, would just return to the flat and catch up on sleep. The three younger men discovered taverns and beer halls where they would not have to spend too much and could sit and enjoy the comings and goings of other young people their age, immigrants from countries like Germany and Sweden, and others American-born. Francesco looked at these attractive young women and mentally compared them to Maria Saggio, the girl he began to think about more and more. None could compare to "his" Maria. Paolo, on the contrary, and even Pietro viewed the young women they saw as exotically superior to the women they had left behind. Watching them flit around from one side to the other, Paolo thought about his possibilities with them. Certainly, it would not be necessary to marry such a woman and still be able to enjoy her, to kiss her, to touch her, even to . . . . One Saturday evening, a young slim woman with long blonde hair approached Paolo. She had seen him there before and was captivated by his striking good looks.

"Hi, honey, wanna buy me a drink?" she asked. Paolo had by this time learned a few words of English, but he could not understand what she was saying. She placed her hand on his shoulder.

"Well, wadda ya say?" Paolo turned to Francesco and Pietro and asked,

"*Voi sapete che dice?*" (Do you know what she's saying?).

"A wop, hey girls, they're wops," the young woman shouted across the floor. Two ruffians who were friends of the girl came over and demanded,

"Are these guys bothering you?" Francesco, Pietro and Paolo looked at them in bewilderment and one of the antagonists pushed Paolo off his stool. A scuffle ensued and Francesco entreated his friends to get out of there as quickly as possible. Paolo was again upset at hearing the by now familiar word of disparagement, but he was afraid of what would happen if the police were to intervene. After that incident, the Longobardesi kept to themselves and found a small church in lower Manhattan offering Masses in Italian. They went there and learned that there was an Italian social club that had meetings on Saturday evenings, so they began to attend these too. Pietro Rogano met an Italian immigrant at the social club, a young woman who went there with her parents and brother. She had been born in Bari and had come to the United States at the age of 12. Now 19, she was one year younger than Pietro. Within a year they married and Pietro was never to return to his native land again.

Paolo Morrone's destiny also predicated that he would never return to his homeland, but the reason was tragically different. Once again Paolo made a mistake that incurred the wrath of Gunther Mueller. Gunther again called Paolo a "wop," and Paolo this time cursed at him in Italian. Gunther knew this curse since he had heard it many times, when Italians among themselves exchanged diatribes. That evening, Gunter waited for Paolo and challenged him to a fist fight. Paolo did not know how to fight with his fists, but being younger and in better shape than Gunther, he was able to wrestle the older man to the ground and pin him down. Gunther, fearing a loss of face, since some of his own compatriots were watching, pulled a knife from his back pocket, one that he used to cut ropes, and plunged it into Paolo's back. Francesco, who was there watching too, ran to Paolo's side and held him in his arms, shouting, "*Aiuto!*" ("Help!"), as his friend expired. Mueller had friends in the police department and they blithely accepted his explanation that he had only taken out his knife in self-defense. Strangely, Francesco himself would enter a plea of self-defense years later, but for altogether nobler reasons. His testimony against Mueller was dismissed before he ever had a chance to offer it to the authorities. His bosses assured him it was useless for an Italian immigrant to fight the system. They tried to placate Francesco by paying for Paolo's burial in a small Catholic cemetery in Brooklyn. This was the end of the American dream for Francesco Nardi, a tragic conclusion to a journey that had begun with much promise. Disillusioned, one year and three months after his arrival in America, having barely paid back his debt for the voyage over, and with just enough money saved to make the trip back to Italy, Francesco returned home. It was his sad duty to inform Giuseppina Morrone that her son did not return with him, and would never return to Italy again. Antonio Pellini comforted Giuseppina when he heard the news and wept for the first time since his own mother had died. Francesco was able to bring Giuseppina only some articles of clothing that belonged to Paolo. With these, a shirt and trousers, she erected a shrine to her son, with images of Mary, who had also had a son killed, of that son himself and of Saints Anthony of Padua and Francis of Paola. Each morning she said a Rosary before her shrine and prayed to Jesus and Mary to look after her son. In her heart, she could never accept his death, but in her mind, God had called him and *la volontà di Dio*, the will of God, was what was important. God had so decreed that her son had to die while still young, and she too must accept it.

Domenico Saiardi's wife gave birth to a baby girl three months after his departure. He learned that he had a daughter two months later when he finally received the letter his wife had written to him the day after the baby was born. The baby was named Nunzia after Domenico's mother, as was the custom throughout Calabria. Domenico continued to work, performing various jobs in connection with the construction of the Williamsburg Bridge until the bridge was completed and opened to traffic in December, 1903. At that point, he had not seen his family for seven years. One of the other foremen, a man of French parentage, had taken a liking to Domenico. He saw that the young man was very capable and soon had him working on various types of construction projects. One Sunday, he invited Domenico to his home for dinner. Henri Michel was married and had two children, a daughter and a son. He lived in Brooklyn, renting part of a brownstone in the Flatbush section of the borough. At Henri's home, Domenico was enchanted with Claudine, Henri's wife. Domenico was much too unsophisticated socially to even think about complimenting Henri for his choice of a partner in marriage. Domenico could see that Claudine was an excellent housekeeper and mother and that her physical attributes were quite striking too. Henri, being much more of a worldly chap, noticed Domenico's suppressed admiration for his wife and said, "Dom," for such was the nickname he had given to his workman,

"If you think Claudine is pretty, wait until you see her sister." Domenico blushed and said in his best English,

"I don't know what you are talking about." Shortly, Claudine's sister Mireille appeared. At that time, Domenico was 27 years old, having been living in the U.S. for three years. Mireille was a year older. She was married to a Frenchman who hadn't liked America and had returned to France. Mireille refused to go back with him and remained in New York, working as a waitress at a deluxe New York French restaurant located near Broadway and 40th Street, not far from the Metropolitan Opera at 38th Street and Broadway. Domenico immediately saw that Henri's assessment of the relative merits of the two sisters was accurate. He was, however, extremely shy and could barely bring himself to respond to questions Mireille asked of him. He did not tell her he was married, but the two slowly warmed to one another and Mireille became captivated by Domenico's reticence, naiveté and unassuming demeanor. She knew too many men who were puffed up with their own self importance, so she looked upon Domenico as a breath of fresh air. Mireille had shoulder length red hair and green eyes. She was five feet, seven inches in height, with shapely legs, a narrow waist, breasts that were not too large but which she made the most of by accenting their round curves with the blouses she wore that were tightly tied and cut low enough to make the desired effect. Domenico was nearly the same height. He had blue eyes and dark black hair which was combed back slickly in the style of the day. The two young people looked as though they belonged together. Later, after dinner had been served, Mireille offered to walk with Domenico back to the trolley. They continued to see one another at Henri's home on Saturday evenings after Mireille finished her shift at the restaurant and whenever else they could steal some time to be together. They became lovers.

In those days, it was hard to send money home on a regular basis. Domenico would send money to his wife whenever he could. When one of his *paesani* returned home he would ask them to take money to his wife, which they did gladly. Serafina wondered when she would see her husband again. Yes, from time to time some money appeared by Domenico's chosen courier and sometimes by mail, and the amount was sufficient to last Serafina and Nunzia for months since their needs were not so great. They lived in a small, rustic two room house owned by Serafina's father and the money was only needed for food and some utilitarian clothing. After seven years, Serafina began to despair that Domenico would return. None of the men who knew him, men who returned to the *paese* had the heart to tell her that he was now domiciled with another woman. After living with Mireille for three years, Domenico and Mireille decided to start their own French/Italian restaurant. Domenico had learned to cook some dishes *alla paesana* after his mother died and he was left to prepare the family meals for his father and two brothers, and Mireille knew some easy but tasty French recipes from her years at *La Table d'Or*. They opened their restaurant on the lower east side of Manhattan on Mott Street and called it simply *Domenico's*. Nunzia was then ten years old.

Domenico's brother Pasquale, the middle son in the family, three years younger than Domenico, had for some time visited Serafina to help her with any tasks that needed a man's hand, and sometimes he would remain to *cenare* with her, have some bread and cheese and drink some wine together. Sometimes after Nunzia fell asleep, the two would sit together and talk about the things they had in common. They discussed the work that needed to be done on the plot of land that Domenico was meant to share with his two brothers and their father, and of course Serafina was obliged to help cultivate her family's part of the land. They discussed the townspeople they liked and disliked, and the ever persistent question as to when Domenico would come home. These meetings were certainly not secret. Serafina always kept her door wide open since she knew that the evil minded *paesani* would definitely criticize her for having her husband's brother in her house so much. But the undercurrent of gossip seeped into every receptive crevice of malicious judgment that all too many of the townspeople harbored. One evening, Serafina complained to Pasquale that her shoulders were aching from the work she had done in the field that day. He stood behind her and started to massage her shoulders.

"It feels so good," she murmured, "Don't stop." Pasquale continued and slowly brought his two large hands, made rough from daily toil in the fields, down over Serafina's breasts. Suddenly, all the sexual tension that had been suppressed for years flowed quickly through her veins and she could not resist Pasquale's desire for her. She wanted to tell him to stop, but only because of the shame that had been instilled in her from an early age. She told Pasquale to wait, got up and closed the door, drew the curtain that separated the area where she slept with Nunzia, and sat down again.

"Continue," she commanded. Pasquale again started with her shoulders and quickly descended to her breasts, caressing them and stroking her nipples until she began to respond with moans of ecstasy. Then, there could be no doubt for either one of them that they had fallen in love, that they cared deeply for one another. Their first sexual union was but a physical manifestation of their love for one another. It would not be their last.

When Nunzia was fourteen years of age, and when Domenico had already been with Mireille for seven years, Pietro Rogano visited Domenico at his restaurant. The two had remained friends and kept in contact with one another. Pietro operated a grocery store with his wife's family on Court Street in Brooklyn. One of Pietro's sisters, Carmela, had written to ask Pietro if she could come to live with his family in America. She was eighteen years old and had dreamed of taking the voyage, seeing the wonderful new world of her dreams ever since she first heard that Pietro was married and raising a family there. Pietro was thrilled that someone of his family would join him, and his wife was happy that she would meet a member of her husband's family and have a sister-in-law with whom she could be close. Pietro wanted to hear everything about his hometown. Who had died? Who married whom? Which of his friends or *paesani* had left for Argentina or Venezuela? He knew about those who arrived in New York since all emigrants kept in close contact with one another and visited each other whenever possible. Gradually, the conversation drifted to the subject of Domenico. Carmela wanted to know if Pietro knew if he would ever go back to see his wife and daughter.

"I doubt it very much," replied Pietro. "Domenico has another wife here now."

"Another wife?" exclaimed Carmela. "Is that possible here? Can a man have more than one wife? Is it legal?"

"Well," said Pietro, "she is not his wife really, but they live together as man and wife."

"Then he should not be so upset that his wife is doing the same thing with his brother," Carmela cried.

"What?" said Pietro, completely taken by surprise, and shocked that such a thing could be.

"Oh, yes," Carmela continued, "The whole town knows it now and all the women in church give Serafina *malocchio* when she goes to Mass. They stare at her to make her uncomfortable. Sometimes they even whisper '*Putana*' as she walks down the aisle past them. They say a sinner such as she most certainly is should not be allowed to come to church until she stops sinning and goes to confession. But she has no intention of stopping. She just disregards everyone's insults. The real pity is that her daughter has to suffer the same kind of insults, and she does not deserve them. What did she do, poor child? She never even met her own father and Pasquale has been like a father to her since she was born."

Pietro pondered what his sister had told him and considered it his duty to inform his friend about what was going on between his wife and his brother. At the first opportunity, the following Sunday afternoon, he went to Domenico's restaurant.

"Domenico," Pietro began somewhat hesitantly, "I have some news for you." When Domenico saw the sullen look on Pietro's face, his heart started to beat faster. He felt light-headed, and from deep inside emotions welled up that had not been tapped for years.

"Did my father die?" he asked.

"No, no," said Pietro.

"Then, what?" demanded Domenico.

"Sit down, my friend," and with that Pietro told Domenico about his wife's infidelity.

"*Putana*," he shouted. It did not occur to him at first that his own brother was as guilty as his wife was, nor did he ever stop to think that he was guilty of the same transgression of his marriage vows. When Pietro went on to tell Domenico about the suffering his poor daughter had to bear, innocent as she was, Domenico became enraged. He decided then and there that he would have to take action. Mireille was left to run the restaurant as Domenico began his return journey to Italy.

The evening he arrived in Longobardi, after an arduous 12 day trip, he went directly to his father's house and spent the night there. His father, Ettore Saiardi, was a wise man who understood the ways that people act in unusual or difficult circumstances. He was also a forgiving man and never exacted retribution from anyone throughout his life, even if he felt that he had been wronged. After greeting his son and offering thanks to all the saints and Jesus and Mary—images of which were hung throughout his modest abode—for allowing him to see his first born son again before he died, he began to try to reason with his son, but Domenico, whose personality traits seemed to derive from another unidentified family member, brushed aside his father's remonstrance. The next morning he walked directly to the home where he had left his young wife and without knocking opened the door. Serafina and Pasquale were dressing to go into the fields. Neither had any idea that Domenico had even been en route. Pasquale looked at his brother and was about to embrace him when Domenico waved his hand,

"Stay where you are," he demanded in a voice of authority and anger. Serafina, who had by this time lost any feeling she had had for her husband, all of it transferred to the man she now loved as much as anything or anyone except for her daughter, merely looked at Domenico with an air of indifference. She had no intention of asking his forgiveness or of asking him if he intended to live with her again. As far as she was concerned, it was out of the question. When she realized that Domenico had no such intention, but was preparing to return to America shortly, she determined that she would not go with him if that was what he wanted. Alas, her apprehensions were unfounded, but she was to become more apprehensive, in fact, quite alarmed when she gleaned his true plans for her and especially for Nunzia.

"Where is my daughter?" he demanded.

Serafina pushed aside the curtain and showed him the young girl sleeping on her makeshift cot. By this time, Serafina and Pasquale slept on a day bed in the main room of the edifice. The girl began to stir and Serafina said,

"Nunzia, come to greet your father."

The girl looked bewildered, but she quickly apprehended that this, finally, was the man she had thought about all these years. For her, he was the man who sent them money and who had also sent from time to time little playthings, trinkets, which she prized more than any other possessions. She jumped up and ran over to embrace her father. Tears came to Domenico's eyes when he saw the display of affection his young child demonstrated towards him. After composing himself, he told Nunzia that she would join him on his return trip to America.

"*Che dici?*" screamed Serafina. "What are you saying? No, never, she will never go with you. She is my daughter, mine! I am the one who raised her for her entire life, for fourteen years while you kept away from her."

Serafina's wrath was so overwhelming, so impassioned, an aspect of her character that Pasquale had never seen displayed by her before, that he could not believe this was the tender woman he had grown to love.

"You will have nothing to say about this matter," Domenico proclaimed. Turning to his daughter he said,

"You, my dear one, do not worry. Get your things ready and I will come back for you, and no one will ever insult you again."

With that, Domenico walked out. He went to visit Antonio Pellini who looked much older than his years, having aged prematurely after the death of his illegitimate son. Domenico told Antonio what he needed and after agreeing on a monetary consideration, Antonio delivered to Domenico an order signed by a judge in Cosenza, stipulating that, as the girl's father, he, Domenico had custody of her. From Longobardi, he left for America with his daughter. Serafina tried as hard as she could to keep her daughter locked in the house, but Domenico appeared with *carabinieri* who took the young girl by force from her mother. Nunzia, distraught at leaving her mother, fantasized that she would one day bring her mother to stay with her in America when she was old enough to be on her own. Serafina suffered a nervous breakdown and was never quite the same again. Pasquale was faithful to her throughout his life. Mother and daughter, in fact, never saw each other again. The system of power in Calabria continued to work for the benefit of the powerful, suffering Serafinas be damned.

Five

While Francesco Nardi was working in New York, and thinking about Maria Saggio, the young woman was working long days to help her family to provide for their basic needs. If the men in Longobardi worked hard, the women worked even harder, for their day sometimes extended from 4:00 A.M. in the morning until 11:00 P.M., at least an hour after the male family members had retired for the night. The Saggio family, consisting of mother Emilia, father Natale, Maria, the couple's oldest child, Pasqualina (who was so called because she was born on Easter Sunday) and nicknamed Lina, and younger brother Agostino, had a plot of land that they worked on behalf of the Pristerá family, another of the *famiglie nobile* of Longobardi. The Saggios were allowed to keep 40% of everything they grew or raised. The Pristerás would supply them with young animals, sheep, chickens and pigs, but the Saggios would have to feed them, fatten them and finally slaughter them when required or at the right time of year. The sheep would have to be milked and the milk brought to the *palazzo* for the landowning family's diet, as would the cultivated tomatoes, onions, figs and other fruit, vegetables, eggs and freshly killed and cleaned chicken. As long as the Pristerás received all they needed for their own meals, the Saggios could take whatever provisions they required and even sell off any excess. However, sales had to be reported and 60 % of the receipts had to be surrendered to the landowners. One year the Saggios had a bumper crop of tomatoes. There were enough tomatoes for the Pristerás, as well as for the Saggios and for some of their friends too. Emilia realized that this would be the case in August when she saw how many tomatoes were ripening on the vines. In fact, they had so many tomatoes ripening each day, beginning in July, that everyone was feasting on them for weeks. Emilia usually sold her excess fruits and vegetables to a particular lady in town who was always happy to get them. One day, when she was bringing this lady some peaches, onions and figs, she asked Signora Pellegrini if she was interested in tomatoes for bottling in September. The two women agreed on *due quintale* (two hundred kilograms) and the matter was left at that. When September came, Emilia was so busy with many other things that she did not get to pack up the tomatoes for Signora Pellegrini until around the tenth of the month. One day she showed up at the Pellegrini's front door, with part of the delivery fastened on the back of her mule, prepared to go back for the rest as soon as she unloaded. When she knocked and was admitted into the dining area, Mrs. Pellegrini asked Emilia what she had brought her.

"I brought you the tomatoes that you ordered last month for your bottles."

"Tomatoes," replied the older woman, "What tomatoes? I already bought my tomatoes for the bottles."

"Excuse me," said Emilia, nervously, "but don't you remember that I came to talk to you about bringing you tomatoes in September, and you told me to bring *due quintale?*"

*"Due quintal*e?" exclaimed Mrs. Pellegrini, in an exasperated tone. "What am I supposed to do with all those tomatoes?"

"Signora, it is not my business what you do with them. With all due respect, my business is to bring them to you after you order them from me."

"But it is already the middle of September!" said Mrs. Pellegrini, her voice rising to a high pitch. "I always get my tomatoes in the beginning of September. When you didn't come, I ordered them from *Maria la canchiera."* *Maria la canchiera* was so named because she provided some of the women in town with meat from animals that she slaughtered herself, purchasing a pig or sheep from one of the *contadini* or farmers from time to time. *Canchiera* was Calabrese for *macellaio* or butcher. Mrs. Pellegrini had actually let the order with Emilia Saggio slip from her mind, but she did not want to admit that.

Emilia was a patient woman, but she was now quite beside herself.

"What does *la canchiera* have to do with tomatoes? I thought she only sells meat?" Emilia asked excitedly, now wiping the perspiration from her brow, for the trip to town with the mule with all the tomatoes had exhausted her.

"Well," said Signora Pellegrini, fanning herself and sitting back, now taking the attitude that this was not her mistake.

"When September came around and I did not have tomatoes, Maria asked me if I had arranged for tomatoes for the bottles. She knows some women who were willing to bring them to me."

This was, in fact, highly unusual, since Maria had never sold tomatoes before. However, since so many of the tenant farmers had large supplies that year, they asked Maria to help them to sell their excess to her meat customers. Maria was only too happy to oblige since she could take a small profit on each transaction.

"This is not just!" Emilia cried. "What am I going to do with *due quintale* now. I could have sold them to someone else, but I offered them to you first since you always buy from me."

Signora Pellegrini began worrying that she would not have Emilia to depend on for future provisions of fruits and vegetables if she made her angry now. She called to her daughter,

"Daniela, go call Maria and tell her to come here now!"

Within a few minutes, the overweight Maria trudged up the stairs, followed by Signora Pellegrini's aunt Marta, who had asked Daniela what was going on.

The slim Emilia was standing against one wall. Her girlish figure had not changed much in spite of multiple pregnancies, including two miscarriages. The hard work she performed in the fields helped her to maintain a steady, low weight. Signora Pellegrini was in her mid-fifties and was some sixty pounds overweight. Her legs were marked by varicose veins and she had difficulty walking or standing for too long. Maria the butcher was in her early sixties, overweight too, but energetic and feisty. Even though she lived in town, she walked barefoot in every season. The bottoms of her feet had taken on an appearance of tough black leather. Her hair was gray and was loosely tied behind in a bun. After entering the room, she sat down on the floor Indian style. Aunt Marta, a seventy-six year old woman who looked every bit her age, walked with a limp. She was a small woman overall, but her stomach protruded making her look heavier than she actually was. Her hair was completely white and although she could hear quite well when she wanted to, she had the habit of saying "*Che dici?*" ("What are you saying?") whenever anyone spoke to her so that the speaker found it necessary to repeat himself. Those who knew her just ignored the question. She came in and sat at a chair next to her niece.

The four women all began to talk at the same time.

Signora Pellegrini: "She wants me to buy *due quintale di pomadori*, but I already bought them from you."

Maria: "So, what have I to do with that?"

Emilia: "You sold tomatoes to her after I sold them first."

Marta: "How can this be?"

Sig. Pellegrini: "She didn't bring them on time so I ordered . . ."

Emilia: "I did bring them on time. We never set an exact date. There is still plenty of time to do the bottling."

Maria: "What's the problem? Just make more bottles."

Sig. Pellegrini: "Are you crazy? Who's going to help me make *cinque quintale*?"

Emilia: "*Cinque*? How do you arrive at five? How many did you get from her?'

Maria: "I sold her *three quintale*. That's what she asked for."

Sig. Pellegrini: "You stay out of this. I can answer for myself."

Maria: "Then why did you call me if you want me to keep quiet?"

Sig. P.: "I called you to see if you can take some of Emilia's tomatoes and sell them. I don't want her to suffer because of your mistake."

Maria: "My mistake? How is this *my* mistake? I didn't even know she was selling you tomatoes."

Emilia: "You knew, all right. You know I always sell her fruits and vegetables. You always see me passing your place to bring her things. And why did you buy three from her and were only taking two from me?" she asked, now addressing Signora Pellegrini. "Did she give you such a good price that you took an extra *quintale*?"

Maria: "I don't interfere in other people's business. I just . . ." she interrupted unsuccessfully.

Emilia: "You interfered in my business here, didn't you?"

Marta: "I think she has a point . . ."

Maria: "Who asked you?"

Marta: "Don't try to get nasty with me. Just remember who you are talking to."

Maria: "An old fool, that's who." But this she said to herself and no one heard her.

Marta: "I think Maria and Emilia should settle this between themselves."

Emilia: "What are you talking about? I can't waste any more time. My husband needs my help in the fields."

Maria: "I have work to do too. I can't stay here to discuss something that is going no place!"

Sig. P.: "You are all making me crazy."

By this time the cacophony of all the voices declaiming, shouting, mixing together reached a level of confusion where no one really knew what the other was saying. If someone could have set it to music and recorded it then, however, all the strands combining would have proven to be almost as enjoyable in its own way as Donizetti's "Sextet" from *Lucia di Lamermoor.*

Marta shouted above the din,

"Ladies, let's settle down. There must be a way to settle this."

"How?" "How?" "How?" came the responses to this initiative from the other three women.

Finally, after a good deal of discussion, it was decided that Signora Pellegrini would take the two *quintale* from Emilia, sell one to Maria who would dispose of it to some of her customers, and Maria and Marta would come to help with the bottling of the additional tomatoes, getting some bottles themselves for their trouble.

In Emila Saggio's family, her daughter Maria, as the oldest of the Saggio children, bore the greatest burden. She had to help work the land, harvest the produce when the time came to reap, process and store it, feed the animals, clean the house, gather wood for the fire, and take the family's clothing and bed linens to the river and wash them. When they killed the pig in the winter, Maria was right there beside her father and mother. Pasqualina and Agostino joined in at this time too. It was one of the most enjoyable times of the year for the children, akin to an adventure. At 3:00 A.M. Emila woke everyone and Natale went to fetch the pig from its enclosed quarters in the farthest part of the garden adjoining their house. The pig was tied with a heavy rope to a pulley-type device in a special storage room next to the main, small house. Natale used a sharp knife to puncture a vein in the pig's neck. The children looked on with horrified excitement as they saw the pig squealing, seemingly knowing that his fateful hour had arrived. The pig had nearly taken on the status of family pet, since the children had been feeding it, each one taking turns, over the past year. Still, they knew that this pet was different from the three cats and one dog that roamed over the land around them. The pig, *il maiale*, or *il porco* in the Calabrese dialect, was a lovable figure for the youngsters, but they knew that it provided a good part of some of the best food they would enjoy during the year, and they had been raised to understand that this was a necessary cruelty, so they reconciled themselves to the slaughter.

When the vein was struck, the blood came pouring out into a large clean bucket that had been properly placed so that nothing would be lost. This having been accomplished, the pig was hauled up with the pulley and left to hang so that all excess blood, the so-called non-clean blood dripped to the dirt floor of the hut-like enclosure. The outside temperature was cold enough, and there was no indoor heating, so once the pig had been split in half by Natale, it could be kept in the kitchen for the next three days, with no possibility of spoilage or rancid odors. The first thing made was possibly the only dessert the family had ever known—*sanguinaccio,* (except for Emilia's occasional *crostetta,* made of flour and sugar with some fruit that was going bad placed on top). The blood was boiled and mixed with sugar, pignoli nuts and other flavors, depending on whatever was available. Natale was skilled at butchering and he taught his children from early adolescence how to cut and separate the meat. Maria was especially helpful in preparing the meat, some to be used while fresh, some salted and preserved for future consumption, some worked into *capicolle* and *soppresate,* various forms of meat that could be salted and dried and later, usually primarily on special occasions such as Christmas and Easter, weddings and baptisms, cut into slices and eaten cold. Emilia was always nervous when she saw Maria holding the sharp knife, fearing that she would slice one of her fingers.

When it was time to do the wash, *andare a lavare,* Maria would go with or without her mother (for Emilia had at times to help her husband in the fields), her sister Lina, who was just a year younger than Maria, and some other women from their *vicinanza,* their narrowly defined neighborhood, and placing the clothes in baskets that they carried on top of their heads, they would walk some six kilometers southwest of the town to the *fiume,* the river, but as already noted, not a river at all but a swiftly running mountain stream. The women in this region were particularly adept at carrying large and even heavy loads on their heads. They took a large piece of cloth, the size of a table cloth that could cover a small table, rolled it up, took the rolled long strip and formed it into a circle with a small opening in the middle. This was placed on top of the woman's head and the basket placed atop the cloth. Various size baskets could be used to carry clothing to be washed and brought back home, fruits and vegetables or any other items that needed to be transported around the town. This practice was so much a part of their everyday activities that it became second nature for the women who utilized it. They could be seen walking along, bouncing even on the rough paths, and not using their hands at all to hold the baskets in place. It was a balancing act worthy of the most talented jugglers or trapeze artists.

On wash days, Maria would take her share of things to be cleaned, or her mother would carry the clothes and linens and Maria would carry the wood for the fire to make the *bucato,* along with some potatoes that they would bring with them to roast for lunch since they would not be back home in time for the midday meal. When they got to the stream, the women found their places where the running waters emptied into reservoirs that were either naturally developed tubs or deep receptacles for the water that the women themselves had constructed with stones and parts of tree trunks. There they first washed all the items they had brought with them that needed to be laundered. They used soap that they had themselves produced at home from used olive oil. After potatoes or fish or vegetables had been fried in the olive oil two or three times, the oil was accumulated in a large jar. When there was enough oil, the following recipe was used to make the soap:

2 liters of used olive oil
½ kilogram of caustic soda
1 kilogram of flour
4 liters of cold water

Mix the flour together with the olive oil, and the caustic soda with the water. Combine the two liquids and mix together thoroughly, but slowly. Pour into a large rectangular pan and allow to sit for a couple of days. Cut the pieces into the desired size soap bars

Some women chose to boil the mixture, while others felt that was not necessary. When the mixture had solidified, the newly made soap was cut into pieces and the larger pieces were taken to the stream. The clothes were first scrubbed and turned and twisted in the reservoir, and then rinsed in the water flowing down from the mountain. The next step was the *bucato*. All the white clothes and linens that had been thoroughly washed were placed in a large vessel, one on top of another. The container had holes at the bottom for the water to slowly seep through. This is why the procedure was called *il bucato* since *buco* means "hole." The linens and clothing were completely covered by a cloth that had been preserved for this purpose. While the first stage of washing was progressing, a fire had been built from twigs and tree branches that had been gathered when the women went *a legno*. A large rustic pot with water was set to boil and into this water was poured a goodly supply of ashes that were saved whenever a fire was made for any purpose at all. The ashes were absolutely necessary for the *bucato* and produced the same effect that bleach would when used in washing machines fifty years later. When the ashes and water were all mixed together, and had reached a boiling point, the mixture was then poured over the vessel and allowed to seep through all the washed items. After everything cooled down, the sparkling white sheets, undergarments, towels and anything else that had been part of the *bucato* were taken and spread on rocks to dry in the hot noonday sun. While waiting for everything to dry, the women had their *pranzo* of baked potatoes that had been cooking while they were working. A fruit, some water, and they were set until *la cena* around 8:00 in the evening. When the clothes and linens were completely dried, they would be folded and placed in the basket to be carried atop their heads on the walk back to their homes.

Maria had been helping her mother with the laundering from the age of ten. By the time she was sixteen, she did the family's laundry by herself since her mother was needed by her father for the work in the fields. Maria went with other young women her own age as well as with the older women who did not have daughters they could rely on. This group of women from Maria's *vicinanza* also joined together whenever it was time to go to gather the wood necessary for their fires, whether these fires were made for outdoor activities or indoor necessities. The day before they set out, the word would spread among the women: *"Domani andiamo a legno"* (tomorrow we go to get wood). The wood gathering party numbered about seven or eight women. Sometimes one of the young men would go along too, in cases where the family had no daughters and the mother was occupied with other chores. *A legno* days started even earlier than *a lavare* days. The women met outside their homes at around four in the morning and walked together up and on upwards into the higher ridges, covering as much as twenty kilometers at times. On their way they would sing songs in praise of the saints and the Virgin, alternating verses and joining in the chorus. The area where they could expect to find the greatest abundance of wood and the wood easiest to manage would take them some two hours or more to reach. One of these areas was called, in the local dialect, *la rupa*. This was a large geological wonder, a boulder some fifty feet high, thirty feet wide and another forty feet deep. It was so much larger and impressive than any other rocks in the area, that some residents believed that it had magical powers, and they would touch it or bow to it and make the sign of the cross on their foreheads. The women sought out these higher places because there they could find many trees that had suffered the ravages of the powerful winds that blew in from the sea in all seasons, and trees that succumbed to the damaging effects of the relatively mild but still sometimes ferocious winters. The women would look for dead wood, twigs and branches that would easily break off with the application of very little pressure when they were bent and pulled from the larger tree branches they had been anchored to. These branches and twigs were placed on the ground until a very large bundle could be made and tied together with cord that had been brought for that purpose. The bundle or bundles of wood were placed upon the supporting turban atop the women's heads for the journey home.

Six

Less than a year after Francesco Nardi had left for America, Maria Saggio and seven women companions left their homes on a late October morning at around five A.M. to go a *legno*. They didn't have to leave as early as they did when the weather was warmer. In late October the days were cooler and the mornings, especially in the mountains, were very chilly, requiring a sweater on top of the dresses or blouses worn by the women. As they began their trek uphill, they sang one of their favorite hymns. This particular hymn was concerned with Beato Nicola the man who had been born right there in Longobardi, and although not strictly a saint, had been beatified by the Church. It would be only a matter of time before he was canonized since many miracles were attributed to his intercession. The oldest woman of the group, Angelina Garasto, known by the townspeople as *Angelina la Gaddina*, or simply as *la Gaddina*, began the singing. The use of nicknames in Longobardi was a long-standing tradition. Sometimes the name referred to the work the person did, sometimes to a physical attribute, and sometimes to something completely external to the person himself or herself. *La Gaddina* acquired her *soprannome* from the fact that when she was quite young she walked around on her tiptoes and bobbed her head now and again, her walk reminding at least some of her neighbors of that of a chicken. *Gaddina* is the Calabrese equivalent of the Italian *gallina*. Another man, Giuseppe Ammerata had a double nickname. Like Giuseppes, he was known by the so-called diminutive Peppino. However, as a toddler, his mother would feed him outside the house and repeatedly say, "*Peppino ven'a pigliare la pappa.*" With neighbors hearing this over and over again, the boy became known as *Peppino la Pappa* and the name stuck throughout his life. Michele Nigro was a shoemaker. Michele Nigro's *soprannome* was related to his occupation. He, too, had what could be called

40

two nicknames joined together. The nickname for Michele, *Micuzzo*, came first and then *u scarparu* because he made shoes (*scarpe*). The Calabrese dialect has many words that are quite different from the Tuscan dialect which became standard Italian, so that instead of referring to a shoemaker by the Italian *calzolaio, scarparu* was preferred. Michele Nigro was known to all in the town as *Micuzzo u scarparu,* and if anyone would call him Michele Nigro, most of the townspeople would not know who was being referred to. For example, some women, both young and old, were better known as the daughter of a father who was well known in the town, so that Caterina Bruno was known as *Caterina di Mastro Timoteo.* When the *soprannome* had a negative connotation, the person who was referred to thusly was never addressed by that name directly. It would have been considered offensive, even if everyone else called the person by the odd nickname.

La Gallina began to sing:
> *Laudi a te, o Beato Nicola*
> *San Francesco ti volle suo figlio*
> *A chi prega dai pace e consiglio*
> *Carità, grazie, fede e virtù.*

The other women would then join in singing:
> *Tu, Nicola dal Ciel benedetto*
> *Desti al corpo ogni strazio crudele;*
> *Fosti al Santo di Paola fedele*
> *Nell'offrire le pene a Gesù*

In this hymn they gave praise to Nicola affirming that all who prayed to him would receive peace, guidance, charity, favors, faith and virtue.

The long walk uphill was quite strenuous, but the women were so accustomed to it that it did not tire them as it would another person who led a sedentary life. They walked along familiar footpaths through the woods, paths that had been well traversed over the years so that little growth impeded their progress. Eventually, with the singing and the discussions about their families and friends, the time passed and they reached their destination. As they arrived, the dawn was breaking and there was enough light to see which branches could be most easily acquired. The women set to work and made up their bundles

Seven

Maria Saggio, at nearly seventeen was, as already noted, a beautiful young woman. She had long dark brown hair that reached below her shoulder blades and which she usually wore in braids, dark brown eyes and an olive complexion. Her skin was unblemished and shined with an aura of wholesomeness. She was slender and taller than most of her companions at a height of five feet and six inches. As a baby she had displayed a beautifully mild and happy disposition, and this never changed. As she grew into early womanhood, her distinctive features, her finely shaped nose, straight white teeth, absence of facial hair and dignified demeanor were noticed by all who came in contact with her. She was liked by everyone. When the women gossiped and spoke slightingly of others, Maria always found something positive to say about the person being disparaged. Francesco Nardi was not the only man who had thought of Maria as a potential wife. There were, in fact, a number of men who were anxiously making plans, developing strategies, to be the man who would win this unique prize for himself. Maria's father had already been approached circuitously by some would-be suitors. The method used by the townspeople was such. No man would go directly to the girl's father to ask for her hand in marriage—at least not as an initial approach. First an emissary would be sent, an uncle, an aunt, the man's father or mother. Then if the initial endeavor showed promise, the suitor would present himself to the young woman's father to confirm the agreement in principle. When Maria's father was approached, he was about to give his consent to one man he liked, for he thought the potential match was quite a good one. But he knew he had to discuss it with his wife and she was adamantly opposed to any union for her daughter until Maria was at least eighteen years of age.

For Maria, the thought of marriage had occurred to her and she sometimes wondered about who her husband would be. She had felt an attraction for Francesco Nardi when they had exchanged glances, but since he left for America, he never came to her mind again. No other man she saw particularly appealed to her, but she fantasized that one day someone would come along who would sweep her off her feet and that she would love him as those women loved men in stories that her aunt, her mother's younger sister, Eugenia, had told her about, the heroes of old who fought to gain the love of the young maidens they themselves were in love with. And although Maria had gone to school only up until the 4th grade elementary, she possessed a native intelligence that was remarkable. Still, she had been sheltered. She knew that men were built differently from women. After all she had seen her mother change her brother Agostino's cloth *panizze* and even changed them herself though only six years old at the time. Her mother had given her some basic sex education, which, however, was but a series of proscriptions as to what not to do.

"If you ever find yourself alone with a man, any man but your father, don't let him get close to you. Don't let his face come near yours. Don't let him talk to you about anything personal or of an intimate nature. If you are in the woods and you have to pee, make sure the women get around you. Men are always hiding and looking to see what they can see. You must save yourself for your husband. This is what God wants of you, for you."

On one of these occasions, Maria asked her mother what this was that she needed to save for her husband, and Emilia replied,

"Don't you know that to make a baby a woman must lie with a man and give him her honor? This is what you must save."

"But what is my honor, where is it?" persisted Maria.

"Oh, stop asking so many questions!" her mother snapped back.

"When the time comes for you to marry I will tell you everything."

Maria had a vague idea about what needed to happen to have babies since she had spoken with some of the girls of her own age after the times when various families got together to help each other killing their pigs or gathering an overabundant harvest. Still, she did not know anything about the kind of passion that could slowly arise between a man and a woman and that could burst forth like a wild torrent and transport two lovers to exalted heights of ecstasy. She had no desire for men, except perhaps in certain undefined, completely ambiguous feelings of longing, a longing for something her body vaguely craved but which she could neither identify nor comprehend. When she saw herself in a mirror, she liked what she saw, but she foolishly, innocently thought that she was very plain. It was not that she even knew anything else but plainness, but she saw other young women in her town who had received simple gifts from visiting family members who returned from Rome or even from America, colorful bows that they arranged in their hair, and she imagined that these girls looked beautiful, when, in fact, their visage could in no way compare to hers. She had never seen herself in a mirror completely nude, so she had no idea of how physically attractive she really was. Her breasts were round and firm, not especially large, but not small either. Her posterior was shapely and perfectly proportioned to complement her beautifully shaped legs, long, slender and curvaceous. Unlike many of her friends, her legs were also free of a large amount of hair, a characteristic of women, however, that was not looked upon with distaste in this late nineteenth-early twentieth-century provincial society. She never touched her sex except when it was necessary to, washing herself, and during her periods. This too was the result of something that had been instilled in her from a very young age: girls must be pure, pure like the Blessed Virgin, like Santa Domenica, Virgin and Martyr, like Santa Innocenza, Virgin and Martyr. This was her orientation as it had been that of her mother and all the other good women in the town. Of the bad women, those women who occasionally but secretly flaunted the decent and proper way of living—for they were found out eventually and their shame would cause them suffering on earth that would be compounded when they were sent to hell—nothing could be said except that their example proved that honor was worth everything and dishonor was to be abhorred.

Maria had assimilated all of these beliefs and assumptions and practices and she looked out on the world she knew as a world of beauty and love. She loved her family and her relatives and friends. She never had a bad thought about anyone. She loved the Gospel injunction to "love one another" and she was certain that this was necessary for true happiness. She had a deeply embedded religious fervor and was sometimes tempted to tell her mother that she would like to join the order of Sisters in Paola and devote her life to God. But she also loved children so much and so wanted to have children of her own, and she knew that the Sisters could not have children, for they were not permitted to be with men. She made the firm decision not to bring the matter up with her mother, fearing that her mother might think it a good idea, even though Emilia would actually never agree to such a life for her daughter.

And so this late October morning, after joining in with her women friends in singing hymns, breaking branches off from trees and gathering fallen branches, Maria was completing the tying of her bundle, one of the largest she had ever put together. Her mother had asked her to bring as much wood as she could carry, since they would need more to keep warm during the coming winter as well as for cooking and everything else the burning of wood accomplished. Then, too, they had to accumulate extra wood and stockpile it since they would have to make a very large fire *"quandu mazzamo u maiale,"* the annual slaughtering of the pig they had raised all year. Maria needed help to tie all her wood together and she needed help again to place it on top of her head. This bundle could not be carried hands free. Maria would have to use her hands to balance it. Due to the size of her burden and its unwieldy mass, Maria was the last to start her descent and fell some paces behind her companions.

On that day, lurking in the area, getting some wood for his own use but lingering because he wanted to see which women had come up the mountain, Massimo Malavolta waited. He pretended to be gathering some herbs and had his own bundle of branches next to him, which he had been pulling along with a length of rope that was tied around and across his considerable acquisition. Not all the women saw him there, but the few who did said to their companions close to them,

"What is he doing on this side? He lives closer to the other part of the mountain. He never comes *a legno* here."

The women did not like him. He was a man of around forty-five and had been married once, but his wife had died mysteriously after they were together for only a year. Furthermore, he was quite ugly and unkempt and mean of disposition. One of the women tried to reason with the others,

"*Povero Cristiano,*" she said, "He has a right to live too."

"*Ah, ah,*" the others muttered, indicating they did not appreciate her charity in this instance.

Malavolta watched as seven women walked by him, perhaps not more than thirty feet away. Then he spied Maria, maneuvering her load of branches, stepping as quickly as she could to keep up. He liked what he saw. He had seen this girl in town and had thought of how beautiful she looked, imagining the softness and allure of her body beneath her skirt and blouse that revealed so very little of what he was certain could please him immensely. Maria had on a long, wide skirt and loose blouse. She had removed her sweater and tied it around her waist, for she no longer felt as cold as she had earlier in the morning. Her long braids hung down and swung from side to side as she walked. Malavolta noticed that Maria was at the back of the line of women and that no one was behind her. It was also not lost on him that she was considerably behind her friends. Any creature other than a man like this, one should say a vulture rather than a man, would have looked at that innocent soul and felt nothing but beneficence for her. Any truly good man would have gone to help her to manage her load. But Massimo Malavolta was not a good man. All of his life he had preyed on weakness. He was a large man and had a strength that made it easy for him to dispatch an adversary with very little effort. For this reason, most sensible men avoided any extended contact with him. Malavolta crept quickly down the hill, through the tall and small trees, across the brush, veering to the left where Maria was walking. When he was close behind her, Maria sensed that someone was there and turned slightly to look, but the bundle on her head made it difficult to turn far enough around, and before she could see who it was, he swung out at the bundle of wood, causing it to tumble off her head and Maria to fall to the ground. Maria was astonished.

"What are you doing?" she asked. Her innocence did not give her a sense of fear or foreboding that such a situation demanded of anyone with enough guile to make the judgment necessary for self preservation.

"Oh, I'm just trying to help you," Massimo said with a smile that was cold in spite of his desire to make her believe him. "Here, I will help you to get this back on your head."

"Oh, thank you," said Maria, still not comprehending how he could have tried to help her. She did not know this man, did not remember ever having seen him, and was unaware of the stories that had spread around the town about his possible complicity in his wife's death. Malavolta was really just buying time. After he pretended to help Maria place the bundle on top of her head again, when he noted that the other women were fairly far down the hill, he gave vent to his lust for the beautiful young woman. He groped at her buttocks and the bundle of wood again fell and Maria found herself once more on the ground. Malavolta pounced on top of her. "*Bacimi!*" ("Kiss me!"), he demanded. He tried to bring his mouth close to hers but she wriggled and kicked out and tried to get up. As she was rising, he reached under her long skirt and groped again, feeling her buttocks and reaching between her legs to feel her sex.

"*Che fai?*" she tried to scream, but Malavolta covered her mouth with his large hand. He held her in that position for a long time. She struggled, but the brute's strength was too much for her to contend with. When Malavolta felt that the other women were far enough down hill so they could not hear anything, he took his hand away, but before she could scream, he took his knife out and told her he would kill her if she made another sound. Maria was stunned, shocked and began to weep. She could not understand why anyone would want to harm her. She began to pray,

"*Madonna, aiutami, Jesu, salvami.*" Malavolta told her to be quiet.

"Just do what I want you to do and everything will be fine," he lied. He felt her breasts inside her blouse and brought his hands under her skirt to lift it up.

"No," cried Maria, over and over again, "No, no, no, no, no!"

As Malavolta tried to position himself to violate his innocent prey, and as he rose to loosen his trousers, Maria jumped up. She ran to a small tree and wrapped her arms around it, kneeling, tucking her skirt under and between her legs. Malavolta tried to free her arms, but the young woman summoned up all the strength that she could find in her lithe and energetic young body. All of the resistance that had been somehow genetically transmitted to her, from all the ancestral women who had fought against and repelled sexual attacks–from the Longobardi themselves, those ancient conquerors whose occupation gave the town its name, from the French who had twice conquered the village in the early 1800's, and perhaps countless others—this accumulated resistance provided Maria with an almost super human power and will to do anything necessary to avoid the onslaught of this villain. When Malavolta could not easily extricate his victim from the tree, he began to stab her arms with his knife. Still, Maria resisted. He took out his hatchet and swung it at her shoulder. Maria resisted and prayed, resisted and prayed until her beautiful young spirit could no longer cope with the assault on her violated body and her delicate psyche. She collapsed and her arms slowly fell backwards, slowly she reclined, away from the tree that she embraced as she one day should have embraced her true lover, her soul's mate, the man who could have brought happiness to her hitherto ordinary life. Massimo Malavolta, seeing the blood running from her wounds, wiped his knife and hatchet with some leaves and ran as quickly as he could back to his hut.

When Maria's wood gathering party arrived back at their homes, Maria's mother was working in the field nearby. She saw them all and looked for her daughter.

"Where is Maria?" she asked apprehensively.

"She's coming," *la Gallina* told her. "She had more wood than all of us so she's walking more slowly."

Two hours later, when Maria had still not returned, Emilia Saggio knew that this was not good, not good at all.

Eight

The populace of Longobardi and other towns throughout Calabria were born Roman Catholics. Perhaps it would be more precise to say that they entered Holy Mother Church soon after birth through the sacrament of Baptism. Most never had any formal training in their religion. Their information about their faith came from their parents, from priests or nuns who spoke to the children on Sundays, before or after the Sunday Mass, and from the sermons they would hear from the priest of their *parroco* whenever they attended Mass. In preparation for First Holy Communion (*Prima Communione*) or Confirmation (*Cresima*), special instruction was arranged for the children who were about to receive these sacraments. Along with the Catechism which they were urged to read and learn (in some parishes no printed material was available, so the priest would dictate what was to be written down, simple questions and answers such as, "Who made me?" with the reply "God made me," and so on) the basic tenets of their faith were heard and reiterated for the young by attendance at Mass on Sundays and feast days. Along with the more or less formal input from the clergy, additional information and bases for belief came via word of mouth, transmitted from one generation to another, including myths, legends, personal accounts of why all they believed was true. This was absorbed and accepted in most cases without questioning the validity of the source or the accuracy of the data. Everything was Gospel truth, whether it originated in the Gospels or came via folkloristic evangelism. Furthermore, each town, village or local area had its own unique credo, peculiar to their people alone. Parents, relatives and neighbors did not have to do anything extraordinary to impart the message. It was lived day by day as the concomitant part of an unchallenged mindset wherein everything that needed to be known about God and all things related to Him had been long since settled upon, with no need to think about it at all.

In Longobardi, Beato Nicola was especially revered by the inhabitants because their town was his birthplace. The house where he was born was looked upon as sacred territory. Beato Nicola was born in 1649 and christened Giovambattista Saggio. For his parents, Fulvio Saggio and Aurelia Pizzini, Giovambattista was the first of their three children. The child demonstrated excessive curiosity about religion from a very early age and became devoted to the Church and its beliefs and liturgy, and was seen by his contemporaries as one of the most humble young men they ever knew. Eventually, he went to Paola, where his devotion to San Francesco was manifested by becoming an Oblate Brother in the monastic convent there. Sometime thereafter, he went to Rome where he became well known for his piety and profound religious fervor and ability to move his followers to embrace their faith with ever deeper devotion. While Nicola was in Rome as a spiritual counselor, Countess Luisa della Cerda, the sister of the Duke of Medinacoeli, the Vice King of Naples, became devoted to Nicola and his work. When it came time for Nicola to return to Calabria, she offered to give him the uncorrupted corpse of the Virgin and Martyr, Santa Innocenza, which had been entombed under the altar of her private chapel. Nicola took it back to Longobardi. After an eight day voyage by boat, the body of the saint arrived near Longobardi, but a tremendous storm arose and no boat, legend tells us, could have survived the tempest. But when it was over, the boat carrying the saint did not have even a drop of water on it. The remains of the saint were then taken up to the town where it was placed under the altar of the Church of San Francesco. Each year on the saint's feast day, the corpse would be taken out and carried in a procession throughout the town. This custom has been followed even to the present day. There are many stories about Nicola that mirror miracles attributed to Jesus. For example, one day he needed fish to feed workers who were building a new church and convent. When the fisherman refused to give Nicola fish to feed the men, he called out to the sea and suddenly numbers of fish came floating to shore, ready to be gathered to feed all the men. After Nicola's death, various miracles were attributed to his intercession and eventually the Vatican consented to his beatification, a step in the process towards canonization.

The Longobardesi have also always been devoted to the 15th century Saint Francis of Paola, whose life was also an imitation of the life of Jesus in many respects. Perhaps the most famous episode was Francis' walking on water, a feat immortalized in a masterly piano composition by Hungarian composer Ferenc Liszt. The Madonna of Taureana, another religious symbol of importance concerned a vision of the Blessed Mother that appeared in the section of Longobardi known as Taureana. High on a hill, the Madonna reportedly stretched out her arms to repel the advances of invading armies. Continually thereafter, this Madonna was venerated, a small church was built on the hill where she supposedly appeared, and a feast day was instituted on which a morning Mass was celebrated in her honor there, followed by special feasting by all the participants.

In this cultural and religious atmosphere of unquestioned faith, undying devotion to Jesus and His Sacred Heart, the Virgin and saints, especially those saints most revered, the news of the murder of Maria Saggio was received by the community with varying degrees of shock, horror, incredulity, repugnance and, yes, with a certain acquiescence based on the conviction that this was *la volontà di Dio,* the will of God and whatever God so wills, even if we do not understand, we must accept. God has a reason for everything and as events over the next months and years were to demonstrate, God had a special reason for Maria to die the way she did. Her body was found with twenty-six stab wounds from the killer's knife, covering both arms, both hands, her back and her buttocks. Another eight large cuts made by Malavolta's hatchet had penetrated her shoulders and neck. At her funeral, barely a soul from the entire *paese* was absent. The eulogy at her funeral Mass was given by Don Gregorio Previteri, the priest that had baptized Maria, given her first Communion and assisted at her Confirmation. He began softly.

"Thirty-four wounds. Thirty-four lacerations. Thirty-four," his voice began to rise, "attestations to the honor the young Maria Saggio has conferred on all of us. Why, 'honor' you ask? Why? Because she has shown us that purity and love of God are important above all else. This young, beautiful, good, exceptionally good young woman chose to suffer, as our Lord Jesus Christ himself suffered. Yes, she chose to suffer rather than to succumb to the devil, to the forces of evil in our world. Jesus made the same decision. Being the Son of God, he could have freed himself, but he knew that he had to die for our sins, and he accepted that. He gave up his own earthly life so that we could live. Maria, too, could have given in to the horrible demands of her killer. She could have taken the easy way out and saved her own life. No one could have blamed her, but she chose to die rather than to compromise her honor." The priest's words resounded so much more forcefully in Italian than can be imagined from the English equivalent, the inflections carrying his message out across the congregation with a sweeping power that left his listeners trembling in their seats. "*Trenta-quattro lacerazione!*" he shouted and some could almost feel the impact of the knife or hatchet on their own skin.

50

As the priest spoke women could be heard weeping and wailing. Some proclaimed aloud after each phrase spoken by Don Gregorio,

"*Lauda sia a Dio*" (Praise be to God). "

"Yes, Maria could easily have saved her own life by surrendering to the illicit desires of this devil incarnate who chose to destroy a lovely flower, a ray of sunshine in the lives of everyone who knew her. But she was raised to love God, to honor His Church and to place honor and the love of God above everything else. Today, I would much have preferred to be here to perform the marriage ceremony for Maria and a man worthy of being her husband and to celebrate that marriage with her family."

At this, the women's and even the men's sobs became palpable.

"But this was not to be," Don Gregorio continued.

"No, today we are here to celebrate her martyrdom. Today she is in a happier place, a place she shares with all the other saints and martyrs. Today she is praying for us. Today we can ask for *her* intercession, yes, for her intercession in all our spiritual needs."

Perhaps knowingly, perhaps not, with this suggestion that Maria could be an intermediary between the people she had known and God, Don Gregorio provided his listeners with a new object for devotion, a new possibility for the confirmation of their belief, as absurd as that may sound, and the people grasped it to themselves with fervor and conviction.

"I don't know what will happen to the assassin, but justice will be done," continued Don Gregorio.

"*Giustizia, giustizia!*" came the cry from many in the church.

"Yes, we will have justice," the priest assured, "We will have justice and Maria's murder will be avenged. But remember this too! Remember the words of our Savior: 'Forgive your enemies.' Forgive as you yourselves have been forgiven by our God. Do not allow your hearts to be filled with rancor."

Looking over at Maria's mother and father, Don Gregorio pleaded,

"You have a right to be angry. You have a right to be sad. You have a right to even question why God could allow this evil to come to pass. In time you will understand more and more. In time you will come to accept the will of God in this as in everything. Believe that God so loved your daughter that He chose to take her to His side at this early and fragile age. He must truly love her to give her a place beside the saints and martyrs of old, to have her join Beato Nicola, San Francesco, Santa Innocenza in his Heavenly abode. She is with our Blessed Mother Maria, her namesake, in communion with the holiest of the holies. She is happy today in her new home."

Don Gregorio completed his sermon and the procession began with a number of men carrying the light coffin up to the cemetery. Two shrines for devotion to Maria were soon erected, one at her graveside and the other at the tree that she had embraced before dying. Years later, her remains were exhumed and buried inside the Church that also housed the remains of Santa Innocenza, Longobardi's saint with the incorruptible body.

After the murder, Malavolta took refuge in his house, not sure whether he was suspected or not. Later that terrible morning, he walked to town and spied from a distance, attempting to ascertain conditions regarding suspicions that he could have been involved. A search party was being formed. He volunteered to join it and went along with the Saggios and a group of men to look for Maria. Her family piled hope on hope that she was alive, perhaps just injured and unable to walk. When Maria's body was spotted, lying next to the tree, the ground suffused with her blood, and as the cries of Emilia and Natale, Pasqualina and Agostino resounded throughout the mountains, none of those present who had gone, praying all the time that the young girl would be found alive, could suppress their own lamentations. A woman who had been with Maria's group that morning and had seen Malavolta briefly, saw through her tears that he was the only member of the search party not crying or bemoaning the sight they had come upon. Immediately, she sensed that he was the murderer and pointed at him.

"*È lui!*" she cried. "He is the murderer. He was there when we were descending. He killed her!"

Hearing this accusation, Malavolta panicked and ran from the group. Later, he did not resist the *carabinieri* when they came to arrest him, maintaining his innocence. At his trial at the *Tribunale* in Paola two months later, the judge was tending towards acquittal, since he felt the evidence was not strong enough to convict Malavolta. Before he adjourned, prior to giving his verdict, Emila Saggio cried out in the courtroom,

"*Giustizia! voglio giustizia per mia figlia! Dio sa ch'è stato lui,*" pointing an accusatory finger at Malavolta. ("I demand justice for my daughter! God knows he was the one"). The sun had been shining brightly all morning. Just then, a crack of thunder accompanied by a sharp stroke of lightning shook the room. The room was suddenly darkened as thick dark clouds covered the sun. The judge quickly retired to his private chamber, calling for a one hour adjournment. He pondered the merits of the case against Malavolta, reflected on the similarity of what had just happened to the events of Good Friday and deemed it to be a certain sign from God. Returning to the courtroom, he sentenced Malavolta to life in prison. Some measure of justice was realized that day.

Nine

Rosina Nardi's younger sister, Laura Pucci, had gone to America with her husband Amadeo Goffreddo after he had made a return trip to Italy to look into finding a bride to take back with him to Pittsburgh. He had originally settled in Caracas and eventually made his way to Pennsylvania, where a company that did business in Venezuela offered him work. He had a younger brother, Giovanni Goffreddo, who had also gone to Caracas and eventually decided to follow Amadeo to the U.S. Giovanni lived with his brother and new sister-in-law for some time after his arrival. Laura showed Giovanni a picture of another sister, Emma, who was the youngest in her family, and Giovanni told his brother that he wanted to marry her. Amadeo, somewhat surprised asked,

"Gianni, how can you say such a thing? You have never even met her."

"I don't care," Gianni insisted. "I like her and she is Laura's sister, so she must be good too."

Gianni had within a few months of his arrival opened a shoe making and repair shop in the center of Pittsburgh, and soon had more work than he could handle. When he felt that the time was right, he hired a man to look after his shop, one who could barely do the minimum, since shoemakers of Gianni's ability were not readily available. Gianni went to Longobardi with a letter of introduction from his sister-in-law and presented himself to Emma's father, for he did not need further intervention in light of Laura's letter. Rosina Nardi was ecstatic to have news of her sister's whereabouts and general well-being and she liked the young man who had come seeking her younger sister's hand in marriage. He was a *paesano*, but Rosina did not remember him for he had been away for almost ten years, having left when he was just nineteen. Now twenty-nine, he was ready to settle down, and Rosina and her family liked this suitor's serious outlook that mixed happily with a ready smile and a good heart. He met Emma, they were married and Gianni took his new bride to America, where the young woman could see her sister Laura for the first time in seven years.

Gianni Goffreddo went back to his shoe shop and worked diligently, amassing a large and loyal clientele. His customers recommended him to their friends, for his work was both excellent and fairly priced. After a year had passed, Gianni was so satisfied with the success of his small enterprise that he never even considered returning to Italy. Emma was pregnant with their first child and everything was progressing smoothly. Gianni had images of Jesus, the Blessed Mother and some saints on the walls of his dwelling as well as in his shop. He thanked God each day for his good fortune and Emma said a daily Rosary for her unborn baby's intentions.

Gianni knew that the men who walked into his store one day could not be customers. They were well dressed, wearing ties and jackets. One of them, the older of the two men, waiting until a customer had walked out, spoke to Gianni in what Gianni recognized as the Sicilian dialect.

"You have a nice business here," the man said in a complimentary and non-threatening tone.

"I do my best, " Gianni replied.

"I'm sure your profits are quite handsome," the Sicilian continued.

"These are my interests," Gianni replied, "and they do not concern you."

The gray haired man smiled a bitter smile and, not deterred at all by Gianni's remark, insinuated,

"But you see, my good man, it is our interest too."

"How so?" Gianni asked.

"Oh, my dear friend," and Gianni winced at the mention of the word "friend," for he did not extend this distinction to too many people.

"My dear, dear friend, and I assure you we will have a friendship between us, for you need my friendship very, very much."

"I don't see what I can possibly need from you," Gianni responded, now with some trepidation.

"Let me explain," came the rejoinder.

"There is a good deal of danger for a man like you, a man with a business like yours. There are those who would come and steal from you, those who would set your shop on fire because they need the business they feel you are taking away from them. Even the legal authorities will eventually try to shut you down. They will say your shop does not comply with the municipal regulations. *We* are your protection. We can help you to avoid these problems. We have all kinds of connections, with the police, with the local politicians, with many. That is why we are your friends. We will take care of any problems that may come to you before they even reach your door."

The gangster's sardonic tone told Gianni that he was not going to like what he was about to hear.

"Why would you do this for me?" asked Gianni, completely bewildered, never having experienced a shakedown in his life before.

"That is our business," the younger of the two men joined in, "Just as you have your shoe business, we have our business, a business of protecting our friends. We make certain that no one can bother you or hurt your business."

"What do you want from me in return?" Gianni inquired, feeling himself slipping, sensing an anger welling up inside him that was so untypical of his personality.

"You pay us for the protection we provide you with," came the assured response of the mobster, speaking now with contempt and disdain. No appearance of friendship was in evidence any longer.

"Someone will be here on Saturday evening to collect our fee," the younger native of Sicily advised Gianni, speaking in an authoritative tone portending disaster if the veiled threat were not heeded. As the two men exited the shop, Gianni could hear the younger man say to the older one,

"Un cazzo stupido!"

When Gianni told Amadeo about his experience, his brother was speechless. After some minutes, Amadeo said,

"È La Mano Nero!" ("It is the Black Hand."). "I have heard about them," he went on. "You must give them what they ask you for. First they will warn you and knock things around in your shop. Then they will knock you around. You have no choice. I have heard it said that they even kill those who resist."

"I will go to the police!" shouted Gianni.

"The police are in their back pocket."

Having said this, Amedeo sat down and placed his head on the table.

"Things were going so well here," he lamented. "The Devil must always get into the middle of things."

Gianni listened to his brother's deprecations and, as though someone had just turned on a light in his head, he exclaimed,

"Yes, they told me they take care of the legal authorities too."

The following Saturday night, as Gianni was getting ready to close, a man walked in who was not as well dressed as those who had visited earlier. He was a burly man, unshaven and unkempt, muscular and menacing in appearance.

"I am here for the protection payment," he said, demandingly. Gianni found that he had to give the man one tenth of his week's net earnings.

La Mano Nero was a late nineteenth century, early twentieth century antecedent of the Sicilian Mafia that would thirty years later control the entire illegal sale of liquor during Prohibition, and continue thereafter to exercise its control over many other American interests. The name "Black Hand" was, in fact used by a number of different groups, including Spanish anarchists and the group of Serbians responsible for the assassination of Franz Ferdinand, the Archduke of Austria, this being the immediate cause of The Great War. However, The Black Hand that flourished for some years in Pennsylvania and New York City had no political motives whatsoever. Their stimulus was simply greed, preying on helpless immigrants whose ignorance of English and distrust of the justice system, a distrust instilled in them in Italy from unfortunate personal experiences, made them easy targets. Gangs of petty criminals enforced the code. Gianni received a personal visit because he had a business, but immigrants who worked in the limestone quarries received letters with an imprint of a black hand. When they saw that mark, they knew they had no choice but to comply with the demand. Eventually, the extortion demands reached twenty per cent of Gianni's net income, then twenty-five per cent. The mobsters informed Gianni that the costs of "protection" were increasing so he had to pay more too. Gianni told Emma that he could no longer tolerate living this way and that they had to return to Italy. Their daughter, born in Pittsburgh two months earlier, an American citizen by birth, would soon be traveling to her parents' place of birth. As Gianni prepared to close his shop, he had another visit from the two well-dressed extortionists.

"Where do you think you are going?" demanded the gray haired man.

"I must return to Italy. My father is very ill and I must go home to care for him and for his interests."

Gianni spoke haltingly, now afraid that they would try to prevent him from leaving. The Sicilians, however, did not react as Gianni expected them to.

"That is an honorable thing to do. Family must always come first. One's father must be respected above all things," and the scoundrel stepped forward to shake Gianni's hand, which he barely took hold of. The matter of family honor was the only thing these villains held sacred. The disposition of the shop was then discussed and the Sicilians told Goffreddo that he would not have to try to sell his shop. They would pay him what it was worth and set someone up to run it.

As Gianni was about to set off on his journey back to Italy, foolishly expecting to receive a sum of money that would at least match his own investment, he was bitterly disappointed but not surprised any longer when a pittance was given him. The rationale according to his tormentors was that their protection funds could not be depended upon until the shop was up and running and this would take some weeks.

Tragically, Gianni contracted a virus on the voyage back, his health deteriorated and he died on the ship before he ever saw Italian soil again. Emma was left to raise their daughter alone.

Ten

Francesco Nardi returned home about four months after Maria's death. He was unaware of what had occurred there. He still entertained the thought of asking his father to approach Maria's father on his behalf. When he saw Maria's mother dressed in black, he assumed that one of her close relatives had died, but certainly not one of her children. Treading lightly, for the matter was a delicate one for him, he asked his father if he had seen Maria.

"Don't you know, Francesco? Only heavenly spirits can see her now."

"What?" Francesco asked agitatedly.

His father told him what had transpired while he was in America. After fulfilling his duty to inform Paolo's mother about her son's ugly fate, Francesco fell into a stupor that lasted for weeks. First he had seen his best friend murdered. Now he had returned home to learn that the only woman he could see himself with had also been murdered. His mental state was in distress and his family soon feared that he himself would succumb to illness, for he ate hardly at all and he refused to even speak to anyone. By and by, Maria's mother Emilia Saggio learned of Francesco's decline and the reasons for it. She went to the Nardi home to visit Francesco and spoke to him gently and encouragingly. She had always admired the young man as he was growing up.

"Francesco," she implored, "I have come to know that you loved my daughter. My family would have been honored if you had become her husband, but destiny did not so decree this for you or for her. Maria wants you to move ahead with your life. I had a dream about her some nights ago and she told me that she wants you to be happy, for she is happy where she is. She wants you to find another woman that you can love." Francesco roused himself for the first time in weeks.

"Truly?" he asked. "Did she tell you this?" Francesco inquired timidly. "Yes," Emilia assured him. "She wants you to live, and to love."

Francesco began to come back to life that same day, and soon he was helping his father in making shoes. A few weeks later, Francesco decided to visit the Saggios, to thank Emilia for her concern and support and to offer to make her a pair of shoes. He had been so moved by the way in which she spoke to him that he wanted to do something special for her. As he entered the house, he saw Maria's younger sister Pasqualina. She was not quite as beautiful as Maria had been. She was of fairer skin with blue eyes and lighter hair. She did not exhibit the sense of serenity and sweet composure that Maria had, but she was also quite beautiful in her own distinctive way. Francesco made a mental note of this young woman. She was then just sixteen years old. There followed a year of courtship, a courtship characterized by occasional visits during which Pasqualina's mother or father were always present, and the young couple could speak only of mundane matters and only when Emilia or Natale were not speaking. This left them very little time to get to know one another in any real sense, but they did come to prize each other's qualities of tenderness, respect for family, and evenness of temperament. Their union was frowned upon by some members of the Nardi's extended family since essentially the Nardi's were on the second rung of the social ladder, but the Saggios were *campagnuoli*, living outside of the town center and working the land. Francesco's parents did not give in to this prejudicial attitude and they gave their blessings to the couple. They were married in 1899 and had two sons and four daughters, Gaetano in 1900, Rosina in 1901, Natale in 1902, Emilia in 1903, Violetta in 1904 and Maria, named after Pasqualina's sister in 1906. In conformity with local tradition, the first son and daughter were named after the paternal grandparents and the second daughter and son after the maternal grandparents. Violetta was a name that Francesco loved. Soon after the birth of Maria, Pasqualina died of a hemorrhage. Her frail frame was unable to withstand the burden of delivering six babies in seven years. The oldest daughter Rosina, just five when her mother died, had to adapt to doing chores and helping her father with the younger children. Gaetano, too, was responsible for various household chores. Francesco had assistance, of course, from both his mother and his mother-in-law.

It was a hard life for these children, with no mother to do all the things that mothers do so well, and, in a very real sense, are irreplaceable in the lives of their children. Francesco was a good man. He was affable and even-tempered, and gave his children as much affection as he knew how to give. He was not well educated and could not imagine that his children had needs that he could, perhaps, have met to a greater extent than he did. He was more distant with his two sons, and they stayed away from home as much as they could once they had fulfilled their duties around the homestead.

Natale learned shoemaking from his father and worked alongside him for a time, but at the age of fourteen he went to live with a man from Longobardi who had moved to Paola and who had a more thriving business there than his father had in Longobardi. When he reached the age of eighteen, he went to America and eventually opened his own shoe repair shop which he operated for the rest of his life. He never returned to his homeland. His older brother Gaetano was called into military service in 1918. He was eighteen years of age, just having reached the age of conscription when he was called up. Any suffering and deprivation he had known in his life until then was as nothing compared to what he faced as an infantryman, living in the trenches, fighting from the trenches, lacking the proper clothing to ward off the cold and rain that chilled his bones and rendered him and his fellow soldiers unable to even assist one another. The one meal they could look forward to consisted of cabbages, potatoes and, infrequently, some bread. While fighting the Austrians in the mountains of Northern Italy, he became the victim of a poison gas attack. The Germans had developed various types of gases. Some killed the person who inhaled it almost instantaneously. The gas that Gaetano had inhaled was carbonyl chloride, otherwise known as phosgene. The Germans developed this gas because other gases they had been using were irritants and as such, sent the infantrymen scurrying to put on their gas masks. Phosgene, instead, a gas of high density and soluble in the body's fat could be inhaled without any immediate discomfort. It was said to even have had a pleasant odor. In its concentrated form the gas brings on a tightness in the chest and a feeling of trauma, but this initial reaction passes quickly and leaves one feeling quite normal. Its effect is delayed until the lungs begin to swell and the affected infantryman feels himself choking and unable to breathe. This is what happened to Gaetano Nardi, and his superiors had him sent home to convalesce.

These were years of severe hardship for the Nardi daughters, with one crisis succeeding another. In 1918 the first cases of the Spanish influenza manifested themselves and the populace began to scatter to try to avoid contagion. Emilia, fifteen years old was stricken and Francesco told his daughters that they must leave her in the care of the town's doctor, inside a quarantine building that had been set up for the purpose, and go with him up into the mountains where his in-laws had a shack. He felt that they would be better off up there, away from the higher concentration of people, before they were all stricken too. Reports were circulating that in some cities healthy men contracted the disease one day and died the next. Some families were wiped out in a matter of days. Francesco did not think of himself as selfish in abandoning one of his daughters, for in one sense that was what he was doing. But he felt that as the head of his family he had to think of the greatest good. Rosina and Maria went with their father, but Violetta, then fourteen, a year younger than Emilia, refused to leave her sister. She stayed in the house with her, nursing her, running back and forth to the town doctor to seek advice and information as to what needed to be done. Violetta did not get the disease, but she watched her sister deteriorate and held her in her arms as she expired after suffering and ailing for weeks. With the care her sister gave her, she almost recovered, but she got out of bed too quickly and had a fast relapse that caused her to succumb to the deadly influenza. Violetta was unique among the four Nardi girls. She possessed the greatest beauty of all the sisters. She was a combination of her Aunt Maria and her mother Pasqualina. She was slightly but firmly built, with long brown hair and large brown eyes. Her face had a sculpted look, with a fine small nose, rich red lips, an unobtrusive chin and finely proportioned ears. It was not just her physical beauty that set her apart from her sisters, for she also had a radiance about her that enraptured all who had any contact with her. In this regard, she inherited some of the traits that had endeared her Aunt Maria to those who knew her. Violetta had a pure, good heart, magnanimously offering to do anything she could to aid anyone in need of her help. She had a ready smile that emitted rays of sunshine that could penetrate the sourest disposition. She was personable, affable, sincere and genuine. Although very religious, she did not wear her religion on her sleeve as many of the other women did. She never said anything to indicate to others that she felt that she was such a good person, in spite of being praised by her family and friends for all the fine things she did. On the contrary, she felt that she should always do more. She felt deep compassion for the suffering of everyone she saw who languished in any way, from physical pain, mental depression, deprivation as to material goods, or anything else that could hurt them. About three months after Emilia died, Gaetano returned home from Austria, suffering extreme pain and weakness and having great difficulty in breathing. The three sisters did all they could for him, but, again, it was Violetta who sat at his bedside night and day, giving him his medication, rubbing him down when his fever got high, consoling him and telling him funny stories to try to make him feel good. Violetta always displayed that unique characteristic of one truly concerned for the welfare of others. Gaetano lingered for two more months and succumbed to the complications set in motion by the poisonous gas, one of 571,000 Italian soldiers who died in the Great War.

Eleven

After the deaths of her sister and brother, Violetta Nardi began to do all that she could to make life for the remaining family meaningful and enjoyable. She cooked special dishes for her father and two sisters, utilizing whatever ingredients she could put together to make the meals tastier. She had a strong desire to flush away the sadness and the pain of their losses and to look at life with renewed zest, to *godere la vita*, enjoy life, for she knew how precious life was. Violetta had a flair for cooking, and unlike most of the town's women who made the usual pasta, plain vegetables and other equally uninspired dishes, she enjoyed experimenting and preparing foods worthy of a gourmet. With eggs, she would concoct *frittatas* that not only smelled and tasted wonderful but also looked so very appetizing on the plate. She would mix the eggs with flour and various cheeses—provolone, goat cheese—peppers, onions, mushrooms, squash flowers and more. The *fritttata* was cooked in a large frying pan, *frissura* in Calabrese, to a golden brown, puffing up to as high as four or five inches. Her pastas would include not just tomato sauce, but *pancetta*, hard boiled eggs, ricotta and whatever other ingredients became available. Her *minestras* of pasta and vegetables, squash, beans, potatoes, cooked with the resulting exquisite odors provided by spices like, rosemary, oregano, basil and fennel, were worthy of the most cherished prizes accorded to chefs. But for all of this, her efforts were not particularly appreciated, for her father and sisters considered her insouciance to be inappropriate in view of what they had been through.

Francesco eventually found a woman to live with and he installed her in a room on the ground floor of the small house. One evening he called her to come up to eat something with them. Rosina, the oldest sister stood before the door and stated with burning conviction,

"That woman will not come into these quarters. If you have so little respect for yourself that you want to sleep with her in the same house with your daughters, then I do not have to tolerate it."

Francesco swung his heavy hand at Rosina's face and shouted back at her,

"Don't you ever tell me again that I have no self-respect." This was the very first time the gentle man had ever struck one of his children. Rosina won the battle, though, since Francesco did not ask that his woman friend be allowed to come upstairs again. He would ask Rosina for some food that he could give to her, and Rosina would grudgingly hand over a small portion of what the family was eating. Violetta, feeling compassion as was her wont, always took something extra to Lisandra so that she would have as much to eat as the rest of the family did.

By 1920, at the age of sixteen, Violetta was already the object of the affection of a number of the town's male population. Whenever Giovanni was approached by these men's families with the suggestion that they expand the *parentata*, that is, join their families together with the marriage of their son and Violetta, Giovanni told them simply,

"You know that I have one daughter older than Violetta. If your son is interested in Rosina, we can talk further."

This was a reference to the Calabrese custom that if an older daughter was still unmarried, a younger daughter could not precede her in the sacrament. None of the men who wanted Violetta would settle for Rosina, so a stalemate ensued for the next two years.

In 1922, a man from the town of Falconara Albanese, a town some 16 kilometers distant from Longobardi, appeared looking for a wife. Carmine Sandreva was descended from a family from Albania that had crossed the sea to settle in Italy. A fairly large number of other Albanians had made the same journey and the town of Falconara developed into a bi-lingual one where both Albanese and Calabrese were spoken interchangeably. Carmine was a merchant who traveled up and down the coast from the south of Naples to Reggio Calabria, returning home twice a year to his home town to spend some time there to rest and to make plans for his next trip. He would buy and sell items such as locally made cheeses, *sopresate*, *capicoli*, dried figs and olive oil, realizing a healthy profit. On his way back from Reggio Calabria, stopping along the way in Tropea, Amantea and other towns as he made his way north with his horse and wagon, he came to Longobardi. Carmine was then thirty-eight years old and he had long thought about marrying and starting a family. He was not a physically attractive man for he had a large frame on a short body and looked disheveled most of the time. As he sat on the front seat of the wagon driving his faithful mare, a horse he had named Stella because of a white spot on the horse's forehead that resembled a star, the dust from the rural roads and the sun beating down on him gave his skin a worn and dirty appearance. His face had the appearance of a man at least ten years older than he actually was. He had stopped to buy some wine from a vintner in Longobardi and was asking the man if there were any young women that he could approach for the purpose of contracting a marriage. While they were talking, Rosina Nardi came by to return some empty bottles and to get some wine. As she waited for the vintner to finish with Carmine, the vintner told the merchant that the young lady who had entered his *bottega* was available. He promised Carmine that he would speak to the girl's father and told Carmine to return in one week to see if there was any interest. When Francesco discussed the proposal with his daughter, she was flattered but wanted to know who the suitor was. Her father told her that she had already seen him, the man who was buying wine while she was there. She recalled this old looking, shabby man and told her father that she was not that desperate to be married. However, when Carmine approached the house a week later, accompanied by the vintner, Rosina saw a much different looking man. Carmine had washed and shaved and was wearing his finest pants, shirt and jacket. While he still did not look like the man Rosina could have seen herself with, he did not look all that bad to her now. Furthermore, Carmine told Francesco that he would not require a dowry and that he would supply all the food for the wedding feast. This was an extraordinary offer since most fathers then had to give the prospective groom a sum of money or some goods of value before the marriage could be effectuated.

Rosina and Carmine were wed and Rosina left Longobardi to live in Carmine's house in Falconara. Within a few months, Rosina was pregnant. She went to see the local doctor who immediately told her she would have to depend on the midwife at her time of delivery since he was much too busy to be available for all the women having babies. This one doctor in the area served the towns of Falconara Albanese and San Lucido. Federico Sansevero was from Rende in the Province of Cosenza and had studied medicine in Rome. He was a typical country doctor, if one can truly refer to any such doctor as typical, for there are those whose compassion knows no limits while others see their patients as "cases." Sansevero had no particular expertise in obstetrics, but over twenty years he had delivered many babies and considered himself an authority on the procedure. He harbored an attitude of condescension towards the local population, fancying himself a father figure to whom they had to defer, not only in medical matters, but in any and every subject that might come up for discussion. He, however, had very little patience for discussion, continually pontificating and refusing to have his views challenged. After some years, he had developed the theory that childbirth was basically routine, that there was nothing one had to worry about except in very unusual cases. Eventually, then, he permitted the midwives to deliver babies without exception. He had made it clear that they should disturb him only in a real emergency, and he stressed the point that such aberrations from the natural course of things would almost never occur.

Rosina went through what appeared to be a normal pregnancy. She could feel the baby moving inside her, growing larger and larger as the months passed. In her ninth month, she became very uncomfortable. Clotilda, the midwife, told her that the baby was extremely large and that since this was her first pregnancy she could look forward to difficult labor and a hard delivery. Clotilda was a good woman and had assisted many of the town's families in bringing their children into the world. She wanted Rosina to know what to expect but she expressed herself in terms of tenderness and compassion."I will be with you the entire time," she assured the young mother-to-be. "I want you to be prepared for some pain. I don't want to lie to you and tell you it will be easy. You have a very large baby inside you. But I have delivered many babies and I have some ways of making it easier for you."

Rosina was happy to be in this woman's hands. She preferred having Clotilda with her in place of that dreadful arrogant doctor. Rosina was happy, too, that her sister Violetta also came to help during the last weeks of her pregnancy.

Early on a Monday morning Rosina's contractions began and continued for some hours. With the breaking of her water, the arduous delivery began in earnest and Rosina's pain was unbearable. Clotilda had nothing to give her to ease her ordeal. She could only caress her head and encourage her to push harder. Carmine stood nearby, totally helpless as Violetta and a few of the women neighbors ran to and fro, boiling water in preparation for the delivery, retrieving clean cloths from their own homes, following Clotilda's instructions as to what was needed. After ten hours of intense labor, by which time Rosina had become totally enervated, Clotilda ordered Carmine to go and fetch the doctor.

"And tell him to bring his surgical tools," Clotilda whispered into the frantic man's ear

Doctor Sansevero was at home in San Lucido and Carmine rode his mule down the mountain to call him. Rosina's labor had begun at around 10:00 in the morning and it was already past 8:00 P.M. The doctor was about to have supper, and his wife did not want to call him outside where Carmine waited.

"But it's very urgent. Tell him my wife could die if he doesn't come." Carmine was shocked at his own words, not wanting to believe that such an outcome could be possible. When the doctor's wife heard the word "die," she ran inside to call her husband.

"Tell him I will come after I have had my supper."

"Federico," his wife urged, "I think you should go right away. He told me his wife has been in labor since early this morning."

The doctor arose and mounted his own horse to make the trip up to Falconara. Carmine informed him that Clotilda said he would need his surgical instruments.

"I have everything I need in my bag," Sansevero replied, obviously annoyed that anyone, least of all a midwife, should tell him what to do.

Upon arriving at the Sandreva home, Dr. Sansevero quickly cautioned Rosina about her screams.

"Try to be quiet. Your screaming takes away the energy you need to push the baby out."

After examining his patient and ascertaining that Rosina's cervix was fully dilated, Dr. Sansevero urged her to keep on pushing. Clotilda took the doctor aside and pleaded with him to perform a Ceasarean section to deliver the baby.

"Doctor, she is very weak. She cannot push any more. The baby is just too big. I have delivered many babies and have never seen one this big! Please, do the Caesarean."

"I only perform a Caesarean as a last resort," the doctor insisted. Sansevero knew that a Caesarean would tie him up longer and make it necessary for him to return to see the patient again, and he wanted to avoid that. After a few hours, when he realized that the woman's strength was depleted and that she would need help to get the baby out, the doctor decided on a most unorthodox approach. Pushing a chair next to the bed, he got up onto it and mounted Rosina with his knees on her stomach, using all his force to press down on her, demanding that the midwife stand in front and help the baby to emerge. The doctor was not a small man and his excessive weight put a great deal of pressure on Rosina's abdomen. As he bounced up and down Rosina cried out, but her evident discomfort did not give the physician pause.

"*Sforza!*" he cried over and over with each thrust. After about fifteen minutes of this maniacal endeavor, the placenta separated from the wall of the uterus and blood flowed down Rosina's legs, followed by the emergence of the baby's head. Slowly the baby came through the cervix, tearing apart the mother's skin. Finally, at around three o'clock in the morning, the baby was completely out and the umbilical cord was cut. Alas, there was no cry. The baby, a beautiful, fully formed eleven pound boy, was dead. He looked as though he could have been two months old. Rosina nearly did not herself survive, and it was ten days before she could even get up out of bed. Fortunately, Rosina had Violetta's capable assistance and moral encouragement to get her through one of the most difficult times of her life. Dr. Sansevero smugly told Carmine that he had done what he could, but the baby was already dead and that was why he was not coming out. Clotilda knew otherwise.

When Rosina was strong enough to get out of bed, Don Luigi said a Requiem Mass for the baby's soul. At the conclusion of the Mass, he sat with Rosina and Carmine, offering his condolences and trying his best to make some sense out of their tragedy for them.

"*È stata la volontà di Dio*," he said with compassion. "God evidently wanted your little boy for Himself, for His own glory. This can explain why he was already so big within you. He was already more developed than babies usually are at that stage. Do not be sad. God wanted this one. He will give you more, I am sure of it."

Rosina and Carmine nodded in agreement. Clotilda, standing nearby, was not convinced by the priest's words. God says "Help yourself and I will help you," she thought and quickly felt guilty at having contradicted the good priest's words, if only in her own thinking. Violetta's faith was so strong that she, too, accepted without further thought the conclusion that God's will had been done. The structure of belief that had been erected within each of them could not be easily shaken. Their Faith demanded of them that they accept God's will and the priest had assured them that this was God's will, hadn't he?

Eighteen months later, after another difficult pregnancy, Rosina delivered a baby boy that she named Filippo after Carmine's deceased father. They were happy together, for Carmine was a considerate man, a devoted husband and father in spite of his long absences.

Three years after their marriage, Carmine was again working his way back to Falconara, stopping in towns that were now familiar to him for he had been making the same journey for some fifteen years. He stopped in a town called Lago and was selling some goods to residents who came to the center of the town to look at his offerings. One man, Gregorio Filippelli, a Sicilian who lived alone in a small house on the road descending to the sea, asked Carmine if he would stop at his house on his way down.

"It's not out of your way," said Filippelli, "and I have some things in my house that I can exchange with you."

Filippelli had bought some items from Carmine on previous stops that the peddler made to Lago, and Filippelli had asked many questions about which towns Carmine stopped in, where he started, where he ended his trip and so on. Carmine Sandreva was not a suspicious man, and being of an open disposition, he could see no reason not to tell his questioner anything he wanted to know. One of the other Lago residents, a regular customer of Carmine's, told him to beware of that man.

"Don't tell him anything. It's not his business," the man warned.

"Oh, what's the harm?" replied Carmine. Filippelli was a dangerous man. He had killed two men in Messina over monetary disputes. In one incident, he had demanded more money than had been agreed upon for working in the fields during a harvest. When the man refused to give him more, Filippelli attacked him from behind, killed him with a blow to the head, and stole all the money the man had put aside to pay the other workers. While making his escape, he killed another man who tried to question him about his sudden departure. The authorities in Sicily were looking for Filippelli, but he escaped by boat to the mainland, making his way up the coast and eventually settling in Lago. When Carmine got to Filippelli's house, he was invited inside, and as Carmine was helping his new customer to place some bottles of wine and oil inside a subterranean space, the evildoer took advantage of Carmine's bending over to hit him forcefully on top of his head with a large shovel. He then covered his victim's mouth with a blanket until the poor man's breathing stopped. Filippelli knew that Carmine traveled long distances and sold many things, accumulating a considerable sum of money before returning home. As soon as he realized that he could easily acquire the peddler's earnings, Filippelli's cunning ways devised the scheme to trick Carmine into stopping at his house, a hovel well hidden by growth from the main road. Filippelli buried Carmine's body behind his house and early the next morning, before anyone was awake, he took the horse and wagon and drove them eastwards, to an area he knew was not part of Carmine's route. He sold Stella and the wagon for a sum that the farmer who bought them considered to be more than fair.

When Carmine did not return during the days that Rosina expected him, she began to worry and had troublesome dreams about her missing husband. In the dreams, he demanded retribution and pleaded for justice to be exacted on his behalf. One dream was particularly vivid. Carmine told Rosina that he had been murdered and that all his money and his horse and wagon had been stolen. Rosina was beside herself and when Carmine had not returned for more than a month after the time he should have, she went to the office of the *carabinieri*, located in nearby Fiumefreddo. The police told her they could do nothing unless she knew where he had been when he disappeared. Violetta went to Falconara to care for her sister since she heard reports that her sister was losing her mind. Night after night, Violetta would watch as her sister tossed and turned in her sleep, uttering unintelligible words in a highly agitated state. Then one night, after Rosina had gone to sleep, Violetta heard her speaking in a voice that was not hers but which was not unfamiliar either. It was the voice of Carmine. Violetta looked at her sister and Rosina, sitting up in bed demanded,

"Justice! Why can I not have the justice that is due me?"

Violetta became frightened, for the voice was exactly that of her missing brother-in-law. She tried to console her sister, but Rosina just fell backwards and fell asleep. As this continued for a number of nights, Violetta went to visit the priest in charge of the Falconara parish, Don Luigi Angelillo. Don Luigi was a good priest and a good man. He had known he had a vocation to the priesthood since he was just sixteen. He devoted his life to God, as he understood the nature of that devotion. He wanted only to serve God, to practice his religion and to do good to all with whom he came into contact. He was ordained a priest when he was only twenty-four, having spent six years preparing for his mission to work for his Lord, and to bring the truth of the Gospels to all, helping his parishioners to live the best possible lives they could in obedience to the laws of God. Don Luigi never spoke disparagingly of anyone, nor did he listen to gossip or seek any kind of advantage for himself, whether material or social. He was kind and gentle, compassionate and caring. Violetta was gratified by the priest's response to her story. He agreed to visit her sister's house to talk to her, and an appointment was made. When Don Luigi arrived at Rosina's home, he came with another priest who was visiting various parishes on behalf of the local Bishop. This priest, Don Alfonso Marozzo, was a much worldlier man than Don Luigi. The two priests spoke to Rosina and heard her description of her dreams and how she always felt her husband was trying to communicate with her. They heard Violetta's description of Rosina's speech in the voice of her husband, who demanded retribution and justice. Don Alfonso asked Don Luigi to step outside.

"This is clearly a case of possession," the visiting priest said. "We must perform an exorcism, for this woman has been possessed by the devil and she will not recover unless it is exorcised."

Don Luigi listened patiently and smiled.

"Don Alfonso," he replied, "I know this woman. She is a church-going, God-fearing woman whose faith is as strong as anyone's I know. I am sure she is not possessed. Perhaps she truly senses something from her husband. Perhaps she has a sixth sense."

"That is blasphemy!" cried Don Alfonso. "There is no such thing. Holy Mother Church does not admit of such nonsense."

Don Luigi did not wish to argue with his fellow priest. He asked Violetta to listen and to see if she could get any pertinent details the next time her sister took on the voice and apparent personality of Carmine. That night Rosina again sat up in bed, awakening Violetta.

"*Giustizia,*" the plaint began again, "*Voglio la giustizia!*"

"What happened to you?" Violetta inquired.

"I was robbed and murdered," the voice informed. "*M'a rubato, m'a ammazzato!*"

"Where did this happen?" Violetta persisted.

"In the town of Lago," came the reply.

"Who killed you?"

But before Violetta could get an answer, Rosina had dropped back into a deep sleep.

One of Carmine's closest friends from Falconara, Rinaldo Ricca, a man who also traveled a good deal throughout Calabria, looked in on Rosina whenever he could. On his next visit Violetta told him about the dream and the disclosure that the murder had taken place in Lago. Rinaldo made a special visit to Lago to see if he could trace his friend's passage though the town. As he approached the town's central piazza, he saw some farmers selling the products they grew, tomatoes, potatoes, fruits and more. He had a sudden sensation of *déjà vu* when he saw a horse and wagon that looked familiar. When he asked the farmer where he had obtained the horse, the farmer stubbornly refused to discuss the matter. Another farmer nearby, however, told Rinaldo that his neighbor had purchased the horse and wagon from a man who used to live in the town. Further investigation brought Rinaldo to the decrepit house where Filippelli had lived, for he had moved on again, and behind which he had buried his victim. Rinaldo's dog sniffed out the grave, and Carmine's remains were easily uncovered since Filippelli had not buried the body deeply. Carmine was identified primarily from the wedding ring he wore and the shirt he was wearing that Rosina had made for him.

Carmine's remains came home and Don Luigi said a proper funeral mass for his soul. Intrusions into Rosina's dreams ended. Gregorio Filippelli was now a fugitive wanted in two provinces, but until then he had gotten away with murdering three men.

Twelve

In 1920 with the Great War over, the Italian Army was still calling young men to active service. In Longobardi, two men who were about to reach the age when they could be called up, decided to avoid this prospect by going to America. Renato Manfredi was a cabinet maker. He came from a long line of artisans, six generations, who worked with wood to create furniture of exceptional beauty. He spoke to his father about going to America to avoid entering the military. His father was not happy about his son's decision, but he gave him his blessings. Renato left with his close companion, Vincenzo Lorelli and the two arrived in New York on October 28th, 1920 after an eleven day Atlantic crossing on the America, a ship that had been built in 1908. It carried 2,650 passengers, in three classes. 2400 of these passengers, including Renato and Vincenzo, were stuffed into third class, the lower portion of the ship housing passengers.

In a clean but unassuming apartment, they joined two other men from their town, who had arrived in the United States some five years before. Renato was an earnest young man with the highest ethical principles and a sense of responsibility that left no room for frivolity. He took his work very seriously and would not compromise in any way when it came to working with wood. Each cut and each joint had to be perfect. Parts of a cabinet were carefully joined with dowels and the use of nails in any fine work was stringently avoided. Like everyone else from his town, Renato had been brought up as a Roman Catholic and his orientation concerning the major tenets of his faith was solidly established. He believed that Jesus was the Son of God, that he was born of a Virgin, the Blessed Mary, that he had died on the cross to redeem mankind and that the Church's saints were to be honored, with celebrations on their feast days. If Renato had been asked about these beliefs, his subscription to them would have been confirmed absolutely, without, however, much real thought since they were just so ingrained. He rarely went to church, though, and he derided the comments of some of his male friends who suggested with a mixture of gravity and banter that he committed a mortal sin each time he missed Mass. Renato, not unlike Italian men from all parts of Italy, was moderately anticlerical. Perhaps the fact that his own great-grandfather was a priest had something to do with this attitude toward the clergy. That sinful action was one that he could not possibly regret, since he would not be alive if the priest in his genealogical lineage had not erred. Still, he decried other things about the Church and he did not have much patience for all of its dictums concerning sexuality. He saw hypocrisy displayed by some of the priests he had had contact with, and he did not feel that he could extend uncritical allegiance to everything his Church demanded of him. Although of a serious nature, he was a young man who enjoyed having a good time. He loved women and could not wait to have a new sexual encounter, since it was some time since he had been initiated into carnal pleasures.

His first experience with a woman came when he was just eighteen. He was working with his father as a *falegname*, a cabinet maker, and a young widow whose husband had died needed a coffin for the deceased's burial. Renato's father allowed him to take this particular job on by himself since he had become a most able and skilled workman, and a coffin was not much of a challenge at all. One day, the widow, one Maddalena Prudente sent a messenger asking Renato to come to her house so she could pay him for the work he had done. Maddelena's family lived in a nearby town, and she had no family or friends to speak of who could comment on her activities. She, in fact, preferred to remain in the house her husband had set up for the couple when they were married. When Renato entered the house, Maddalena was quite alone. She was dressed in black according to the local custom. In practice, when a woman's husband died in this town and in towns throughout southern Italy, the wife would dress in black for the rest of her life, unless she remarried. Maddalena's mourning dress was long and clean, not yet soiled by household chores. Its tapered fit enhanced the young woman's ample feminine attributes. Her curly black hair hung loosely on her shoulders and her seductive green eyes sparkled with anticipation, although Renato could scarcely determine what this engaging glance meant. He was not naive, but he would hardly have thought that a recent widow would flirt with another man. He brushed aside these provocative thoughts and told himself he was being foolish. Maddalena suggested that he sit down, but Renato demurred saying that he had to get back to work.

"Come now," Maddalena persisted, "You must accept something. Shall I make you warm milk? Or do your prefer a small liqueur?"

Renato accepted the offer of a *liquore dolce*, not wishing to offend by declining the proffered hospitality, and as Maddalnea turned to pour the drink, Renato looked at her as she bent over to retrieve the bottle from a low shelf. He saw her slim form, her black stockings, imagining how she looked underneath her clothing. He turned his head, feeling ashamed that he could have such lustful thoughts about a widow. Maddalena poured two glasses and they pronounced the traditional "*salute*" and drank slowly, looking at one another. Maddalena said,

"You know Renato, I'm so lonely now. My husband was sick for so long and I miss his company. When a woman is accustomed to having a man near her, she comes to need it, and she needs that company."

Renato, listening incredulously, could not contain his annoyance at hearing these words, sensing an impropriety that went against everything he had been brought up to respect.

"Why do you tell me these things?" he demanded angrily.

"Oh, Renato," replied Maddalena gently, prodding him with her sweet manner, "Don't be angry. I was sure that you are a man who has compassion for others. That is why I am telling you about my loneliness."

"Well, what can I do?" he asked.

"Come here and I will show you," and Maddalena led him into her bedroom. Slowly, she unbuttoned her dress and stepped toward the young man, whose desire for her had been stimulated to the point of no return. Maddalena looked down at the young man's buttoned trousers and saw the bulge there that told her she would have her way with him. Renato did return to Maddalena after that first experience, and when he told her he was leaving for America, she wept and told him that she had been hopeful that they would marry, for she had come to love him more than she had loved her husband. Renato consoled his lover, but he knew in his heart that he could never marry such a loose woman. Everything he had been raised to believe in would not allow such a union.

If Renato had the desire to boast about his conquests—something he had no desire to do, for deep down he was convinced that he had done something shameful—his male companions would have thought he was just boasting, and they would not have believed him. There is no doubt that they would have acted similarly, and there was absolutely no doubt that Renato would not cease to exploit the opportunity that had been offered to him. If one of Renato's female relatives or the female relatives of Maddalena had been confidentially informed that such and such was happening, a typical reaction would have been,

"I don't believe that for even one second. No. I will place my hand on the fire (*metterei la mano su fuoco*) that such could not happen. It is impossible. It is merely the evil minds of people who need God's forgiveness for their bad thoughts."

The reasons for this type of reaction had to do with their religious upbringing. They were taught that certain things should never be done, that illicit actions were so horrendous in the eyes of God that only those smitten by the devil could perform them. The more credulous among them believed that in their town, it was certain that no one was so smitten, for hadn't they all been brought up the same way. Hadn't their mothers and the priests, hadn't the entire teaching canon of the church mitigated against such things happening? Oh, yes, in the cities it was possible, but not here in their small village. This type of denial was necessary for these good people to carry on. They had to believe that the faith that had been imparted to them all was indeed working for all, against any interference from outside forces. This is not to say that there were no skeptics, for indeed there were, but they were looked upon by the more innocent souls as malcontents.

Renato immediately found work in a shop in Manhattan along the Bowery. The owner was German, but he had four Italians working for him already, and being a fine craftsman himself, he appreciated the skills the Italians brought to their work. Renato had but a few tools he had carried from Italy, and the German told him that every cabinet maker needed to come to work with his own tools. One of the other Italians who had been working there for some time, a cheerful fellow from Naples, told the boss that he would let Renato use his tools until he could buy his own. This particular woodworking facility was then making cabinets for beauty parlors and barber shops. Some of the designs were quite extravagant, with curved corners, and carvings in the wood that had to be made manually. Renato had soon earned enough money to buy his own set of tools and he made his own fine wooden toolbox to contain them. He sent some money home to his father too. His tools were a special joy, providing him with the same satisfaction any collector obtains from whatever it is he is collecting, whether the objects are stamps, wines or paintings. With woodworking tools, however, Renato could make beautiful furniture and still have his tools to hold and admire. His toolbox was filled with hammers; screw drivers; carpenter's pliers; a dowel jig; a number ten Stanley carriage maker's rabbet plane used for making rabbet cuts in hard woods; a Stanley ten inch brace hand drill; a Stanley smoothing plane; a sash pocket chisel; swans neck and mortise chisels; a Stanley Bedrock Jack plane with a corrugated bottom for working with soft woods; a twelve inch steel back saw; a Stanley bench plane; a handled tongue and groove plane; a jointer plane; a router; a miter square; a dovetail saw; a Disston panel saw; a crosscut saw; bevel edged chisels; a Boxwood handled mortise chisel; a spanking new wooden ruler and more. Renato had never used many of these tools before, but he quickly made himself familiar with their special attributes and learned to use them with skill to shape and smooth and join and finish the various types of wood he loved.

On weekends he frequented dance halls where he enjoyed watching couples flying by him as they danced a waltz or a polka. He loved these dances and wanted so much to be able to dance himself, that he went to a studio that gave lessons. Soon he was bowing to the women standing alongside the walls of the ballroom and flying across the dance floor with them. No conversation was needed and his English was not good enough for him to dare to strike up a conversation with one of his partners. It was just the dance and the bow. One evening he danced a number of dances with a woman who seemed to like him. The last dance of the evening was a slow waltz. The melody was from a then popular song, "Three O'Clock in the Morning." It was by now close to 3:00 A.M.., and the strains of the popular hit signaled the end of the evening's program. As their hands disengaged, Renato asked his dancing companion if he could walk with her outside. She heard his accent and snapped,

"Italianisches?"

Renato said,

"Yes, I'm-a Italiano."

With this disclosure, the woman smiled and graciously said, "Good night," walking away quickly. This experience discouraged the young immigrant and he was thereafter loath to try his luck at attempting any even tentative seduction.

After he had been working in the U.S. for six years, Renato returned to Italy and soon visited the father of a young woman he had known while growing up, one whose looks he had admired, but who now looked completely different to him. Gaspare Ferrara gave his consent to his daughter's marriage to Renato. They were married within three months of his return, and a month later the newly married couple set off for America. Paola Ferraro blissfully imagined that her new life would be one of relative leisure compared to her life in Italy, but she was about to discover a world in which her toils and tribulations would change incrementally.

Thirteen

Vincenzo Lorelli had no specific trade as did his friend Renato. In Longobardi his father had a small store in the center of town where he sold products that were mostly obtained from the nearby farmers—fruits, vegetables, goat's milk, olive oil, wine and other commodities. Vincenzo went to America with very little idea as to what he could possibly accomplish. Renato had a connection, a *paesano* who promised him at least two or three contacts with woodworking companies that were interested in the labor of a good craftsman, and so it was very easy for Renato to find work quickly. Vincenzo, with the help of one of the men he was sharing rooms with, found a job in a grocery store in East New York, a section of Brooklyn, New York. The store catered to an Italian clientele, so Vincenzo found himself right at home. With fine native intelligence, a positive attitude towards his job, including a willingness to work hard, and an exceptional ability to relate to people, Vincenzo soon became indispensable to the store's owner, Mario Migliardi and gradually learned everything there was to learn about the business.

Vincenzo was not one of the men who had sought the hand of Violetta Nardi in marriage when the young beauty was only sixteen, but he had certainly thought about her and had gone to bid her father farewell before he left for America. Francesco and Vincenzo's father Geraldo had been *compare* for many years, since Francesco had been godfather to Geraldo's first daughter, Nilda. Among the Calabrese, to be asked to be a godfather was considered a great honor and would result in a lifelong connection between the families. In the Calabrese dialect, those who so joined with others were said to have *u San Giuan'* (after St. John the Baptist) and this bond was not a matter of mere social exigency. It had to be respected and it superseded all other matters, so that if an argument came up and one of

77

the antagonists expressed a desire for revenge, the reply that would always come forward would be,

"Oh come on now, *avite u San Giuan',*"

and it would be unheard of not to settle amicably. Vincenzo, then, showing the proper respect, went to take his leave of his *compare.* Violetta gave him her hand, too. It was not customary for a woman to extend her hand to a man in this culture, and a man would not presume to extend his own hand to a woman that he was not related to. In the case of family, however, two quick kisses, one on each cheek, would suffice for a greeting or an *addio.* But Violetta was a woman who did not defer to all the traditional customs. She acted spontaneously and had no inhibitions when it came to showing others that she had a heartfelt concern for their well being. And so, she urged Vincenzo to be careful.

"I will pray to our Blessed Lady for you to have a safe voyage," she said, and her voice was so sweet, and her manner so sincere, and her bearing almost regal, that Vincenzo wondered why he had never noticed this aspect of her before. In fact, she was much younger the last time he saw her for any extended period. It was at another Baptism celebration and Vincenzo did not really notice her. As he walked out of the house, he was almost thinking about canceling his trip to the New World. He had a sudden inspiration and called Francesco outside.

"*Compare,*" he said somewhat timidly. "If I do well in America, I would like to come back for Violetta. Please see what you can do for my interests."

Francesco smiled and replied,

"*Compare*, let us be honest. Who knows how long you will be away. There are some men here in Longobardi who have been seeking her hand since she was sixteen. It has to be her decision as well as mine. I would not force her to marry anyone she does not care for. I don't believe in these antique customs."

"*Va ben*" replied Vincenzo. "I will keep my hopes alive."

When Francesco went back inside, Violetta asked him why Vincenzo had called him out.

"Ah, *figlia mia,*" sighed Francesco, "He too wants you."

"Yes, from America," laughed Violetta.

Fourteen

Renato and Paola Manfredi settled into a small two-bedroom apartment in Brooklyn. Renato had found work with a cabinet company nearby and could walk there, return home for lunch and be back in plenty of time. This gave him a chance to see his wife and to allay her loneliness somewhat, for she had no one with whom she could speak. One of her neighbors, a lovely Irish woman, tried to talk to her and made motions with her hands to help Paola to understand. Gradually, with the help of Mrs. O'Brien, Paola learned some English and began to feel more comfortable in her new surroundings. Within a year, a son was born to Paola and Renato, and fifteen months later, in November of 1929, they had a daughter. The young Italian immigrants had all they could handle. Renato was working long hours and Paola had two babies to care for. Every diaper change for each infant required a clean cloth diaper and since Paola had a limited supply she was constantly washing diapers, hanging them out to dry, washing again, feeding first one baby at her breast, then the other, preparing pastina for the boy and feeding him that while the girl was at her breast again. While the children were asleep, she cleaned the house and hand washed her own and Renato's undergarments, her house dresses, his shirts and workpants. Every minute of her day was accounted for and there was no longer any time for her to sit with Mrs. O'Brien as she had before having her babies. By early 1930, the United States found itself deep into the Great Depression, and Renato lost his job. No one could afford the type of cabinet that his employer had been producing. He had managed to save some money in the hope of opening his own shop, having his own little business, but with no income, he had to be extremely careful about all expenditures. The winter of 1930 was harsh and bitter. The Manfredi's landlord could not or would not provide any heat. Paola did all she could to keep her babies warm, wrapping them in blankets and rushing to change their diapers before they could experience the extreme cold that pervaded the rooms. The young couple wore their winter coats inside the house throughout the day, with gloves that Paola had knitted covering their hands. Food was scarce and the money they had could not be spent foolishly since they did not know how long Renato would be without work.

In March, 1930 Paola was again pregnant. Renato decided that it would be best if he took the family back to Italy where the weather was better, where they would not have to pay rent since they could stay with his family, and where most other conditions were more favorable at that time. For his wife and children, this was the best solution. They arrived in Longobardi in early April, but Renato could not see himself sitting around with a family to provide for, so by the beginning of June he returned to America to see if he could earn some money while keeping expenses at a minimum.

Paola still had much to do with the two children. Gennaro was nearly two and Gilda was seven months old. Towards the end of Paola's pregnancy in November, 1930, little Gilda became ill. She had a bad upper respiratory infection and the doctor was called to examine her. A simple antibiotic, something that would be taken for granted a quarter of a century later, was not even heard of by doctors in Calabria, and in spite of the doctor's and Paolas's best efforts, baby Gilda's condition grew worse. When Paola went into labor, she suffered a great deal and begged her relatives to care for her daughter.

In spite of the difficulty of her labor, she asked again and again if Gilda was being taken care of. Paola gave birth to a beautiful baby boy, but a day after his birth, Gilda succumbed to pneumonia and died. Paola remained weak from her labor. The doctor gave her a sedative to permit her to get some rest. In her dreams, she saw her baby daughter, smiling and playing in her crib. Then a sinister looking figure would snatch the baby and Paola would scream out in her sleep. Each time she woke up, she would ask her sister or her cousins who were there assisting her and caring for her children if Gilda was all right. They could not tell her the truth. When Paola was strong enough to get up, she walked to Gilda's crib to look at her daughter. When she did not see her baby there, her sister broke the sad news. Paola cried and sobbed for days and could find no consolation whatsoever. The parish priest came to talk to her.

"Your baby is with God," he said. "God has called her to his bosom. You do not have to worry about her. This was God's decision and does God not know what is best for each and every one of us?"

The priest's words could not help. Paola nodded her assent to each thing he said, but in her heart she did not agree, she did not understand why God had taken her beautiful baby from her.

"Pray to our dear Lady," the priest insisted. "Did she not lose a child too? Talk to her and she will console you. She will help you to be courageous. Talk to her."

Paola nodded, but was listening to his words not at all. She had an aching feeling deep inside her that told her tacitly but forcefully that this pain she felt would never cease, that she would live with it for the rest of her life. Not even the act of suckling her new baby gave her any sense of respite from the dolorous sensations that permeated her entire being.

She knew that she had to write to Renato, but she could not bring herself do so. Her father wrote to his son-in-law instead. Renato shuddered when he saw the letter, for the envelope had a black band around it at the bottom. He knew this meant one thing and he did not want to open the letter, fearing what it contained. When he read about his daughter's fate, he could not contain his grief, nor did he wish to. He thought about that beautiful little face that he had seen smiling at him six months before. A profound gloom gripped him and he began to blame himself, imagining that this death could have been avoided if he had done something differently. Now he questioned all of his efforts to accomplish anything for his family. What was the good of all their toil and the hardships they had endured if one of the things they most cherished could just be taken from them, so swiftly, so senselessly? Within months the young husband and wife were exchanging letters that in some measure provided them with the balm they both needed to bring a measure of healing to their deep and shared wound.

Renato remained in America for five years. He started his own small shop and his earnings were good. In 1935, he sent word to Paola that he could now bring her and their two sons to America again, where he hoped they would prosper and thrive. Seven year old Gennaro and five year old Matteo came down the gangplank holding onto their mother's skirt. Renato embraced his wife and kissed her. Then he looked down at his two sons.

"Kiss your father."

Paola pushed the boys towards Renato. Gennaro immediately obeyed and hugged his father, exclaiming,

"Papà, Papà." But Matteo was bewildered. He did not know this man. How could he be his father?

Renato had opened a cabinet making shop on Coney Island Avenue in Brooklyn. Custom made cabinets, doors, tables, shelves were his specialty, but he also accepted repair jobs on anything made of wood. His establishment, which he called Gilda Cabinet Company in honor of his deceased daughter, kept him occupied six days a week. Sundays were set aside for Mass and for family. The apartment he had rented prior to Paola's and the children's arrival consisted of two large bedrooms, a nice sized living room and an eat-in kitchen, and was in walking distance of the shop. The boys were enrolled in a Catholic school nearby. After school, they were instructed to go directly to their father's shop so that they could sit and do their homework under his watchful eye and play in the yard behind the shop.

The Catholic School they attended, St. Anthony's, was staffed completely by nuns of the Order of St. Joseph. They were extremely strict and would tolerate no mischievous behavior whatsoever. Gennaro had started in second grade since he was seven, but Matteo had to wait one year to enter first grade. Gennaro's English was not good and his teacher, Sister Mary Dominic had little tolerance for these immigrant children who could not understand her.

"What kind of name is Gennaro?" she asked. When she saw that the boy did not understand her question, she just quipped,

"Never mind. It sounds like Jenny, but that's a girl's name. I'll just call you Jerry."

It was thus that Gennaro became known as Jerry in that school and forever as far as America was concerned. Matteo was called Matt, a known diminutive for Matthew, and one of the priests who had studied in Italy told Matteo's teacher that Matteo in Italian was the name on the Gospel of St. Matthew when he had looked at an Italian language Bible. Not all of the nuns at St. Anthony's were equally daunting from their students' perspective. There was a second grade nun, Sister Frances, who smiled at all the children, those in her class as well as those in other classes. She, too, would tolerate little nonsense, but in her classes, there was very little if no attempt at all to veer off the path she had set her students on. She proved, if anyone was prepared to listen—and few other nuns, for sure, were so prepared—that she could achieve more with a sweet approach than with one of challenge and rancor. The other Sisters, who followed the example of Sister Mary Dominic who was the mentor of some of the nuns, were stern and would bridge no dissent whatsoever. Jerry Manfredi would look on with fear and horror whenever one of his classmates was called up to the front desk, ordered to bend over and given five to ten whacks on their behinds for infractions as innocent, so Jerry thought, as whispering to a classmate when Sister Mary Dominic was writing on the blackboard. She always knew exactly who the culprit was, even if that child was not the true culprit. Jerry feared that she would mistake him for someone else who was talking, in spite of his vigilance in avoiding anything that could be misconstrued by his teacher. He knew that there was no point in complaining at home either, for once, when he told his father that the nuns hit the children, Renato expressed his approval for the policy and told his son that he had best beware of finding himself in such a situation, for if he heard that one of his sons had to be disciplined, he would make sure that they received that and double that when they came home. Sometimes the Sisters actually seemed to get a perverse pleasure out of disciplining the children in their care. One day, Sister Mary Dominic's class was joined in the small school auditorium by two other classes, one third grade and another fourth grade. They were gathered together to select participants for a religious pageant that was being organized While the three nuns were talking amongst themselves at the front of the room, and absolute silence was demanded of all the children, one fourth grade boy laughed when he saw one of his classmates peeing in his pants. The boy who wet himself was so intimidated that he could not bring himself to raise his hand and ask permission to go to the bathroom. He also knew from past experience that if he did ask, he would be told that he could hold it in, and in fear of bringing any attention to himself, he waited until he could wait no longer and let go. When the sisters heard the laugh, they turned around quickly. Sister Angela Patricia, the fourth grade teacher demanded,

"Who laughed?" No one spoke.

"The person who just laughed had better admit it, or all of you will be punished." As his classmates looked at him, the boy who laughed knew he had to accept responsibility for his action. He raised his hand.

"Come up here!" Sister Angela Patricia ordered in a stentorian tone. The boy went to the front of the room and the nun said aloud to her colleagues,

"I think we have to make an example of Tommy today." The other two nuns nodded their assent. Tommy Britten was a sensitive boy and he could not tolerate pain very well.

"Sister, please don't hit me," he pleaded, "I didn't mean anything."

"If you don't be quiet, you'll get even more punishment," the nun warned.

She pushed him over and gave him three whacks as the boy cried out, stunned by the pain.

"Now it will be worse for all the noise you're making," and she gave the board to Sister Mary Dominic who administered her three whacks with even more vigor, handing the instrument of pain to the third sister for her contribution to the cause of enforced good behavior. As Tommy cried aloud continually, during and after the corporal punishment meted out to him, the three nuns could be seen smiling at one another, obviously pleased at their collaborative coercion. The boy was then sent back to the classroom to cry alone until he was ready to return and obey the rules.

There was a high concentration on religion in the classes at St. Anthony's, first in the lessons devoted exclusively to religion and then in almost every other subject that was taught as well. One day during Lent, Sister Mary Dominic discussed the death and resurrection of Jesus.

"And just remember," she told her impressionable students, "Our Lord Jesus was killed by the Jews. The Jews are the killers of Christ. Remember that. You should avoid any contact with those people since they were evil then and they are still evil today. They are Christ-killers!"

Jerry could not understand what he was hearing. He knew very little about Jews. He really had only met one Jew, a boy whose father ran a dry cleaning store next door to his father's shop. Sometimes the boy, Alvin Greenberg, would be playing and would ask Jerry if he wanted to play a game where they had to bounce a ball over the fence. The person on the other side had to get it to bounce back over with less than two bounces; points were gained or lost depending on the number of bounces the ball had taken. One day Alvin asked Jerry, "Are you Jewish?"

"What's Jewish?" Jerry asked, puzzled by the question.

"It's what I am," said Alvin. "My family is Jewish. It's our religion."

"We believe in Jesus and God and Mary and the saints," Jerry replied.

"Oh, then you're not Jewish for sure," said Alvin smiling.

Jerry liked Alvin and could not understand why Alvin was a Christ-killer if he had not even lived when Jesus lived. He wanted to raise his hand and ask Sister Mary Dominic how this could be so, but he thought better of it and decided not to. That evening he asked his mother about this and she suggested that he must have misunderstood the teacher.

"She probably meant that Jews had killed Jesus back then, but she could not mean that Jews living today are responsible in any way.'

Paola's words made Jerry happy, especially when she said,

"There are good and bad in all groups of people, my son. There are many Jews who are as good and as devoted to God as any of us Catholics are."

Jerry smiled at his mother and felt warm inside, for he did not want to believe that his friend Alvin could be a bad person. Paola had also become friendly with a Jewish woman in her building who was as nice as anyone she had ever known. The six family house had three floors, and two families lived on each floor. Mrs. Moskowitz lived in the apartment opposite the Manfredi's flat, and was always offering to help Paola with shopping, watching the children, or anything else that she needed.

One day as they usually did after school, Jerry and Matthew went to their father's shop on Coney Island Avenue. They sat at a workbench that was not being used, and worked on their homework lessons. After about an hour, the boys went into the back yard to get some air and to see if their friend was out. Alvin was not there, but in the yard on the opposite side, a fourteen year old, the son of the owners of the hardware store to the right of Renato's shop, was holding a bee-bee gun and shooting at cans that he placed on a tree branch at the back of the yard. Jerry was eight years old and Matthew just six. Fourteen year old Hank Smith saw that the two young boys were watching him with considerable interest.

"Watch this," he boasted, and proceeded to hit one of each of five cans he had placed on the branch.

"Can I try that?" Matthew asked, obviously impressed by this display of shooting prowess.

"Oh, no, you're much too young to handle a gun," and Hank walked closer to where the boys were standing on the other side of the fence.

"But I'll tell you what I'll do, just to show you what a great shot I am. You put this on top of your head and I'll shoot it clean off."

He was directing his remarks at Jerry, but Jerry walked away quickly, refusing any part in the proposed display of marksmanship. Matthew, though younger than Jerry, was more of a daredevil. He was a youngster who craved excitement, and though rarely getting any, he let his imagination take him on flights of fancy in which he was always at the brink of extreme danger. "I'll do it!" he cried out. Quickly trying to protect his brother, Jerry said, "No you won't, Matthew!" Matthew asked the sharpshooter to give him the can and Jerry ran inside to call his father, sensing his brother could be in danger. Before Jerry got back with his father, Matthew had placed the can on top of his head, Hank backed up and aimed, and the shot burst forth entering Matthew's left eye with a force that sent the youngster flying backwards across the yard. He screamed with pain, excruciating and intolerable, and most bewildering, too for one so young as Matthew. When Hank saw what happened, he ran quickly into his parents' store. Renato found his son on the ground, screaming and holding his eye, blood pouring out profusely. Renato picked up his son and ran. He got a clean towel and held it over Matthew's eye, running through the shop out to the front. He knew that the Smith's owned a car and ran into the hardware store holding his son in his arms, begging for help. The Smiths knew what had happened since their son had run in and told them.

"Please," Renato pleaded, "Can you drive me to the hospital?"

Mrs. Smith got the car keys, gave them to her husband and motioned for him to get going, but Mr. Smith refused.

"I can't leave the store now," he said.

"Then please," Renato begged, "Please let me use your car."

"No, no," Smith said nervously, "I can't do that." Smith's mind was turning somersaults. He thought about the repercussion of his son's act and was trying to decide how to proceed, fearing that his son's action could cost him dearly in a number of ways. Renato could wait no longer. His son's screams and cries were penetrating in their intensity and that part of him deep inside that had never healed from the pain he felt when his baby daughter died became raw again with this new wound. He ran out to the avenue and hailed a taxi, instructing the driver to take him to the closest hospital.

The driver took him to Kings County Hospital where Matthew was admitted and a staff eye surgeon was called in to look at him. Dr. Maurice Simpson told Renato Manfredi that it was not likely his son would ever see out of that eye again. After a week in the hospital, when everything possible was done to make the boy comfortable, the doctor called his parents in for a consultation. Dr. Simpson told them that he was able to preserve the eye, so that after a period of healing, Matthew would still have his own eye, but in order for him to look normal, the boy would need surgery. If his eye were to have a normal look to it, and if there was the slightest chance that he were ever to have sight in that eye again, an operation was mandatory. Renato, without hesitation, informed the doctor that whatever needed to be done should be done. He wanted his son to have sight in his left eye again. Dr. Simpson spoke slowly and deliberately, fearing that these immigrants did not understand all that was involved.

"Mr. Manfredi, Mrs. Manfredi," the doctor looked first at one, then at the other.

"Your son needs surgery if he is to see again. Surgery is very costly. Where will you get the money to pay for it?"

The bee-bee, a solid metal ball about the size of a pea, had entered the boy's eye with such force that it tore through all the delicate portions of this incredibly developed human organ, an organ that is a true marvel of intricacy and interrelated and interdependent parts. The extraocular muscles that regulate the motion of the eye were severely damaged. The retina, that innermost layer of the eye composed of nerve tissue which senses the light entering the eye, was compromised by the damage the bee-bee caused, so that the nerves that send impulses through the optic nerve and back to the brain, translating these messages into images one sees, could no longer do its proper job. Each part of the eye that contributes to sight in one manner or another was either destroyed or so badly hurt that the possibility of restoring sight seemed quite hopeless, even to a skilled surgeon. The cornea, the transparent dome which serves as the window of the eye and which is the primary structure focusing light entering the eye was damaged, it appeared, beyond any reasonable hope of repair. The optic nerve containing approximately 1.1 million nerve cells had been splattered, and the transparent crystalline lens of the eye, located immediately behind the iris seemed irreparable. The macula lutea is the small, yellowish central portion of the retina, and it is the area providing the clearest, most distinct vision. The damage here appeared to be permanent, extending through the macula, called the fovea centralis; the fovea is the point of sharpest, most acute visual acuity. The iris, visible through the clear cornea, the colored disc inside the eye, is a thin diaphragm composed mostly of connective tissue and smooth muscle fibers. These fibers had been torn apart by the blast from the boys' gun, along with the pupil. Initially, the surgeon was convinced an enucleation would be an absolute necessity for Matthew, but Dr. Simpson wanted to save the boy's eye and avoid fitting him with a prosthesis. He had had few challenges in his career that made him want to prevail against the odds as much as this one

Renato sat silently. It was not that he hadn't thought of the costs involved, but, foolishly perhaps, he did not want that to be the determining factor in whether or not his son would ever see out of that eye again. Paola was beside herself. Pregnant again and not feeling strong, this latest blow, this severe injury to her youngest son brought her to the depths of despair. All of the pain she experienced in losing her daughter had not really gone away. It was just lying inside her, not even dormant, for her anguish and that sadness that allows of no respite, that penetrates to one's very soul and beyond, that can never be completely overcome, that pain and sadness and disillusion were to be a part of her forever. Now her son's pain brought it all back to the surface and she could not contain her grief. She cried softly as the doctor spoke.

"Doctor," said Renato, seeking a solution some way, somehow,

"I am a fine cabinet maker. I have my own business. Can I not pay for the operation little by little until it is paid in full?"

"Mr. Manfredi," Dr.Simpson replied, "I am not even sure if one operation will suffice. The costs can be quite excessive. Let me look into this and I will let you know."

Dr. Simpson went home that evening and thought about the Manfredi's. He lived with his wife and two children on Bedford Avenue, one of the finest residential areas in Brooklyn in that period. They lived in an oversized colonial house with twelve rooms. One of these was the doctor's study and he had books all over, on tables, piled up on the floor, on top of his desk. Adjoining the living room with its huge fireplace was another room that was designed as a library, and this is where his wife kept all her books and magazines. The collection had outgrown the minimal number of shelves that were originally provided, however, and both Dr. Simpson and his wife continually discussed what needed to be done. As Dr. Simpson looked over the disarray in his study, Manfredi's words, "fine cabinet maker" came to mind. He called his wife in and told her his idea. He would perform the surgery free of charge and Manfredi would build whatever cabinets and shelves were needed in both rooms. The doctor's wife agreed that his idea was a good one. The next day Dr. Simpson stopped at Renato Manfredi's shop and asked him if he could come over to his house the following Saturday morning. Precisely at the appointed time, Renato presented himself at the Bedford Avenue residence and listened to Dr. Simpson's proposal, agreeing that he would take care of all the doctor's needs if he would take care of securing his son's eyesight.

Over the next two years, Matthew underwent four operations, and still he saw nothing out of his left eye. Renato completed all the agreed upon cabinets and shelves for Dr. Simpson, working some evenings until 10:00 P.M. so as not to interfere with his other jobs. As one operation succeeded another, Dr. Simpson suggested additional projects—shelves for his daughter's room, a cabinet for his son's rock collection, and still more. After the fourth operation, Matthew could see some shadows, but little else. He had missed two years of school and fell behind other boys his age in his knowledge of the basic subjects. Finally, he could stand no more.

"Please Papà," he entreated, "No more operations. I don't want this any more. My eye hurts all the time. Just when it gets better, another operation makes it worse again. Please, Papà, I want to go to school again."

Renato did not know what to do. He wanted his son to see, but he could not stand to have him continue to suffer as he had for the past two years. He didn't care about the work. He would continue working late into the night if it could benefit his son, but after the fourth operation, even Dr. Simpson admitted that he had done all he could and he was not sure if he could do more. He had not restored the boy's sight, but at least he had managed to repair the sclera to the extent that the extraocular muscles, to which it was attached, could allow the eye to move. This combined with some skillful cosmetic surgery around the eye, made it appear to anyone looking at Matthew that his blind eye was totally normal.

Some weeks after the final operation, Matthew returned to school where Christian compassion was not very much in evidence. The students poked fun at their classmate and the Sisters had no patience for Matthew's ignorance of things that boys his age knew quite well. The pain was not the thing that bothered the young boy most. With just one eye to see out of, he felt totally off balance and easily bumped into things. He became an object of ridicule for some of his classmates, who laughed at his clumsiness. He was made to feel inferior and even stupid, but the youngster's pluck never deserted him, and he determined then and there that he would show everyone what he was really made of.

Fifteen

The grocery store where Vincenzo worked gave him very little free time. It was open from 7:00 in the morning until 7:00 in the evening, Monday through Saturday. Mario Migliardi, the sixty-four year old owner of the store was from a section of Palermo in Sicily, a fairly large city with distinct, closely knit neighborhoods. He had started his business some fifteen years earlier, having worked as a tailor in Manhattan from the time he first came to America at the age of thirty. He married his first wife in Sicily when he was twenty-eight, and the couple came to the United States together. They were childless and Matilda died from a blood disease when Mario was fifty-seven. He was very lonely and lost without a woman to cook for him, wash his clothes and clean his dwelling. Some men can get along very well on their own, experiencing no difficulties with cooking and taking care of their own laundry, but Mario was not one of these men. He decided to return to his village and to seek a new wife. When he returned to Palermo, to the section of the city known as Fiumicello, Mario visited some friends and relatives whom he could count on to point him in the right direction.

"But, more or less, Mario," asked his cousin Enzo Tallarida, what kind of woman are you looking for."

"What kind of woman?" Mario shrugged and laughed nervously. "A woman like all other women, with the things women have and with the good will to work with and help her husband."

"Certainly," Enzo continued, now taking on a tone of condescension. "But do you want a young woman, a woman your age, a woman with a big behind, large breasts? What are you looking for?"

Mario now felt like he was being made a fool of.

"What kind of questions are these? Are you trying to turn this into a comedy?"

Enzo backed off, "Please, cousin, no offense is intended. But seriously, if I were in your place, I would be looking for a good looking young wife who could make me feel young again."

Mario was not one of these men who never lose their appetite for lust. He thought of sex, but it was not an overriding concern as it is for many men who, even at Mario's age of fifty-eight, cannot keep themselves from looking after a female form that they find attractive.

"I feel young," Mario countered. "I am young. What? Do I need a young woman in my bed to make me feel young again?"

However, the persuasive power of suggestion had taken hold in Mario's subconscious, or perhaps a bit higher in his consciousness and not so very "sub."

"Do you know any young women in our town here who would have me? Whose fathers would agree to their daughter's marrying a man twenty years younger than they?"

"Oh, so now you're interested in a woman in her thirties?" Enzo teased. "Mario, Mario, women in their thirties are not attached to a man for very good reasons. Either they are ugly, or they are widows . . . and you don't want a widow!"

"Why not?" Mario asked, now becoming agitated. "Am I not a widower?"

"Yes, yes," Enzo laughed, "But most widows here have children. Do you want a ready made family? How many people do you want to take back with you to America?'

Mario took this more seriously than it, perhaps, had been intended, and he sheepishly asked his cousin, whom he now began to view as a very wise person, indeed,

"Well, what age woman should I be considering marrying?"

Enzo now had Mario where he wanted him.

"Mario, I don't know if we can pull this off. But there is a woman here who is only twenty-four. Every bachelor in town wants her with a passion that has them dreaming about her night and day. But she wants none of them. Her father died and she has no brothers, so she has been able to avoid anyone and everyone who cannot offer her what she is looking for. And her mother cannot control her and force her to marry."

"What is she looking for?" Mario asked, now intensely interested in this unusual and, even if unseen by him, this fascinating and provocative, potentially palatable prospect.

"She does not want to live her life out in this town and end up like all the other women here whose lives, she feels, are devoid of excitement and, yes, even of any real meaning. There was a man she wanted to marry. He left for America and promised her he would be back for her. But he never returned, and that is why she is twenty-four and still unmarried. She was eighteen when he left—six years ago!"

"And what makes you think she would be interested in me if she has this young man she is waiting for?" Mario's question was almost rhetorical. He was not really expecting an answer, but his cousin surprised him.

"Don't you see? She wants to get out of here. She dreams of going to America. She has waited for six years! At this point, she will marry any man who can guarantee her passage to a new life, to a new world. And she is an intelligent woman too. She can be of great help to you in your business in New York." Enzo licked his lips, satisfied with his own rhetoric and the impassioned manner in which he had delivered it.

Mario was now quiet and thoughtful. He wondered if this is what he truly needed in his life, at this point in his life.

"I don't know . . ." he began. "I don't know if such a woman is what I need."

"Oh come now," Enzo persisted. "If she is too much for you in bed, I would be willing to help you out." He quickly lowered his voice, fearing his wife would hear him from the other room.

"That's not what I mean and you know it!" Mario snapped. And now, that masculine defense that is present even in men who are not particularly concerned about their own virility came sweeping to the fore.

"I can handle any woman—any woman's needs. Would that I can find one to keep up with my own."

When Mario saw Rosaria Rondinelli, even before he was first introduced to her, he could not believe that such a superb specimen of female form and sensuality, a woman whose very bearing imparted a scent of sexual abandon, that such a woman would have any interest in him at all. However, when they were formally introduced and Rosaria spoke to Mario as though she were honestly and truly interested in him, the middle-aged grocer started to fall in love. Rosaria was actually a unique woman, a woman much wiser than her years could possibly suggest. She was very self assured and confident. She had had good training, for when her father died, and she was left to take over all of the activities that he had been responsible for, and considering that her mother was a completely lost soul without her husband, Rosaria adapted with remarkable ease and self-reliance to her new situation. She presented the same exterior to Mario that she displayed with everyone with whom she had any contact whatsoever, and that is to say that she was completely personable and thoroughly engaging. Her physical attributes combined with her spontaneous and piquant personality to immediately endear her to anyone, man or woman, for that matter, with whom she had any contact whatsoever.

She had been told about Mario before their meeting, so she knew what he was looking for. Although Mario had dressed up for the occasion and looked quite dignified, if not especially distinguished—some gray steaks highlighted his dark black hair—Rosaria could see that he was old enough to be her father. This in itself did not bother her. If Mario had been a man even older than he was, but with some fire in his eyes to match her own, some panache, a man who could just look at a woman and symbolically initiate a meltdown, that peculiar but pleasurable sensation she had only felt with one man in her entire life, the man who left her and failed to make good on his promise to return; no, if Mario had even the minutest trace of that kind of charisma, Rosaria would have jumped at the opportunity, advanced age notwithstanding. But she was not quite ready to say no just yet. He was 58, but he owned a business in America, a business she could certainly help him to run. Hadn't she helped run her mother's dressmaking business since she was sixteen? Her mother was an excellent seamstress, but she was useless when it came to setting prices, writing bills of sale, keeping records. Rosaria did all of this and more. She even helped her mother with the pressing of the garments, but more importantly, she really ran the business while her mother's contribution was limited to making the items that the business sold. This, Rosaria, felt was a key distinction.

Rosaria pondered the pros and cons of the offer. Perhaps, most importantly, she wanted to get even with the man of her dreams, the one who, she felt, had betrayed her. She fantasized that she would meet him in New York, someplace, somehow, and that he would see her and regret that he had ever left without her. He would look at her beauty, for she knew she *was* beautiful and entertained no false modesty on that count, and he would look at the woman he had settled for, a woman, she imagined, who had already lost the allure that had first attracted him, and he would bemoan the day he had let Rosaria slip away. Rosaria gave her consent, with the stipulation that her mother came as part of the package. The mismatched couple was married in a small ceremony with only close relatives and a few of Rosaria's very close friends in attendance. No honeymoon was planned since Rosaria wanted to leave for America as soon as possible. Their first nights together were not emotionally satisfying for either partner, but physically speaking, Mario's interest in sexual intimacy was abundantly revived at the sight of Rosaria in her very brief attire. She would not allow him to see her completely naked, however, and she insisted that there be no light on during intercourse. When Mario ejaculated, she would quickly leave the bed, and reach orgasm alone, typically fantasizing about her lost idol, the one true love whose betrayal continued to haunt her.

Sixteen

Vincenzo Lorelli arrived at Mario's grocery establishment five years after Rosaria had come to America. He had been working at odd jobs for two years and was now twenty. Mario was then sixty-three and Rosaria twenty-nine. Rosaria had been insisting that Mario find someone who could make a real contribution to the business, not just a young kid who could only work after school. Mario felt that they could not afford the salary, but Rosaria, who had taken over most of the ordering and bookkeeping, insisted that not only could they afford it, but that they absolutely needed more help since their business had expanded. They had some help that put in part-time hours waiting on customers, unpacking and arranging stock, and making deliveries, but Rosaria wisely calculated that they were losing business by not taking advantage of new opportunities that presented themselves since she and Mario were already quite overwhelmed by their customary duties. When one of Vincenzo's housemates, a *paesano* of both Mario and Rosaria, asked his friend if he could use a good man in his business, a young, strong Calabrese who was not afraid of hard work, Rosaria did not even wait for Mario to reply.

"Send him over," she commanded.

Vincenzo soon became indispensable. He was a fast learner and mastered ever aspect of the grocery business in a short period of time. He was trusted to open and close the store, making Mario's and Rosaria's hours more manageable. He helped Rosaria in ordering and controlling the inventory, paying the bills and even doing some general bookkeeping. After Vincenzo had been with the Migliardi's for two years, at just twenty-two years of age, he began to take on so many additional duties that he found it necessary to stay in the store after the 7:00 P.M. closing, to settle up the day's cash account and maintain the books among other things. He had a small desk in the back of the store where he worked. The lights in the front of the store would then be closed and a single gas light would burn above Vincenzo's head. When the young Calabrese first came to work for the Migliardi's, Rosaria looked at the eighteen year old as just a kid, if a somewhat attractive one. She had become so immersed in the business that she had little time to think about anything else, and by evening was so tired that she just went upstairs, where she lived above the store with her husband and her aging mother. During the prior six months, however, she became attached to her young employee, almost treating him like a son. They shared a number of activities in the business, and often had to discuss strategies and plans such as bringing in seasonal items and changing or adding new suppliers. Late on a Saturday evening, as Vincenzo sat tallying the week's receipts, he heard the door open and close at the front of the store.

"*Son'io*," he heard Rosaria's voice. Most of their conversation was still in Italian, or more precisely in the Sicilian and Calabrese dialect, except when they needed to discuss anything with anyone who could not speak Italian. Then they would manage in their "broken" English. Rosaria and Vincenzo were able to converse fluently, even though they would sometimes share a laugh when she did not understand a Calabrese word or he was puzzled by a Sicilian expression.

"I came down to get some milk for the morning. How did we do this week?'

"Very well," Vincenzo replied.

Rosaria came around to where he was sitting and sat up on the edge of a table opposite him. She had on a loose bathrobe, which she had put on after her bath. Vincenzo looked at her, stared at the whiteness of her legs as she crossed them, the front of the bathrobe slipping slightly to either side. Sometimes, when they were working together in the store and he had to go around her behind the counter or in the aisles, he would brush up closely against her buttocks and she would look after him smiling gently. He would wonder if this meant anything. Rosaria was as sensual as ever, and every man who entered the store looked after her longingly. Vincenzo resented their glances, feeling, justifiably or not, that this right was reserved to him. Although he, himself, sometimes looked at Rosaria with a suppressed longing to hold her in his arms, he never dwelled on these lustful glimpses, for he felt a strong sense of loyalty to Mario and his strict upbringing instilled in him a sense of respect for another man's wife, especially the wife of one who had given him work and trusted him completely. As the gas light flickered and seemed to be dying down, Rosaria reached sideways and above her towards where Vincenzo was sitting. As she moved to adjust the level of the flame, she uncrossed her legs and the bathrobe opened, revealing the insides of her milk white thighs and her pink undergarment. Vincenzo found himself staring, and after Rosaria raised the flame she looked back at him, noticing the young man's penetrating gaze.

"What are you looking at?" she teased, and she crossed her legs and closed her robe.

"Uh, uh nothing," he stammered. Then, daringly, for he was not sure where his remark would get him, even causing him to lose his job, he ventured,

"Rosaria, I have never told you this, but you are the most beautiful woman I have ever seen." Later that night, as he lay in his bed, Vincenzo felt a twinge of guilt, for since he had seen Violetta on the day he left his *paese* for America, he had felt that she, as she looked to him that day, was the most beautiful woman imaginable. He felt that he had somehow betrayed his bride-to-be, for he was convinced that he *would* return to marry her. Violetta still was the most beautiful woman he had ever seen, he thought, convincing himself that what he had said to Rosaria was true, but not totally true. Rosaria had a different type of beauty than that of Violetta. She was earthy, sensual, provocative and tempting. Violetta, on the contrary, was virginal, innocent, and refined, with a beauty that had an ethereal quality that needed to be appreciated in an entirely different manner.

Rosaria looked at Vincenzo, and although she had heard his remark, she was unsure as to just what it could mean.

"What did you say?" she asked rhetorically.

"I said you are the most . . . ." Thinking about Violetta, Vincenzo hesitated. "You are a very beautiful woman. Even your legs are perfect."

Rosaria was certainly worldly enough to know that her young assistant was attracted to her, as she knew that most men who saw her were. But in the case of Vincenzo, he came across as such an innocent young man, so timid in so many ways, that she never imagined he would ever make a move on her. For her part, those brushes in the tight spaces sparked wild thoughts about how much enjoyment his young, firm body could provide her, so unlike Mario's flabbiness. Once when he came behind her a second time, having passed her a moment earlier, she could feel his erection against her thigh.

"You are a handsome young man yourself," she replied after hesitating briefly. Her compliment had a salutary effect on the assistant's level of confidence and he rose from his chair. Without further discussion, without another word being spoken, the Sicilian beauty and the Calabrese initiate came together, kissing passionately, embracing, tearing one another's garments off. Rosaria's pent up desires for a man who could satisfy her in every way she needed to be satisfied, then gave vent to an explosion of sexual fire that left her inexperienced lover gasping for air. Rosaria had not wanted this to happen, for she feared it would compromise their business relationship and worse. Now that her suppressed thoughts materialized in this wild abandon, she felt happy, fulfilled and glad that her misgivings had, almost by chance, been cast aside. She would come to realize that her foreboding had not been without substance.

Seventeen

Vincenzo and Rosaria continued with their trysts for months afterwards. She would wait until Mario was asleep and slip downstairs to the store where Vincenzo waited expectantly. Now that he had experienced the pleasure a woman could give him, he could never get enough. During the day, during working hours, Rosaria would tolerate not even the slightest suggestion of their shared intimacy. Vincenzo placed his hand on her thigh one morning when she came down to begin her work, but she stepped back quickly, giving him a look of such astonishing annoyance that he was dumbfounded. Later, when they were alone in the back room for a moment, she told him pointedly,

"Don't ever try that again when we are working."

Rosaria had no misgivings or guilt about her affair with her young employee. She had no scruples about wronging Mario in any way. By this time, sexual relations between the young wife and her aging husband were almost non-existent. Occasionally, she would tolerate Mario's thrusts from behind as she lay there coldly, impassively. She saved her heat for her lover. She didn't give much thought to where this relationship was going. Mario was apparently in good health and would be around for some time to come. She had a confidence and self respect that made her very different from many other women. She didn't need her lover to be with her all the time. Yes, she loved him and wanted him to make love to her, but she was not in love with him in the usual way, where one's entire outlook is concentrated almost exclusively on the beloved's approbation or absence of it. Still, she was visibly shaken when Vincenzo told her he wanted some time for a return trip to Italy. Their affair had been going on for two years already, and it had taken on an aspect of the routine. It was really just sex, for they never even went out together to share a meal or just to walk romantically hand in hand

"Why do you want to go back there?" she asked sarcastically. "Don't you have everything you need right here? Work, money, me?"

"I have to go to see my parents. My mother is not well," he lied.

"But I need you here," Rosaria complained, adding quickly, "I need you for the business." She had too much pride to give him the impression that she could not get along quite well without his lovemaking. A compromise was arrived at so that Vincenzo would go back to Italy during the summer months, when business was just a little slower than usual.

In Longobardi, Violetta Nardi had become engaged to a man whose persistence paid off, or so he thought. Giacomo Gianicco, a Longobardi native who worked in construction in the city of Cosenza, visited the Nardi's each time he came home for a few days and always expressed his admiration for Violetta. He had time and again asked Francesco if he would consent to their marriage. Francesco Nardi always gave him the same answer, "I will see if she is interested," and later tell Giacomo that he was sorry, but although Violetta liked him and admired him, she was not interested in marriage. Violetta had been thinking of Vincenzo, but she soon began to lose hope that he would ever return. Suddenly, in a moment of weakness, she gave her consent and almost immediately regretted that she had done so. She realized that she had acted out of a sense of compassion for the man. She felt sorry for him and didn't like to see him going back and forth trying to win her over. After a while she began to think that perhaps she shouldn't be so fussy. After all, most of the married couples she knew settled into comfortable routines after being married for a year or two. Perhaps she was expecting too much. Her sister and her close friends told her that as long as a man is good, provides for his family and respects his wife in all the ways he should respect her, then what more could a woman ask for. It was in this milieu that Violetta weakened and yielded to Giannico's requests that more and more were sounding like demands. She couldn't quite accept the idea that she was compromising certain ideals she had always tried to live by. How could she possibly marry a man she didn't love? Was her belief in love just an old fashioned, foolish girl's thing that had to be discarded when one had attained a certain maturity? No, this was one principle she could never renounce. Giacomo continued to visit her over the next six months and was determined to set a date for the marriage.

"You'll see," he told Violetta, "We'll have a lovely home in Cosenza. You'll love it there."

But Violetta kept putting him off. Finding herself in such a position was difficult for this young woman. She had always prized honesty above everything, in all her dealings with everyone. Now she had involved herself in a very serious matter, having given her consent to a marriage that she did not truly believe in, and she did not see how she could solve the dilemma, for she did not wish to hurt anyone, and by going back on her word, she knew she would be hurting Giacomo. But the more she thought about it, the more convinced she became that she had to recant.

One Sunday, Giacomo arrived at the Nardi's door and presented his presumed fiancée with some flowers he had brought for her. He was determined that on this day they would make final arrangements to marry one month hence. After he had handed the flowers to Violetta, he spoke softly but firmly.

"Violetta, you know that I have been very patient. Now I must, with all due respect, insist that our marriage take place at the earliest possible date. We have to go to Church for *la promessa*, and then one month from now we will be married in *la chiesa madre*. Giacomo felt good now that he had completed his statement and felt certain that it would be accepted.

"Giacomo," began Violetta, hesitantly, carefully, aware that she was going to hurt this good man, but convinced that she would hurt him even more by consenting to a loveless marriage.

"I'm glad you came today, since I wanted to speak to you, too, about this very subject."

Giacomo smiled, expectantly.

"Oh, my dear, I'm so happy that you have been having the same thoughts that I have been having."

"Well," continued Violetta, "My thoughts have been somewhat different from yours."

"What do you mean?" Giacomo asked, now losing his composure and beginning to perspire.

"Giacomo, you're a good man. Any woman who marries you will be fortunate indeed to have a husband like you."

"Any woman?" Giacomo demanded, halting Violetta's momentum.

"What I mean," she continued, "is that you will find the right woman who will be your wife, but I am not that woman. I am sorry, but . . ."

Violetta could barely complete her expression of apology when Giacomo stood up and shouted,

"This is outrageous. Do you think you can make a fool of me?"

The expression Giacomo used, *"Tu pensi che tu pigli a me per fesso!"* represented a declaration of outrage for an act that Calabrese—Southern Italians, generally, in fact—abhorred and stood ready to defend against.

"No," Violetta, said, "No, not at all. I'm only being honest with you. I made a mistake in saying I would marry you. I want to correct that mistake before it becomes a bigger mistake."

"There is someone else, then?" Giacomo bellowed. "Who is this traitor who would betray his own *paesano*?"

"There is no one else, no one now," Violetta said, expressing herself with solicitude.

"What do you mean not now? Do you mean that once I walk away, then he will come in to take my place?"

Giacomo could barely contain his rage.

"You would like that, wouldn't you? After you make a fool of me, when everyone is laughing at Giacomo, then your cavalier will ride in from the wings."

The reference to theatrical staging was lost on Violetta, for she had never been inside a theater in her life.

"I'm not trying to make a fool of you," pleaded Violetta, and then she could not hold back her tears and began to weep.

Francesco, who had heard everything from the other room, walked in and addressed his daughter's suitor.

"Giacomo, accept the fact that Violetta made a mistake. She has tried to explain how this happened, but you will not even listen."

"No, I will not listen. If she does not marry me, she will marry no one! I will be avenged for this insult" Having made this solemn declaration to defend his honor, Giacomo walked out. He made his way quickly to his father's house, retrieved a rifle that his father used for hunting small animals in the mountains, and hurriedly turned to return to the Nardi home to seek his revenge for the incredible slight that had been so callously and unjustly, he felt, visited on him. As he reached the front door, which Violetta closed after he walked out, he kicked at it and the door flew open. Violetta was sitting at the table sewing, for she had become a seamstress and was doing work for neighbors who needed items of clothing. Violetta saw the gun and pleaded, speaking in a frightened tone,

"Giacomo, don't be foolish. Put that gun away!" Francesco, who had gone to the room below, heard his daughter's voice clearly. He picked up a small hatchet that he used for chopping wood and ran around to the front of the house. The door was still wide open and he could see Giacomo raising the gun and pointing it in Violetta's direction. Seeing the danger his daughter was in, Francesco's feelings of paternal love totally overwhelmed him. There is a special relationship between a father and a daughter that cannot be gainsaid. A true father will do anything in his power to defend his daughter against anyone or anything that threatens her well being. Francesco knew this instinctively so he came in behind Giacomo, and seeing the rifle in position to be fired, quickly hurled his hatchet at the would-be perpetrator. It struck Giacomo at the base of his neck and he hurtled forward, his rifle falling under him. As he fell, his eyes met those of Violetta for a split second, as if in supplication to her to recant and to accept him again.

Giacomo's death was ruled a justifiable homicide by the tribunal in Cosenza. The *carabinieri* had testified that the rifle was still in Giacomo's hands when he fell with it, and that his finger appeared poised to pull the trigger. Nevertheless, Violetta had not wanted things to end this way. She appeared to be in a trance during the following months. She felt guilty and responsible for Giacomo's death. If she had never accepted his proposal, this terrible tragedy would not have unfolded as it did. She did not want to leave the house. She was convinced that the townspeople would blame her for the unfortunate man's death. Why did she have to be so headstrong, they would say. Why couldn't she just go through with the marriage? The man was a good man. She had always been a good woman, so why change now and drive the poor man crazy, drive him to run home and get a gun. Violetta prayed day after day, asking God's forgiveness for her unwise decision—not to refuse to marry Giacomo, since she knew that she did not love him, and she wanted so much to marry only for love—to have agreed at all when she knew deep inside that he was not the man for her. Violetta would never forget this. She would spend the rest of her life, in one way or another, atoning for her part in Giacomo's death. She had always been a giving person, selfless and filled with compassion, but after this event, she was to become ever more the giver. She would practice the virtue of charity daily, for the rest of her life.

One year after the tragic event in her home, Violetta heard from some neighbors that Vincenzo Lorelli had returned to Longobardi after six years, and that he was asking about her.

Eighteen

Vincenzo was happy to learn that Violetta was still not married. His father told him about the unfortunate events that had unfolded and of Giacomo Gianicco's attempt on Violetta's life. Vincenzo became concerned that Violetta did not know her own mind, and he worried that if she did agree to marry him, she could change her mind afterwards. He thought it would be best to visit first, to see if he was still attracted to her and then make his decision about proposing marriage or not. The entire time he was with Rosaria, he tried to convince himself that once he was with Violetta, he would forget Rosaria completely, at least in terms of intimacy. With the time and distance factor, however, he began to miss his lover. He thought about her allure, her curvaceous body, the way she moaned with pleasure after they had connected physically. He tried to force himself to forget, but the images kept recurring. In his dreams he would see Rosaria in the store. He would watch as she walked to the back with one of the men who delivered the milk or the bread. He would nervously wait for them to come out, and when they did not, he would go to the back room, where he would see Rosaria lying across the table with the delivery man on top of her. He would wake up in a cold sweat, in a state of agitation.

When Francesco received word that Vincenzo was coming to visit, he asked his daughter if she had any interest in him, provided, of course, that Vincenzo was still interested himself.

"What makes you think he would not still be interested?" she asked.

"Well, dear, for all we know he may already be married."

Violetta looked up suddenly, with a worried expression on her face.

"Oh, so you do have an interest, then?" her father asked.

Violetta opened up to her father and confessed that the reason she could not marry Giacomo was that she had always thought about

Vincenzo since he left and knew that he was the man she wanted to marry. She gave in to Giacomo's proposal in a moment of weakness, when she felt that her hopes for a union with Vincenzo were fruitless.

Vincenzo appeared on a Sunday morning and knocked apprehensively on the door. Violetta came to open it and extended her hand in greeting. Violetta was joined by her father and younger sister Maria, and they all spent the next hour catching up on the many things that had happened to the Nardi family during Vincenzo's absence—except for the confrontation, which was not mentioned at all—and to what Vincenzo was doing in America, his work, whether he saw many of the other *paesani* who had also emigrated and whether he had come home to stay or had plans to return. As he stood to leave, he asked Francesco to walk out with him. Seeing Violetta again, he was convinced that she was even more beautiful than he had remembered. Looking at her as she spoke, he could not help but compare her to Rosaria, and the things about her that had kept Violetta alive in his thoughts these past years proved even more engaging now.

"*Compare*, remember when I left for America, I asked you to try to save Violetta for me. I'm happy that you did not give her to anyone and that you even protected her from that madman and saved her life. I ask you for her hand in marriage now."

"I'll speak to her," Francesco promised, "and you will have your answer tomorrow."

When Vincenzo appeared the next day, he was apprehensive lest his proposal be turned down. He knocked timidly at the door. Francesco called out,

"Come in, the door is open."

Vincenzo waited, not wanting to enter unless he was sure he was going to be accepted. He was a proud man and did not want to beg. He had already determined that he would not wait around to ask a second time if there was any hesitation on Violetta's part whatsoever.

"Come in, come in," said Francesco. "It's yes. Your answer is yes."

Violetta and Vincenzo were married in the *Chiesa Madre* and went on a brief honeymoon to *La Sila*, the nearby mountain area to the northeast. They stayed at a type of *pensione*, where their meals were included and they could relax and become acquainted with one another. Vincenzo liked everything about Violetta and she could not imagine any other man who could make her as happy as he did. He was gentle as he initiated her into the ways of sexual expression, and although he was the first man she had made love with, Violetta was not disappointed. Although she was nearly twenty-one, Violetta had never even kissed a man before she kissed Vincenzo. There was something about Violetta that convinced Vincenzo that he would never stop finding her attractive or desirable, and that above all, he would never fall out of love with her. With Rosaria, perhaps because that aspect of love was missing, the aspect that considers the beloved as more than an object in sexual terms, their relationship could not progress beyond a point that had set its own limits. Violetta and Vincenzo shared a mutual tenderness of immense proportions that would make every day of their lives together meaningful and happy.

A month after their wedding, the devoted couple left for America. Francesco had been there himself, one of his sons lived there, a son whom he did not expect to see again, and now his beautiful, cherished daughter was going away to that unforgiving land too! The day that she left, a piece of him died.

When they arrived in New York, Vincenzo took Violetta to his small apartment, really just a room with an adjoining kitchen, and apologized to her for taking her to such a shabby dwelling. Violetta brushed aside his regrets, though, telling her husband that as long as they were together she was happy, no matter the surroundings. When Vincenzo reported to the grocery store the next morning, Rosaria and Mario took his hand and gave him the customary two kisses, one on each cheek. As Rosaria moved from one side to the other, she whispered in Vincenzo's left ear, "*stasera*," (this evening). Mario asked about his trip and Vincenzo told him that everything had been very nice.

"How is your mother, or was it your father who was ill?" Rosaria inquired in a tone of sarcasm.

"Yes, they are fine now. They were very happy to see their son find a good wife."

"Oh, did your brother get married?" Rosaria asked in a voice that indicated she was not sure that her question made any sense.

"Not my brother, but I." Vincenzo replied.

"*Auguri*," Mario exclaimed, smiling and embracing his wife's former lover, for Vincenzo knew that he would never make love to Rosaria again. Rosaria, however, was still, not sure that this meant anything in terms of her needs.

"*Auguri*," she chimed in. "And your wife? Will she remain in Calabria?'

"My wife is here with me," Vincenzo declared proudly, smiling a broad smile.

Rosaria still was unconvinced that this changed anything between herself and Vincenzo.

"Well, when are you going to bring her to meet us?" Rosaria asked, continuing in a gracious and hospitable fashion. "We invite you and your wife to have dinner with us this coming Sunday, isn't that so, Mario?"

"Oh, yes, of course," Mario agreed. "By all means, we must meet your wife and Sunday dinner would be perfect."

Sunday was the only day possible to have guests for dinner since the store occupied Mario's and Rosaria's time fully on the other six days of the week. In those days, almost all stores were closed on Sundays. It would be many years before Sunday store openings became commonplace.

Rosaria was not concerned that Vincenzo's marriage would change anything in their consensual relationship. For his part, Vincenzo was similarly unconcerned about anything Rosaria could possibly do about his current lack of interest in making love to her. Even if she disclosed their affair of the past to Violetta, he would not deny it, but would admit everything to Violetta, explaining to her that this had happened, yes, but it would never happen again. She only needed to be concerned about his actions after their marriage. What happened before was irrelevant. After all, everyone knows that a man cannot live like a saint–that if he is alone in a foreign country, it is only natural that he would couple with a woman. Vincenzo knew some of his *paesani* who were married and whose wives were still in Italy, and they were certainly not living celibate lives. Of course he would not mention this to Violetta, for she surely knew some of these men. But he, Vincenzo had brought his wife with him and he would forevermore show his fidelity to her. He was sure that Violetta would see it from his perspective.

At first, Rosaria said nothing when Vincenzo did not work late after closing the store. She viewed it as a period of adjustment. Then she asked him if he was going to neglect some of the duties that he had taken on before he left. Vincenzo assured her that he was taking care of them, and that he was, in fact, bringing the books home to work evenings after he had had supper with his wife. It wasn't fair to keep her waiting so long, but he was fulfilling his obligations to his job. Then, when she could wait no longer, Rosaria asked Vincenzo to stay for a few minutes after closing. She needed to talk to him. Vincenzo complied.

"Come to the back," Rosaria said, smiling seductively.

Vincenzo followed her and waited as she turned around towards him. She began to unbutton her dress in the back and to lift it over her head. Vincenzo looked at the familiar torso and for a brief moment, the lust that first attracted him to this voluptuous example of divine womanhood, came to the surface, but only momentarily.

"Put your dress back on!" he commanded, but in as gentle a manner as he could bring himself to use. He still cared for Rosaria as a person. She had been good to him. They had shared many moments of blissful abandon, pleasure and yes, even love at times. He did not wish to hurt her.

"Don't you care for me anymore?" Rosaria spoke proudly. She was not pleading, but asking her question with a tone of subdued astonishment, as if it was impossible for her lover not to still desire her as much as he always had.

"Rosaria, please understand. Things are different now. I'm a married man."

Rosaria laughed, conveying by her laugh the notion that his statement was so ridiculous, so beside the point that he must certainly be joking and that he would soon get back to taking things seriously again. Her dress dropped to the floor and she started to unhook her bra.

"Rosaria, don't make a fool of yourself. Put your clothes back on. Thing are different now. I have a wife!" Vincenzo started to turn to walk towards the front of the store.

Rosaria ran towards him and took his arm, swinging him around. "And I have a husband. So what!" She moved her face towards his mouth and tried to place her lips on his, but he pushed her away, walking quickly to the front and out the door. Rosaria felt humiliated for the first time in her life. She had never allowed a man to get the better of her, and had never permitted anyone, man or woman to have the upper hand in any dealings she had ever had with them. She composed herself, and determined then and there that things would not finish this way. No, she would decide how the drama would play out.

When Rosaria met Violetta on the following Sunday, she could not help but like her "rival." Violetta's personality, her sincerity and the way she drew people to her, totally disarmed them, and even a woman as sophisticated as Rosaria certainly was, could not help but succumb to the new immigrant's charms. Rosaria enjoyed herself, in spite of herself that day, but she was still calculating that she would have the last word when it came to Vincenzo.

On the Monday after Sunday dinner, Rosaria began her strategy which she was convinced would have Vincenzo eating out of her hands before too long. She began to wear clothes that were more seductive and appealing. She spoke to Vincenzo only when absolutely necessary, giving him very little confidence and treating him with a cold contempt which would, she was certain, bring him to his knees. Vincenzo, however, was happy with the results of his actions. From his perspective, she needed to act the way she did in order to save face, and he did not wish to take that away from her. But he began to think about his future, the future of his family, and he did not see that it had anything to do with Mario's grocery store in East New York.

Nineteen

Vincenzo opened a small grocery store in Bensonhurst, a neighborhood in Brooklyn where Italians were beginning to settle in greater numbers. Above the store was a three bedroom apartment, and the building's owner, Nathan Kaplan, the son of Jewish immigrants, gave Vinnie, as he insisted on calling his new tenant, a special "deal" for renting the store and the apartment. Soon, all the customers were calling Vincenzo "Vinnie" too, and the next stage in his Americanization was thus established. Nathan liked the young Italian immigrant and enjoyed telling him how much Jews and Italians had in common: their love of family and so much more. Vinnie taught Violetta all he could about the business, and soon she was helping him to run the store. He told her that once they had children, he would not expect her to continue working in the store, and that as far as he was concerned, her primary place would be in their home taking care of their babies. Violetta assured Vinnie that she agreed with him that caring for their children would be her primary activity, but the energetic wife was beginning to feel that her contribution to their store was making a difference, and she looked forward to doing even more. She visualized becoming an integral part of the business and foresaw her active participation in it even if she did have children. After their first year in the new business, many customers would ask for Violetta specifically and seek advice on how to use particular foods and how to prepare certain Italian dishes. Gradually, she understood English better, and she was able to express herself with improved articulation as time passed.

Meanwhile, upstairs, Violetta had decorated the apartment so that it truly looked like a comfortable home. She hung drapes in the living room, curtains in the kitchen and bedrooms and decorated the walls with framed pictures that reflected her religious upbringing. Dominant among these items, aids to devotion, as the priest once told Violetta, was a ceramic crucifix above their bed and a small statue of Our Lady of Pompeii on their dresser. The statue had a circular receptacle attached to its front which held a candle that could be lighted. The Blessed Mother had a serene look on her face and her long gown was of a deep blue color. Her arms were extended and her hands outstretched to impart blessings on all true believers. At her feet, a snake was coiled up and one foot was trampling it. Around the bottom of the circular candle holder, the inscription, "Our Lady of Pompeii, Pray for Us" was inscribed in small blue letters. Violetta hung a pair of Rosary beads from the Lady's right hand. On her kitchen wall was an image of San Francesco di Paola. As time passed, other religious figurines, statues and paintings would be added to the walls and to the tops of the family's furnishings. Violetta went to Mass every Sunday morning at 7:00 A.M., and Vinnie would accompany her, but not always. On Sunday afternoons the couple would visit their *paesani* or be visited by them. A musical event became a special part of these visits, a concert of sorts by Vincenzo on his mandolin. When he was working at Mario's, they usually tuned the radio in the store to a station that played traditional Italian music. Vincenzo loved the sound of the mandolin that accompanied many of the Neapolitan songs. He visited a store that sold musical instruments and saw a used mandolin on display. The price was not too high and Vincenzo purchased it. Completely self taught, he soon played as if he had had lessons for years. He had a natural affinity for the mandolin and an inborn talent for making music. Sometimes he would sing a few verses of a song and get everyone to join in. The immigrants did not have much time for any form of entertainment or enjoyment, so these Sunday afternoons became very special to everyone who participated, and the memory of those gatherings would fill each of them with pleasure for many years to come. Even when they could eventually be able to afford much more elaborate forms of entertainment, the simple pleasures they shared in times of hardship would not be surpassed.

Violetta had arrived in America some months before Paola Manfredi came over, and although she knew Paola in Longobardi, the two women had not had much contact with one another. Violetta became Paola's best friend. She was there to assist her when she had her first two children, for she knew that Paola had no relatives in America, and she and Vincenzo saw their friends off at the piers when they returned to Italy. When Renato came back alone, Violetta kept after Vincenzo to invite his friend over for Sunday dinner. Renato appreciated the good woman's hospitality, and for many years thereafter remembered her kindness and showed his respect for her by offering to construct items that she needed in her home, and being helpful to his friends, generally, in any way he could. When Paola returned with her two sons, Violetta visited her upon her arrival and the two women wept together as Paola explained how she had lost her daughter just as her son was born. At that time, Violetta and Vincenzo were still childless and they had been married for seven years. When Paola's son lost his eye, Violetta thought about how difficult and even heartbreaking it could be to have children. She certainly had a full life now, for her participation in the business was something that took up so much of her time that she could not imagine how she would handle everything if she had a child to take care of too. Nevertheless, she felt that she was missing something important in her life. Having a business was fine, but she was a woman who was born to have children. She had so much love to give. She wanted to have a child to give this love to. Her maternal instincts were crying out to have this need fulfilled. When three more years flew by and the Lorelli's were still without children, Violetta decided to make a Novena for the special intention of becoming pregnant. Her parish, St. Philomena's, announced a special Novena that would be conducted by a visiting Dominican father, a priest who had traveled to every major city in the eastern United States, and whose inspiring sermons, it was said, had transformed the lives of hundreds of men and women. At Sunday Mass, Violetta heard the priest announce,

"If you have a special intention, whether it be for the recovery of a loved one who is sick, for the soul of a deceased relative in Purgatory, for any worthy and holy purpose whatsoever, come to Church on nine consecutive mornings beginning next Sunday, for the 9:00 A.M. Mass, receive Holy Communion, remain for the sermon and for the communal recitation of the Rosary, and your prayers will not go unheard. The intentions you pray for will find their realization through our Lord, through his Blessed Mother whose special prayer, the Rosary, will be the focus of our veneration."

Violetta believed in her heart that if she made this Novena, she would become pregnant. Each day, then, beginning on that Sunday morning, she went to Church to hear the Mass, to receive Holy Communion, and to listen to the Dominican priest speak and lead the congregation in the recitation of the Rosary. The celebrant, Father Timothy O'Byrne, was a young priest, having been ordained only three years prior to his then current Novena crusade. The head of his order realized what a charismatic speaker Father O'Byrne was, and suggested that he undertake this initiative by traveling to cities such as Boston, New York, Baltimore, Philadelphia and Pittsburgh, visiting key parishes and accomplishing these objectives: promulgate the Faith; increase devotion to our Blessed Mother and to the recitation and veneration of the Rosary; provide incentives for the faithful to live their faith more fully; assist the Order financially. The last objective would be accomplished with the cooperation of the pastor of the parish who agreed to host the Novena. Collections would be taken, and fifty per cent would remain in the parish and fifty per cent would go to the Dominicans to assist them in their work.

The following Sunday morning Violetta went to Mass and received Communion. After Mass, a number of parishioners left the Church, but Violetta along with some fifty other women and perhaps another ten men remained as Father O'Byrne led the faithful in the five decades of the Rosary. Each decade was preceded by Father O'Byrne's description of one of the Mysteries of the Rosary, fifteen altogether which recalled events in the life of the Virgin Mary, Jesus' mother. Some of these happenings, as the description makes evident, recalled joyful, sorrowful or glorious events. Since the Novena began on Sunday, the five Glorious Mysteries were to be meditated upon. These Glorious Mysteries would also be their focus on the following Wednesday and Saturday. The Joyful Mysteries were reserved for Monday and Thursday, and the Sorrowful Mysteries for Tuesday and Friday. Then, "Hail Mary, Full of Grace, the Lord is with Thee. Blessed art Thou amongst women and blessed is the fruit of thy womb, Jesus. Holy Mary, Mother of God, Pray for us sinners, now and at the hour of our death, Amen." Violetta, not knowing the words in English would join in the recitation in Italian, "Ave Maria, piena di grazia, . . ." Fifty times the words were repeated and the monotony was not felt at all, for the faithful were absolutely convinced that each repetition of these sacred words proved the sincerity of their petitions, and insured that the intentions they so fervently prayed for would find resolution according to God's will.

At the end of the Rosary, Father O'Byrne asked the petitioners to repeat after him the following words: "O my Jesus, forgive us our sins, save us from the fires of hell, lead all souls to heaven, especially those who have most need of your mercy." He then looked out at the faces of those gathered in the Church and began his sermon:

"The words we just spoke are sacred words because our Blessed Lady instructed us to conclude our recitation of the Rosary in this manner. She gave us these instructions as recently as some twenty years ago, at Fatima in the month of July in 1917. Isn't it wonderful that our Lady loves us so much that she has continued to provide us with the inspiration and the encouragement to honor her with this very special prayer or series of prayers over the centuries. As some of you know, I am a priest from the Dominican Order, a religious order founded by St. Dominic. St. Dominic was instructed by our Blessed Lady concerning the Rosary in 1214. St.

Dominic wisely and reverentially saw the power and the benefits to mankind of this same Rosary 700 hundred years ago. Pope Benedict the Fourteenth, whose Papacy lasted from 1740 to 1756, acknowledged the contributions made to the propagation of the Rosary by St. Dominic and conferred a most special honor upon the Dominican Order as the order that was especially consecrated to spread the Rosary tradition, and to ensure that its promulgation be manifested throughout the world. Continuing in this ancient tradition, I and other priests in my order conduct Novenas like the one you good people are now making, for we know that such a Novena can benefit all of us in so many positive ways. I know that many, if not most of you are making this Novena for a special intention. I can assure you, and I have personally seen this happen time and again, yes, I can assure all of you that your prayers *will* be heard. Our Blessed Lady knows about you, about your sufferings and your special needs. She will intercede with our Heavenly Father on your behalf, but she needs to see that you are serious about truly desiring God's help. You will show that you are indeed serious about seeking this help if you continue to appear in this church for the next eights days, nine days in all, that is the meaning of *novena*, nine, and especially if you show your devotion by praying the Rosary with your whole heart, your whole soul and you whole mind. The Rosary is, after all, a series of prayers, of words that are recited, but in order to gain the maximum benefits from saying the Rosary, we must also, while reciting, meditate on the sacred mysteries from the life of our Blessed Lady."

Violetta listened with rapt attention, not quite understanding all the words expressed by the priest, but feeling in her heart that she was truly faithful, and at the same time wondering if she was praying in an effective manner. She put her head into her hands and fervently asked for Mary's blessings on her and on her family.

"Don't imagine for one minute," Father O'Byrne, exclaimed, his voice rising to a pitch that roused Violetta from her meditative prayer, "that anything you can possibly ask is beyond the power of the Mother of God. Your prayers will be answered, your special intentions will be realized, even if not in the manner you may expect them to be. You will see that our all-wise heavenly Father will not disappoint you. Remember that Jesus himself said that anything you ask for in his name will be granted. It is the same with anything asked of his Holy Mother Mary. I am looking forward to speaking with some of you individually as our novena progresses. Perhaps you will find that your petition will be fulfilled even before the completion of this special devotion. If so, I pray that you share this knowledge with me."

"Please now, make every effort to continue throughout the coming eight remaining days. Our ushers are coming around to accept your offerings so that we can continue this important work. Please be generous"

Vincenzo was not pleased that Violetta was not in the store each morning, for that was one of the busiest times of the day. When he realized that she would also need to go to church on a Saturday morning, he pleaded with her to be reasonable.

"You know all our customers want your advice on what they need to buy for their Sunday dinners."

"I will just be gone for two hours at most," she countered, "and they can come back if they need to talk to me. Vincenzo, it's important for us. Don't you want to be a father?"

"Oh, Violetta, please don't be so naïve. Praying will not produce babies."

"I will prove you wrong," she said, proudly, confidently.

Three months after the completion of the novena, Violetta found that she was pregnant for the first time. Her faith was strengthened beyond measure and this faith would be transmitted, by word and example, through every fiber of her being, to each of the four sons she would give birth to during the following five years.

Twenty

Giovanni Lorelli was born in 1938, named after Vincenzo's father. Alberto arrived in 1939, Daniele in 1940 and Stefano in 1942. Violetta had a difficult first pregnancy and she wrote to her sister Rosina in Falconara, asking her to come and live with them, since she needed help desperately. She would not give up her work in the grocery store, and she believed that her sister would have a better and fuller life in America, too. Rosina arrived with Filippo, now twelve years old, as Violetta entered the second trimester of her pregnancy. The sisters were overjoyed to be together again. Rosina had been very lonely in Falconara since no one from her family lived there. Her life had become one of routine monotony, with nothing new ever happening, and her loneliness was only assuaged by the affection and the antics of her son. Filippo was a boy with a jocular personality and he constantly did things that made his mother laugh. She depended on him for the only levity possible in her dreary existence. Rosina again became everything for Violetta that she had been during her childhood. She was the mother the younger sister never had, since her own mother had died when she was so young. Rosina was more like a grandmother to Violetta's and Vincenzo's children, for she did everything a good grandmother would do for her grandchildren. With Rosina's help, Violetta was able to continue working in the store. Violetta never neglected her sons, however, and always went upstairs to spend time with them, to play with them and read to them, to teach them their prayers and tell them stories about the saints and martyrs whenever possible. With Violetta's constant supervision, Rosina looked after the youngsters' needs and tended to them whenever their mother was not present.

Gradually, as World War II ended and an economic boom brought prosperity to the United States, the Lorelli's business got better and better.

116

Vincenzo and Violetta bought the building from Nathan, which included two additional stores on either side of theirs, and expanded their store to include these. With the family now numbering eight, the Lorelli's also decided to buy a larger house, a real house, not an apartment over a store. They moved to an area in Bensonhurst where new one and two family houses were springing up. It was still very convenient since the new house was not too far from the store. The house was a new brick building with a large yard in the back, where the children could play without concerns about their safety, and it was in a quieter and more residential area. Rosina now had her own apartment, with a separate entrance on the side, but she still spent most of her time with the boys in the main part of the house. Filippo was a teenager and he worked in the store with his uncle and aunt after school and on Saturdays. Violetta came up with the idea of offering home made dishes, Italian *pastas, minestras, antipasti,* and other delicacies, for which orders were placed in advance by their customers, and which became so popular that she was having trouble keeping up with the demand for them. When the new expanded store was being planned, discussions about its name occupied a good amount of time during Sunday meals at home. Everyone agreed that *La Cucina di Mamma* was a great choice for a name since Violetta's kitchen-prepared foods had made their store particularly distinctive in the neighborhood. However, in keeping with their feelings of gratitude for what the United States had done for them—both Vincenzo and Violetta had become U.S. citizens—they felt a name that combined Italian and English would be appropriate, so the store was called *Mamma's Kitchen.*

Another reason why Mamma's Kitchen was popular and why customers were so loyal was the manner in which both Vincenzo and Violetta treated them. There was never a question about the honesty of the store's owners. On the rare occasions when something was found to be unsatisfactory, the customer was always given the benefit of the doubt and anything the customer deemed unsatisfactory was either exchanged or their money was refunded. Violetta lived her religion in her dealings with everyone. She was always, kind, considerate and helpful. She extended credit to customers who promised to pay when they got some expected funds, she gave food to poor souls who stood in front of the store, knowing that she would come out and feed them, and she always made certain that anything weighed on the scale would be slightly over what the customer requested, rather than under, never charging for the extra weight. Sometimes Vinny would get upset with her.

"We are running a business, not a charity," he would insist.

"Oh Vincenzo, what does the Gospel say? Are we not to love our neighbors and to help those who are less fortunate? We are doing well. Why shouldn't we help others when we can? We can only be blessed for our good deeds. We cannot lose." Vinny knew her argument by now, and he knew it was useless to contradict her.

Filippo Sandreva, now known as Phil, joined his Aunt's and Uncle's business when he completed high school. He had worked in the business throughout his teen years and became an invaluable asset. He spoke English as though he had been born in the United States and handled much of the paperwork entailed in running such a business. He was a happy young man and was grateful for the opportunity that had been accorded him. As the Lorelli brothers grew up they seemed to take it for granted that they too would enter the family business when they completed their education through high school. This was especially true of Giovanni, Alberto and Stefano, though Stefano was the youngest brother. Daniele, the penultimate son never quite expressed the same enthusiasm that his brothers did about becoming grocers like their father. Daniele's dreams focused on a life that would take him away from the mundane world of family business with its inherent restrictive scope. He had an artistic bent and from the age of six or seven enjoyed participating in school plays, contributing poems to the school bulletin, and singing in school pageants. Daniel was unusual in other ways too. Violetta noticed this and would often say to her husband,

"I wonder who our Daniele takes after."

She insisted on calling him Daniele, becoming visibly upset if his brothers called him "Danny." The name was always pronounced in the Italian manner in the Lorelli household. Outside, everyone called him "Daniel" in the English pronunciation. Violetta noticed that although Daniel was not shy and had an open and engaging personality, he would sometimes turn inward and appear to be off in another world. Violetta always remembered the Sunday evening when, only three years old, her son said to her,

"Mom, that park we went to today?

"Si, Daniele, Prospect Park, what about it?"

"I remember I was there before."

"That's not possible, son. Today was the first time your father and I ever even went there."

"But Mom," Daniel insisted, "I know I was there. I even remember the lake and other things about it—the trees, the hills, the way the sun shines through the trees in certain places. I just feel that something important happened to me there."

Violetta just attributed her son's words to something he had seen someplace else. But during the next two years, he would tell her about other things that felt familiar to him, including certain scents or feelings about people that he remembered from someplace, from some other time. After the age of five, Daniel only mentioned his sense of *déjà vu* occasionally. Thereafter, Violetta did not attach too much importance to her son's imaginings, aware nonetheless that Daniel was different from her other children, even if she did not know precisely why.

Around this time, the Lorelli family went to the wedding reception of a young couple, the daughter and son of families they had known in Longobardi. The young man's parents knew the parents of the young woman but the two first met during a visit one family made to the other's home. The wedding reception was held in an American Legion hall, and it was the kind of reception that became known as a "football" wedding. The food served consisted of various types of sandwiches made with Italian rolls. If one person went up to the table to get a sandwich, he would call over to family members and friends,

"Hey, Johnny, what kind of sandwich do you want?"

"What do they have?"

"*Salami, provolone, ham, capicolla.*"

"I'll take a salami."

With that, Vito would toss the salami across the room to Johnnie, toss it like a football, hence the term, "football wedding." These wedding receptions were quite enjoyable. People mixed freely, speaking to one another throughout the evening, dancing, making the most of their time together.

In one corner of the room an upright piano provided the evening's music. A man played songs requested by the guests who would dance to the music and stand around the piano singing some of the popular tunes of the day: "Sioux City Sue," made famous by Bing Crosby; "Ole Buttermilk Sky," a hit in the version by Kay Kayser and His Orchestra; Perry Como's "Prisoner of Love"; "To Each His Own" by the Ink Spots; "Managua Nicaragua," a great tune to dance to; "Linda," "Chi-Baba, Chi-Baba," and others. In the 40's and continuing on into the late 50's, pop music lovers kept abreast of new songs, and through their purchases first of the breakable 78's and then the non-breakable 45's, helped determine which songs would be hits, make the top ten and even become number one for one or sometimes many more weeks. A large cross-section of the population listened to pop music and when a song became a hit, it seemed as though everyone was humming it or playing the recording. The pianist at the wedding, therefore, had to know all the top songs of the day.

During a break for the pianist, Daniel, who had been avidly watching the pianist's fingers flying across the keyboard, sat on the bench and began fingering the keys himself. He had never played a piano before, but after a few minutes, he was able to approximate some of the sounds he had heard played by the wedding pianist, even using both hands. When the pianist came back, he heard Daniel and asked him how long he had been taking lessons. He could not believe that this little boy, correctly matching a melody with chords, had never before in his life even touched a piano.

"Where are your parents?"

Daniel's oldest brother John had already gone to call Vinny and Violetta over to hear what Daniel was playing.

"Mr.?"

"Lorelli," replied Vinny..

"Your son here tells me that he never touched a piano before today. This kid has a natural talent. You should send him for training. Play something for your parents, kid."

Vinny was not surprised, since he had started to play the mandolin the same way.

"He takes after his father." Violetta said.

"But I thought he said he never touched a piano before today?" the pianist asked, now somewhat puzzled.

"No, I mean he must have his father's musical ability. My husband plays the mandolin quite well, and he never had a lesson in his life."

Vinny and Violetta discussed this amazing discovery and agreed that they would have to buy a piano and send Daniele for piano lessons.

His brothers were good students, but they rather enjoyed math and science while Daniel excelled in subjects like spelling, reading, music and art, at least to the extent that these latter disciplines, especially, were made available, being a smaller part of the curriculum. The Lorelli boys, each and every one, attended Mass on Sundays, but their parents were unsuccessful in enrolling them into the Catholic school that was attached to the parish. Even though the Lorelli's were very devout, practicing Roman Catholics, the lack of participation in parish activities by the parents, due, of course, to the little time available after long business hours, made the church's pastor unwilling to accommodate them. To be fair, it must be said that the number of seats in each grade was limited by the size of the school itself, and the pastor made his decisions for admission based on how much he saw of the parents of prospective pupils, how active they became in things like the altar society for women parishioners and the ushers' society for the men. Financial contributions to the Church influenced the selection of children to attend the school too. The Lorelli's, generous and charitable people that they certainly were, did not have a tradition of giving a meaningful portion of their income to the Church, as, for example, Irish Catholics or American Protestants did. In Italy, when the Longobardesi went to Mass, they either made no contribution at all because of their lack of money, or gave a token sum that was more symbolic than financially meaningful for themselves or for the Church. If someone had told the Lorelli's that they could get their sons into the Catholic school by donating money, there is no doubt that they would have gone to the pastor and asked him what needed to be done. As a result of the lack of sophistication of their parents, all four Lorelli boys went to the local public elementary, junior high and high schools. In the days following World War II, this was not a bad place for children to get their education. The public schools were staffed by well trained, conscientious and devoted teachers. The level of education of most of the public school teachers was considerably higher than that of the nuns and the few lay teachers who taught in the Catholic schools. In those days, the mention of God in the public schools was not frowned upon and individual teachers who were themselves religious could "get away" with preaching to a certain extent. Since about half of the students in the classes attended by Violetta's sons were of the Jewish faith, teachers would not generally discuss religion in terms of Jesus. It was safe to merely talk about God in a general way. The boys had to learn their Catechism by attending "religious instruction," sometimes also known as "released time." On Wednesday afternoons, the public schools set aside the afternoon for those who wanted to attend religious instruction. It didn't matter what religion you were, the time was there if you wanted to take advantage of it. Roman Catholic pupils, whose parents signed the necessary forms, could leave at Noon, go home for lunch or have lunch in school and then appear at the Catholic school for instruction in Catechism from 1:00 to 3:00 P.M. Most of the public school pupils made their First Holy Communion at the age of seven, usually in the month of May. About a week before the ceremony, the public schools excused the Catholics making their First Communion for the entire week prior to the ceremony. That was a tough week for the public school Catholics, for they had to sit in an auditorium for about five hours each day, listening to the nuns instructing them on why they were there, on the meaning of First Holy Communion, and on what needed to be done when they went up to the altar to receive the body and blood of Jesus Christ. Daniel Lorelli was very excited about making his First Communion. Violetta told her son what a great event this was going to be and how fortunate he would be to receive Our Lord for the first time. He didn't mind a change of scenery either, going to the Catholic School instead of his usual Public School classes. As so often in life, however, reality can be quite different from one's imagined perception of an event. After the first day, sitting still for so long, with no chance to talk or even to get up and walk around made the experience an ordeal. The unpleasantness was compounded further by a disturbing occurrence. This particular day, the combination of one irascible nun and one incorrigible boy combined to intensify tensions throughout the auditorium. Seven year old Michael Bevilacqua made a comment to the other boys sitting nearby when Sister Annuciata spoke about how the communion wafer was the true body and blood of Jesus and when you swallowed it, you were actually swallowing that body and blood. Michael had told his friends that if that's what it was, he wanted no part of it. The other boys didn't laugh, for they already knew what such a reaction could bring them in terms of discipline. The long wooden ruler was still used to redden the behinds of any trouble-makers. Sister Annunciata shouted in Michael's direction and walked down the aisle. As she approached the area where the sound came from, she looked around and noticed that the other boys were staring at Michael. The girls were all segregated from the boys on the other side of the auditorium, actually a gymnasium, where folding chairs had been set up for the Communion preparation activities.

"Do you have something to say?" barked Sister Annunciata.

Michael was used to being questioned by his public school teacher, and he usually got no more than a punishment assignment of homework for misbehavior, which he never did anyway. He always managed to get laughs from the other kids, the kind of laughs that are for you, not against you, and Michael won a measure of popularity because of his daring. He saw this question from the Sister as an opportunity to extend his luster to these kids, many of whom knew him not at all.

"Oh, I was just saying that if there's really blood in that wafer, I'm not going to eat it. No, Ma'am, no blood for me."

Some of the children wanted to laugh because of the funny way Michael expressed himself, but they hesitated and thought better of it.

"That is sacrilege!" the Nun shouted. "I am going to tan your hide. You go up front and assume the position and you will get your comeuppance for daring to say something so disgusting."

Unafraid, Michael had the temerity to answer her still.

"Disgusting is right. Drinking someone's blood, what you said, that's disgusting."

At this new outburst, Sister Annunciata could not contain her rage. She reached into the row and grabbed Michael's shirt, pulling him off the seat.

"I'm going to teach you a lesson now, you rude child you."

She pulled the boy towards the front and tried to force him to bend over. She whacked him as hard as she could, the ruler hitting his back instead of his buttocks. The boy screamed out, "Ow! Ow!" and pulled away, running to the back door He opened the door and ran out. Michael was one boy who did not receive the body and blood of Jesus Christ the following Sunday, in spite of his mother's pleas to Sister Annunciata that Michael would behave henceforth.

Daniel Lorelli sat quietly throughout the five days of lectures and instructions, written tests and oral tests. On Saturday morning, all the First Communicants were brought into the Church to give their very first confession.

"Bless me Father, for I have sinned, this is my first confession." As Daniel said this, he hesitated.

"Yes, my son," said the priest. "What are your sins?"

Daniel had thought about this, but he really did not think he had done anything that could be called a sin. He always obeyed his father and his mother. He never fought with his brothers. He was always respectful to his teacher and to his fellow students. He never really got angry about anything. What could he say?

"Would you like to tell me your sins?" the priest asked again. "It's all right if you are nervous. Take your time."

"Father, I don't think I have any sins to confess now," Daniel ventured.

"No, sins. What is your name? "

"Daniel."

"Ah, Daniel, the name of the prophet. Daniel, we are all sinners. Only God is perfect, and among human beings, only our Blessed Lady was conceived without original sin, the sin of Adam. You know about that don't you."

"Yes, Father," Daniel replied, "We learned about it in religious instruction."

"O.K, then. Since we are all sinners, you are a sinner too, so you must have some sins. Do you ever get angry?"

Daniel thought about this and remembered that he had been upset one day when his friend borrowed his homework and soiled it so that he had to write it over. He told this to the priest, but he could not convince himself that this was a sin.

"Well, now, see Daniel, the sin of anger. And be careful, my son, for if you continue to think that you are sinless, you will have committed the terrible sin of pride, the sin of Lucifer, and then you will have to confess that at your next confession. For your penance say five Hail Mary's. Now say your Act of Contrition."

"Oh my God, I am heartily sorry for having offended Thee. And I detest all my sins because I dread the loss of Heaven and the pains of Hell, but most of all because they offend Thee, my God, who art all good and deserving of all my love.

I firmly resolve, with the help of Thy grace, to confess my sins, to do penance and to amend my life. Amen."

As he was saying these words, Daniel could barely see the priest through the screen, see his hands moving and hear the Latin words that signaled that Daniel's sins were being forgiven, that the priest was acting as God's intermediary and that although he was forgiving the sins, God was in reality the One who forgave and whose forgiveness was radiating down from Heaven.

When Daniel came out of the confessional, he noticed the other children waiting on line staring at him. When they left the church, one of his friends told him that everyone was whispering that he really must have had many terrible sins to have been in the "booth" so long. Daniel knew that he was bound not to say anything about what went on during Confession. The priest could never tell anyone else what a penitent told him. Even if a man admitted he had committed a murder, the priest was bound by the secrecy of Confession never to tell anyone, even under torture. The penitent, too, was bound by the same secrecy, and Daniel remembered those stories of martyred priests in times when the Church was persecuted, and how they chose death rather than divulging anything told to them in Confession. At least this is what Daniel was convinced of as he faced his friends, even though he wanted to tell them that he really had nothing to confess

That evening as he lay in bed, Daniel thought about the priest's words. He had to find out about the prophet Daniel. And who was Lucifer, whose sin of pride he could be guilty of? With these thoughts going through his head, Daniel fell into a deep sleep. The following day, he did receive his First Holy Communion. That morning, Violetta dressed her son in a new navy blue suit with short pants and a jacket. Under the jacket he wore a white shirt and tie. He had a new pair of black leather shoes with shoe laces and a pair of navy stocking that reached up to his knees. The First Communion package that parents were obliged to purchase for this special day included a small black prayer book, a pair of rosary beads and a scapular with images of Mary, Saint Joseph and the Infant Jesus. Also included was a satin white cross that was to be pinned to the right sleeve of the jacket. As he walked up to the altar with the other children, a line of girls on the left, a line of boys on the right, Daniel smiled as he passed his mother and father, his three brothers, his aunt and cousin, seated at the end of one pew. He kneeled at the altar and the priest placed the communion wafer on his tongue, uttering some unintelligible Latin words. As the seven year old walked back to his seat, he lowered his head and made certain that the Communion wafer did not touch his teeth. He kneeled and tried to lock out all thoughts but those concerning this Communion with God, with Jesus.

"Oh God," he prayed, "Please help me to do Your will always and in all things. Help me to be a good person and to show love to everyone, just as you show us Your Love, always and in all things."

After Mass, the Lorelli family went to a local photo studio where Daniel was photographed holding his prayer book in front of him, palms open, the Rosary dangling, draped over the book. A midday family feast followed which included a special First Communion cake that Violetta had made herself. Renato and Paola and their three children were invited too. Daniel felt so special that day. He was the center of attention, and everything about the ceremony and the liturgy, and the sense that God was with him made him feel certain that he belonged, indeed, to the One True Faith.

Twenty-One

In 1948, eight year old Daniel Lorelli was in third grade. His brothers were ten, nine and six. The United States was in the throes of a post-war boom that reflected not only economic well being, but widespread feelings of positivism. There was a general sense that the future was bright, that only good things could happen from then on, and that the world would continue on a path leading to greater riches, happier experiences and more exciting developments in all fields. New and fantastic inventions would contribute to helping this wonderful state of living come about. World War II had been fought, a terrible war to be sure, but a war that would end wars. After what had happened, man would not go to war again. Everyone had learned an important lesson. Daniel read accounts of the unspeakable things that had been done to civilians, to Jews in concentration camps. He saw pictures of the survivors in popular magazines like *Life*—living skeletons whose eyes peered out in agony and incomprehension at those who came to rescue them and to document the inhumanity they had suffered at the hands of other human beings? Was it possible? Shooting babies in their mothers' arms? Gassing people who thought they were going to shower, to cleanse themselves? Burning them in ovens? No, it was too much. How could this have happened? One day, a boy in his class was showing him and another boy a story in the *Daily Mirror* that described one of these camps and had a black and white picture of a mound of naked corpses being pushed into a large, mass grave.

"How could the Germans treat people like that?" Daniel asked, rhetorically.

The other boy looking over their shoulders nonchalantly replied,

"They deserved it."

"Who deserved it?" asked Daniel.

"The Jews, they had it coming to them. My father told me all about how they always had all the money and took advantage of everyone else."

Daniel stood, dumfounded, not understanding how anyone, any group of people could "deserve" such a fate. That evening, he asked his mother about it and told her what the boy said.

"That is a lie," Violetta told her son. "Some Germans were inspired by the Devil, and they were in power then. The Devil exists in the world, my son, and he made his home in Germany during the war. Not all Germans are bad either, but many took part in these terrible deeds. This could never have happened in Italy. Italians would never do such things. As for the Jews, don't ever believe such lies. Remember that I always told you there are good and bad in every group of people. Even though our faith is the one true faith, there are still some Catholics who are not good, mostly those who do not practice their religion, for if they did they could never do the bad things some of them do. The Jews are the people who gave us the first part of our Bible, the Old Testament. I first learned all about this when I went to a Novena and the priest talked about how the Old Testament was fulfilled in the New, but that Jews do not accept it. They are in error, but they are still good people and good friends. If it had not been for a Jewish man, we would never have had the business we have today. This man—Nathan was his name—he gave us the chance to start our business. He was fair to us and then he sold us the building."

Daniel felt somehow good inside. He felt bad about what had happened to the Jews, but at least he was confident that Italians could never have participated in such horrors. Nevertheless, there was something inside him that would not leave him, this gnawing recognition of evil, an evil that came about without any good reason, but worse still, found justification in the minds of some. Daniel had been exposed to anti-Semitism, had witnessed blind hatred, and this was merely the beginning of his immersion into the mindless arena of intolerance.

Thinking about those people who had been so cruelly treated and who lost their lives under such horrible conditions in the Second World War, especially the children, Daniel began to think about religious teachings concerning life after death. So many of these children had had no chance whatsoever. Some had not even begun to live. And the Church taught that Jews could not go to heaven, that un-baptized babies were sent to a place called "Limbo." He remembered his early childhood recollections of having been here before. One day he read an article in a magazine about reincarnation. It made sense didn't it? How else could there be any true justice in the world? If those children who had been killed in the war could live again, it wouldn't matter so much that they had died at such an early age. They could live again. They would live again. They would have another chance, and another and another, until they reached a state of perfection where they could return to God. But Daniel had asked a priest about this in confession, and the priest told him to forget "that nonsense." You could not be a Catholic and believe such "stupidity." As a Catholic, you must believe in the Resurrection. Just as Jesus rose from the dead, so would all those souls who had been true to their Faith. After the final judgment our souls will be reunited with our bodies, and we will see such sights as the eye has never seen before, as St. Paul instructed us. This is what the priest told Daniel, and Daniel wanted to believe it, and he was determined to believe it, but still the gnawing doubts persisted.

In spite of negative factors, the world still appeared headed in the right direction. Then, in mid-1948 the Soviet Union's program to develop an atomic bomb, like the one the United States had dropped on Hiroshima and Nagasaki, took on a new urgency. On August 29, 1949, the Russians exploded "First Lightning–Joe 1," their first such device, and a new era had begun. By 1955, the Father of the Soviet Hydrogen Bomb, Andrei Sakharov, had developed the RDS 37, the first Soviet super-bomb, a true H-bomb. This news was disturbing and preparations got underway for American citizens to protect themselves.

In the Fall of 1949, Daniel's teacher, Miss Martinson, who was very nice most of the time and would only raise her voice if some of her twenty-five or so pupils disobeyed her instructions, discussed the new civil defense procedures that would have to be followed in all American schools, and especially in cities like New York that would be the primary targets of the Russians when they were ready to drop their atomic or hydrogen bombs. Miss Martinson showed her pupils pictures of what such an explosion looked like, and how the stages of the explosion could kill people who did not take adequate cover. The blast itself was bad enough, but then there would be flying glass and other objects, tremendous winds, fires and more. At the signal, students had to act quickly, get down on their knees in the aisle next to their desks and cover their heads with their hands. But all of this talk about the possible destruction of American cities, the pictures of atomic bomb explosions, the smoke rising up into a cloud that looked like a mushroom, these disturbing images gave some of the more impressionable youngsters a feeling of foreboding. Daniel was one of these particularly sensitive children and he began to wonder if he would live to adulthood himself. He thought about it more and more, read about people who were building bomb shelters so they would survive an atomic bomb attack. Daniel and others like him who feared this new danger developed an almost irrational attitude concerning it. They worried about the bomb being dropped on their homes. They could see the giant mushroom shaped cloud above New York City, see it clearly in their imaginative ruminations. Daniel thought of this fear he and others had, and even though he knew nothing about psychology, he had heard the term *complex* in connection with so many mental aberrations that he thought he himself possessed a complex. He thought of it as *a mushroom complex*.

At the age of ten, Daniel was confirmed in his Faith. Bishop McCabe visited the parish and conferred the sacrament on the children and even on a few adults, two women and two men who had never received it because they were either converts or didn't have parents who saw its importance. Daniel chose Phil Sandreva, his cousin, to be his godfather and selected the name Michael as his Confirmation name. Now that he had confirmed the choices made for him by his godparents at Baptism, Daniel was a true soldier of God. He decided that it was time to become an altar boy, and went too see Father Manning, the best liked priest in the parish. He was the favorite of the children, and on Saturday afternoons, when confessions were heard in the church, Father Manning's line was the longest. The other priests had perhaps four or five adults waiting outside their confessionals, while Father Manning had fifteen to twenty youngsters. It was common knowledge among the kids that Father Manning would never speak harshly, no matter what sins you committed, and he was very lenient about the penance he meted out too. Father Manning gave Daniel a book with all the Latin phrases that he had to learn. First came the priest's prayers at the foot of the altar. In the 1950's the priest still faced the altar, with his back to the congregation, but this was to change with Vatican II which opened in 1962 under Pope John XXIII. The priest would thenceforth face the congregation. Vatican II also paved the way for the mass to be said in the vernacular, with the congregation providing the responses to the priest's words that the altar boy was responsible for in the Latin Mass. Daniel's desire to serve as an altar boy required him to learn all the Latin responses. In the book given to Daniel, the priest's words came first, followed by the altar boy's responses in bold print.

"Take this home and try to learn all the Latin responses as quickly as you can. You just have to memorize the words, those in bold print. When you come to the meetings, you will learn what they mean and have practice in responding. Meetings are on Thursday nights in the Church basement at 7:30." Father Manning smiled at Daniel and assured him that he would be a very good altar boy.

"I'm sure you'll enjoy ringing the bells."

Daniel was very enthusiastic and went home and began to study. The first responses followed the priest's invocation of Psalm 42, "I will go up to the altar of God."

In nomine Patris, et Filii, Spiritus Sancti. Amen. Introibo ad altare Dei.

Ad Deum qui laetificat juventutem meam.

Judica me, Deus, et discerne causam meam de gente non sancta: ab homine iniquo, et doloso erue me.

Quia tu es, Deus, fortitudo mea: quare me repulisti et quare tristis incedo, dum affligit me inimicus?

Emitte lucem tuam, et veritatem tuam: ipsa me deduxerunt, et adduxerunt in montem sanctum tuum, et in tabernacula tua.

Et introibo ad altare Dei: ad Deum qui laetificat juventutem meam.

Confitebor tibi in cithara, Deus, Deus meus: quare tristis es, anima mea, et quare conturbas me?

Spera in Deo, quoniam adhuc confitebor illi: salutare vultus me et Deus meus.

Gloria Patri et Filio, et Spiritui Sancto.

Sicut erat in principio et nunc, et semper, et in saecula saeculorum. Amen.

Introibo ad altare Dei.

Ad Deum qui laetificat juventutem meam.

Adjutorium nostrum in nomine Domini.

Qui fecit caelum et terram.

The Mass opening was followed by the *Kyrie, Gloria, Credo, Sanctus, Benedictus and Agnus Dei,* and in all these parts of the Mass, Daniel had responses to learn.

The Latin sounded strange, but it had a musical quality that Daniel liked (years later, as a professional musician Daniel would love hearing these Latin words to the music that they had been set to by composers like Bach, Haydn, Mozart, Beethoven and others). He was proud of himself when he arrived at the Church basement the following Thursday evening. He had memorized all the responses and was ready to prove how well he could do. Seven other boys were present, two being the senior altar boys. Father Manning came in and assigned one of the senior altar boys, Charles, to read the priest's words and have the younger boys respond. When Daniel's turn came, he remembered the responses perfectly, only mispronouncing a few words. There was a discussion as to what the Latin words meant and Father Manning, for the benefit of Daniel and one other new boy explained the significance of the Latin Mass which they were participants in. The Mass, he told the boys, was known as the "Tridentine Mass" because it was codified by the Council of Trent in the 16th century.

This Mass had been used by the Catholic Church for 1500 years. That evening, Father Manning told the boys about the universality of the Latin Mass.

"You can go anyplace in the entire world, and if you go to Mass, you will hear the exact same Mass that you hear right here in our parish." The priest said this with a distinct display of pride

When the meeting was over, Daniel started to walk out, following Father Manning. Charles called after him,

"Danny, wait a minute, we are not finished yet. You, too, Joseph." Charles and the other teenage altar boy told Daniel and Joseph that since they were joining the altar boys they had to undergo an initiation.

"What's an in initiation?" asked Joseph.

"It's something you have to go through when you join a new group," the older boy replied, sounding annoyed at the question. Charles then placed a blindfold over Daniel's and Joseph's eyes and took them to a room off the main room. They were told to bend over and hold onto a bar that ran along the wall. Daniel was finding this hard to understand. But it's in the Church, he thought, on Church grounds. How could anything bad happen? Joseph's pants were pulled down and Charles hit him across his buttocks. When Daniel heard the slap, he pulled his blindfold off and saw Joseph's bare red bottom.

"I'm not staying here!" he asserted and walked out of the room. As he approached the doorway they had been led through, he could see Father Manning looking at what was occurring through a window from an adjoining darkened room. Daniel could not understand how Father Manning could know about this and still permit it. He never said a word to his mother or father because he felt they would not be able to understand either. Daniel told his mother that he had changed his mind about being an altar boy, and although Violetta was disappointed, she wanted her sons to learn to make their own judgments and was resigned to avoiding any kind of unreasonable control over them.

Twenty-Two

By the age of thirteen, Daniel began to notice indefinable, mysterious changes in his body. A small amount of hair was growing in his pubic area, but this did not baffle him as much as certain feelings of restlessness, a longing for what he knew not, an anxiety that had no apparent cause. His mother and father never spoke to him about sex. Vincenzo felt that boys learn from other boys as he had, and that was all there was to it. Violetta would have spoken to her son if she had realized it was necessary, but she just assumed that this was something her husband would know about and take care of. Besides, the brothers were close in age, they would probably help each other out in these matters. This would have seemed logical, but John and Albert worked in the store everyday after school, wanted to work there, saw it as their own future business and were too tired to talk about anything after eating supper and doing their homework. It was understood that Daniel's time was better spent going home after school and practicing the piano. He had weekly lessons on one day of the week and the other days he practiced for a minimum of two hours. His father had bought him a fine upright piano, and after some six years of lessons, his playing was superb and his parents were very proud of him. Daniel, then, was quite innocent at the age of thirteen. Television was in its early stages in 1953, and there was absolutely nothing in the medium that shed any light whatsoever on sex for the benefit or, some would say to the detriment of, young boys and girls. One Saturday evening in summer, as he was riding his bicycle home from a friend's house, it began to rain and he quickly sought shelter. There was a movie theater nearby and he rode around the side. He took refuge under some wooden steps that led up to the doors to the box office. It was a brief summer shower and he was about to take his bicycle and leave when he heard some laughter above him on the steps. He looked up and could see in between the cracks, under the dresses of some young women who were standing there waiting to go inside. He couldn't really see very much, but the sight of their legs under their skirts or dresses and the white or pink or blue panties he saw somehow excited him. He went home and again experienced this strange restlessness, something that needed a resolution, but he had no idea as to what it could be. After that day, he went back under the steps as often as he could, always sensing the excitement of something forbidden, for he knew that this was something he would probably have to confess the next time he went to confession, and going home to again and again feel that strange restlessness.

In a junior high school gym class, as Daniel was seated with other boys around the edge of the gymnasium waiting for their turns to be tested on the parallel bars, two boys next to him were discussing masturbation. They were calling it "jerking off." Daniel had no idea what they were talking about, but he listened intently as one boy said to the other,

"It's so great when it gets hard and you start to rub it up and down. I think about that girl in my math class with the big tits and I can't even hold it in. It shoots out a mile!"

Daniel had no idea that such a thing was possible, and he wondered as to exactly what shot out. Was it like peeing, only it shoots out suddenly?

The following Saturday, he again went under the steps of the theater. When he got home his restlessness was greater than ever. He went into the bathroom, sat down and thought of the legs he had looked up at. He tried to perform the act described by the boys in his class. This was new. After some moments, he suddenly felt a release, the release from that restlessness he had been feeling, a sensation he had never before experienced, somewhat pleasant, but troubling too. Seeing a white fluid, he worried that he may have damaged something, but soon realized that this was what the boys had been discussing, for it had shot out suddenly. That night, he told his brother Albert about his experience.

"First time? No kidding. I've been doing it for a long time. You know, you have to tell that to the priest in Confession?"

"To the priest? Why? I can't tell that to the priest. It's too private!"

"Oh, you have to if you want to go to Communion. It's a sin of impurity."

This started for Daniel the long series of confessions and the lectures on the value of being pure, the necessity for chastity.

"Bless me Father for I have sinned. It's been one week since my last confession."

"And what are your sins?"

"Well, I used bad language a few times."

"Yes."

"I was disobedient to my mother—not really disobedient, I just didn't want to finish my dinner."

"Anything else?"

"Yes, Father. I had impure thoughts."

"Is that all?"

"No, Father, I committed impure acts too."

"How often?"

"Every day."

"Every day?"

"Yes, Father."

"Did you confess this sin at your last confession?

"Yes, Father."

"And when was that?"

The priest's voice seemed to be taking on a tone of impatience.

"Last Saturday, Father."

"Last Saturday? And didn't you solemnly swear in your Act of Contrition that you would amend your life? Do you know what that means? It doesn't mean that you go right back and commit impure acts again every day!"

The priest now sounded angry, but he kept his voice muffled.

"Now, are you going to make a serious effort to stop these impure acts for once and for all?"

"Yes, Father."

"O.K. Say a good Act of Contrition, and for your penance say ten Our Fathers and fifteen Hail Mary's and ask our Lord to help you to overcome these temptations. Remember, God's grace is sufficient for all of us, all of us, even for you. After Communion tomorrow morning, you will be in a state of grace and there is no temptation that can be too strong for you to resist. Do you understand?"

"Yes, Father."

More easily said than done.

Daniel began to think there was something wrong with him. Then, one day he was sitting in the Confessional waiting for the priest to open the screen on his side. The priest was talking to a boy who was a couple of years older than he. Daniel had seen him going in on the other side before him. The priest's voice was louder and angrier than usual. Confessions were heard on Saturday afternoons from 2:00 P.M. to 5:00 P.M. and it was almost five. The church was nearly empty.

"Weren't you here before?" He heard the priest demand.

The boy apparently confirmed that he had, indeed, been there that very afternoon.

"Then why did you come back? You don't go to confession twice in one day!"

Again Daniel heard a muffled sound, and this time the priest fairly lost his temper.

"You mean right after leaving confession you went home and committed another impure act?"

The priest must have realized that he was dealing with a case that needed special spiritual attention, for he lowered his voice and talked for so long that Daniel walked out and went to another confessional that was empty.

After receiving Communion, Daniel always felt so good, so clean, so pure. He knew that God's grace was sufficient for him. That is, it was sufficient for awhile, but then temptation took over again. At night he would look out of his bedroom window, look up at the stars and stare at the moon when it was visible. He would pray with all the fervor pouring forth from his truly pure heart,

"Oh, God! Please show me a sign."

He looked at the stars and waited to see if God would send a star hurtling down to earth to show him that He wanted Daniel to serve him in some special way.

"God, please, show me what I need to do to honor You. Send me a sign and I will dedicate my life to your Glory."

A few years later Daniel went on two day retreats, and within that atmosphere of supplication and devotion, he felt such profound piety that he began to think in terms of becoming a priest. One evening during Vespers, he saw a novitiate of the Passionist order playing the organ, accompanying the singing. The young man of perhaps twenty or twenty-one years of age had a rapt expression on his face, but his entire bearing displayed a serenity that seemed so other-worldly and beautiful. Daniel thought,

"That's how I would like to be. God, help me to know Your will. I will follow wherever You lead me."

Gradually, Daniel began to feel that God had shown him what He wanted of him. Hadn't he been told time and again that he had a God-given talent for music? After seven years of lessons, after studying scales and arpeggios, Czerny *Etudes* and Bach *Inventions*, Daniel had mastered Haydn's early *Sonatas*, Mozart's *Fantasia in d minor* and some early Beethoven *Sonatas*. By and by, he excelled in works like Beethoven's "Moonlight," "Pathetique," and "Appassionata" Sonatas, flying through the difficult third movement of the "Moonlight," with virtuosic skill. His first teacher, a Mr. Carducci, had a school that he ran out of an old three story house. Most of Mr. Carducci's students had a communal type of lesson. The teacher would bring together six or seven students of similar ability. Each would play the piece they had worked on for the past week in front of the other students and Carducci would ask for comments as to what was done well, what not. When he felt it necessary, Carducci would sit down himself and play specific passages the way he wanted his students to play them. Daniel easily surpassed all the other students so that Carducci was obliged to give him lessons by himself. After a year of tentative endeavors, Carducci suggested to Mrs. Lorelli that Daniel needed a teacher who could more effectively stimulate the youngster's "God-given talent" (that phrase again!). To Carducci's credit, he knew his own limitations. Violetta heard from one of her customers of a woman piano teacher who had a good reputation. She had annual concerts when her pupils' skills were presented to parents and relatives. Daniel studied with Mrs. Jorgensen for the next six years. Mrs. Jorgensen too, honestly and admirably, told the Lorelli's after the annual concert in June, when Daniel was thirteen, that he needed to have advanced work that she felt inadequate to provide him with. She suggested that he attend a school in Manhattan, a conservatory that was well known for turning out some of the best concert pianists. The Lorelli's felt their son was too young to travel to Manhattan alone, and the exigencies of their business did not allow them the time necessary to accompany him. Mrs Jorgensen then said that she had heard of a piano teacher nearby who was a Russian immigrant and who himself had been a concert pianist in his native country. Vinny Lorelli took his son to see the teacher, a large man with a wild beard, tall and overbearing in appearance. His unkempt appearance somehow added to the aura of mysteriousness that his brusque manner provoked. Vinny was unsure as to whether he wanted his son's musical development entrusted to such an unsympathetic looking individual.

"Sit down and play!" Vladimir Vronitsky commanded in a tone of unmistakable authority. He pointed to a large Steinway grand that dominated the sizeable room.

"What would you like to hear? I can play . . . "

But before Daniel could complete his sentence, the teacher stopped him with one word,

"Play!"

Daniel began the first movement of Beethoven's Sonata No. 21 in C, Op. 53, the "Waldstein" Sonata. Three minutes into the first movement,

Vronitsky stopped the youngster and asked for the second movement. He listened to two minutes of this "Adagio molto" and said almost defiantly,

"Let me hear the 'Rondo!'"

Vin Lorelli watched Vronitsky as he lowered his head and seemed completely immersed in the music. Having an innate feeling for music himself, Vin sensed that this gargantuan figure knew music and that he knew it intimately. When Daniel completed playing the third movement, Vronitsky said simply:

"I accept him as a student. My fee is $7.00 for a one hour lesson." Turning to Daniel he commanded,

"Be here on Saturday morning at 9:25. Your lesson will begin at 9:30. Be on time!"

Daniel's lessons with Vronitsky were elucidating and inspiring. The teacher rarely played himself, but when he did, at times when he wanted to demonstrate a point that Daniel did not apprehend after three or four verbal suggestions, his command of the instrument was so overwhelming that Daniel just wanted to sit and listen to him forever. With the dour but inspiring Vronitsky, Daniel studied Chopin's *Etudes, Nocturnes* and *Ballades*, Liszt's *Funerailles* and selected pieces from *L'Années de Pèlerinage*, including all of "Switzerland" and "Italy," a number of Piano Sonatas by Schubert and other works by Schumann, Weber and Rachmaninov.

One day as Daniel was waiting in the room adjoining the room with the Steinway Grand, he looked at the books inside a bookcase and saw a few books on Christian Science, including a copy of *Science and Health with Key to the Scriptures* by Mary Baker Eddy. This coupling of the words "Christian" and "Science" aroused the interest of the sixteen year old whose religious training somehow inculcated in him the concept that the two terms were contradictory. He had been with Vladimir Vronitsky for three years and the two had never discussed anything besides the music at hand. Vronitsky liked his young student immensely and was very proud of the way Daniel played the piano, not just technically, but "musically" as well, especially musically. He always imparted the simple concept that one's touch on the keyboard was more important than most other aspects of playing the piano.

"Remember, Daniel," he would say, "a delicate but firm placement of the fingers on the keys is what helps one to make *music*, to truly make music. Many pianists think it is necessary to bang on the keys to make an effect. That is nonsense! When loudness is called for, it comes from the coordination of the arms and the hands, and it is natural, it unfolds in an unforced manner."

The one hour lesson flew by and there was never time for discussion about anything else but the music. At the end of the lesson, Daniel asked,

"Mr. Vronitsky, may I ask you a question about something not related to music?"

The teacher smiled, a reflex the student had almost never seen before.

"You know there is very little time between lessons, but today you are in luck since my next pupil cancelled due to illness. So, go ahead. Sit down."

"It's just that while I was waiting next door, I noticed you have some books on Christian Science. I have heard about this, but I don't know anything about it. Is that your religion?"

Vronitsky frowned and said,

"You know Daniel, this is something I would rather not discuss."

Daniel picked up his music and prepared to leave, feeling embarrassed that the first time he tried to talk to his teacher about anything besides music, he had touched on a bad subject, an unacceptable subject as far as his teacher was concerned. Flustered, he quickly expressed his regret and began to walk away. Vronitsky saw the boy's pained expression and thought to himself that he should talk to his young student. Yes, he could. Why not?

"Daniel, come back. Sit down again." The boy obeyed and looked inquisitively at his teacher.

"I didn't want to discuss it because it brings back some bad memories." As Daniel listened, mesmerized by his teacher's words and his serious tone of expression, Vronitsky proceeded to tell his young student all about his family background. He came to the U.S. from Russia, from Odessa. His parents were impoverished Jews who could not afford to provide the means whereby their only child, Vladimir, could exploit his special talent. They emigrated to the United States and settled on the lower East Side of Manhattan. Vladimir was eight when they arrived. Vronitsky did not go into detail on the ups and downs of his career as a soloist, skipping to the time when he met his wife.

"My wife was also a pianist. We were very happy. We had two children, a daughter and a son. My daughter became very ill when she was only six years old."

Vronitsky sighed deeply and Daniel wondered if he had any right to touch upon such a personal and intimate subject, but he sat there spellbound.

"We tried many doctors, many therapies. Nothing worked. Then my wife got interested in Christian Science. She read all about Mary Baker Eddy, the founder. She lived during the nineteenth century and was often quite sick herself. She discovered things in the Bible that helped her to heal herself and she wrote the book that you saw in the bookcase, *Science and Health with Key to the Scriptures*. My wife was convinced this would help our daughter. She was grasping at straws. Our daughter died."

"But why is it called Christian Science?" Daniel asked.

"It's the idea that Christ is the ultimate scientist. That's why they call their church the Church of Christ, Scientist. Jesus was known for his powers of healing, and the work of the Christian Scientists is concerned with healing any illness by using instructions they draw from various Biblical passages. Even though my daughter died, I don't think what they believe is absurd. There are Eastern religions that practice similar philosophies."

"Do you believe in it yourself?" Daniel, now emboldened by his teacher's openness, dared to pursue the subject.

"I don't believe that Jesus has anything to do with it. I think that a person can heal himself if he is able to concentrate fully and get in touch with inner powers that we all probably have but which we know so little about."

Daniel was disturbed, for it seemed that Jesus, his Lord and Savior was being somehow belittled.

"But don't you believe that Jesus is the Son of God and can help us to do anything, even to heal ourselves through his intercession? Look at all the miracles that occur all the time in Lourdes, things like that." Daniel was perspiring. His emotions were driving him and he wasn't sure if he should have said anything like this.

"Daniel," Vronitsky replied, gently if with a touch of condescension in his words,

"I told you I was born Jewish. Jews do not believe that Jesus was anything else but a man like any other man, perhaps an extraordinary philosopher, but a man nonetheless." Vronitsky stood up and indicated that he had to get ready for his next student, abruptly terminating the discussion. Daniel felt his beliefs had been maligned, but he dismissed these thoughts, convincing himself that not everyone was as fortunate as he was in belonging to the One True Faith and knowing that Jesus is Lord and ruler of the world, with his Father and the Holy Spirit, the sacred Trinity.

Over the next few months, Vronitsky told Daniel more and more about his life. The young piano pupil never even had to ask again. It seemed that the teacher found a needed outlet in Daniel's patient and sympathetic attention to every word he uttered. He had waited very long for the chance to purge himself of his own inner demons. It was ironic, he thought, that the instrument of his purgatorial impulses was this innocent young boy.

"After my daughter died, my wife was never the same. When she was only thirty-five, she herself got sick. She had a terrible cancer . . . terrible." Vronitsky stopped and seemed absorbed in his thoughts. He did not speak for a long time. Then he started again,

"Even though it didn't help our daughter, she was again convinced that Christian Science was her only hope for recovery. She tried everything. We contacted some of their ministers . . . wonderful people, really. They tried to help but, but it was hopeless. Finally, against her wishes, I sought medical help and the doctors took tests and confirmed that she was dying. Her pain got worse and worse. She cried in agony day and night. The doctors gave me pain killers, morphine, but even these did not help after some time. She begged me to give her something so she would die." Vronitsky stopped again. He put his large head into his large hands and bent over. Daniel knew that he was sobbing, but his sobs were not outwardly apparent. The pain was still directed inwards. Slowly, he raised his head and continued.

"She cried out to me, 'Please, please, I want to die.' Finally, I loved her so much. I could not let her suffer any more . . . I help . . . helped her . . . die."

With this ultimate admission of his part in his wife's death, Vladimir Vronitsky let go. He cried aloud, shaking, completely overcome by emotions that had lain dormant for too, too long. Daniel was astonished. He didn't know what to do. Getting up from his chair, he approached his teacher. He put a hand on his shoulder, patting him gently, saying no words, for there were no words that were adequate at that moment. After what seemed like a long agonizing time, Vronitsky wiped his eyes with his handkerchief. He got up and said, "I'm sorry Daniel for sharing this heavy burden with you, but thank you, thank you so much for listening. I had to tell someone, sometime. You are an intelligent boy. You do understand, don't you?"

Daniel thought to himself, what can I possibly say? I must tell him I understand. At that point, Daniel could not be doctrinal, dogmatic and dismissive of thinking that he had been brought up to abhor. His personality, the sensitivity that gave impetus to each and every act he performed would not allow him to turn to the principles that had been embedded within him since birth. Instead, the conclusion he came to was not arrived at intellectually. He looked at Vronitsky, looked him directly in the eyes and said,

"I understand. It was the only choice you had."

That night Daniel thought about all he had heard. "He killed his wife," he thought. "He had no right to do that. No one has the right to take another person's life. Only God can do that." Daniel thought and thought and pondered every aspect of what he had heard. "He really loved his wife. There is absolutely no doubt about that. She was begging him for relief. She was in agony. How would I act in such circumstances? Still, to take a life?" This boy, this soldier of Christ, this Communicant and receiver of the body and blood of Jesus thought about his Faith and concluded in his head that his teacher had committed a serious sin. But in his heart, he somehow understood why what happened did happen and he did not judge Vladimir Vronitsky. No, he did not judge him in his heart.

After that day, teacher and pupil developed a new respect and love for one another. Vronitsky usually never played for his pupils, except for demonstration purposes alone. But Vronitsky got satisfaction and pleasure playing for *this* pupil. In some ways, these little concerts taught Daniel more than all the regular lessons. Hearing his teacher play works like Beethoven's *"Hammerklavier" Sonata*, especially in the passionate second movement, and in Franz Schubert's last three *Sonatas,* written shortly before the composer's death in 1828, Daniel knew that Vladimir Vronitsky's personal tragedies made his playing of these works especially meaningful, powerful and transcendent. These were compositions that eloquently evoked the sadness and suffering permeating human life, along with the perennial quest for spiritual renewal.

During the summers of his sixteenth and seventeenth years, Daniel had the opportunity to attend a summer music camp. Vronitsky was an old friend of the camp's director, and when he recommended his pupil, the director immediately accepted him. Interestingly, Vronitsky had been solicited for talented pupils for a few years already, and always told his friend he had no one he could honestly recommend. The camp was part of a minor but important music festival in the Catskill Mountains. The program was the brainchild of a violinist with the New York Philharmonic who wanted to give something back to music. His idea was to have famous musicians, or failing that, professional musicians with impeccable credentials, working as performing musicians and as teachers. The violinist, Anastasio Giuffre, came from a family that owned a large twenty-two room house and some ten acres of land outside of Stamford, New York. After renovating the house to include bedrooms for the teacher-performers, two dormitories, one for the young male students and another for the young female students, practice rooms and a fairly large dining hall, Giuffre wrote to friends and colleagues and was gratified by the response. Not all orchestras had summer programs where the musicians could supplement their incomes, so this was a good opportunity to earn money and enjoy the summer months in an almost idyllic setting. An old barn was renovated to serve as a concert hall, boasting excellent acoustics, and programs in chamber music as well as solo instrumental recitals were offered to the general public. After only five years, the program had grown impressively and ticket orders from local towns as well as New York City and other eastern cities came pouring in. During the two summers that Daniel was at the Festival, the professional musicians included masters of the piano, violin, cello, viola, clarinet, French Horn, oboe, flute and harp.

Music students like Daniel Lorelli were given free instruction by the professionals as well as room and board. In exchange, they had to agree to work in the dining hall, serving breakfast, lunch and supper. At the end of the summer, a grand finale provided the students—all highly capable players in their own right—with the opportunity to perform a major work with one or more of the professional musicians. Daniel loved the rustic setting, his encounter with nature and the total identification with music that the Pastoral Summer Festival (named after Beethoven's *Sixth Symphony*, one of Giuffre's favorite works) provided. In the early morning Daniel would go to the window and look out at the fields behind the house. His heart leaped each time he saw the beautiful graceful deer prancing across the high grasses. This was his first exposure to the special delights of the country–the quiet, the sounds of birds chirping, the magnificent view of mountain peaks within close range. After sundown, he could look up at the sky and see the stars and constellations as he had never seen them before in the city. Everything about the surroundings and its connection with the music he loved, conspired to give a sensitive young man like Daniel one of the most exhilarating experiences of his life.

Each student was given certain tables he or she was responsible for. The dining hall provided meals for the performer-instructors as well as for visiting guests, including attendees at the Festival who arrived early, provided there was space in the dining hall. The smaller tables could seat two or even a single guest. Some of the musicians preferred to dine with old friends, so tables accommodating eight people were also available. For such tables, two students worked together doing the serving. Daniel's partner for serving meals was a young black woman from Philadelphia, Rebecca Bailey. Rebecca was a talented musician, having studied the violoncello since the age of seven after discontinuing the piano lessons she had taken since the age of four. As she told the story, once she saw a cello when she went to a concert at Academy Hall in Philadelphia at the age of six, she knew that the cello was "her" instrument. And she was right, for every teacher who taught her felt that she was born to play the instrument. Rebecca's ambition was to play cello in one of the major symphony orchestras. She was intelligent and attractive, around five feet, nine inches in height, of slim build, with long slightly curly black hair. She and Daniel developed a liking for one another and sometimes discussed the musical compositions they were studying that summer. One day, Rebecca came back to the kitchen in tears. Daniel saw her, off in a corner crying with her head buried in her hands, her shoulders shaking. He went to her and inquired as to why she was upset.

"That man." Rebecca said, crying even more.

"Which man?" Daniel asked.

She took him to the window of one of the swinging doors and pointed to a man sitting by himself.

"What'd he do?" asked Daniel, not quite understanding what could have happened in such a public place. Rebecca wiped her eyes and composed herself,

"When I brought his plate to him, he pushed it aside and said 'Niggers here too! Isn't there a white girl who can serve me?'"

Daniel could not believe what he was hearing. He had never had much, if any, experience with non-whites, whether they were black or yellow, but he knew instinctively that this was unacceptable.

"Don't let him upset you Rebecca, I'm going out there to tell him off."

"Oh, don't waste your time, Daniel. People like that will never admit they are wrong."

"Just the same, he has to be told."

Daniel marched through the swinging door and confronted the man, a somewhat pathetic looking figure in his fifties, not particularly well dressed and bearing a scowl that indicated a temperament marked by rancor and animosity.

"A young lady brought you your lunch and you insulted her. How dare you?"

"Can't you find white people to work here any more?" the man replied, completely unfazed by Daniel's remark.

"You're an ignorant, mean person. You owe her an apology." Daniel was trembling now. He was totally unaccustomed to the confrontation he was engaged in.

"Get lost, you nigger lover!" the man replied. "I'll take my business elsewhere, where whites still count." He got up and quickly walked away.

Daniel walked back into the kitchen and apologetically said to Rebecca,

"I'm sorry Rebecca, he refused to apologize."

"I heard what you said and his answer to you. Thanks for trying to defend me, but I told you it was useless. Just forget it."

"Forget it? Come on Rebecca, you were so upset. I'll bet this never happened to you before."

Rebecca laughed. "Never happened? Ha! That's how much you know. I was upset because this is my third year here and I always felt normal in these surroundings. It's as if my color doesn't matter here. That's why I got so upset. I never expected such a thing to happen here."

There wasn't time for further discussion, but about a week later, one evening after that night's concert, people were walking along the paths surrounding the barn turned into concert hall. Daniel saw Rebecca and asked her if she would like to walk with him. As they walked, Daniel asked,

"Has that kind of thing really happened to you a lot Rebecca?"

Not wanting to discuss a subject that had so many unpleasant associations, Rebecca tried to play dumb.

"What kind of thing?"

"You know, what happened in the dining hall."

"I would rather discuss something different."

Daniel was so much like his mother Violetta. He had this innate desire to help people, whether he knew them well or not. He wanted to reach out, to comfort and to reassure those he sensed needed help in some way. He was still too naive, too inexperienced in human relations to know that sometimes some people just don't want your help, don't need it, don't appreciate your efforts and would prefer to be left alone. Rebecca was not one of these people. She was gracious enough to realize her friend's sincerity, but she knew he could do nothing to help, so why discuss it?

"All right, Rebecca, if not for your benefit, then for mine. I want to better understand the situation you find yourself in."

"Why"

"Well, my father told me once that when he first came over people would call him and other Italians 'wops,' and would insult them."

"O.K. Take that and multiply it by a million. That's what happens to Negroes all the time."

"I can't believe it. This is the United States."

"Boy, are you naive. Where have you been living? Don't tell me this is the first time that you have seen a Negro being maligned by a white!"

"It is," Daniel insisted. "I never even see Negroes where I live."

"Oh, I guess that explains it. You live in a lily white neighborhood where all the whites are too good to have anything to do with us."

Feelings of guilt now began to overcome this white boy. He had an uneasy feeling that he had failed to do something he should have done ... somewhere, sometime.

"I'm sorry Rebecca. Tell me what I can do."

"What do you mean tell you? Tell you what?"

"I want to help in some way so you will not have to take those insults again."

"Oh, really? Are you Superman? Are you that guy in the red cape? You really think you can do anything? Anything at all to make a difference?"

"I would like to." Daniel was thinking how totally foolish he must sound to this young woman.

"Well, then, start in your own life. Start by never prejudging anyone no matter what color or religion or whatever she or he is."

"I never do." Daniel sheepishly replied.

"You know, it's funny, but I believe you. You've probably had such a sheltered upbringing that you really don't bear animosity towards anyone."

On subsequent evenings, Daniel and Rebecca had conversations on many other subjects, excluding race. One evening a few weeks later, they were again walking together after a concert. Rebecca had substituted for the cellist who was to play the cello part in Brahms' *Second Sonata for Cello and Piano.* She had been playing the work with the cellist, taking the piano part during one of her instruction sessions, and when he developed a stomach virus, he suggested to Giuffre that Rebecca be allowed to perform that evening in his place.

"Rebecca, you were great tonight. You are every bit as good as the man you replaced."

"Oh come now Daniel! He is a first desk with a major orchestra."

"I don't care," Daniel continued enthusiastically. "Maybe he has a larger repertory than you right now, but you are as good a player as he is. I'm sure of it, technically, certainly, musically without a doubt. You should pursue a career as soloist when the time comes. Why do you want to settle for a seat in a symphony orchestra?"

Rebecca sighed. "Oh Daniel! Do you remember our conversation about all the prejudice around us? It's the same with music, especially classical music. I'll be lucky if I can ever get a job playing in one of the top orchestras. They have these auditions when a place in an orchestra opens up. You play behind a closed curtain, and after they hear all those who came to play, they pick someone. But that someone is not chosen based on who was actually the best player."

Daniel interrupted, "What do you mean? What's the purpose of having the auditions behind closed curtains, then?"

"It's all political. Don't you *understand*? They have to do it to look good, but they already know who will get the seat in the orchestra."

"That's crazy." Daniel offered his demurral without much conviction.

Rebecca looked at this handsome young man she knew for such a short time. Suddenly, she could see his goodness, could see his innocence, and her heart, so cautious, so reserved and suspicious opened to a possibility. They had now walked a good distance away from the barn and were quite alone.

"You know Daniel, now I would like to kiss you."

She turned towards him and moved her lips towards his. He moved back, away from her, turning his head sideways as he did so

Taken aback, Rebecca, composed herself, straightened and said,

"Let's go back. I should have known for all your words you would never kiss a Negro. I guess my big lips don't appeal to you."

Daniel was even more surprised at this sudden reprimand than he had been at her impulse to kiss him.

"No, you are wrong. It's not that I don't want to kiss you," he said pleadingly, for he was now so sorry he had inadvertently hurt her.

"Then, what is it."

"It's just that, well . . . can I be honest?"

"Of course."

"Well, I've never kissed a girl before." With that admission, Daniel suddenly moved towards Rebecca and placed his mouth, forcefully, amateurishly against hers and held it there. She parted his lips with her tongue and returned his feeble attempt at a kiss with the real thing, a kiss he would never forget for the rest of his life.

"Now what do I do?" he thought to himself. He moved his right hand over her breasts and she did not object. Slowly, as they continued to kiss, he brought his left hand down around her thigh and moved his fingers into the crevice between her legs from behind, and from there to her front, but before he could lift her long skirt high enough to feel her better, she pulled away.

"Don't believe those stories you heard about dark girls being easy. This black girl stops here. This is as far as we go."

Daniel pulled back quickly and expressed his confusion.

"I'm sorry. I didn't know what to do. I thought you expected me to keep going."

"You really are a virgin, then? What luck. I get to deflower a young white boy, if I choose to, that is. It's tempting, but I'll pass for now." Rebecca was very wise for her years, street-wise with a balanced perspective when it came to sex. The promise of a career in music was predominant in her outlook, and she did not want a relationship to pull her away from her goals. They walked back and as they left one another, Rebecca kissed

Daniel again in the corridor. She was clearly the one calling the shots. He was so excited and his hormones were at such a high, fevered pitch that he had to go into the bathroom to relieve the tension that was gripping him. Summer ended, but they did not get to make love. Rebecca had to leave suddenly due to a death in her family and he had no telephone number or address where he could reach her. He tried calling some numbers he found in a Philadelphia telephone directory, about four or five under the name Bailey, but there was no Rebecca at any of them.

Daniel had lessons with Vladimir Vronitsky until the age of eighteen. At that point, Daniel had a repertory that included twenty of Beethoven's thirty-two *Sonatas*, six *Sonatas* by Schubert, various works by Schumann, including the splendid *Fantasy in C*, and four concertos that he performed with Vronitsky playing the orchestral parts: the Beethoven *Third*; the Grieg *Concerto*; the Schumann *Concerto* and the Mozart *Concerto No. 25*

Twenty-Three

John Lorelli entered the family business right after high school, as did Albert, one year after his older brother. Mamma's Kitchen was thriving and John developed a new branch devoted to direct home catering. The food was so good that word spread quickly and the catering part of the business soon almost outpaced the store in profits. John was a serious young man and his outlook was fairly simple and conventional. He wanted to make a lot of money, marry a beautiful girl that he would have to be madly in love with, have a large family that would be housed in a magnificent home and enjoy wonderful vacations with his family. He knew that the family business was developing into something that could provide him as well as his parents and brothers with a sensational life style. He even foresaw a time when the business would reach a standard of success so the family members could manage things without doing too much of the routine daily drudgery. Stephen was very much a follower, and he would simply emulate his older brother in most things, doing his share, but not being innovative in any way whatsoever. It would remain for the second oldest brother Albert to bring the business forward to the point envisioned by John and beyond.

John hired a young woman who had taken a commercial course in high school and was now studying Business Administration in evening college. The daughter of Italian immigrants, too, Sofia Romano (she later changed the spelling of her name to Sophia) was determined to have her own business some day. A woman of independent thinking, Sophia did not wish to have a subservient position in life like that of her mother. She convinced John that she could handle the job he needed filled, and she saw it as a learning opportunity by which she could acquire a good amount of practical experience and have the flexible hours she needed to continue her studies. Sophia had striking good looks and an open personality that fairly disarmed people. Unlike many beautiful women who know they are beautiful, Sophia would look at men directly, purposely avoiding any coquettish mannerisms or flirtatious instincts, while displaying a confidence that left her admirers and hopeful seducers befuddled. Her job working for the Lorelli's involved public relations catering management. Her duties included scheduling, pricing and advertising. Although she had nothing to do with food purchases or preparation, she was responsible for order fulfillment. This meant that she had to insure that an order was delivered to the right party at the right time and that payment was received and deposited. Vinny told his son that he thought the young woman was too young and too inexperienced to handle the work involved, but John Lorelli insisted on hiring her, assuring Vinny that he would replace her after a short period of time if her promise was not fulfilled. Sophia met and exceeded John's expectations. She ingratiated herself to the customers, who recommended the service to friends and relatives, placed inexpensive advertisements in local bulletins and newspapers that brought in amazing results, and made deliveries herself if she felt that there was the slightest chance the normal panel truck could be late.

Sophia's office was around the side of the building. At that point Mamma's Kitchen included what had originally been three stores along the avenue. When the catering began to take hold, an entrance was opened on the side street, another in the back, with a driveway that ran to the back entrance for loading the food. The side entrance had a counter with brochures where walk-in customers could place their catering orders. Sophia's office was just behind that reception area. John could enter the catering area from an interior door at one side of the store. Sophia found it amusing that both he and his younger brother Albert made so many visits to her office when they had no reason to do so. Depending on what Sophia was wearing that day, the brothers would increase or decrease their visits. If she was dressed conservatively, they would still visit, but if she had on tight pants that revealed her curves, or a low-cut blouse, or a fairly short skirt with stockings that conjured up images of sublimity, they would walk in to ask her questions or to make suggestions that made no sense whatever. One day, John walked in and stood in front of Sophia's desk, practically staring at her.

"Is there anything I can help you with John?"

"Uh, Sophia, uh, I just wanted to ask you a question."

"Go ahead and ask."

"Well, I was just wondering, uh, do you have a boyfriend?"

Sophia looked up at John and smiled, seductively, confidently,

"*A* boyfriend? I have lots of boyfriends."

John stood there, bemused, taken aback somewhat, not understanding or wanting to understand if what he understood was what he thought she *might* mean. Then, thinking she was joking, playing with him, he laughed nervously and returned what he would have liked to have been a volley, but it was too late. Hers had already touched the ground.

"Ha, that's funny. Yeah I understand. But do you have a special boyfriend?

"All my boyfriends are special."

John did not know what to say anymore, so he just said,

"That's nice," and walked back into the store.

Later that day, Albert walked into Sophia's office and stood there for a brief moment before sitting on her desk. He was a bit more confident than his brother.

"Sophia?"

"Yes, Albert?"

"Do you have a boyfriend?"

"What's this? Are you and your brother studying the same script?"

"What do you mean?"

"He was in here earlier with the same exact question."

"Yeah, and what did you tell *him*?"

"I told him I do."

"Oh, O.K. Lucky guy," Albert's attempt to tell Sophia that he thought she was special. She understood. He walked out without another word.

Sophia knew that both brothers liked her. She found them both attractive too, for the Lorelli brothers were good looking young men. They had classic Italian features, dark hair and blue or green eyes, a muscular build combined with a lean body, and they respected women. She saw the special way they all treated their mother, but Sophia was not ready for a relationship. She had her game plan worked out, and it did not include getting serious with any man until she had completed her education, had sufficient work experience in her chosen field, and was herself settled financially. She saw herself with a man who would be able to give her everything she desired, but she wanted the ability to make things come together for herself too, so she would not be dependent on any man if she chose not to be.

A few weeks after these discussions took place, John informed his father that he was leaving early that Saturday evening to go to the City with some friends. Tony Bennett was appearing at the Copa and John was a fan. Their table was at the back of the room, fairly far from the stage. This was John's first "live" concert of any kind and the atmosphere was electrically charged.

When Bennett came out and began to sing, the audience went wild with enthusiasm. In between songs, the pop idol walked among the tables and patted John on the back. When he sang "Rags to Riches" and "Stranger in Paradise," the women were swooning. John looked around at some of the other young couples and imagined himself at a table with Sophia. He thought he would ask her to go out with him and tell her he wanted to take her to the Copa. "I'll bet none of her other boyfriends ever took her to the Copa," he thought.

After the show, one of John's friends suggested they go down to the Village. They took the subway downtown to 8th Street and walked towards Fifth Avenue, winding through some of the side streets above and below The Avenue of the Americas (Sixth Avenue). In the late fifties, Greenwich Village was a quite distinctive section of New York City. It was a place where one could see modes of behavior that were then considered outlandish by the general population. Sometimes curiosity seekers from other parts of the City and the country would go there to be titillated by the sights—women kissing other women, men embracing men and kissing each other on the lips, all this in the open, in cars parked along the curbs, in bars, walking down the streets.

"Look at these queers!" John said.

"Disgusting!" concurred his friend Joe.

"These people are not normal," chimed in Bob.

"They're all going to Hell," another judgment from John.

As they walked along they passed a café, and sitting at a table inside, barely visible through the window John saw . . . was it possible? Sophia? John looked closer and saw that she had a companion, a Negro! John, now concerned that Sophia would see him, walked beyond the store and peeked through an opening in the window at the other side of the door. "So that's it!" he thought. "One of her boyfriends. A Nigger no less."

"What are you looking at?" Joe asked.

"Oh, nothing, let's go."

On Monday morning John went into Sophia's office and told her that he would have to let her go. She was taken by surprise and completely baffled at this turn of events.

"Why? I thought you said I was doing a great job?"

"Well, my father told me you were too young, too inexperienced."

"But you even told me your father was satisfied with the job I'm doing."

"I promised my father that I would keep you until I was sure one way or another."

"Well, what aren't you sure about."

"Look, I don't want to discuss this. I'm giving you a week's notice."

Sophia was not going to just accept this without a fight. She knew she could find work, but she didn't understand why she should be fired after bringing in so much new business and she had to have a better explanation than that given to her by John. She walked into the store and addressed Mr. Lorelli directly,

"Mr. Lorelli, your son John wants to fire me and he won't even give me a reason. You know the kind of job I've done here for the past six months. Do you think that's fair?"

"What?" Vinny asked. "He wants to fire you. He didn't say anything to me about this."

"See, and he's trying to make it look like it's what you want."

"Listen, Sophia, let me talk to John. We'll get to the bottom of this."

That evening, when the family was together at home, Vinny asked his son why he wanted to fire Sophia

"Dad, I'm responsible for the catering part of the business. You shouldn't question me."

"When did my son get to be such a big shot that I can't ask him a question?" Vinny was visibly annoyed.

"You can always ask me questions, Dad, but why about this. I hired her, even against your better judgment, and now I think I need to fire her."

"O.K. Fine. But what is your reason now for firing her. When you hired her you gave me some good reasons for doing so, and I think those reasons are still working in her favor."

Frustrated and knowing his father's logic was correct, John had no alternative but to approach the matter illogically, emotionally.

"Look Dad, she has a Nigger for a boyfriend!"

"A what? I don't believe that. Why would a beautiful girl like Sophia go for someone of another race?"

"That's what I'd like to know. But she does. She wouldn't go out with me, but she'll go out with a Nigger!"

"What do you mean she won't go out with you?" Vinny suddenly shared his son's apparent dismay at being slighted. "You asked her to go out and she turned you down?"

"Well, she didn't turn me down, but she said she had a boyfriend."

Finding this opening, Albert decided to tell his story too.

"I asked her the same thing and she told me that too."

John looked at his brother with a shocked, hurt expression.

"You, what? Why did you ask her if she has a boyfriend?"

"I wanted to see if she was free to go out with me."

"Oh, that's great. Two brothers going after the same girl and she turns us both down. She has to go!"

Violetta had been quietly listening to the conversation and had said nothing, but now she was sufficiently disturbed by what she saw as her son's complete lack of charity and unfair judgment of another human being. First she spoke to Albert.

"What did she say to you when you asked her, Albert?"

"She said that my brother and I must be reading the same story or something like that, and when I asked her why, she said that he had asked her the same thing. Then she told me she has a boyfriend and I said he's a lucky guy."

"You jerk!" John shouted.

"Listen, you two. It seems to me that she didn't turn either of you down. You were both too dumb to actually ask her to go out. Why ask her if she has a boy friend? Why didn't you just ask her if she wants to go to a movie or dancing or something like that? And the . . . how do you know she has a boyfriend—a Negro boyfriend! I don't like that other word, and don't let me hear you say it again."

"I saw her in Greenwich Village Saturday night, and she was with this Nig—Negro."

"How do you know he is her boyfriend? And is that a reason to fire her? What if you saw her with a white boyfriend? Would you still fire her?"

"Well, uh, no. . . ."

"I'm glad you are being honest with me. Is this the way I brought you up? All people have dignity in God's eyes. Have you ever seen me or your father show disrespect to people who are not like us? Maybe Sophia sees that more than my own children do. She told you she has a boyfriend. If you saw her with a white boy friend, you wouldn't like it. Jealousy would take over, but you wouldn't fire her. But because she could have a Negro boyfriend—no business of yours by the way!—you decide to fire her, a young woman who is doing a great job for you, for us. I am ashamed of you John!"

Listening to his mother's impassioned delivery, John realized she was right. Fortunately, he had been raised in a home where any kind of hatred, racial or otherwise, had never been instilled or tolerated, so he could see that his bias was completely illogical, something he had picked up from friends and associates who were not taught differently.

"O.K. Mom. I guess you're right."

"Good, then tomorrow I expect that you will talk to Sophia and apologize for your foolishness."

The next morning John approached Sophia timidly and told her that he did not want to fire her.

"Good," she said. "I'm glad you came to your senses." She wanted so much to know what had precipitated the initial decision and how it had been overturned, but her pride would not allow her to question him. This was another area where she felt that women were traditionally weak. They always had to know why, and how, and when and where. And this was another type of female dependence. Men knew this weakness and took advantage of it in different ways.

"Don't you want to know why I changed my mind?"

"Not really," Sophia replied, with a supercilious air that made John wonder if he should tell her anything. This was beginning to be humiliating. Nevertheless, he thought of his mother's words and he felt ashamed at how small he came off in his own self-perception.

"I'd like to tell you anyway," he said, raising his head to show that he still had his pride and that he was acting out of noble motives. After he described seeing her in the Village with the Negro, and how what he saw stirred his basest instincts, Sophia began to laugh, heartily.

"Now you are mocking me," John said in a surly manner.

"No, I'm not mocking you. I just think it's funny. You're jealous! I didn't think you cared that much."

"I'm not jealous," he retorted.

"Yes, you are. And for your information, that man is my marketing professor. He agreed to have a coffee with me outside of school because I wanted to ask him about his thoughts on some marketing ideas I have–for *your* business! He's a brilliant teacher."

"He's a professor?"

"Yes, do you think all Negroes are uneducated? You must be dumber than I thought you were!"

John was now even more apologetic than before and he found the courage to ask Sophia if she liked Tony Bennett. She did and he arranged to take her to the Copacabana.

Sophia liked the fact that John was able to admit he was wrong. There aren't too many men, she thought, who are capable of that. This augured well for their future relationship as far as she was concerned.

Twenty-Four

Daniel Lorelli was awarded a full scholarship to the Curtis Institute in Philadelphia, one of the finest music conservatories in the country. Each student was accepted only after intensive auditions since free full scholarships were provided. The professor on the pianoforte faculty who oversaw Daniel's activities was the well known Moritz Levanski. When he saw Daniel's *curriculum vitae*, he called the young student into his study.

"I see that you studied for five years with Vladimir Vronitsky," Levanski noted. "How did you enjoy your studies with him?"

"I don't expect to ever find a better piano teacher," Daniel said, matter-of-factly.

"I cannot contradict you there," Levanski agreed. "You know, don't you, Daniel, that Vronitsky is a legendary figure in classical piano circles. Those who heard his recitals when he was still giving concerts say that there was no one who could approach him technically or musically. His Rachmaninov was in no way inferior to Horowitz's and his Chopin was every bit as good as Rubinstein's."

"I know he is a great, great pianist," Daniel agreed. "He played for me often, over the past two years especially, but he never spoke to me about his career."

"After his daughter died and his wife came down with incurable cancer, he had no spirit left for playing concerts."

"I know about his wife and daughter, but I didn't know that was why he gave up his career." Daniel thought about his conversations with his teacher, and a bittersweet melancholy overcame him.

"Well, you were very fortunate to hear him, especially in such private circumstances. May I ask what pieces he played for you, what truly impressed you?"

"Everything he played was absolutely beautiful, impeccable. But I recall three works that especially enthralled me, when I just felt he was one with the piano, the composer and the work."

"This is amazing. Please tell me, what are the works?"

"Beethoven's *"Hammerklavier" Sonata*, Liszt's *Sonata* and Schubert's *Sonata in B flat, Deutsch 960."* Daniel's eyes closed as though he could still hear the magic of the performances.

"Of course, of course," Levanski remarked, as though he had heard the same performances and remembered how wonderful they were. "You know, "he added, "I did hear him just once. It's the reason I decided not to pursue a concert career and to go into teaching instead."The older man had never admitted this to anyone before. Without another word, Daniel understood everything. He stood up, shook the teacher's hand and walked out.

Studying in Philadelphia made it easy for Daniel to practice his Faith. Philadelphia is known as "The City of Churches," and a Roman Catholic Church was close by. Most days, Daniel had lunch with a small group of fellow students, and they seemed to prefer discussing philosophical topics rather than anything related to music, since they were immersed in music most of the time. Some of the students frequented a local restaurant and Daniel usually dined with Diana Santiago, a cello student; Marilyn Schwartz, a violin student; Sam Halstead, who studied the oboe; and Jeanne Simpson, a flautist. Marilyn had already been at Curtis for two years when Daniel arrived. Jeanne and Sam had completed one year and Diana, like Daniel, was a new student. Daniel usually didn't start the conversations, but he was determined to finish them if a topic was brought up that he had strong feelings about. At the age of eighteen, he was still an ardent Roman Catholic and was convinced that his religion was the one true faith. One day Jean told the group about a Catholic friend who had married recently, but who had stopped going to Church. She had gone to Confession and the priest told her she could not remain a practicing Catholic if she used any form of birth control besides the Rhythm method.

"And everyone knows that doesn't work," Jeanne said.

"Why did she get married if she doesn't want to have children?" Daniel asked.

"She wants children, eventually, but not right now. She and her husband are still struggling to finish school and they want to buy a house and get settled before having babies."

"That's just selfish!" Daniel replied. "These people–they want the pleasure without the responsibility."

"Can you believe this guy?" Marilyn said, shaking her head.

"Yeah, Daniel, I'm Catholic too, but this birth control thing is ridiculous," Diana opined.

"What's so ridiculous about it? One of the primary purposes of marriage is to procreate. If a couple can't fulfill one of the primary purposes, why get married?"

"Oh, so they should just live together and get married when they decide to have children?" asked Sam sarcastically.

"No, sex before marriage is immoral too." Even though he thought he had come close with Rebecca, Daniel was still a virgin.

"Oh, what a good boy we have here," laughed Marilyn.

"Daniel, you are so naïve! I see all these women going up to Communion every Sunday and most of them have been married for years and have only one or two kids. Do you mean to tell me that they don't practice birth control?" Diana took Dan's hand and put it on her arm. "Here, try pulling my arm since you're not succeeding at pulling my leg."

Another day at lunch the question of abortion came up. The Roe vs. Wade decision legalizing abortion was not yet the law of the land. Jeanne and Marilyn felt that abortion should be legalized, but Daniel, Sam and Diana adamantly opposed any such legal sanction of something they called "murder."

"Diana" asked Marilyn, "You agree about birth control, but you don't think a woman has the right to have an abortion if she becomes pregnant? What's the difference?"

"It's different because a fetus is already growing. It's a living organism and abortion kills it. With birth control, you are not killing anything, just preventing a fetus from even forming." On this subject, Daniel and Sam allowed the women to do most of the talking, since the women became emotionally excited, and Marilyn and Jeanne argued that men had no business even having a say in the matter. A woman's body is her own to do with as she sees fit, and men should stay out of it. That was how they saw the situation.

"But aren't there certain natural laws that transcend gender?" Daniel asked.

"What kind of natural law applies here?" Marilyn countered.

"The sanctity of life!" Daniel asserted.

Jeanne slapped her hand on the table,

"It's a question of when life begins. If a woman has an abortion in the first three months of her pregnancy, there is no life there to speak of."

"Anyway," Marilyn stood up and looked at Daniel straight in the eye, "My mother has a cousin who had to have an abortion because she feared her father would disinherit her if he found out she was pregnant. She was in college and would not dare tell her father she was pregnant. Because there is no place a woman can go in such a situation, she had to go to a butcher, a doctor who performs abortions just to make money and doesn't even have sanitary facilities. He ruined her for life. She is married now, but she will never give birth to her own child."

Daniel wanted to maintain his rigid position and was about to say something that Marilyn would have found abhorrent, and he knew this, so he kept still. Then he said,

"I guess there is no black and white in situations like these."

"You bet there isn't!" Marilyn shot back.

Daniel always found this conflict within himself. He wanted to maintain his beliefs, the beliefs of his Church with respect to faith and morals, but more and more he found that the simple answers that he had been taught to uphold, the staid affirmations that provided no room for compromise did not suffice in every life-and-death situation. Increasingly, as he got to know others who had not been brought up with his beliefs, Daniel felt compelled to look at the other side of the coin.

When he was not at Curtis practicing, performing, interacting with his professors, Daniel's free time was spent more and more with his friends, particularly with Marilyn and Jeanne. Marilyn and Jeanne shared a small apartment on the South side of Philadelphia, next door to Daniel and Sam's two bedroom flat. The two young women enjoyed talking to each other about Daniel even if the game they were playing did not allow for too much honesty where their own feelings were concerned. Each saw in him a desirable stimulus for her own budding sexual impulses. Daniel's striking good looks–deep blue eyes, dark wavy black hair, muscular lithe frame–and his intelligence and musical talent combined to make him a most desirable sexual partner. Marilyn's appreciation of this likeable fellow student encompassed, additionally, what she saw as a most unusual sensitivity–an almost feminine ability to gauge others' needs and to shoulder them himself. She realized that his personal beliefs about all the heavy topics did not even come close to her own, but this did not concern her. She saw no problem in confronting these peccadilloes and effecting change.

After some months, Jeanne and Marilyn found themselves thinking about Daniel more and more, even apart from activities they shared at the Institute. Part of the curriculum involved performing with other students, preparing some of the great works of chamber music to develop that aspect of a student's repertoire and perfecting the performances for eventual presentation before an assembly of faculty and fellow students. Those performances that received accolades from the teachers would be offered on future concert programs that were open to the general public.

Curtis promoted an on-going schedule of such concerts. One day after an intense session of practicing Prokofiev's *Flute Sonata in D, Opus 94* with her friend playing the piano part, Jeanne went back to her apartment and thought of Daniel sitting at the piano, seeing him with his fingers dashing across the keyboard, his hair flying about as he moved his head back and forth, feeling the music, living its emotions. She thought about how she saw him as she herself swayed to and fro, catching glimpses of his obvious passionate commitment to what he was doing. That night as she lay in bed, she ran her hands across her body and thought about him, soon drifting off into a deep sleep.

Marilyn had never been attracted to a non-Jewish man before, and she was surprised at herself when she entertained romantic thoughts of Daniel. She had never, ever envisioned herself with anyone unlike the men she grew up admiring–her father's younger brothers who were not much older than she, her cousins' husbands, one a Reformed Rabbi, a man dedicated to a modern Judaism that combined aspects of Humanism with teachings from the Torah.

Returning to their apartment one night after a late movie with Sam and Daniel, Jeanne asked Marilyn the inevitable question, "Do you think he's still a virgin?"

"Who?" The game was in session again.

"Who do you think?"

"Sam?"

"Oh, come on. You know very well who I mean"

"Yes, I think Daniel is still a virgin."

"Let's play a little game."

Marilyn laughed, "I thought we were already playing one."

"Well, we are. But let's add a prize to the rules. Let's see which of us can take his cherry."

"Do men have cherries?"

"Oh, come on!" Jeanne began getting nervous, worrying that her suggestion was not finding favor with her friend.

"O.K. Sounds like an interesting game to me. What's the prize?"

"He's the prize, silly. If you get him that way, isn't that prize enough?"

Marilyn and Jeanne both thought how it would be if Daniel became *her* "prize." The obstacle each envisioned was how to get him in a suitable place, all alone.

The following afternoon, Jeanne saw Daniel walking back to his flat and joined him.

"I have to get something in my room. Where are you headed?" he asked innocently.

"I left some music at home that I need too," Jeanne lied.

When they reached 4th St., Jeanne quickly went to her flat, got the music to Mozart's *Flute Sonata* and rang Daniel's bell.

"That was fast," he said. "Can you wait a few minutes before we go back? I still have to look through some music." Things were going according to Jeanne's improvised plan. Daniel was sitting at a table and Jeanne sat in a chair next to him. She looked at the naïf she was about to try seducing, drinking in his profile, the small sharply etched nose, delicate ears, and exquisite neck. On a sudden impulse, she ran her fingers through Daniel's wavy black hair. Surprised, he turned and looked at her.

"You have such great hair."

Daniel looked into the eyes of his would-be temptress and liked what he saw. He had liked Jeanne from the first moment he met her. Her shoulder length blonde hair was complimented by her striking green eyes. At five feet eight inches, her height nearly matched his, and her figure was perfectly proportioned.

"Your hair is so beautiful too." This was said in a hesitant manner and he had an impulse to touch her hair, but did not have the confidence to do so. He turned back to his music. Jeanne ran her hand down from his head to his shoulders and slowly, slowly continued in a circular motion until she reached his waist, continuing down to his thighs. She felt for his penis through his pants as his organ of desire began to enlarge.

"What are you doing?" he asked, his heart beginning to beat faster and faster.

She stood up and pulled his arm.

"Come here," she murmured, softly but in a tone of voice allowing of no dissent.

She sat him down on the sofa and unzipped his pants, pulling his erect organ to her mouth. She smiled, kneeling next to him.

"Don't you know that flutists give the best blow jobs?" she asked. She actually had little experience to prove or disprove the theory. Once in high school one of the macho football players, a crude fellow who nonetheless was pursued by many of the best looking girls, had asked her, teasingly,

"Hey, is it true that flute players give the best blow jobs?"

Jeanne shrugged off his remark, revealing her contempt for him as she turned quickly and walked off. However, since that day, the thought erotically charged her from time to time.

Daniel put his head back and surrendered, seemingly, to the heat of the moment, nearly incredulous at how he was about to experience what he had been dreaming of for so long. Just then, footsteps were heard coming up the stairs to the apartment. Jeanne jumped up and Daniel quickly zipped up his pants.

They sat at the table again before Sam opened the door and saw them, apparently busy at work.

Jeanne didn't know if she should tell Marilyn about the experience. Negative. After all, she had not changed the status of his virginity. Oral sex, to her way of thinking, unless at least reciprocal, could not count. Days passed before Jeanne saw any possibility of being alone with Daniel again. "Why don't I just come out and ask him when we can meet to do it?" she thought. "After all, I broke the ice. The rest should be easy." But the object of her desire was having feelings of guilt. The next Saturday, he went to confession and was astonished at how nonchalantly the priest accepted what had occurred. He asked Daniel about his age, occupation and the nature of his relationship with his accomplice. He asked if Daniel had full carnal knowledge of the woman and whether she was married or not. Daniel confessed to very limited sexual contact, none by himself, and almost none on the part of his "woman friend."

"Ah, *coitus interruptus*, "the priest commented, self satisfied with his ability to use a Latin term with sexual and moral implications.

"No, Father, the woman wasn't even undressed," Daniel explained.

"Same thing. *Coitus interruptus*."

Once established that Jeanne was not a Roman Catholic, the priest smugly advised his penitent that he should avoid the company of women of other religious orientations. It was obvious, the priest insisted, that non-Catholic girls had no moral base.

Daniel walked away, wondering if he could possibly avoid Jeanne's company. In spite of what had happened, perhaps even because of it, he liked her very much. He thought of how the scene might have unfolded if Sam had not walked in. Confession was neither as comforting nor as reassuring as it had been when he had confessed to sins of a sexual nature in the past.

Meanwhile, although Marilyn had indicated, if somewhat tacitly and not wholeheartedly, that she would join Jeanne in her strategy to see which of them could give Daniel his first taste of sexual union with a woman, she failed to disclose the fact that she was not herself very experienced in sexual encounters with men. Two dates had erupted into necking and touching sessions that became extremely heated, falling short of full sexual intercourse. Both were high school dance dates. She also had a brief affair with an attractive Jewish athlete at the University of Pennsylvania, where she was concurrently enrolled for non-music courses. That ended quickly when Marilyn realized that she was just another trophy in his narrative display case. With Jeanne, she hated herself for not coming right out and saying directly that she was not interested in such "games," and as she thought about it she knew that she did not want to appear to be "square," an accusation that had even been leveled against her by other Jewish young women she was friendly with. She promised herself that she would not compromise again whenever a specific principle she lived by was at stake, but as far as she was concerned, there was no principle involved in pursuing a good looking man like Daniel, even if he was not Jewish. The Sunday after he went to Confession, Marilyn asked Daniel if he could stop by her apartment to go over a passage in a composition they were performing together. Jeanne had gone home to New York for the weekend, so Marilyn had the apartment to herself. Daniel questioned how they could go over the work, Beethoven's *"Spring" Sonata*, if there was no piano in the apartment.

"That's it exactly," Marilyn said. "I just want you to listen to the violin part of the first movement without the piano, just so you can advise me on questions of tempo. Besides, as you know, your piano is not available this afternoon." The piano that Daniel used for practicing chamber works with Marilyn and other students was in service for a private concert that evening. Marilyn realized that this would be the perfect opportunity for her to try to win the bet with Jeanne, but she had no intention of going in that direction.

"I don't see how it makes any sense, if I can't join in with you."

Even if Marilyn was referring to anything else but music, which she convinced herself she was not, Daniel was again, even now after very limited but actual sexual contact with a woman, unable to assay any ulterior intent, whether it was present or not.

Marilyn winked at him and said enticingly,

"Don't worry. I'll let you join in." She realized this was a flirtatious kind of remark and added as an afterthought,

"With your opinion about the tempo, I mean."

Suddenly, as if a bright light had been turned on in his head, Daniel was cognizant of something extraneous here, apart from the "normal" or usual exchange of words. The thought entered his mind, only to be slammed back and submerged by the cumulation of experiences that suggested that he was being tested, that evil spirits were seeking his downfall. But he looked at Marilyn again. She smiled innocently. He saw only her goodness and her beauty, a beauty different from that of Jeanne, to be sure, but present in every word she spoke, every look she exchanged with him, every step he saw her take. Marilyn had long, black, straight hair. Her grey, soulful eyes had an inner light that made her appear to be smiling even when she was not, and that looked out from a face notable for its engaging simplicity and lustrous beauty. Unlike her friend Jeanne, who already entertained thoughts about someday marrying Daniel, Marilyn had only fantasized that she could enjoy him for his friendship and for the sexual gratification they could provide one another. Her family was not religious in the conventional sense, but they had a very strong identification with their Jewish roots, and intermarriage was especially deplored since it diluted the Jewish presence in the world and contravened all they held to be sacred. Marilyn shared her family's feelings on intermarriage, even if she sometimes thought that Daniel *would* make the perfect husband. However, she was certain that their differences could not be accommodated in a lasting relationship. But there was nothing wrong in sleeping with a man whose animal magnetism was so tangible. She had to once again convince herself that this had nothing to do with renouncing the principles she was determined to honor. Marilyn was one of the new breed of modern women who wrote their own agendas when it came to things that concerned them personally. This is not to say she would totally abandon her family's values, but she would make what she considered reasonable deviations from wholly standard practices.

Daniel followed Marilyn into her apartment and sat on the sofa she directed him to. Marilyn played sections from all three movements. After discussions that both musicians considered fruitful, Marilyn offered Daniel a drink. She took out a bottle of white wine and poured two glasses, handing one to Daniel.

"Cheers! Here's to good performances for us both. I know we have to temper the heat of the moment with a balanced perspective." Daniel returned her "Cheers!" and wondered why his own natural reticence always prevented him from following up on what he considered such an obvious advance, as this one almost certainly was, he thought. He was not completely sure. He was not a man who could take the initiative in matters of intimate contact with women. Marilyn sat down next to Daniel on the sofa.

"Daniel, do you like me?" she began.

"You know I like you Marilyn. I like you very much."

"I mean, do you like me as a woman, aside from the respect we share for one another as musicians and friends?"

Marilyn was so smooth and confident in her manner of prompting him that Daniel momentarily wondered how often she had performed this very scene. The distaste he momentarily felt quickly dissipated as her smile modulated into its disarming mode. Her charm having relaxed him somewhat, Daniel replied with greater assurance,

"Marilyn, I really like everything about you: your looks, your talent, your personality, your ...."

She did not let him finish, placing her mouth firmly against his, allowing her tongue to part his lips, engaging his tongue in rapid swirls. His heart was beating fiercely, pounding in his chest. His hands moved across her breasts, reaching inside her bra to caress them. Marilyn knew for certain, now, that Daniel was a virgin and that she would have to provide the leadership in this encounter. Daniel was moving much too quickly for her, typical of a young man tasting the sweet fruit he has anticipated savoring for so long. She had to take control, slackening the pace, submitting to her lover's impetuosity with restrained accord, taming his ardor, insuring a measured but more pleasurable experience for both. Daniel stayed the night. They made love three more times before Daniel returned to his own flat. He was physically and emotionally exhausted and slept for eight straight hours until five that Sunday afternoon. He had missed going to Mass for the first time in years.

Jeanne returned Sunday evening to find Marilyn in a state of exhilaration. She knew there was something different about her friend, but she could not pinpoint what it was. A sudden insight caught her by surprise and she was almost afraid to ask.

"Marilyn," she began, hesitantly. "Did you make any progress in our game while I was away?" Marilyn no longer liked the idea of the game. What had happened between her and Daniel was much too meaningful to be relegated to the status of some jocular pastime.

"I really don't want to discuss it, but I *will* tell you that Daniel and I have become lovers."

"I don't believe you!" Jeanne shouted, exasperated, disappointed that she had come so close, only to be preempted by her friend while she was away. Marilyn did not honor her remark with any reply. A subdued but pervasive tenseness developed between the two young women. Jeanne also noted that Daniel was avoiding her. She determined that she would confront him. About a month after her initial attempt to seduce Daniel, Jeanne learned that Sam was going to be away for the weekend. She knew that Marilyn had spent Friday night in Daniel's bed and waited for an opportune moment to go over when she was not there. After Daniel opened the door, awkwardly inviting her in, Jeanne hinted at what had occurred between them. Daniel's character, alas, was imbued with a basic honesty in all of his contacts. He could avoid a person, as he had been avoiding Jeanne, but once confronted, he could no longer defer or deny an open and totally sincere exposition of his feelings.

"Jeanne, I'm involved with Marilyn now, and I cannot do anything to hurt her."

"What makes you think you would hurt her if you made love to me?" Jeanne's wrath was obvious from the tone of her voice. There was anger, tinged with a sarcasm that indicated she had little patience for nonsense of any kind here.

"Well," Daniel's course was compromised now by this unexpected response, "we have a relationship, and it would be wrong for me to be with anyone but Marilyn now."

"Oh, really? Well, let me tell you something: you are so naïve. Marilyn and I had a bet about you."

"A bet?" Daniel had no idea where she was going in this exchange with him.

"Yes, we made a bet to see who could fuck you first. I almost succeeded, and if Sam had not walked in, I would have."

"I don't believe you!" Daniel could not reconcile the wonder of his intimacy with Marilyn with something as trite as a bet.

"Well, ask Marilyn then."

Daniel looked at Jeanne and she appeared so desirable at that moment. He had finally tasted the sweetness of a woman's body and he looked at this other woman with lustful longing, but his sense of loyalty and fidelity was uppermost in his mind.

"I'm sorry Jeanne. I really like you and I'm totally flattered that you want me, but I cannot be two-faced. I don't think we should. . . ."

Jeanne walked out, slamming the door behind her. Marilyn returned that afternoon and embraced Daniel, running her hands down his side and around his back. Daniel spoke nervously,

"I have something to ask you, and you must be completely honest with me."

"My God, this sounds ominous. What's wrong?"

"Did you make a bet with Jeanne that you could get me to bed before she did?"

"That *bitch*!" Marilyn cried. "She was the one who suggested that we make such a bet. I just said O.K., but that had nothing to do with what happened between us."

Marilyn's explanation, followed by intensive love making convinced Daniel that he was not taken advantage of and that Marilyn's attentions were based on her true feelings of love for him. "Love?" Daniel thought about the word and what it meant to him. He loved God, his mother, father, brothers and so on. But did he love Marilyn? Yes, yes, a thousand times yes. Perhaps he didn't love her before he knew her intimately, but he certainly loved her now. He decided he would bring her home to meet his parents.

"Are you sure you want to do this?" Marilyn asked, fearing the direction their relationship could take if she met his parents.

"I'm sure. I love you. Why shouldn't I want you to meet them?"

"You love me?"

"Yes, of course I love you."

"You never told me you loved me before."

"Well, I'm telling you now. Why, don't you love me too?"

"I don't know . . . ." Marilyn's puzzled look disturbed Daniel.

"You don't know if you love me? How could you have acted the way you did with me if you didn't love me?"

"Daniel, I do love you. Our expressions towards each other mean very much to me. I care for you very much."

"Well, isn't that love?" Daniel's question had an urgency to it that Marilyn found discomforting.

"Yes, I suppose it is."

"Well, then, come home with me to meet my family."

"O.K."

That ended the doubt, and during Spring break Marilyn accompanied Daniel home to meet his family. By that time Marilyn and Jeanne had made other living arrangements and the two women avoided one another as much as possible. Since she was obliged to perform with a pianist and Daniel was one of only three student pianists then enrolled at Curtis, Jeanne and Daniel continued to see one another and even maintained a friendly relationship.

Violetta installed Marilyn in Daniel's room and had Daniel sleep with Albert. The family liked Daniel's young friend and there was never a question as to what their relationship entailed or where it was going. After Daniel returned to Philadelphia and he telephoned his mother to get her reaction, Violetta assured her son that she liked everything about the young woman.

"Ah. Mamma, I knew you would love my future wife?"

"*Moglia?*" Violetta asked.

"*Si, mia moglia, cara Mamma.*"

"*O Dio!*" Violetta sounded positively upset.

"What's wrong Mamma?"

"Daniel, I like Marilyn very much, but you must marry someone of your own faith. I will never tell you whom to marry. That is your decision, but it is my obligation to warn you against marrying a woman of another religion. And besides, you are still much too young to think about marriage. You are just getting started in your career."

"But Mamma," Daniel implored, "I never expected this from you. You always taught us that Jews are good people, very much like us in family ways, and the Old Testament is part of our religion too, so there is not that much difference between our beliefs."

"That is all quite true," Violetta admitted reassuringly, "But marriage is best when a husband and wife have as much in common as possible, and difference of religion can be a serious obstacle to a good marriage. They do not accept our Lord as their Savior."

Daniel was devastated.

"*Va bene, Mamma.* We shall see, but you may have to change your mind in this."

"There is nothing for me to change my mind about. It is my duty to tell you. As your mother I must tell you these things, but you know that I will support you no matter what you decide to do with your life. You must consider this matter with the utmost seriousness. I know that marriage is difficult enough. Two individuals always have natural differences, and when you add differences that go back to the very roots of their upbringing, well, it is something not to be taken too lightly."

Violetta sighed a heavy sigh and threw a kiss to her son over the telephone. She replaced the receiver and went directly to the statue of the Blessed Mother, lit a candle before it, and clasping her hands together, prayed fervently.

"*O Madonna mia*, please guide my son Daniel along the right path. Open his eyes so that he may see the will of your Son clearly, and make all the right decisions that will affect his life forevermore. Let his decisions be such that he will never have regrets about them. Thank you blessed Mary, Amen." Years later, on Daniel's wedding day, Violetta would think back to this particular day, to her impassioned prayer, and she would know in her heart that the Blessed Mother had intervened for her, had brought the light to her son's mind. Of this she would never have the slightest doubt, and no one, no one at all could convince her otherwise.

Twenty-Five

John Lorelli dated Sophia Romano for two years, during which period she continued her studies towards a B.B.A. degree and managed the home catering department of Mamma's Kitchen, expanding it to the point where two additional chefs needed to be hired in addition to three new personnel to help with the presentation and delivery of the food. One morning John walked into Sophia's office and held a colored plastic box in front of her.

"What's that?" she asked.

"Oh, I came across a new type of food storage container. I just wanted to see what you thought about it." John opened the lid of the 24" x 36" x 10" container.

"See, the potatoes and vegetables go here," he said pointing to a lid some 3 inches deep that he pulled out.

"Then the meat or fish go into this large container," and he pulled that out too, leaving a bottom layer with small compartments with closable lids.

"And what goes into these small compartments."

"Well, usually, you can put the condiments into each and close the lid so nothing spills out. But take a look at this compartment. It really holds something special."

"What?" Sophia asked, totally confused as to why such a compartment would have anything special in it. She lifted the lid and saw a velvet covered box.

"Take it out," John suggested. "Open it."

Sophia opened the box and found a 3 Karat gold diamond ring shining before her unbelieving eyes.

"Will you marry me?" John smiled a smile of happiness, anticipation and assurance that he had won the heart of his beloved.

"Oh, John," Sophia said, her voice indicating an interrogative response before words came forth that John was not prepared to hear. "It's beautiful, but why?"

"What do you mean why? Why not? What kind of reaction is that? I was expecting to hear you say, "Yes, yes, yes, not why!"

"John, you know I love you and I will marry you someday if you still want me, but I cannot make that decision now."

"Why not?" John's temper, his inability to suffer foolishness of any kind, a trait he had inherited from his father Vincenzo, rose to the fore.

"Who said you have to decide now? This is an engagement ring. People can be engaged for years. Oh, give me the box!" He snatched the box with the ring, took the plastic container and walked back into the store.

The following Sunday, Sophia was having dinner with the Lorelli's as she did from time to time now. Albert, who had enrolled in a B.B.A. program at Baruch, full time, majoring in marketing, was sitting with Sophia in the family room. She and Albert had gotten to be good friends, and now that he was attending the same school she was, albeit in the day session while Sophia attended afternoon and evening classes, they had even more in common. Sophia confided to Albert that although she loved his brother very much and did want to become his wife, she had made a promise to herself that she would only marry after she was settled in her own business and had become successful in it.

"But Sophia," Albert said, speaking with assurance and obvious concern,

"Within a short time, you and I will have our B.B.A. degrees. I have some fantastic ideas about taking this business to the next level, and I know that you have even greater ideas than I do. When we put our heads together, my parents and brothers will have no choice but to follow our lead, and believe me, they will be happy to do so. They will see results they never imagined possible. And with you married to John, this will be your business as much as anyone's. John will see to that and I will be with him 100%. And I know you will settle for nothing less than full partnership with the rest of us, and you will have it!"

Albert discussed certain concepts that the two had only touched on in prior conversations, and Sophia's eyes lit up. She could envisage everything Albert was describing and her imagination encompassed myriad possibilities. Just then, John walked into the room and saw how excited Sophia was.

"What's going on here?"

"John, where's the ring?"

"It's upstairs in my bedroom. Why?"

"Al just convinced me that I should accept your proposal."

"What?" John asked, obviously pleased and muddled at the same time. "It takes my youngest brother to convince you? What magic power does he have?" John laughed.

Albert explained to John his plan to include Sophia in the business as an equal and how their ideas would bring things to a new apex.

"Of course, it will be her business as much as it's mine. Why would you think differently?"

John put his arms around Sophia and they kissed so intensely and with such abandon that Albert became slightly embarrassed.

"Hey, guys, I'm still here," he teased.

After dinner, John stood up and announced that he had special news.

"What is it?" Violetta asked, smiling.

He opened the box with the ring, bent over to place it on Sophia's finger and said,

"Sophia has made me a very happy man today. She has agreed to become my wife."

"*Auguri, auguri!*" Vincenzo and Violetta shouted, clapping their hands, obviously very pleased at this news. They both liked Sophia very much and admired her beauty, personality and enterprise. "Congratulations!" from Stephen and Albert.

Violetta sent Vinny out to buy a special cake to celebrate the occasion. That evening Sophia and John cut the cake, a cake made with canola cream inside, whipped cream outside, adorned with a figure of cupid and his arrow, with the words, "Congratulations John and Sophia" written atop the cake. They telephoned Daniel who was thrilled at the news, for he, too, had the highest regard and affection for Sophia Romano.

"See," Sophia said, pointing to the cake, "This is something we should be selling too. There's no reason our business should not encompass every type of Italian delicacy, dessert and what have you."

"*Brava!*" came the expressions of approval from Sophia's soon-to-be new family.

John and Sophia were married six months later. Daniel brought Marilyn to the elaborate wedding. At the Mass celebrating John's and Sophia's marriage, Daniel was the only member of the family who did not receive Communion. Violetta noted that this was the first time since his First Communion that she had ever seen her son at a Mass where he did not receive. At the reception, she watched as her son and Marilyn danced, holding each other tightly. She knew her prayer would be answered one way or another, and her faith was strong enough to include any possibility.

Who knows, Violetta thought, she may even convert! That would be wonderful. My son could help to save this lovely girl's soul.

After a honeymoon on the Amalfi Coast (Violetta urged her son to go to Calabria to visit his relatives while in Italy, but John had no desire to share his new bride with anyone), Sophia and John returned with Sophia determined to truly make her mark now in the business.

Soon Mamma's Kitchen had an arrangement with an importer of Italian foods—*pomodori, funghi, caponata, olivi,* etc.—to place the "Mamma's Kitchen" label on specially packed cans and jars of products that first had to have Violetta's and Vinny's absolute approval. Indeed, Violetta had an uncanny ability to determine quality by sniffing and slightly tasting something. When the business began to attract attention on a much wider scale, Violetta was asked by the interviewer for an Italian magazine if she tasted everything that left the premises. She laughed and merrily proclaimed,

"Se mangiassi tutto sarei gia cinque quintale!" (If I ate everything I would already weigh over 1,000 pounds). In fact, at the age of fifty-six, she was still quite slim, burning more calories with her ferocious activity than those she consumed.

Albert was not satisfied with merely having the corporate name and logo emblazoned on labels affixed to cans and jars, even when they did wind up in stores and supermarkets across the country. He had more ambitious ideas. After graduating from Baruch with his B.B.A. degree, Albert decided to attend law school. With the plans he had for the business, a good lawyer in the family was an absolute necessity. Vinny and Violetta, his brothers and sister-in-law all supported him fully, so Albert's next four years were devoted to the study of law, with gratifying results for the entire family. He graduated Summa cum Laude, at the very top of his class. He had made some excellent connections at the Ivy League Columbia School of Law, so after graduation he began to plant the seeds for the family business's future development, an expansion that would eventually make it a multi-national company. In everything he did, he was particularly mindful of the necessity to consult with Sophia, for he felt an obligation to her based on the promise he had made to her the day she and John became officially engaged.

Albert entered into financial agreements with bankers whose sons he knew from law school and soon the first Mamma's Kitchen Italian diner opened in a large mall in Westchester County. Hot and cold food was available throughout the day, including various kinds of pizzas, hero sandwiches, rice balls, Italian potato and eggplant croquettes and many other delicacies. The diner was a huge success and the bankers wanted to invest money to open additional stores throughout the eastern part of the United States, in malls in Baltimore, Atlanta, Norfolk, Philadelphia, Boston, Providence and eventually other cities. Albert was intelligent and enterprising, and a less competent administrator would have tried to persuade his family to give in to the temptation of offers whereby they would realize amounts of money they had never dreamed of. Instead, Albert always insisted that his family maintain a ¾ or 75% controlling interest in the business.

Philip Sandreva was more like a brother than a cousin. Having worked in the family business nearly since its establishment, he was considered an equal partner with his working cousins John and Albert. Phil was in charge of food purchases and knew the ins and outs of buying imported delicacies, and staples too for that matter, better than anyone. By the time he was thirty years of age, however, Phil was not quite the astute businessman the company needed, but his cousins did not have the heart to criticize him or take him to task about any of his deficiencies. Instead, John and Albert would repair his mistakes, quietly cover his lapses in judgment, and always act with tact and discretion in their day-to-day dealings with him. They appreciated all that he did, but at one point they wondered why his performance in the company had so declined, and it did seem to be an interminably long time since he was "himself." The reason for the drastic change in his behavior stemmed from events that followed what his family considered an unfortunate marriage.

Philip had worked conscientiously and dutifully for Mamma's Kitchen and was happiest when he saw that his efforts helped the company to develop and achieve unprecedented success. Unlike his cousins, he never even socialized very much. When they would go dancing on Saturday nights, he preferred to go home to watch sports and relax after a grueling week of work. He had not had any real experience with women. Physical contact with them was something he had experienced in ways that did not give him any real satisfaction. A couple of his good high school friends finally convinced Philip to accompany them to a hot spot in the City, a dance club where it was easy to meet someone nice to "score" with. There, he met Vivica Simpson, a vivacious and flirtatious young woman who was attracted to Phil's sharp good looks. He was a good dresser whenever he had the opportunity to dress up, which was very infrequently—weddings and funerals—and Vivica immediately latched onto him, asking him to drive her home while still early in the evening's proceedings. After a short conversation, having learned that Philip was a businessman with a successful business of his own—at least this is how she interpreted the little he had told her about his work—Vivica thought to herself, "Ah, perhaps this is the man I have been looking for." She liked much of what she saw and heard in her brief encounter with the socially inexperienced young man, and she was smart enough, not to say conniving, to size him up and see that here was someone she could manipulate. She was not herself educated beyond high school, but she had all the street smarts a woman in her position needed to survive and flourish in what some called a "dog-eat-dog environment." When they reached her apartment on the upper west side of Manhattan, a five room flat with three bedrooms that she shared with two other young women, she asked Philip if he wanted to come up.

"I don't think so," the shy novice replied. "It's getting late and I have to get back.

"Late?" Vivica laughed. "You call 11:30 late? Why it's just the beginning of the evening." She laughed again, an infectious, laugh that Philip found pleasing and even sexy. He followed her up the stairs, eyeing the shape of her legs and her buttocks as she moved on up the stairs ahead of him. He thought of what his friends had said about scoring and his heart raced in anticipation of an experience he had been thinking about every time he saw an attractive girl in the store. Were his fantasies about to become reality? Vivica sat him down on the sofa in the common living room (each girl had her own bedroom), and brought over two bottles of beer. As they drank the beer, Vivica sat closer to her intended prey and plied him with questions.

"Tell me more about your business?" "Where do you live?" "Do you live alone?" Vivica quickly determined that there were two things she didn't care for about this Phil: he was a bit on the short side—in heels she was slightly taller—*and* he lived with his mother. But these were not exactly things that made such a big difference in light of the positive things she had enumerated in her mind about him. One, he was really good looking; two, he was well built and slim (Philip was a weight lifter); three, he was well off financially; four, he was a gentleman, a quality she did not find very often, if at all. Most of the men she met were pawing at her as soon as they got alone with her and were interested in sex and not much more. There didn't seem to be much of a chance of a real relationship with any of the men whose paths had crossed hers over the past few years. Vivica was a very attractive young woman, twenty-five years of age, with long dirty blonde hair, long, shapely legs, and sensual curves in the places that drive men crazy with desire. After they finished their wine, Vivica led Philip into her bedroom. Her housemates were not at home, and she assured Philip that they would not be for some time. They sat at the edge of her bed and Vivica put her arms around Phil and kissed his neck, his cheeks and his lips. Their kisses multiplied and Vivica's hands moved down and inside Philip's trousers. He mustered up the courage to move his own hand under her dress and she did not stop him. He felt a dampness there that stimulated him even more and he thought to himself that he had better start to undress and to help her to undress. Isn't that what I should do now, he thought. However, just as things were approaching the point of no return, Vivica suddenly stood up and straightened her dress. She really wanted him, but she was a cunning woman. She did not want to show her full hand all at once. She felt certain that she had to hold something back, to give him something to look forward to. Then, next time, their mutual lust would have its consummation and she would have him. Too much all at once could drive such a frail creature away.

"Look, I hardly know you. I think before we get too involved we should see a little more of one another."

"All right. Yes, I think you are right. When can I see you again?"

Vivica knew from his response that her instincts were correct. After that they saw each other every weekend and even sometimes during mid-week, when Philip would drive directly to Manhattan after going home for a quick shower. Rosina would plead with her son to eat something first, but he hurriedly explained that he did not have time. When Rosina complained to her sister about the sudden change in her son's behavior, Violetta would try to reason with her.

"Rosina, he's a man. He is twenty-eight years old. He has to have his own life. Let him be."

After some months, Philips brought Vivica home for Sunday dinner. Afterwards he brought her around to meet Vincenzo and Violetta too. Rosina detested her son's girlfriend from the start. She was not Italian, and that was bad enough, but she was not even a Roman Catholic. "*Nemmeno è Cattolica*," she lamented to her sister, but Violetta, always willing to give a person the benefit of the doubt, tried to reason with Rosina. "Perhaps she will convert once she is in the family. Think how wonderful that would be! I once heard a priest say that converts are usually better Catholics than those brought up in the faith." Violetta, however, who never found anything wrong with anyone, was wary of the young woman too, but she would not say anything to her nephew. She didn't feel it was her place, and besides, her sister was saying enough along those lines already. And deep down she wanted to believe that things would work out for the best.

After having known one another for only a year, Vivica and Philip married. Vivica did not convert, but she agreed to have a Catholic ceremony. Philip was very happy and totally devoted to his new wife. He would do anything at all to please her. But his happiness was short-lived. He arrived home early one day to surprise her with a gold bracelet that had just arrived from Italy. A friend, an importer of cheeses who traveled frequently between Rome and New York had brought it in to Philip that very day. Philip had seen the bracelet in an Italian magazine and asked his friend to pick it up.

Vivica usually got home two hours before Philip, so he thought he would get there a half hour ahead of her and surprise her with his special gift. When he arrived, after unlocking the door, he heard sounds coming from their bedroom. Entering quietly, he found his wife in bed with another man. If he had a gun, Philip would have killed the two on the spot. He was so disillusioned and filled with despair that he walked out and sat in a nearby park for hours, going to his mother's place to sleep that night. He wouldn't speak to anyone and wouldn't tell anyone what had happened. Rosina knew it had to do with that "*strega*," that undeserving wife of his. It was Albert, finally, Albert who had been Phil's best man at his wedding, who was able to get through to his cousin, to get the details from him and if not console him, at least get him to come back to work, where he could bury his cares in his activities. Vivica apparently needed this one last fling. She had met an old boy friend that she had been in love with, a man who did business with the company she worked for. He had simply used her and wanted to subject her once again to his brand of lovemaking that thrived on instant gratification. Vivica told him she was married, but this did not deter him. He followed her when she left for lunch and tried to persuade her to go to a nearby motel with him. At first, Vivica was adamant in her refusal to have anything to do with him, but gradually, as they sat in a booth at a nearby diner, he brushed her thigh with his fingers and she felt the old sensations she remembered from some passionate encounters the two had shared. Her mistake was in accepting his offer to drive her back to her apartment. He just wanted to see where she lived. Lunch had been late that day because of a report she had to complete for her boss, and since he had left for an important conference, she wouldn't be missed. All of Vivica's instincts told her she should walk away from this deft manipulator, but she had never been capable of acting in a truly mature manner, and it would take some serious soul searching on her part before she could discard the vestiges of self-loathing that she had grown up with.

But although Philip and Vivica had a reconciliation and continued to live together, Philip was not the same. To her credit, Vivica made a solemn pledge to her husband and to herself that she would never betray him again. But Philip never trusted his wife from that day forward and was never able to bring the same level of concentration to his work as before. Even after they had children together and their mutual love for their children gave their family a stability and sense of happiness envied by some of their friends, Philip's suspicion of his wife, buried within him, would occasionally manifest itself in spite of all his efforts to suppress it.

Twenty-Six

During Daniel's second year at Curtis, a visiting professor from L'Accademia di Santa Cecilia in Rome joined the faculty. Professor Carlo Maria Stagione's specialty was conducting, and students interested in conducting were invited to apply for one of the limited places in his class. Daniel applied, was interviewed and accepted. The young pianist decided that if he were to have a career in music, he would have to expand his scope somewhat. His professors and fellow students continually encouraged him to pursue a career as a concert pianist, but Daniel knew that no matter how good a pianist he was, and he certainly was quite extraordinary, the competition was fierce. Even those who had taken first place in important international competitions found it difficult to get enough engagements—solo recitals, invitations from important orchestras, recording contracts—to insure an ongoing and lucrative career. Besides, Daniel had started to explore other areas of the classical repertory and he found so much excitement in the variety, power and beauty of many orchestral, choral and opera compositions. He began to listen avidly to recordings and to attend performances at the Academy of Music in Philadelphia. Listening to the great Philadelphia Orchestra, he imagined himself at the helm, and this image continued to inspire him and drive him to learn all he could about the orchestra, all of its instruments and how a good conductor could bring everything together to deliver memorable performances. Little by little, in the intricate way a conductor gets to know musical compositions, he became familiar with Beethoven's *Nine Symphonies*, his *Missa Solemnis* and the opera *Fidelio*. Brahms' *Four Symphonies* and his *German Requiem* were revelatory works for Daniel. It amazed him how works like Cesar Franck's *Symphony in d minor*, the Sibelius *Second*, Tchaikovsky's *Fourth*, *Fifth* and *"Pathetique," Symphonies* and Rachmaninov's *Second and Third Symphonies* could each in its own special way capture distinctive, original sounds from the orchestra and bring everything together for an overwhelming emotional experience. Hearing Stravinsky's *Rite of Spring* for the first time at the Academy of Music was a true turning point for Daniel. The exotic rhythms and the powerful orchestral attacks were like nothing he had ever heard before. He just had to conduct an orchestra in that work one day.

Toward the end of his one year residency at Curtis, Professor Stagione stopped Daniel after class one morning.

"Daniel, I am very impressed with your musical abilities. As a pianist you can sight read better than anyone I know. This is a very important factor in becoming a fine conductor. The *feeling* you bring to your performances, on the piano as well as when you conducted the Curtis Chamber Orchestra the two times you had occasion to do so, is a rare commodity these days. So many young people are technically brilliant but without any real sense of what the music is about. When I heard how you shaped the phrases in Schubert's '*Unfinished*' *Symphony* the other evening, how you gave the strings the proper weight and had the winds dominate in the places they should, no truly the way they *must,* I was confirmed in my belief that I had come upon a most unusual and extraordinary talent."

Daniel was elated. He had no idea the Professor felt this way since Stagione was a man who continually made corrections on his students' endeavors, finding some fault in almost everything they did.

"Thank you, Professor. I appreciate your kind words."

Stagione waved away Daniel's expression of gratitude,

"Never mind that," he said.

"The reason I am telling you this is because I would like to invite you to come to study in Rome next year, at L'Accademia di Santa Cecilia. I think it is important for you to continue your studies in conducting."

Daniel didn't know what to say. He loved the idea of going to study in Rome, in the country where his parents were born. He knew this was a great opportunity for him too, and perhaps an important step in his career as a conductor. But he knew now, too, that he was in love with Marilyn. How could he leave her for a whole year?

"Professor Stagione, I feel honored and I want you to know how grateful I am to you for this consideration." Stagione interrupted, "Daniel, you do not have to decide this minute. That would not be fair. I have no right to expect you to decide immediately. Take your time. I will be here for another two months. If you decide you would like to come to Rome, I would need to know in about five to six weeks to notify my colleagues so that your place there will be assured. I am also recommending you for the special Pietro Mascagni Scholarship in Conducting and this has to be approved by the Council of Composers and Conductors. I have no doubt that they will honor my request once I write to them about you."

"That is what I needed to know. I appreciate your willingness to extend the time for me to reply. I must discuss this with my parents and family. You know how Italian families want to be consulted," and Daniel smiled a broad smile as he said this.

"*Sei non soltanto una musicista eccezionale, ma anche un figlio straordinario!*" Stagione said, having come to appreciate Daniel's ability in spoken Italian.

"*Grazie, Professore, grazie,*" Daniel said, grasping Stagione's hand and shaking it firmly.

Daniel's head was swirling as the idea of spending his junior year in Rome began to penetrate. Curtis actually did not have the traditional freshman, sophomore, junior and senior years as most colleges do, since students could take as much time as they needed to finish their studies, with the input of professors helping to determine the time necessary for conferral of a degree or diploma. The only thing he found difficult to reconcile was how he could possibly bear being away from Marilyn for a full year. Of course she could come to visit him during school breaks, and he would come home for Christmas, but she was now so much a part of his life that he could not envision being separated from her. They didn't live together. He wanted to, but she was concerned about her family's reaction since her parents came to visit from time to time. Daniel did suggest they move in together, but Marilyn politely refused. Besides, the school frowned upon male and female students living together. In cases where the school helped students with living arrangements, they kept tabs and made suggestions for partners sharing rooms or apartments. This was how Marilyn and Jeanne came to room together, and also how Daniel and Sam got to share their quarters. But students were free to make their own living arrangements and Daniel wanted to look for an apartment where he and Marilyn could live together. He had not been to Mass since his Confession about his conduct with Jeanne, because his intimacy with Marilyn began right after that. Marilyn told her parents she had a boyfriend, but refused to elaborate on the details. Her mother asked if he was Jewish and she lied, saying he was. Moving in with Daniel would surely complicate matters since her parents would learn the truth the first time they visited her. On one of their visits, her mother asked about the boyfriend and Marilyn practically ignored her questions. On a subsequent visit, Marilyn's mother again asked, this time persistently, and Marilyn went over to fetch Daniel.

"Now don't, please don't tell her you are a Catholic. Anyway, Daniel *is* a Jewish name." Marilyn's facial lines revealed her excessive anxiety.

"Listen, Mar, you know I can't lie."

"Why can't you? Can't you tell a little white lie for me?"

"Mar, it goes against my principles."

"What principles?" Marilyn was nearly crying.

"Every principle I live by."

"You mean your religious principles?

"Yes, those too," Daniel said, but this time without conviction.

"Oh, so fucking me is all right. That doesn't go against your religious principles, but telling a little white lie—in *your* religion certainly not as serious as pre-marital fucking!— that's too much to ask for?"

"Mar, do you have to be so crude?

"Crude? Is that what concerns you? All this talk about love, and the first time I ask you to do something for me, it's a problem."

Daniel suddenly felt like the biggest hypocrite on earth. She was right. He had a selective approach to morality. What he enjoyed, even if he knew it to be wrong, he did. But the rules he could easily comply with, without them interfering in any way with his desires—these he followed to the letter.

"You're right. O.K. I will do anything you want me to do."

"Fine." Marilyn was obviously relieved and she hugged Daniel.

"If the subject of religion comes up, just tell my mother that you are Jewish. Tell her you are not a practicing Jew because your parents are Jewish Bohemians and don't really have much to do with religion. They never let you have a Bar Mitzvah. You don't know what the inside of a synagogue looks like; you never even sat at a Passover Seder. Say anything you want to say about being a Jew, but don't let on you are anything else."

"O.K. I'll do my best, but you know, I do know things about Judaism, so I don't have to appear like a complete fool. I have read quite a bit about the Jewish faith."

"Daniel, I think it would be better if you do it my way. When my mother hears you play in the concert in June, she's going to be convinced that anyone who can play the piano like you do has to be Jewish."

The meeting with Marilyn's parents was a success. Batia Schwartz, Marilyn's mother liked Daniel immensely and actually took some pleasure in learning that his parents had neglected to teach him his Jewish heritage. This way, if he and her daughter got together (she didn't want to jinx anything by even thinking the word "marriage"), she would have a formidable but enjoyable and gratifying job making him a respectable member of the tribe.

Following the meeting with Professor Stagione, Daniel thought about that day some three or four weeks before. After her parents left, Marilyn went over to Daniel's room and kissed him over and over.

"Thank you, my love; I know that was hard for you, so please accept my gratitude."

"I accept," said Daniel sheepishly.

"Now I want to show you how grateful I really am." Marilyn was wearing a sweater that accented her ample breasts. Slowly, she pulled it over her head and dropped it, revealing a bright red bra that pushed her breasts together to make the most of her cleavage. She undid the tight black skirt and worked it down to the floor. Standing there in her brief panties, the same red matching the bra, Marilyn appeared to Daniel as the epitome of womanly beauty. "How can this be wrong," he thought, "when it feels so right?" He had fallen in love with the one woman he was destined to be with for the rest of his life. This fact, this certainty that Marilyn would be his wife one day, helped to allay the guilty feelings that surged up in him from time to time. Everything he had been taught to believe about his faith, God's will, sexual conduct—all the prescriptions and proscriptions—haunted him and prevented him from surrendering completely to the moment. There was always that subconscious sensation that rose to full consciousness when he least wanted to acknowledge it, that he was not being faithful to his deepest self.

Marilyn helped Daniel to undress and she made love to him that night with more passion, greater concentration and wilder abandon than ever before.

"Oh, Daniel!" she cried as she reached orgasm, "I will never love anyone as much as I love you."

Thinking back as he prepared to tell Marilyn about Stagione's offer, Daniel knew that that day had brought him to a full realization of just how much he loved her too. It was almost obsessive. He couldn't stop thinking about her. Fortunately, his overwhelming love for her benefited his musical performances. Indeed, that entire week the lovers practiced every day for a performance of Cesar Franck's *Violin Sonata in A*, to be given before a select group of faculty and students the following Friday evening. Their intensive love making seemed to fuel their performance of the *Sonata*, and by the time they played it for their private audience, they were able to bring a new dimension to the music. Those in the audience who were familiar with the work acknowledged that they had never before heard such an impassioned performance of a piece that itself was the epitome of romantic expression.

Daniel always saw himself and Marilyn together in the future, two musicians, playing and living and loving together, always together.

That evening he wanted to tell her the news, and he was prepared to tell her he wanted to turn down Professor Stagione's offer. Instead, Marilyn opened a different and unexpected door and said,

"I had some great news today!" She looked at Daniel and saw that he had been about to tell her something too. She knew him so well.

"Wait a minute, do you have something to tell me?"

"Yes," he smiled, now more relaxed, "I do, but I want to hear your great news first."

"No, you first."

"No, I insist," firmly now, Daniel took Marilyn's hands in his, "Tell me my love."

"O.K. I'll go first. Today I was informed that I will be playing Beethoven's *Violin Concerto* at the school orchestra concert in June."

"That's great, Mar!" Daniel's excitement was genuine and heartfelt. He loved the work. It was one of his favorite compositions in any genre. He remembered hearing it for the first time on a recording with Jascha Heifetz performing. The opening with the timpani beats sets the mood, and when the violin enters, joining the Boston Symphony Orchestra, the magic unfolds uncovering a beauty of expression that he had never experienced before from anything or any work of art whatever. He loved the five *Piano Concertos* and the *Triple Concerto*, and being a pianist those compositions were more personal, but the *Violin Concerto* was totally captivating. Seeing Marilyn as she looked that night when she confessed the depth of her love, Daniel thought, "Beethoven must have had that kind of beatific vision when he composed the work." Hearing Marilyn practicing each of the three movements from time to time told him that she had the true measure of the composition. Thus, he was not surprised that she was selected to perform it.

After many more kisses and embraces, it was Daniel's turn to give his news.

"Daniel, that's great! It's exactly what you need to spur your conducting career."

"I know, Mar. It is great, but I don't think I can accept it."

"Why can't you?"

"I can't see myself away from you for so long."

"Oh, you are so sweet," she said, holding his head with both hands and kissing him firmly on the mouth.

"No really. I've given this a good deal of thought. The only way I will go is if you come with me."

"Oh, don't be foolish. How can I come with you? You know I can't leave my studies here.

"If we get married, you can join me. Then we'll come back together and continue together, always together. I'll ask Stagione about your taking classes in Rome too. We don't have to have children right away."

Marilyn was totally overwrought by her lover's words.

"Marriage? Children? What are you talking about?"

"We're going to get married sooner or later, so why not make it sooner?"

"Daniel," Marilyn spoke slowly and almost apologetically, "You know we can never get married. What makes you bring this up now? Why do you want to spoil the beautiful relationship we have?"

"Never . . . get . . . married?" Daniel was shocked by her words. He put his head down into his hands, burying his face, trying to see somehow by blocking the light, as if darkness could bring him the truth he needed to see. He rallied a bit and asked,

"Mar, what do you mean? Don't you know I can't live without you?"

"I don't want to think about that now, but I always made it clear to you that my family will not tolerate my marrying any man who isn't Jewish."

"Then I'll convert." As soon as he said it, Daniel knew how ridiculous the idea was. Imagine him telling Violetta Nardi Lorelli, the niece of a woman that many people considered a saint, that he Daniel Lorelli, her son, would no longer be a Roman Catholic.

"That's ridiculous!" Marilyn allowed.

"But Mar, don't you remember what you said to me that night?"

She immediately knew what he was referring to.

"Yes, I said I would never love anyone the way I love you."

"Well, then, how can you marry anyone else?"

"I don't know. Maybe I will never get married, but I cannot marry you. Even though it is killing me inside, even though I never fall asleep thinking about how miserable I will be without you eventually, I know that certain things in life cannot be avoided."

"But, Mar, darling, what you are saying doesn't make sense. Please think about it." Daniel was pleading, earnestly trying to convince his beloved to begin to think clearly.

"When we first got together it was lust, on your part as well as mine. I never expected things to turn out the way they have." Marilyn sighed a sigh of longing, of hope abandoned but ever so close to being recaptured, if only . . . .

"I told you early on that I would someday have to marry my own kind." She corrected herself, "My family's kind. There are times in life when we make choices and those choices can help us or hurt us. When I made the choice to become your lover, to hold you in my heart above all other people or things, I knew that I was making a hurtful choice. Honestly, I didn't really think I would be hurting you as much as myself. I never expected you to fall in love with me. I just thought our liaison would be a good time for you and that you would move on. Isn't that what most men do? But you are not most men. I realize that. I'm sorry that this has to be hurtful for you too. I made the choice knowing I would have to give you up, but I convinced myself that having you for a month, six months, a year, two years? This would be better than not having you at all. I have cherished each and every moment we have been together, and I *will* love you, Daniel, as long as I live, but I must face the reality of the life I was born into."

"I don't understand. When two people love as we do, nothing is impossible. There are those who have died together rather than forsake the kind of love we share."

With tears moistening his eyes, Daniel pleaded,

"Please Marilyn, think about it."

"I have never stopped thinking about it. I never will."

That night, lying in bed, Daniel thought about the irony of the situation. Here he was, always religious until he met Marilyn, always in Church and at Confession and believing all the tenets of his Faith, but he just went against everything when he met her. And he would go against everything to marry her since he could not get married with a Mass, in the Church of his infancy and childhood and early manhood. These were the things he dreamed of whenever he thought about marriage. . . before he met Marilyn. And there she was, not religious at all. She believed so much of the Old Testament was nonsense, fine for the time it was written, but out-of-date now, except for a few things. And she didn't practice her religion. She admitted that she did not care about any of the holidays. She saw the holidays of Rosh Hashanah and Yom Kippur as just ordinary days with no special significance for her. And yet, and yet she would give up the man she loved for the sake of some cultural mandate. He couldn't understand. *This*, Daniel felt he would never understand.

Twenty-Seven

Sam Halstead never questioned Daniel about being away so many evenings, not sleeping in his room. Sam knew that Daniel and Marilyn were lovers. They had been out for drinks together, to movies, and Sam saw how intimate the two were. Nonetheless, he never asked Daniel any questions. After a while, Daniel, would tell Sam that he would not be sleeping in their flat that night, that he was staying with Marilyn. Daniel felt he would give Sam the opportunity to invite a woman friend to stay over if he wanted to, without worrying about anyone walking in. Strangely, the subject of women never came up between the two friends. Sam was a good looking young man. He had straight brownish blonde hair, prominently parted on the left side, large brown eyes, a thin pointed nose, finely shaped lips and sparkling white, small teeth. He was taller than Daniel at six feet one inch. The female students found him attractive, but he was completely unresponsive when they hinted at any kind of interrelationship beyond music making. Diana Santiago approached Daniel one morning outside the school's main building.

"Dan, you know that I am playing cello continuo to Sam's oboe in some baroque oboe works."

"Yes, I passed the room where you were practicing the other day. It sounded wonderful."

"Well," continued Diana, "I wanted to ask you something since you two are roommates and you must know him quite well."

"Yes, about what?" Daniel asked, puzzled that Diana would be asking him anything about Sam.

"Well, since we've been working together, I suggested that we could go out for a bite one day after practice. He politely refused. Then I suggested going to see a new film one night, and he again turned me down. O.K., I figured he's not interested in me as a woman. After all, *de gustibus* and all that, but he wouldn't even have coffee with me one morning. I saw him in the coffee shop, sat down next to him, and he, very nicely, I'll admit, told me he was sorry, but he had to get going. What's with him? While we're practicing he's very nice and complimentary, but what is it that he doesn't like about me? He's done things socially with you and some of the other women, hasn't he?"

Daniel thought for a minute, looked at Diana and was surprised at his own reply.

"You know, now that you mention it, he does things with me and Marilyn and used to do things with me and Jeanne, but only when I was there. I don't think I have ever seen him with any girl alone."

"Is he gay?" Diana asked in an almost annoyed sounding tone of voice.

"How should I know? I don't think so. I mean, he's never made a move on me. If he were gay, wouldn't he have tried something by now?"

"I guess," said Diana.

Daniel had no real knowledge concerning homosexuality. As a Roman Catholic, as far as he was concerned, it was an abomination. It had to be a sickness. It wasn't normal. Maybe those who practiced it couldn't help themselves, but one had to admit that it was a totally depraved way of life. How could anyone argue otherwise? After all, two men or two women having sex? There was no way they could possibly have children. Having children, at least in the scheme of creation, that is what sex was all about–the propagation of the species—wasn't it? Daniel, in his limited knowledge of this phenomenon, could not see any other possibility.

The next time Daniel saw Sam in their flat, alone together, he decided to probe. Daniel had this character flaw as some would have it, or this open approach to people, entirely commendable according to others, of confronting friends, acquaintances, even those he did not really know, and of asking them personal questions. Nothing *that* personal, mind you, but still too personal for some. It was almost never the person asked who minded, since his manner completely disarmed the individual being interrogated.

"Sam. . . ." Daniel began, tentatively, "You know Diana Santiago?"

"Yes, of course I know her. We're working on some Baroque pieces together."

"Well, you know Sam, I think she has a crush on you."

Daniel thought to himself how stupid that sounded, "a crush."

"Really? What makes you think so?"

"She told me."

"Well, I'm sorry, but I'm not interested."

"You don't find her attractive, Sam?"

"Truthfully, I neither find her attractive nor unattractive. She just doesn't interest me."

"Oh, I see," Daniel said, "I know what you mean. There are women who are attractive to other men, but I just don't see it." Daniel was trying to decide if he should dig deeper.

"Sam, what about Jeanne?"

"Not interested."

"How about Marilyn? If I were not seeing her, could you find her attractive?"

"Why all these questions, Dan? You never seemed interested in my interest in women before."

"Well, I just wondered. Is that it? You like Marilyn, and you're being honorable by not pursuing her?"

"No, I'm really not interested in Marilyn either."

"What?" Daniel could not see how any red blooded man could not be attracted to Marilyn. Anyone, man or woman, would have to admit she's an absolutely stunning woman.

"Look Dan, I'm not interested in any women."

"Not interested in *any* women? Then you mean you're. . . .?"

"Yes, I'm gay. O.K. Are you happy that you now know my sexual orientation?"

"Oh, Sam, I'm sorry. I. . ."

Daniel was momentarily at a loss for words.

"You're sorry? *Sorry*? Well you needn't be. I'm completely happy being who I am."

"You are?" Daniel knew he was not using the right choice of words and even felt he was being insensitive.

"Yes, I am. Now, now that you know, what are you going to do?"

"Nothing! What do you mean?"

"I mean, now that you know I'm gay, are you going to move out?"

"No, why should I do that?"

"Because straight people always act irrationally when it comes to their dealings with gays, except for the few enlightened ones."

"No, no, I don't want to move out? But how is it you never made a move on me if you're gay?" Daniel knew that his remark was stupid as soon as it came out of his mouth, but he wasn't quite sure just why it was.

"See, that shows how much you know about homosexuality."

The term "homosexuality" gave Daniel a shudder. "Gay" just didn't have the impact for him that "homosexuality" did.

"What do you mean? What should I know?"

"Look Dan, I'll admit when I first met you I found you attractive."

"You *did?*"

Daniel experienced a wave of disgust coming over him. He suddenly felt that he was vulnerable. He had never known what it could be like to be the object of a *man's* lust.

"Yes. You are, after all, a very handsome fellow."

"Fellow?" Daniel thought. "That sounds so *gay!*" He merely said, "Uh huh?"

"Yes, but as soon as I saw the way you looked at the girls, I knew you were straight and I dropped you from my thoughts then and there."

Daniel wondered about Sam's thoughts of him, and the mild nausea returned.

"But Sam, have you ever gone for treatment? Maybe you can be cured?"

"Dan, you're really a nice guy, but you don't have a clue. My father sent me for therapy. It turned out that the therapist was gay. He wanted to have an affair with me, but I threatened to report him. I found him repulsive. You see, not all gays go with just anyone. We are not all promiscuous, even if some of us are, just as some . . . many? straight people are."

"I'm sorry, but I don't understand. How can 'homosexuality' [he said the word with evident revulsion] be justified? I mean if you lean that way, I guess you can't help it. But how can you put it on the same level as a man and a woman?"

"Look Dan, you're an intelligent fellow."

"*Fellow* again, ugh." Daniel thought.

"Let me just explain something to you and leave it for you to ponder. I was born the way I am, just as you were born the way you are. My parents are, quote, unquote, *normal.* There are scientists doing research now who think there may be a chromosome that makes certain people gay. I had no choice. Can you understand that? I had no choice in the matter. The same way that you find women attractive, I find men attractive. Just as you have no choice in liking women, I have no choice in liking men. This has been going on for centuries. I don't think of my inclinations as any more unpleasant as you do yours. I enjoy being with men, as much as you enjoy being with women, with Marilyn."

Sam's mention of Marilyn's name made Daniel wince. Not knowing what to say at this point, Daniel thrashed about mentally and came out suddenly,

"But what about the Bible?"

"The Bible. Do you believe everything written in the Bible?"

"Well, yes."

"Do you eat pork?"

Suddenly Daniel had a vision of his mother's tales of killing the pig in Italy.

"Yes, of course."

"Well, Dan, the Bible also proscribes eating pork, certain seafood. It condones cruelty towards women in certain cases. Look into it."

"I don't know what you're talking about."

"I'm not surprised. You know Alexander Pope's dictum, 'A little learning is a dangerous thing. Drink deep . . .'"

Daniel now felt a little foolish. He was intelligent enough to realize that he was not very well informed about the Old Testament. His Catholic training had never really devoted any time to a study of that part of the Bible. He couldn't even discuss the subject intelligently. He was sorry that he had sounded uncharitable to Sam.

"Sam, I'm sorry if I seem to be unsympathetic. I really don't know much about the things we are discussing. I will try to be better informed."

"Daniel, you are a good person. I want you to know that contrary to what many so-called religious people think and say, I have never tried to influence anyone to follow my sexual orientation. I only have relationships with men I like and who like me in the same way. I would never force myself on anyone."

"Thanks for enlightening me," Daniel said, but he was not convinced he meant it. Secretly, he was happy that he had a short time left to live in the apartment with Sam before leaving for Rome.

Twenty-Eight

Daniel Lorelli arrived in Rome at the age of twenty. He had always wanted to visit the country of his parents and forebears, but the opportunity never presented itself. Violetta and Vincenzo always talked about returning for a visit, but they were always too busy with the business. Both had become naturalized American citizens and were proud to be voting Americans. Every year on Election Day, they would go to the polls and vote, whether for President of the United States or for a local assemblyman. The immigrant type that Vincenzo and Violetta represented was quite different from the kind who arrived from Italy in the 1960's and 1970's. That generation of Italians saw America as a place for the quick buck. Just make the money, work long enough for an American pension and go back to Italy. America was worthless for anything but making money. Many of these quick-buck immigrants realized to their dismay that by staying too long, their children would not go back with them, so at least in some cases they were unwilling residents after some time.

Daniel had promised his mother that he would visit their relatives before he started his conducting program at "Santa Cecilia," and since he had a few weeks before his enrollment took effect, he made the trip South. He took a train at Rome's *Stazione Termini* and after some six hours got off in Paola. His Aunt Maria, Violetta's sister and her husband Luigi Caroselli, with their three children Domenica, Roberto and Archangelo were there to greet Daniele. He was moved by the extraordinary reception he got. These people whom he had never seen before received him with such obvious affection and enthusiasm, love and regard for his comfort, that he was totally overwhelmed. Even his aunt's husband, who was not a blood relative, acted as though Daniel were his own son. They provided him with his own bedroom and opened their home to him as he had only seen his own mother open her home to anyone who came to visit. Well, after all, he thought, they are sisters.

Daniel was very interested in visiting the place where his grandmother's sister Maria had been murdered He had heard his mother tell the story many times and some of the images haunted him. Luigi and Maria drove him up towards *il pagliarone*, just below the *pineta* and the highest elevation of *Monte Cocuzzo*. There next to a tree was a cross and the following inscription carved on a piece of wood:

In Questo Luogo
Maria Saggio
Martire della Purezza
Fu barbaramente Uccisa

There wasn't much to see: an overgrown field, a path leading down through the woods, the same path Maria had walked up and was never to walk down again. Daniel closed his eyes and stood still, and for a brief moment he had a vision of Maria, of her struggle and her determined effort to ward off evil, to stand firm against the barbaric elements in her world, no matter the cost. Daniel thought of the possibility of one day writing or commissioning a musical composition symbolizing her ordeal.

The following Sunday Daniel went to Mass in the Church of San Francesco. Just as when his father was his age, the women in the church were separated from the men. Throughout the Mass the women's voices predominated and at first Daniel thought they sounded at times like the cackling of hens, and then again like the screeching of the brakes on a bus in New York. But wait, suddenly above the din, one voice dominated and soared over the others. The voice was that of a woman known as *l'Usignola*, the Italian word for "nightingale," except that the ending was feminized to apply to her. Here was a voice that with the proper training could certainly have adorned the great opera houses of the world. Daniel marveled at her beauty of expression and the sheer power of her voice. In one hymn, a beautiful sacred melody that he had never heard before, she sang solo, and the other women joined in for a lovely chorus. Their gusto overcame their lack of musical ability, but *l'Usignola's* contribution was extraordinary. The experience in that ancient Church brought Daniel back to the time before he became involved with Marilyn, when the mystical in his psyche subjugated the sensual. Returning to Rome, Daniel went to confession. At St. Peter's, priests were available to hear confessions in English. Daniel could have confessed in Italian, but he found what he had to say easier to express in his native tongue. The priest was not judgmental.

"What you were confronted with is something many young people today face. The attractions of the flesh are powerful and not easy to resist. All but the strongest, the saints among us, fall easily. That is why we need the sacraments, daily Mass and Communion to keep us on the path of righteousness. The woman you sinned with is far away now, you say. Temptation is distant, so you rightfully turn to God again. Think of how truly free you feel now. You feel whole again. That is why you have come to confess and that is what you must always remember. When sin presents itself to you the next time, you will be stronger because you will have turned closer and closer still to God. In time, through the sacrament of marriage, you will be able to enjoy the pleasures of sex in the way that your Creator intended. Pray for strength, pray for others and pray for me. Now say a sincere Act of Contrition."

After praying, Daniel left the church and returned to his room near Santa Cecilia. He thought about what the priest had said about feeling free. But why was it, he thought, that he did not feel free. He felt trapped in a maze of his own making. Why did he confess? It was obvious that he was still torn between his religious upbringing, all he had been taught, all that had been instilled in him since he was old enough to understand, and then that other part, that "enlightened" perspective as he sometimes thought of it, the intellectual refusal to submit to this enforced creed that warred against natural desires. The inclination to make love to someone you loved was also sacred, beautiful, elemental, and worthy of honor and respect. Could it only be seen this way in the context of a sacrament? After this first confession he had made in more than two years, Daniel did not feel "whole," as the priest maintained. He was sorry that he had compromised the incomparable relationship he had had with Marilyn for nearly two years by discussing it with someone else, as if it was something abominable, when, in fact, it was truly sublime.

The last night they slept together, before his trip home and his flight a week later to Rome, Daniel and Marilyn had pledged their undying love to one another.

"All you have to know is that I will love you forever, always and forever. Even though we cannot be together the way we would both like to be, my love will not die."

"Nor will mine," he said.

They agreed to write to one another, and he kept alive a hope that his absence would cause her to see that they could not remain apart for too long. In his room, he looked at her photos and remembered each and every important moment they had shared. He forced himself to think about specific days and nights over and over, fearing that somehow he would forget them, and these were things he never wanted to forget.

Thinking back on his confession, Daniel realized it was not a valid confession, for he was not sorry at all for the way he had lived, and he did not feel as though he had sinned. Still, hoping to achieve a new mystical experience, he did attend Mass and received Communion the next day, but he could not recapture the same transcendence he remembered from years before.

Twenty-Nine

Professor Stagione greeted his young recruit and Daniel soon became involved in a series of lectures, readings, mock performances and eventually actual performances as conductor of a small group of talented instrumentalists. Of course, daily practice on the piano was mandatory, and if Daniel did not play for at least six to seven hours per day, he would feel as though a part of him had been cut off. Professor Stagione arranged for Daniel to conduct chamber ensembles that could give him the experience he needed in specific aspects of conducting such as cueing up, baton wielding and eye contact with the players. After a particularly difficult day when he conducted six string players in Tchaikovsky's *String Sextet, "Souvenir de Florence,"* Daniel walked off the podium and heard Stagione call to him.

"Daniele, come over for a moment. Do you know that your viola player is a *paesano* of yours?"

Hearing the word *paesano*, Daniel quickly assumed the Professor meant the young woman was from Calabria.

"*Oh, si, Calabrese?*" Daniel asked.

"*Veramente, Piemontese, ma Americana purtroppo.*"

The young woman smiled, looked at Daniel in a self conscious manner, he thought, and said,

"I'm from Boston."

"Well, I'll leave you two to get acquainted," the professor remarked and quickly scurried off.

Annemarie Taviani was a scholarship student at Santa Cecilia. She had been accepted for a year of study after showing exceptional ability at Harvard as a music major. She was nineteen, a year younger than Daniel and the daughter of a second generation Italian-American father, whose own parents were from Piemonte, and a mother whose great grandparents had been immigrants from Ireland. Annemarie had demonstrated musical ability at a very early age. She started with the piano at the age of four, switched to the violin at the age of eight and finally settled on the viola as the instrument that best expressed all that she wanted to say through music. The viola's lower tones were better suited to Annemarie's personality. The high register of the violin was much too flamboyant for her. She was noticeably low-key, and although she seemed shy, Daniel's first impression was that she was "reserved." She was an extremely confident young woman and would speak with complete self assurance whenever conditions called for her to do so, but she was certainly not what one would call an extrovert. After exchanging some words about one another's backgrounds, Daniel excused himself and went to the room he used for practicing. A German Steinway was the piano he preferred at Santa Cecilia and Stagione had arranged the *permesso* for Daniel to use it as long as no official functions were being held in the small concert room that housed it.

One day while Daniel was practicing, Annemarie walked by the room and heard the piano. Quietly, she opened the door and sat at the rear of the room. Daniel did not notice she was there. He was playing Schumann's *Fantasy in C*. Annemarie was familiar with the piece, having heard it a number of times in concert. She also owned a recording of the work. This was the work Schumann composed for his beloved Clara. As Annemarie listened, she was astonished at Daniel's complete mastery of it and his total identification with the work. When Daniel played the last notes and slumped exhausted over the piano, Annemarie suddenly burst into energetic applause. She walked up to the piano saying, "Bravo, Bravo." Then, "I hope you don't mind my eavesdropping."

"No, not at all" Daniel smiled.

"You know," Annemarie continued, "I have heard a number of performances of the Schumann *Fantasy* and I love the recording I have at home by Arrau, but I have never heard it played any better than you did just now."

Daniel did not know how to respond to such an extravagant appraisal of his playing, especially coming from one as talented as this young violist certainly was.

"Why, thank you. That is high praise indeed."

Annemarie looked at this other American studying music in Italy, and was not sure as to whether she should continue conversing or not. She wanted to say more and to learn more about this unusual young man with whom, she felt, she had so much in common.

"As I was sitting here listening to you, I wondered why someone, not really someone, but you, enormously talented as a pianist, would want to go in any direction other than that of pursuing a career as a concert pianist. Why conducting?"

Daniel had never been asked this question before and was not even sure he knew the answer to it. No one had ever asked him the reasons for his interest in conducting. He had always been congratulated on choosing to pursue such a glamorous career. His hesitation in replying prompted Annemarie to continue.

"I mean, I realize that conducting brings with it a certain prestige and has the potential to take a musician to a higher level overall than that possible as a *mere* soloist." She said this with a false giggle.

"But even under the most ideal of circumstances, it is rare, I think, for a conductor to really and truly place his very own imprint on a performance to the extent that you, for example, can as a solo pianist. As a conductor, you must depend too much on what all the other musicians are willing or able to give to you, so that the mélange adds up to more than the sum of its parts, but only if all things come together."

Daniel thought the young woman's comments were somewhat irrelevant, but the way she made her point lent it greater validity than he would have at first been willing to admit.

"I guess you are right, in a way. But just because I become a conductor doesn't preclude my continued activity as a pianist. There are many examples of conductors who even conduct from the piano."

"Yes, that's true," Annemarie admitted, "but that usually happens only with works like a Mozart Piano Concerto or something from the Baroque or Classical period. Can you imagine conducting the Rachmaninov *Third Concerto* from the keyboard, while playing it?"

"Yes, that would be a very big order. I think that being a conductor opens up so much more for a musician than being a soloist on one instrument. It's almost like playing on all the instruments at once. Then it's a question of the much greater variety of musical works a conductor can be involved with. When I first started to play the piano, there was so much to discover, and there still is so much I have not performed, so much I have not even begun to delve into in the repertoire of the piano. But as a conductor, one can become familiar with, on an altogether different level, all the great symphonic and choral works, not to speak of the entire world of opera."

"You certainly sound enthusiastic. I have a feeling that you *will* be successful no matter which direction you take."

196

Annemarie's smile and the sense of confidence she exuded set Daniel at ease and he found himself asking her if she had some free time to continue the conversation outside of school hours. It wasn't as if he was asking a woman for a date. He was much too consumed with his love for Marilyn to even think of another woman in romantic terms. She just seemed so young and agreeable, like an old friend from home. If he had even thought about it, he wouldn't have found her attractive as a woman at all. He could just as well have been speaking to a young man.

Daniel's hectic schedule quite consumed all of his time. He usually woke up at six and spent an hour each morning jogging around Rome. Returning to his room, a modest bedroom with a small adjoining study in a *pensione*, he showered in the common bathroom and had breakfast in the common dining area where he sometimes conversed with other students, a few from L'Accademia and some from other colleges in Rome. The breakfast usually consisted of dark Italian coffee, known in the States as *Espresso*, with warm milk and some bread and marmalade or a *cornetto*, a sweet type of Italian cruller. Students who chose a full pension could have their midday *pranzo* and evening *cena* at the *pensione* too, but Daniel usually had these meals elsewhere. Two hours of practice on the piano would be followed by three more hours of intensive lectures and study in conducting. There was usually then a break for *pranzo* and rest until around four in the afternoon—the Italian way of life that invariably seemed so strange and alien to transplanted Americans—when additional work would have to be completed, either in the library or, whenever possible, in workshop type gatherings that benefited students' various interests and sought to cultivate the dynamism inherent in their individual purposes, which profited from joint endeavors. In this way, Daniel would gain knowledge and experience in his chosen field of conducting while a violinist or cellist would obtain similar invaluable benefits concerning performance practices that took into consideration their instrument's specific place in the orchestra. Professor Stagione insisted that his students studying conducting had to become familiar with each and every instrument of the orchestra. Ideally, he would point out, a conductor should have the ability to play each and every instrument, not as a virtuoso of course, but on an elementary level. This kind of familiarity would prove to be a boon for the conductor in many compositions where the individual timbres and capabilities of each instrument are exploited by the composers for a specific purpose. This, Stagione insisted, is why many conductors turn in performances of works that sound so unidiomatic and even downright ugly.

One evening, after a long grueling day, before returning to his *pensione*, Daniel stopped at his favorite pizza restaurant, a small bistro that had the best pizza he had eaten while in Italy. He knew about pizza, since Violetta made it from time to time, usually for Sunday night *cena* when the store was closed, at least in the early years of the business. Then, too, she used to make various types of pizza for sale in the store, hot slices at lunch time and varieties packaged for home consumption after re-heating. *Tempo Romano*, located in Via Dei Borghi, a small street behind the *Chiesa di Santa Maria dei Angeli*, was owned and operated by a Neapolitan, Salvatore Salerno, who used a wood burning oven to make pizzas with a thin but firm crust, the tastiest tomato sauce prepared with just the right combination of olive oil (very little), basil and garlic. The individual sized pizzas were covered with evenly spread mozzarella so that no splotches were visible. An appetizing looking pizza was set before the customer, and its consumption fulfilled the expectations that its presentation promised. This particular evening Daniel sat at one of the six tables that occupied the tight premises, and noticed that there was only one other person in the restaurant, a boyish looking young woman who sat sideways to him. At seven o'clock, it was still too early for the real Romans to dine. They would come in later in the evening, starting at around nine o'clock. Daniel was aware of this and thought this other person was either a tourist or one of the exchange students. The young woman turned her head and he saw that his hunch was correct. Annemarie Taviani smiled and Daniel asked if he could join her. He felt awkward since weeks had passed since he had spoken to her about getting together for a meal. He felt the need to apologize.

"Well, we finally get together, accidentally as it turns out. I really meant to call you or leave a note about meeting to continue our conversation, but things have been so hectic."

"That's quite all right," she replied. "No need to apologize. I know how overwhelming this Italian life style can be. Add to that our American compulsion to achieve as much as possible as quickly as possible, and no time is left over for anything else."

Daniel detected a tone of irony in her comments, especially with the word "overwhelming." He thought she was mocking him, tenderly, yes, without evident derision.

"The important thing is that we have another chance to talk, if you have the time, of course."

"Certainly."

"Do you come here often?"

"Not very often, but I've been here a number of times since I began attending the Academy. Another American recommended it to me. He's from New Haven and insists that the best pizza in the United States can be found in New Haven. He claims that American pizza originated in New Haven. Have you ever been there?" Daniel said he had not.

"We used to drive down from Boston to visit my aunt, my father's sister, and I remember that there seemed to be many more pizzerias than in Boston, even considering the Italian section in North Boston."

"You know it's really opportune that I ran into you tonight."

"Really? Why?"

"Professor Stagione insists that his conducting students become familiar with each and every instrument in the orchestra–not just familiar, one must also be able to play the instrument, at least in a rudimentary fashion."

"One cannot argue against the principle involved."

"Exactly."

"Still, it has to be a huge undertaking."

Daniel laughed, grateful for the opportunity to solidify his earlier contention.

"Yes, so you see why I unwillingly neglected to contact you?"

Why does he have to be so self-righteous, Annemarie thought. She couldn't understand why he found it necessary to prove his point. She was already well beyond that.

"And why was this meeting so serendipitous?"

"Because I was thinking about your instrument today and I had a technical question and wanted to ask your opinion about it."

"Shoot," she said, matter-of-factly.

"Actually, it doesn't really have to do with playing the viola, but with the viola's placement in the orchestra."

"Its placement? I'm afraid I don't understand your question."

"Let me explain," Daniel continued. "I was looking through a book of orchestras of the world, complete with photographs. I noticed that some orchestras from Germany and Austria place the violas on the outside, while all the American, French and English orchestras and most other orchestras throughout the world place them inside, with the cellos outside."

Annemarie smiled since this was a question she had herself wondered about and had done some research on.

"I guess the easiest answer would be 'tradition,' but in actual fact tradition would dictate that the second violins be placed on the outside on the right. I found in my readings and study that this was the normal practice everywhere until the beginning of this century."

Daniel was very impressed by the young musician's seriousness in replying to his question, and especially impressed that she knew so much about a topic that he had so little knowledge of himself.

"Please go on, this is fascinating." Annemarie acted as if she didn't hear what he said since she had every intention of continuing.

"As a violist, this is quite an important point for me. I feel that the viola in a good deal of the repertoire, especially the heavy Romantic orchestral works, gets lost among all the other instruments. Not having the especially high or low voice of many of the orchestra's other instruments, it doesn't have the same impact on the listener. Of course, any good conductor or sensitive and attentive listener would notice its absence immediately if it were somehow missing. This is exactly why these German and Austrian orchestras place the violas on the left. This way, their unique and beautiful sounds can be better heard. And after all, many composers have written wonderful music for the instrument, even within the confines of the orchestra."

"Wow! Thank you for explaining that to me. I know I'll have a much greater appreciation of the viola in the orchestra from now on. When the time comes for me to have any say in the matter, I'll experiment with its placement."

"You'll be in good company."

"How so?"

"Leopold Stokowski has been experimenting with instrument placement for some time."

"Really?"

Daniel liked Annemarie's manner, the way she spoke, her serious but gentle demeanor, her radiant smile and the way it lighted up her face, making him feel as though he were the only thing that mattered to her at that moment.

Afterwards, they walked back to their *pensione* together. Annemarie's was close to Daniel's. He left her, taking her hand in his lightly, but she, as if to prove that she could be decisive, grasped his hand firmly and shook it like a man would.

"Thank you for your help with my viola question."

"Anytime," she replied, turning quickly and entering the building.

Walking back to his room, Daniel thought about this interesting but somehow strange young woman. There was something about her that he found fascinating. She seemed to be strong and determined, forthright and sincere. And yet, thinking of her purely as a woman, comparing her to Marilyn or even to Jeanne, she held no appeal for him whatsoever. But still, there *was* something about her that made him want to get to know her better. Certainly her deep blue eyes, penetrating and scintillating, held a promise of the extraordinary.

Thirty

During the first three months of Daniel's stay in Rome, he and Marilyn communicated on a weekly basis. At first, her letters were impassioned love letters that made Daniel very happy and gave him hope that she would eventually change her mind about marrying him. As late as Thanksgiving, she had written:

"My love, I miss you more than ever. My bed is still cold and uninviting without you. I long for you in every fiber of my body, in every mental image I have throughout the day, in every dream I dream at night. Even my music making is less inspired without you here to listen and to give me the impetus I need to bring it to a higher level."

She asked him to try to make it home for the "winter break." She could not bring herself to write "home for Christmas," even though she knew that was what his family expected of him. Daniel's letters were always filled with statements of love and devotion, paeans of praise for her beauty and loveliness, epistles expressing the longing he felt for her day in, day out, day and night, night and day. In late November he wrote,

"My beautiful love, my darling Marilyn: the only thing that keeps me going is the knowledge that I will soon see you when I return home for the Christmas break. After being without you for the past three months, I know I cannot live without you indefinitely. You are everything to me. My career, my future only holds meaning for me because I have convinced myself that you will always be a part of it. Please tell me this is so."

When Daniel arrived in New York on December 15th, he telephoned Marilyn in Philadelphia. Getting no reply, he tried her parents' home in Silver Springs, Maryland. The phone rang and rang, but there was no reply. The next day, Violetta gave him a letter. It was from Marilyn and she explained that her parents had decided at the last minute to invite her to go with them to Israel, and she decided to take advantage of the opportunity since she had never been there and could possibly make some contacts for future performances in that area of the world. She knew that he would understand. Daniel became depressed and even though he kept assuring his family that he was all right, it was easy for them to see that he was not. Marilyn's letter was strangely devoid of any intimations of regret about canceling their planned reunion. It was as if they had never even discussed how they would do all the things their hearts were set on, enjoying the pleasures they had both come to cherish. Daniel could not stop thinking about it, blaming himself for having again brought up, if only indirectly, their eventual union in marriage. Before returning to Rome, he received a post card that simply and coldly gave him her greetings, not even a "miss you," or "wish you were here," to mollify the hurt he felt so intensely. Thereafter, when she returned to Curtis, her infrequent letters were disappointingly different. Even though he kept up the heated rhetoric in his epistles, she did not reply in kind. In March, she wrote about a professor from Israel who had come to Curtis for the Spring semester and, after hearing about her first trip to Israel and how much she enjoyed the country and the people, and then hearing her play the violin, suggested that she come to Tel Aviv for a year to continue her studies at the Institute for the Violin there. The professor's close friend, Seymour Slotnick, ran the Institute and had trained many of the finest Israeli violinists who were now in important positions in the finest orchestras worldwide. A few were involved, too, in successful solo careers. Daniel wrote back quickly, asking her to stop in Rome on her way to Israel. They could spend a week together. He felt like he was pleading, but he didn't care. Her reply came, not as quickly as he had hoped, but it might not have come at all, for it was curt and dismissive of his idea. He couldn't believe what he read. How could she do this? How could her attitude change so drastically in just a few months? He wrote back each day, asking for an explanation for her change of heart. Only once after that did she write anything that appeased his thirst for some tenderness from her.

"Just remember," she wrote, "what I said about my feelings for you and how they would never change no matter what happens. But we must both be sensible and move on."

She did not write again, either from Philadelphia or from Tel Aviv. The high level of Daniel's work declined and Professor Stagione, noticing that his student had a serious problem spoke to him about it one morning.

"Daniel, I know that you must be going through some personal crisis and I am not sure if it is something you want to discuss with me.

202

Nevertheless, the quality of your work has suffered and you will not be able to complete in one year what I had hoped for from you. I realize that everyone has problems from time to time, but having seen what you are capable of, I am willing to extend your stay here for an additional year so you can complete the course and leave with the highest marks. But it's up to you. Take some time, decide and let me know. However, if you stay, you will have to fall into line."

Daniel thanked his professor and assured him that he did want to complete the course. He appreciated his understanding and support.

Afterwards, Daniel went through days of self-recrimination, prideful attacks of blame against Marilyn, regrets, feelings of foolishness, and doubts about his own ability to maintain relationships. One day, walking by a record store, he heard a recording of Neapolitan songs. He had loved many of these songs ever since he first heard them years before. In his apartment he had an LP of *Canzone Napolitane* sung by Giuseppe Di Stefano. There was something in his bittersweet mood that was reflected in these songs, but he found that listening to songs like "Core 'ngrato" and "Una Sera e Maggio" only intensified his feeling of loss, the hurt he felt deep inside. Eventually, he threw himself into his work with renewed energy and determination. He practiced the piano for as many as seven hours each day. Still another seven hours were devoted to preparing scores to conduct, rehearsing, practicing playing other instruments in order to better appreciate their individual characteristics and the way they combined with other instruments or instrument groups. Stagione noted with pleasure this new thrust from his student, and was gratified that his initial hunch about the young man's promise was correct. His student's drive fed his own passion for hard work to achieve the extraordinary, and he found himself with a renewed vigor and a determined approach to fulfill his intense love for music by channeling his own energies through the intellect and emotions of one he identified with so closely. Stagione himself was on the road to a successful conducting career when, at the age of twenty-eight, he suffered a stroke. Intensive therapy provided him with a nearly complete recovery, but his right arm, the arm that he used to wield his baton, was left in a weakened state and he was unable to lift it higher than his waist.

Daniel's new assignment was Richard Strauss's *Metamorphosen for 23 strings*. The Professor loved the work and felt that the composer had poignantly expressed the extreme sadness that any sensitive person could not help feeling at the end of World War II, but this *tristezza* as he called it, was combined with a need for reconciliation and rapprochement among peoples, even those who had been enemies with one another. Having lived through the war years, serving in the Italian Army, Stagione could never forget the horrible scenes he had witnessed. He found that his young student brought such intensity of feeling to many of the pieces he conducted, especially to *Metamorphosen*, that he wondered how it was possible for someone who had not himself gone through personal tragedies to have such a sublime musical vision. The group conducted by Maestro Lorelli, as the students teasingly called him, was not the 23 strings called for, but a mere total of eleven. Annemarie Taviani was one of the two violists. When Professor Stagione heard the first non-rehearsal performance, he could not suppress the tears that came to his eyes. In Lorelli, he felt he had finally come upon the one man who could successfully convey his own principles concerning the art of conducting.

Annemarie Taviani watched Daniel Lorelli as he led the group she was part of and felt herself drawn in by this extraordinary conductor, this fellow-American whose impulses transmitted to her and to the other musicians a sureness about the way the music had to flow. Looking up at him from the music, his charisma was tangible. He was as the Italians would say, *simpatico*. She watched as his eyes closed when the music reached a point of intensity so moving that he became as one with it. She saw his abundant hair waving to and fro, and she thought to herself, this is a man I could see myself with.

Daniel became so involved with his work that he had little time for anything else. His parents telephoned and rarely found him available. They became concerned, but he eventually returned their calls, assuring them all was well. In the fall of Daniel's second year at l'Accademia di Santa Cecilia, a young soprano from Poland arrived for studies there. Margareta Komorowski already enjoyed a successful career in her native country. She had appeared in leading roles as Lucia in *Lucia di Lammermoor*, Mimi in *La Bohème*, and Violetta in *La Traviata*. She had been advised by her teachers in Poland that if she wanted to have an international career, she would have to have additional study. One of her Polish teachers had been the student of Professor Bruscantini at L'Accademia, and he agreed to accept her for advanced study. Bruscantini was a specialist in *bel canto*. He spoke to Stagione about his need for a sensitive and musical pianist to accompany Signorina Komorowski in some arias he had assigned to her. Stagione spoke to Daniel, and his young conducting student expressed regret, but indicated that all of his time was already accounted for. Daniel saw the professor's look of disappointment and quickly recanted, saying,

"I'm sorry, Professor. Even though my time is extremely limited, I will do it since you ask me."

"Daniel, I am not asking you only for personal reasons. Of course, I would like to comply with Bruscantini's request since he has always been cooperative with me. But over and above this, I hear that the young soprano is extremely talented and I think that practicing with her can give you important insights for conducting opera, an area you have not yet worked in at all."

It was agreed on, and Daniel was asked to appear at a special rehearsal area the following morning at 9:00 A.M. Daniel was on time. Bruscantini arrived at 9:15, but Signorina Komorowski was nowhere to be seen. Finally, at 10:05, she walked into the small hall. A real *prima donna*, Daniel thought. Daniel didn't mind too much for he used the hour to practice on the piano. However, when Signorina Komorowski walked in, she spoke to Professor Bruscantini in poor Italian, telling him she was ready and asking impatiently if the pianist had the right music, since Daniel was still playing the first movement from Schubert's *Sonata in G*. Daniel stopped playing, looked her directly in the eyes and said,

"I have been here waiting for you for an hour. In fact you have been delaying me as well as Professor Bruscantini. I trust this will not happen again, for my time is valuable."

Signorina Komorowski, turned her head quickly to the right, looked at Daniel sharply and said to Bruscantini,

"I don't need to be addressed in such a manner. Who is this upstart? I would prefer another pianist."

Daniel did not hesitate for a moment. He picked up his music, bowed his head to Professor Bruscantini, spoke three words, "*Buona mattina, Professore*," and walked out.

The next day, Signorina Komorowski arrived at the room where Daniel was conducting a small group of students in Mozart's Symphony No. 25 and sat in the back and waited. When the session ended and all the students had left, she walked up to Daniel and said in halting English,

"Maestro Lorelli, I think I owe you an apology. I was rude yesterday. You were right to walk away."

"You don't have to address me as Maestro. You may call me Daniel."

"Margareta," the young soprano replied, extending her hand.

"I wish you would reconsider. I do need the best pianist available and I know you are that person."

Daniel agreed and for the following three months, he accompanied Signorina Komorowski two mornings each week and found that all that he learned was well worth the time expended. Bruscantini's remarks encompassed so many aspects of the operas and of opera performance itself, that Daniel would remember important points he made years later when he himself conducted the operas they had worked on together.

At the end of a session one morning, Margareta asked Daniel if he would like to join her for supper that evening. Daniel hesitated. He really did not want to socialize with any woman since his wounds from the hurt inflicted on him by Marilyn were still fresh. The best thing was to keep everything business-like. He needed to keep his head clear, but the weakness in his character, as he sometimes thought of it, his inability to turn someone down if they asked him for something, even if he felt it was not in his best interest, this character flaw, for thusly he himself thought of it, had him saying,

"Yes, I would be delighted."

Margareta was a woman that most men would have gone after within a heartbeat. She had long blonde hair which she usually wore pinned up, light blue eyes, and a figure that boasted dimensions that fit together perfectly. Men could not take their eyes off her. In Poland, those who saw photos of her before hearing her sing would bet that her voice could not possibly match her looks. Those bets were all lost once the beauty of her voice was heard. Daniel was not so enthralled. Images of his dark haired love still burned in his imagination. This blonde was pretty, yes, but nothing so special as far as he was concerned. He admired the quality of her voice and her musical intelligence more than her physical beauty. Then too, what he interpreted as her haughty personality was off-putting for Daniel, and he did not even once consider the possibility of an amorous exchange between them. As a man with natural desires and inclinations towards the opposite sex, he could not help stealing glances at the shape of her legs under black, white or flesh colored stockings, or the manner in which her hips gracefully swept around to meet her shapely posterior when she wore tight fitting slacks. But as Daniel sat at the piano accompanying the young singer, he forced himself to look away from these potentially stimulating exposures.

After a light repast, during which they both enjoyed a conversation wherein each could sense the passion the other brought to his or her involvement with music, Daniel accompanied Margareta back to her quarters, an apartment that was being lent to her by Italian friends of her Polish teacher. She asked Daniel to come in for a drink, and he reluctantly agreed to do so.

Malgorzata Komorowski—she took on "Margareta" when she had been singing professionally for a few years, believing the non-Polish sound would make her name easier to remember—was born and raised in Warsaw. Her father was a director of a local theater specializing in contemporary Polish drama. Her mother began her own attenuated career as a cabaret singer, a diversion at best, until Malgorzata came along, followed soon thereafter by Stanislaus, three years younger than his sister. Teresa Staniszewski was an opera singer at heart, but she never had the opportunity to study opera or to pursue a career therein. When Malgorzata was born, the first thing Teresa said to her husband Kazimierz about their daughter, "She will be an opera star," was indicative of her determination to direct her daughter towards that goal.

Kazimierz laughed and replied jocularly,

"Not if I have anything to say about it. I prefer a dramatic actress in the family."

"In the world of opera, she can be both," Teresa countered, and of course Kazimierz's say in the matter was totally ignored. A year after Malgorzata's birth, the Warsaw Opera's home, the Wielki Theater was bombed and almost completely destroyed. Teresa wept bitterly when she saw the condition of the building she had loved, an edifice that had been considered one of Warsaw's most imposing and beautiful structures. She had worked inside the building, serving refreshments to the opera's patrons and stealing each and every opportunity she could to see parts of performances. During the remaining years of the War, the company was silent, but in 1945, they began to perform on various stages available throughout Warsaw and its environs while their permanent home was being rebuilt. It finally re-opened in 1965.

Teresa played old records for her daughter, arias from operas by Rossini, Donizetti, Verdi and Puccini, for she loved Italian opera above all others. Later she would introduce her to Gounod, Massenet and Bizet, giving her young daughter a taste for the different if still impassioned sounds of the French composers. When Malgorzata was seven, Teresa took her daughter to any opera performances she could possibly arrange to attend. One of Kazimierz's friends worked in the financial end of the Warsaw Opera and he provided Teresa and her daughter with passes, sometimes even for seats in the front of the orchestra when a late cancellation came in. It was in viewing performances from this vantage point that the young Malgorzata developed her own love for musical drama, for she could see the expressions on the faces of the singers as they performed their roles. Some of the venues were small, adding to the intimate feeling and connection with the singers. Even though she hardly ever knew exactly what they were singing, her mother had sketched out the action for her before their trip to the opera house, and she accurately guessed the nature of the various emotions by the gestures of the singers and the twinkle or tears in their eyes.

By the age of ten, Malgorzata was accepted for singing lessons by a former member of the chorus of the Warsaw Opera, a soprano who was highly respected locally for her ability to identify and nourish native talent. These first lessons were merely attempts to provide the young girl with an understanding of the relationships between the human voice and the musical sounds that it was possible to encompass, specifically the female voice. Although at an early age it is not fully possible to determine the future range the voice would adapt to, Olga Toniuszko accurately predicted that Malgorzata's voice would develop into a full throated soprano, capable of performing dramatic and *bel canto* roles.

At the age of seventeen, Malgorzata got a lucky break. She had been engaged to sing in the chorus of a secondary but important opera company that performed in and around Warsaw, and prior to the season opening a well known Polish soprano who was slated to sing Mimi in a new production of *La Boheme* came down with bronchitis. The company's music director, Tomasz Zagorski was a man of vision with a strong sense of the dramatic, even outside of operatic performance. He had come by his own first important appointment as a result of another conductor's indisposition, and he thought it would be exciting and fascinating to find a new singer who could capture the public's imagination. As a publicity device for the theater, it could also provide a much needed boost. And so, while the chorus master was rehearsing, Zagorski interrupted and made the announcement that he was looking for a replacement soprano, but he needed someone who already knew and could sing the role of Mimi. Four sopranos indicated their interest and he asked them to visit him in his rehearsal room the following morning, at half hour intervals. If he selected one of them, she would have to spend the rest of the day in rehearsal. Malgorzata was the only one of the four who truly knew the role, and she also had the best voice. Zagorski felt that his plan was working out much better than he had hoped for, since the young soprano was extremely attractive physically with a voice that was exceptional without additional considerations. The performance was a sensation, Malgorzata received seven curtain calls and her career in Poland was launched.

Malgorzata continued to sing leading roles with Zagorski's company for the next four years and was being considered for a major role with the Warsaw Opera. Poland's most important opera company was still not in their rebuilt home theater, and the Director suggested to Malgorzata's mother, who was still acting as her agent of sorts, that her admittedly talented daughter needed additional vocal training if she were to be prepared for an international career. Her talent was obvious, but if she was to avoid the lances that would surely be hurled at her by the critical press, and survive the obvious jealousies of all those in the world of opera who were not prepared to make room for talented newcomers, she would have to work hard to eliminate some of the idiosyncrasies in her technique. By going to Italy to study with the Director's old friend Bruscantini, she would certainly, he felt, return to Poland prepared for her place as one of the country's leading sopranos, and from there receive invitations to sing at the world's major opera houses–La Scala, the Vienna State Opera, the Deutsch Oper, Berlin, the Metropolitan Opera in New York!

Once in Italy, Signorina Komorowski decided to henceforth use "Margareta" as her professional name. As she and Daniel Lorelli were sharing the bottle of Pinot Grigio she opened, Margareta filled Daniel in on her professional life to that point. She felt comfortable enough to talk about her family and prodded Daniel to tell her about his own personal history.

"So your family are Roman Catholics?"

"Of course," Daniel laughed, "Do you know any Italian families that are not?"

"It seems to me that most of the people I know in Poland are more devout than the Italians I have met here. The churches that are not filled with tourists are basically empty for Sunday Mass."

"Yes, that's true," Daniel agreed, "But back home, at least where I grew up in Brooklyn, the churches are filled every Sunday–each Mass from the Six O'clock Mass to the Twelve-Fifteen."

"So you are a practicing Catholic?"

"Yes, of course!" Daniel asserted with a mixture of matter-of-factness and pride.

"That's good to hear." Margareta's tone was now much gentler and less arrogant than what Daniel had become accustomed to. Her accent, too, which he found grating at times, now possessed a lovely appealing lilt. "I will look for you at Mass on Sunday. You do attend?"

"Yes, I do," Daniel said somewhat hesitantly since he did not make a point of going to Mass each and every Sunday anymore, even if he did attend when the spirit took hold of him. Then, looking into his young colleague's eyes, which had not seemed so open and honest to him before, he admitted,

"Not every Sunday, but I do attend when I can   .   .   . or when I want to, I should say."

"Bravo," Margareta said, smiling approvingly. "I know what you mean. I am the same. But if you don't mind my asking . . ." and she hesitated.

"Go ahead, ask me anything you like," he offered disarmingly.

"I am curious about just how much you believe of your Faith and how much you adhere to the teachings of the Church. I mean, I have friends and relatives in Poland who believe each and every article of faith, and whatever the Pope says must be done, they go along with, without even questioning anything."

"Well, if you are a Catholic, you must believe these things. The Pope is infallible in matters of faith and . . ." Daniel broke off because he suddenly felt like a hypocrite about the "morals" part that was to finish his statement. He had reservations about the Church's teachings on premarital sex, but he did not feel comfortable bringing this up with Margareta.

"What about birth control in marriage?" the young soprano asked. "Do you think the Church should tell young couples how to act in their private lives?"

"There are methods of birth control that the Church approves," Daniel offered, adhering to an argument he had put forward when he was still in high school, although he himself had been more convinced of its validity at that time than he was on this day, talking to Margareta, whose provocative tone forced him to think twice.

"Oh, of course, you mean the, how do you say it in English, a musical word?"

"The rhythm method," Daniel said.

Margareta laughed,

"Yes, of course. I have a cousin in Poland who wanted at most three children. She spoke to her confessor and he told her that she must absolutely not fall into the selfishness that is the 'scourge of the modern world.' I think that's what he said. He told her that he understood the difficulty of raising children and that the Church understands and makes it possible for young couples to enjoy their conjugal experiences and still not interfere with the natural order!" Margareta was quite agitated at this point and Daniel was slightly embarrassed. Not knowing exactly what to say, he asked,

"What did she do?"

"What did she do? She followed his advice—the advice of an old man who never took care of a child in his life—and now she has six children with another on the way. And the woman is a wreck!"

Daniel suddenly felt stupid.

"I guess people need to make their own choices."

"Yes. That is what I intend to do. How can I maintain my career if I become pregnant every year or two? Suppose you and I were married. As the husband of a talented singer, you being a talented musician yourself, would you dare to ask me to give everything up because of some silly rule that a bunch of old men who have never even been married want to impose on the members of their church?"

Daniel drifted off into thoughts of being married to Margareta and appeared to her to be staring into space.

"Well?" she asked.

"Oh, I'm sorry. You are right. I think it's something people have to decide for themselves, but I don't think one can be truly a member of the Catholic Church if one does not at least try to follow its precepts."

"I think that is a naïve attitude."

"Possibly," Daniel hesitantly agreed. "It's late, I should get going."

"I'm sorry. I didn't mean for this to turn so serious."

"Oh, that's all right. I really don't mind. I enjoy discussing these things. I'll think about what we've discussed and we can pick it up again." With that, Daniel took Margareta's hand and she leaned over to kiss him on the cheek.

The next time they practiced together, Margareta appeared more beautiful than ever to Daniel. As they worked together on "Casta Diva" from Bellini's *Norma*, one of the most difficult of all roles for sopranos, Daniel admired the way she worked, so diligently, completely devoted to what she was doing. There was no time for distractions of any kind. Professor Bruscantini was pleased with his student's progress. Her singing was so limpid, so passionate. Once or twice he stopped her to comment on her accenting of certain words.

"Bellini was one of the greatest composers for setting words to music, and if you can make the most of what is already there, your identification with the role will be complete–your performance will be truly masterly." Bruscantini smiled and Margareta and Daniel both felt fortunate to be beneficiaries of the older man's wisdom. Daniel was hoping to organize an opera performance when he returned to the States. He wasn't sure yet which opera he would choose for his debut as an opera conductor, but he knew that he would consider Bruscantini's advice quite seriously.

At the end of the session, Margareta seemed overcome with emotion and completely in another world. Daniel was about to leave the room without a word, but suddenly as he was turning she called out to him.

"Daniel, you played beautifully, as usual. I hope we will be able to share recitals when we are both active in our careers. Imagine us both at Carnegie Hall in New York some day!"

"Yes, that would be wonderful," Daniel said, marveling at her sudden transformation from a state of total concentration on her singing to her best social demeanor.

"Daniel, we must have another supper together one evening."

"I would love it."

"This time I will cook for you," and seeing the professor listening to her as he gathered some papers, she added,

"Professor Bruscantini could join us too if he would do me the honor."

It was settled, and a week later, on a Friday evening, Margareta prepared her own version of a Roman *cena*. The two guests were complete gentlemen, praising her culinary skills, even if they did not match her main attributes as a woman and a soprano. After two hours the Professor excused himself and Margareta and Daniel were left to finish the bottle of wine started during the meal. Daniel felt guilty about his new feelings towards the young woman. He was in love with Marilyn. He had determined that he would find her and convince her that they must be together. He would do that before returning to the United States. Why, then, was he feeling this new attraction towards Margareta? How could he be so shallow? As they sat next to each other on the sofa, Margareta's leg was touching his. She was wearing a tight skirt that rode up as she crossed her legs, the heel of her shoe touching his leg. Perhaps buoyed up by the second glass of wine, Daniel turned, facing Margareta and whispered,

"You are so beautiful."

"What?" she asked, laughing gently.

"You are so beautiful. Excuse me, I guess the atmosphere, the food, the wine are making me bolder than I should be."

"Not at all. Please tell me more."

"Well, you know that at first we did not hit it off, and I saw only that side of you."

"Which side?"

"Well, how shall I characterize it? The abrupt side."

"That's generous. Why don't you say the truth: the obnoxious side? I know I can be a *prima donna* at times, and I would not admit this to anyone. But with you, I feel differently. I feel I can open up to you. There is something about you that makes a person want to confide in you. Perhaps it's your total lack of guile. Even Bruscantini admires this about you."

"He does?" Daniel was surprised that the Professor had any personal thoughts about him at all.

"Yes. And I will tell you something because I care for you. Don't mention to him that I told you this!" Daniel looked at Margareta and quickly agreed,

"No, of course not,"

"Well, you must know that he admires your musicianship."

"Yes, I guess so."

"However, he told me that he is worried that you may not have the career you deserve because you are too, what is the word, too gentle. No, *gentile in Italiano vuole dire un'altra cosa.* Well, I guess it could mean gentle too, but kind, too kind. He thinks you need to be much more assertive and even selfish if you are to succeed as a conductor. He said the only time he saw you act out of character, at least what he considers to be out of character for you, was the first day when you were walked out because I was late and nasty too."

"Yes," Daniel mused, "I guess that was unlike me, but it happened on a day when I was very upset about a personal matter."

"Can you tell me about it?" Margareta's tone, the expression on her face, the sincerity apparent in her every gesture, all conspired to soften Daniel's resolve to avoid discussing Marilyn with anyone. He told her about their relationship and about the hurt he felt and continued to feel because of her incomprehensible actions. He continued, telling Margareta about his feelings of guilt in even thinking about her as a desirable woman because of his sense of loyalty to Marilyn. Margareta, seeing his obvious emotional turmoil, put her arms around him and hugged him tightly. Then she slowly pulled back and looked at him directly, becoming herself mesmerized by his striking blue eyes, now sparkling less than usual due to some moisture that was forming, not just yet into tears. When Daniel said all he could say, Margareta spoke,

"I had a lover too, the only man I was ever intimate with. He was the tenor who sang opposite me when I got my big break. Fifteen years older than I, he knew how to manipulate a woman. Even though I did not want to get involved with a man, he convinced me that he loved me. But once he got what he wanted, he went on to his next conquest. If he had been anything like you, I would surely have married him."

This was the second time that Margareta had referred to marriage involving him and her. A slight frown came over his face. She noticed.

"Oh, don't worry. I am not suggesting anything. Now I am determined to devote myself solely to my career. Marriage will have to wait."

Daniel moved towards her and she met his lips, pulling him towards her with both hands behind his head.

"Daniel, I want you to . . . make love to me."

"I want to, too, but Margareta, what about, you know? Are you sure?"

"Again the restrictions imposed by celibate old men? Daniel, I am a woman. I know what sex is. I have a natural need for it. I have not slept with anyone since I slept with him. I am not promiscuous, and you are not either. That is why I want to make love to you. You are a man. I know you desire me. I can tell by the way you look at me at times." That was all Daniel needed. He unbuttoned her blouse and ran his fingers up inside her thighs.

In their next session practicing music together soprano and pianist were both at the top of their form. Margareta sang "Pace, pace mio Dio," from Verdi's *La Forza del Destino.* Bruscantini glowed.

"I can find no fault with either of you. You are both perfect today. Being old and wise, Bruscantini knew that his two young musicians had shared intimacies that made their making music together more powerful and beautiful than ever before. He knew, of course, that this did not work for and with everyone, but for these two sensitive souls, he knew that it had worked very, very well indeed.

Thirty-One

Before Violetta Nardi's first son was born, Paola Manfredi already had four children. At the time of Matthew's accident, Paola was pregnant, and in 1936 a daughter, Caterina, was born, followed a year later by a son, Giuseppe. Renato Manfredi had developed a very successful cabinet making business. He specialized in fine furniture for homes, offices and stores. He refused to work with anything but real wood, the finest wood available. As his business was developing, inexpensive furniture was becoming the norm in American homes. Pressed wood dominated the market and Renato received offers for jobs that could have turned his company into a goldmine, mass production type runs of thousands of cabinets, but he refused these offers each and every time. In order to continue doing the fine work he was accustomed to, however, he needed real artisans and to get them he had to sponsor cabinet makers from southern Italy, making it possible for them to get the necessary papers to emigrate and helping to pay their voyage over. Invariably, these men would work for Renato for a year or two and then move on to another job where they could earn more. But Renato's company prospered. There is always a need for fine furniture, and his company was one of very few around that could meet this need.

From a very early age, Giuseppe or Joseph Manfredi had problems breathing. He was diagnosed with asthma while in first grade. The condition persisted throughout his childhood and Joseph wanted to know more about this illness. In high school he became determined to become a doctor and to do research in pulmonary medicine. He was an extremely intelligent young man and gained entrance to medical school without any problem whatsoever. Like Daniel Lorelli, Joseph Manfredi had vivid feelings about having lived before. He would always remember distinct sensations he had had at the age of four or five, when he could vaguely recall having been in situations like those he now and then found himself in. Family gatherings, certain smells, tunes he heard on the radio as his mother listened to the Italian station—all these things triggered a certain recognition, indistinct but amazingly evocative. He also had disturbing dreams, dreams that recurred over the years. These dreams always involved an aspect of being smothered, of not being able to breathe.

When Joseph had completed his first year in medical school, Paola and Renato decided to visit Italy. It was to be their first trip back to the land of their birth since Paola returned to America in 1935. Joseph had had a very intensive year, and he accepted his parents' offer to join them. He agreed to take a much needed two-week vacation and meet them in Calabria. Everything about the country fascinated him and he was interested in meeting some of the relatives he had never known. For some weeks before the trip, he again had disturbing dreams about suffocating, but now the cause of his problem was clear, at least in his dreams. He was breathing poisonous gas and he was involved in a war. More and more he felt that going to Italy, to Calabria was somehow connected with his dreams. When he arrived, his dreams became more intense. Walking through the town, Joseph felt sensations of recognition. The buildings, the streets, the churches, the view towards the sea—all seemed somehow familiar in a way he could not quite fathom. One day, as he was walking around Longobardi with his mother, they passed a house that attracted his attention more than any of the others. It was like a radar detector, where the signals get stronger and more frequent the closer one comes to the radar being sent out. He stopped and said to Paola,

"Mamma, whose house is this? Did our family ever live here?"

"No, I showed you the house we used to live in, the house where I grew up and where your father grew up, and the house where I was living when my baby died."

"But Mamma," Joseph persisted, "I know I have been here before. Can we go inside?

"Don't be silly."

"Please, let's knock and see if we can just go inside."

Paola knocked and was greeted by a young woman who, after introductions, asked them to come in. Paola had known the young woman's grandmother who now lived in Rome. Her mother and father used the house for summer vacations, usually the entire month of August. She herself was studying medicine in Rome and was in Longobardi for a brief vacation, but while her parents went to the seashore, she preferred to stay at home to study. Speaking Italian, haltingly, Joseph asked the woman about the families that lived in the house before. Silvana Truscello indicated that she had studied English, so the conversation proceeded with words from both languages. She could not really go back too far, but through a series of questions and some discussion, Paola was able to recall that this was the house that Violetta Nardi had lived in before she was married, the house that belonged to Francesco Nardi, who had died about ten years earlier. As they looked about the house and entered a bedroom, Joseph's inner turmoil was obvious to his mother and to Silvana. He excused himself, saying he could not talk just then. Later, he told his mother that he had dreamed of lying in a bed in that exact room the night before. He was lying there being assisted by a woman. He was again, just as in all his dreams, having difficulty breathing. There was another woman too, a woman he felt an attraction for, standing near the bed looking at him, smiling with tears in her eyes. That woman was Silvana Truscello. He had seen her in his dream the night before. Paola dismissed all of her son's thoughts as mere fantasies.

"Joseph, you have always had a vivid imagination and this is just another example of it."

"But Mamma, since I was a kid I have had dreams involving breathing problems. You know that I have always thought I lived before this life. I think I may have died in that house we were in today. And I think that Silvana Truscello was there too."

"Joseph, I think you should talk to a priest. You know these beliefs are against our religion. These are beliefs of other religions, not ours,"

"That's not strictly true. There are references to reincarnation in the writings and traditions of most religions."

"I never heard of any reference in Catholicism, and I have been a Catholic all my life."

"That's because you never looked into it, but there are actual indications."

"I don't believe it," Paola said, now angry and intent on dropping the matter, but she continued, "Look, I can't tell you what to believe. You are old enough to know what you want. Why don't you go to see our old friend Violetta Lorelli when you get back to New York? She lived in that house. I'm sure she can set you straight. And be careful, because she is a very strict Catholic, more religious than I am."

"I remember the name, but refresh my memory. Who is she?"

"We used to visit one another's families when you kids were small, but they got very busy with their business and we lost touch. They are the family who own Mamma's Kitchen."

"Oh, now I remember," and making a mental note to look her up, Joseph let the matter drop there.

Before leaving Longobardi, Joseph visited Silvana again and took her telephone number and address in Rome. The young woman did not know exactly why, but she felt a strange attraction to this young American. Perhaps it's because we are both medical students, she thought.

Upon arriving in New York, Joseph Manfredi was determined to meet Violetta Lorelli. He went to the family's original store in Brooklyn and asked for her. He was greeted by John Lorelli who remembered Joseph's parents and graciously offered to be of any service he could. He told Joseph that his mother was at home that day and gave him her address. Joseph went over to the family's expansive house, surrounded by a fancy wrought iron gate. As he opened the gate and was making his way up the walkway, Violetta looked down from her terrace. Immediately, she was overcome by a feeling that this was someone she knew. Of course she had known Joseph as a youngster, but she had not seen him in over fifteen years. There was something about him that stirred her soul. She came down to open the door and when Joseph asked, "Violetta?" her heart seemed to flutter. Joseph felt an immediate affinity with this woman. He knew before she replied that she was the person he was seeking. Violetta, now in her late fifties, was still quite a beautiful woman. Years of hard work had neither diminished her physical appearance nor dimmed the luster that shone in her eyes and made those who came into contact with her certain that here was a woman who could be trusted. Suddenly, looking at Joseph, almost involuntarily she inquired,

"Gaetano?"

"No, "Joseph replied, "Giuseppe, Joseph. I am the son of old friends of yours, Renato and Paola Manfredi."

"Oh, Paola and Renato," Violetta exclaimed. "I have not seen them for such a long time. We were always good friends, but you know what the life in this country does. In the early days we used to visit all the *paesani,* but now it seems the only time we see anyone is at a wedding or a funeral."

"Why did you call me Gaetano?" Joseph asked, anxiously, sensing that his hunches were correct all along.

"Gaetano was my brother. He died after the War. I don't know why, but when I saw you, for a minute I thought I was seeing him again."

"Do I look like him?"

"No, not at all."

"Then why?"

"I don't really know, " Violetta replied, "But something about you just touched off a memory that was so strong for a moment that I just said his name without even realizing it." Violetta smiled her warm and engaging smile and Joseph knew this smile, this tenderness that came from the older woman's face and bearing.

"I know why you called me Gaetano," Joseph said, measuring each word.

"You do?" Violetta laughed. "Tell me then."

"I was your brother Gaetano in my last life."

"I am Catholic and as a Catholic, I don't believe in those things. But it's funny, my son Daniel also believes in past lives."

"Is he here?"

"No, actually, he is in Italy, studying conducting. He is a musician, a very talented musician if I say so myself."

"Oh, that's a pity. I just returned from Italy and would have liked to have met him."

Joseph went on to tell Violetta about his visit to Longobardi and his feelings about the house he had seen that was her house at one time, as he had been informed by his mother. He told her about his dreams and about the specific dream he had had of lying in a bed in that house. Violetta was amazed. Some of the details he mentioned concerned things that only she knew about, things she had never mentioned to anyone.

"In my dream there was another woman, a woman standing near the bed who was smiling with tears in her eyes."

Joseph's words brought everything back to Violetta with sudden force.

"Yes, yes, there was such a woman. It was Silvia. She was in love with my brother and he loved her too. He wanted to marry her when he came back from the war, but he came back too sick to do anything but lie in bed and die, suffering greatly because he could not breathe."

"What happened to Silvia?"

"After Gaetano died she became totally depressed. She had survived the Spagnola, but she came down with an infection and died three months after he died. She just didn't want to live without him."

"That's incredible!" Joseph remarked. He went on to tell Violetta about his asthma, how he decided to study medicine because of it, how he had had these recurring dreams for many years, and how they had intensified when he went to Italy for the first time. Violetta did not scoff at the young man's remarks, for being the open person she was and having an expansive attitude and outlook towards life, people and yes, even religion, she took Joseph's hands in hers and said,

"Son, there is so much we do not know. Who knows? Perhaps you are right. Perhaps we did live before. I have great faith in the teachings of my

Church, but this does not mean that we know everything. Yes, we believe it is the one true faith, Catholicism, but it is possible that for whatever reason the Church does not reveal everything about the afterlife. Maybe it is a combination of things. We could be born again and eventually go back to God as our Church teaches."

Violetta was a devout Catholic, a woman devoted to her faith and to its precepts, but unlike many others who believed as strongly as she did, she did not, could not by her very nature scoff at or deride what another person believed.

Joseph was impressed by this woman's wisdom. Unlike others he had spoken to who just thought his beliefs about reincarnation were nonsense, she listened, evaluated and allowed that he could be right.

As Joseph Manfredi continued in medical school, he gradually decided to change his direction. Instead of pursuing pulmonary medicine as his specialty, he decided to go into psychiatry. He met a doctor on the teaching staff who had written a number of articles about past life regression. Joseph approached Dr. Franklin Peabody and asked for a conference. He told the doctor about his dreams, his experiences in Calabria and his meeting with Violetta. Dr. Peabody became very excited when he heard his young student's story. Dr. Peabody had fast garnered a reputation as one of the foremost psychiatrists exploring the use of this form of therapy to resolve conflicts in patients when traditional methods failed completely. His success was catching the attention of many who had previously scoffed at such ideas.

"How is your asthma now?" he asked.

"It's not as bad as it used to be, but medically speaking this could be a result of growing out of it. I think I know what you are getting at, and to go further, I do still have dreams about suffocation. Do you think a past life regression can help me?"

"From what you have told me," the older doctor continued, "I am fairly certain that you already know who you were in your last life, but we can see about ascertaining this through regression therapy."

After further meetings between the two men, when they got to know each other better, Dr. Peabody placed Joseph under hypnosis and explored the young man's prior life. He spoke in vivid detail about the hardships he had faced as a foot soldier and how he and his fellow soldiers had to face the constant danger of gunfire and poisonous gas. He recalled how he had succumbed to the gas after not using his gas mask quickly enough. There was something about the gas's odor which was different from what they had been accustomed to. Vividly, he saw how he had been carried away on a stretcher. He had glimpses of the care he received from his sisters, one of them being especially attentive to his needs. And he saw the woman he loved, feeling frustrated at not being able to carry on a conversation with her. Gradually, Dr. Peabody took Joseph back to a life prior to his life as a soldier in the Great War. He had been a farmer in Sicily in the early 1800's, dying peacefully at home as an old man around the end of the 19th century. Joseph planned to make past life therapy an important part of his practice as a psychiatrist. He flew to Rome whenever he had any time off and after a two year, mostly long distance courtship, he married Silvana Truscello, with both families celebrating the wedding in Rome. Having received her medical degree, Silvana studied and took the boards in New York and began to practice her specialty, gynecology. Joseph wanted her to undergo a past life regression with Dr. Peabody, but Silvana was too much the scientist to give much credence to theories that could not be tested in the laboratory. As a form of fantasy, she liked to think that she had been the Silvia who stood next to Gaetano's bed and died soon after he did, and that her husband and she had come together in a new life to fulfill their great love. She would tease Joseph about psychiatry.

"You know as well as I do that psychiatry is the least scientific and therefore most questionable of all the branches of medicine."

Joseph would merely smile, certain that one day he would prove the validity of his theories to his beautiful and intelligent wife.

Thirty-Two

After his first night of intimacy with Margareta, Daniel had feelings of guilt from two different perspectives. One was religious while the other was ethical, but an ethics independent of religion. As a believing Catholic, he still felt some guilt, if not very much, about having sexual relations outside of marriage. He was becoming too cosmopolitan to allow those feelings to interfere with his natural desires. Besides, Margareta, though a Catholic herself, had wanted to make love to him, and she had initiated it. This was revelatory for one whose upbringing somehow dictated that women did not pursue sex as men do, that woman, perhaps, did not even enjoy sex. He remembered overhearing a conversation between his mother and a customer one day in the store. It was late, near closing time, and Violetta, being the concerned and solicitous person she was, listened attentively as the woman complained about her husband. Daniel had walked in to ask his mother a question and Violetta was unaware he was there.

"Try to approach him in a sweet way. Sometimes, this works when nothing else will. Are you affectionate? Try to rekindle the warmth that was surely between the two of you in the beginning."

"Oh, please!" the woman replied. "Affectionate? My husband doesn't understand the word. Listen, he wants sex. He does what he has to do in bed, but that's it, without even kissing me."

"You have to use those times to re-build your relationship with him," Violetta persisted.

"I only do it because I have to. I have never enjoyed sex."

"I see," Violetta said. She turned to her work, closing the conversation by saying, "I wish you the best." She knew that further discussion at that point was futile

Daniel never forgot that conversation. At times he had wondered why his mother did not try to persuade the woman further, eventually recognizing her wisdom in the matter. But this and other things he had heard woman say left him with the general impression that woman could take sex or leave it. It was not as important for them as it was for men. His relationship with Marilyn helped to change his viewpoint, for she seemed to genuinely crave and enjoy sex, and she was often the initiator when they made love. Now he had this further proof from Margareta. She had told him she had a need for sex, hadn't she? And after their first time together, she was the one who arranged every subsequent encounter. On one occasion when he wanted to act as the aggressor she did not respond. Daniel went to her apartment one evening, filled with desire for the soprano, but when Margareta came to the door, she made it clear she was not prepared to satisfy him that time. His feelings of guilt were concerned with what he himself considered disloyalty to Marilyn, whom he continued to love and to feel he would still one day marry. Daniel's character encompassed what he would one day himself come to think of as a flaw—an inability emotionally to allow a relationship to end. He felt an obligation to maintain contact, a need to continue to somehow prove that all he had "promised," his words and actions, would not merely dissolve with time. This was true of his relationships with men as well as with women. There were not many that he called "friend," for he disliked using the term loosely. He had few true friends, and when this special bond was established he would never do anything to sever it. He had known one of his best friends, Ernesto Savalla, from early childhood. They had been in the same classes from elementary school through high school. After college, Ernie became a successful investment banker, met his wife in college and eventually settled in Greenwich, Connecticut. Daniel never failed to at the very least telephone his old friend whenever he was in New York and they would sometimes meet for lunch in Manhattan.

Daniel felt guilt, too, because he made love to Margareta without completely loving her, without giving her his heart. But how could he do this when his heart was still owned by Marilyn? And, in view of that love, how could he make love to another? Oh, yes, one time would be a temporary slip, but continued lovemaking should not go on without a sense of commitment between two people. Gradually, though, this intimate merging of his flesh with hers brought feelings of love to this relationship too, and Daniel began to suggest that there could be more, that the two could have a future together. For her part, Margareta genuinely liked Daniel, but she could not see anything permanent between them. They were much too different. Their backgrounds were markedly dissimilar and even this would not be such a problem if they were both going to be in the same place for a prolonged period of time, but she knew this could not be the case since their individual careers would keep them apart regularly. Besides, Margareta's determination to work out everything according to her plan to become an international opera star was so great, that she would not allow anything or anyone to change it. She saw her relationship with Daniel as one that could be practically useful for her future.

When they parted company on Margareta's last day in Rome before returning to Poland, she kissed her young American friend and reminded him of her expectations of him.

"Don't forget, Daniel, if you get to the Metropolitan Opera before I do, you must find a way of inviting me there."

"And what if you get there first?" Daniel teased.

"In that case, I will use my influence to get you good seats for the performance!"

She winked and laughed, and Daniel would never forget the final kiss she gave him. It seemed to say, "I would be yours forever if I could, and I will never forget you." And for the first time since he had known her, Daniel saw tears coming into Margareta's eyes.

Soon after Margareta's departure for Poland, Daniel returned to Curtis to complete his course of study there. His time in Rome with Professor Stagione would prove to be one of the most valuable periods of his artistic life. Up to that point, he had a fairly extensive background in music for the keyboard. And although he possessed a natural musicality—not just a superb talent for performing on an instrument, but an overriding identification with the *music* itself—he had been basically ignorant about much of the music that had contributed substantially to the development of western classical music, that canon of works that any well rounded musician needed to be aware of. As Professor Stagione had told him,

"You need to know about these composers and their works, but for you to become the great conductor I know you can become, you need to make these composers and their compositions an essential part of your musical being."

Stagione had spent hours with Daniel, himself sitting at the piano, playing key passages, singing the vocal parts of works by composers whose major area of composition involved the voice. With his masterful and astonishingly extensive knowledge of the music of composers from every period in music history and every European country, Stagione provided his student with a wealth of information, both practical and theoretical. He walked him though, or perhaps "played" him through each musical period from the Renaissance down to the Twentieth Century. His insights were remarkable, to say the least. They had discussions on Josquin, Lasso, Palestrina, Byrd, Gesualdo, Monteverdi, Schutz, Purcell, Bach, father and sons, Vivaldi, Gluck, Haydn, Mozart, Beethoven, Rossini, and on and on. Stagione showed Daniel Lorelli how a knowledge of composers like Gesualdo and Monteverdi, Vivaldi and Bach, could help him to better prepare works by Twentieth Century composers like Stravinsky and Berg. Indeed, Daniel's Roman education, accomplished in the short time span of just two years, would serve him well throughout his artistic career. Naturally, the full impact of this preparation would become manifest when he actually began to conduct in earnest, but the seeds were planted, the soil was fertile and artistic growth was assured. Stagione also made Daniel aware of the important difference a conductor made as an accompanist when a soloist—pianist, violinist, cellist, or whatever instrument was involved— performed a concerto or other work with orchestra. Many conductors just plodded along, and this seriously affected the outcome of the performance, even when the soloist's excellence was otherwise apparent. Since Daniel was himself a solo performer, he could appreciate everything the conductor pointed out, being entirely receptive and gaining exceptional insights.

After Daniel's graduation from Curtis, his parents arranged a reception to honor his achievement. They booked a trendy Italian restaurant in midtown Manhattan, La Bella Epoca, owned by friends of *paesani*, and invited scores of guests, friends of Daniel, Lorelli family friends, and friends of each of the brothers. Marilyn had been invited, too, but her mother wrote a note to say that she was still in Israel and could not attend. It was a beautiful New York Saturday afternoon in June, and a sumptuous dinner was complemented by live music from a string quartet made up of musicians from Curtis who knew and loved Daniel, as well as some vocals with piano accompaniment by singers and pianists from the Institute too. All were thrilled to be a part of Daniel's celebration. Albert invited a number of his colleagues from law school, wisely realizing that these contacts could be of great help to Daniel in his career. Some of the attorneys worked for important companies that contributed to the arts in various ways and thereby had influence over appointments and engagements pertaining to positions, appearances and sponsorship. Some of these men, upon greeting Daniel, gave him their business cards and mentioned certain endowments and subscription series that their companies were involved with. Albert, standing beside Daniel, always astute in matters of business, quickly jotted down the names of the musical connections his colleagues mentioned on the backs of each card. One of these was to result in Daniel's first important engagement as a conductor.

A week after the reception, Daniel received a telephone call from a woman who had attended. She had been invited at the suggestion of one of Albert's colleagues. Scott Newall had told Albert that this woman was influential in a particular New York musical circle that was involved—he didn't know exactly how—in a series of periodic concerts by an orchestra of local musicians. They performed at venues in Manhattan and Westchester. Mrs. Hope Desmond lived on the Upper East Side in a spacious apartment, luxuriously appointed. She reminded Daniel that they had spoken briefly. She told him she was very impressed with his credentials. She had studied the piano, was a passionate devotee of classical music and helped to organize some very interesting concerts.

"I would love to meet with you privately to discuss how I can help you. One of my principal interests is helping young musicians to get the break they deserve, if they deserve it, of course, and I am very confident that you are *most* deserving."

The way she said "most," with an emphatic thrust gave Daniel pause, but he did not want to do anything to spoil what could be a very good opportunity, so he replied with a somewhat feigned enthusiasm,

"Oh, thank you Mrs. Desmond. Just tell me what day and time is most convenient for you and where you would like to meet."

"Why don't you come to my apartment? It is in Manhattan, but high up on the 23rd floor here it's very quiet."

"I would be delighted to come over." Daniel hung up the telephone with a mixture of anticipation and foreboding. He was not a very political person, but he knew he had to try to adapt his ways, since he was well aware that a successful conductor needed to exploit social contacts as well as musical ones. Professor Stagione had told him about a few of his students who had gone on to successful conducting careers in Europe, and whenever they stopped in Rome and visited him, the one thing they would complain about was the need to be nice to people they actually detested. One of these, the conductor of a major orchestra in eastern Europe told his old teacher that he was thoroughly disgusted with that aspect of the "business," pointing out that he, like many other sensitive musicians he knew, hated that word when applied to their beloved artistic endeavors. This conductor described how some of these members of the board of the orchestra, who knew next to nothing about music, tried to tell him how he should conduct this composer or that piece, and always made suggestions as to repertoire, suggestions that were ludicrous, he felt. Nevertheless, he noted that he often had to be a "phony," agreeing with ideas for the sake of expediency. Naturally, Stagione pointed out to Daniel, once you became established you could thumb your nose at all of that, but until you had a secure foothold, you needed to play by the rules of the game. Daniel had given this a good deal of thought, and he knew it was truly against his nature to act in a false manner, but he was determined to try to bridge his own sense of truth and honor with practical necessity to ensure an auspicious outcome.

The following Friday evening Daniel arrived at Mrs. Desmond's apartment at the appointed time, 8:00 P.M. A maid opened the door and Daniel was ushered in to an expansive living room, dominated by a Yamaha grand piano. After a few minutes, Hope Desmond entered the room. Daniel did not actually remember seeing her at the party, but there were so many people he did not know there. However, he didn't want Mrs. Desmond to know that, so he said,

"It's so nice to see you again, Mrs. Desmond."

"It's nice to see you too, Daniel. Now, let's not be so formal. Call me Hope."

"Thank you, Hope."

Hope Desmond was a widow. She and her husband had been married for fifteen years when he died of a massive heart attack while at work. He had been a partner in a prestigious law firm and was ten years older than Hope. She was thirty-eight years old when he died five years before. They had been childless. Hope was still a very attractive woman who looked younger than her age. She had reddish blonde hair that was cut short, smartly arranged to accent her narrow face and small forehead. Her hazel eyes sparkled as she spoke with a good deal of animation, using her hands almost compulsively to emphasize a point she was making. She was tall but not quite statuesque, and walked with natural poise. Her husband had left her quite well off. In addition to a sizeable life insurance policy that gave her a large amount of cash to work with, she had holdings in a number of blue chip stocks, bonds and other assets. She owned the apartment she lived in as well as a "weekend" home in Westport. The Connecticut house was not very large, but it was surrounded by about three acres of land that included a small lake in the back. Technically, it was anything but a vacation home. All the other residents in the area lived there year round. Hope had studied sociology in college and had worked for a think tank for a few years before meeting her husband. She devoted her time now to managing her own investments and to various social activities, one of which was the community orchestra that interested Daniel.

"What would you like to drink?"

Daniel hesitated. He was not much of a drinker, so he ventured,

"I'll have whatever you are having."

"Well, I'm having white wine. Miranda, bring that chilled bottle of Chardonnay and two glasses." She spoke to her maid with respect if also with a small measure of haughtiness.

They made a toast.

"To your future success as a conductor," Hope announced confidently.

Then she plied Daniel with one question after another. Each time he tried to turn the conversation over to anything to do with her life, she gave incomplete replies to his queries and again shifted the conversation back to him. She asked about his family, their background, his education, his time in Italy, seeking minute details about each and every facet of his life up to that point. Actually, Daniel liked her. She seemed to be down to earth and sincere. Aside from the few comments he heard her make to her maid, she did not seem to be pretentious at all. Eventually, the conversation got around to her piano. She told Daniel that she thought the Yamaha was one of the best pianos then being built. Of course, it can't compare to some of the older Steinways, but it can hold its own against any contemporary piano. Daniel had performed on various Yamaha pianos over the years and he could not disagree with her assessment, but he was curious as to why she thought the older Steinways were superior.

"At my home in Westport I have a Steinway that dates from around 1900. It is still in top shape. I have a technician who works on it regularly to keep it that way. In fact, you may be interested to know that Rachmaninov played on it quite often when he lived in New York."

"What?" Daniel asked, incredulously. "Rachmaninov played on it? How do you know that for sure?"

"I purchased the piano from a woman who lived on Riverside Drive, and 72nd Street. The piano was in a penthouse there, and Rachmaninov was living on West End Avenue. He often visited the family and performed for friends there."

"That's amazing!" Daniel exclaimed with unfettered enthusiasm. "Can I . . . would it be possible for me to hear this piano, to play it?"

"Of course," Hope said, replying with her own positive spin on his request. "I was going to suggest that you must come to the house for a weekend. I will invite some important people too, people you really need to meet who can help you to further your career. But first, I have a request of you."

"Yes, of course, anything," Daniel agreed, maintaining the vigor of his mood.

"Will you play something for me now, on the Yamaha, one of my favorite pieces?"

"Certainly, but why don't you play first," Daniel said, trying his best to be diplomatic.

"Oh, no. My playing is not up to the level to which you are accustomed. The only way you will hear me play is if you agree to give me lessons."

"Well, if I had time I would . . ."

"That's quite all right," Hope interjected. "I just meant that if you were giving me lessons I would have to play for you, but I realize that you have other fish to fry right now."

"What piece did you have in mind?"

"Chopin's *Third Ballade*. You know it, of course?"

"Oh, yes, all four Chopin *Ballades* are in my repertory."

Daniel sat down to play, and as his body swayed, his black hair flowing from side to side as he moved with the music, Hope Desmond became completely captivated by the young man's talent, good looks, the magic of the moment. Never had she heard anyone play like this in her home. There was something about this music that encompassed an old world nostalgia that she could feel, but not completely identify. It reminded her of something from her childhood, a certain elegance, an understated but evident sensation of something noble. Daniel, for his part, was totally into the piece. When he played, he became almost as one with the music, with the composer, with the very soul of the music he played. It was just such a natural phenomenon with him; during the time he was playing, nothing else existed. So intense was his concentration that when he ended the *Ballade* with the final four emphatic chords, he sat there for a minute, unaware for some seconds where he was. After dropping his hands to his sides, looking up, he returned to the present, brought home by Hope's enthusiastic applause.

"Magnificent, beautiful! Oh, thank you so much. Your playing was so lovely."

Daniel nodded, stood up and spontaneously embraced his admirer, thanking her for her words.

"Dare I ask you for one more, the *Fourth Ballade*?"

Without hesitation Daniel sat down again and began to play the delicate introduction that led into the bitter-sweet melody that Hope again identified with something from the past, her past and that of her family, memories that were stored in her subconscious from tales she had heard as a child. The difficulties inherent in the *Fourth Ballade* seemed not to present any problems for Daniel, and when he again ended majestically, again with four final chords, Hope could not contain her enthusiasm.

"Oh, that was wonderful! Beautiful! I know why I love the *Third* so much, but your playing of the *Fourth* makes me wonder if I don't love it even more now."

This time Daniel did not embrace his host, merely taking her two hands in his, indicating that he should now take his leave of her.

"Thank you for coming. Daniel, I really want to help in any way I can. And you want to, you *must* play the Rachmaninov piano. Will you come to Westport for a weekend? As I said, I will invite some important people who have connections that should prove beneficial for you."

"I would be delighted. Thank you so much. I enjoyed our time together."

"The first of many, I trust," and Hope smiled a flirtatious smile that went completely over Daniel's head.

A few weeks later on the only weekend that Daniel did not have a recital on a Friday or Saturday evening, he drove up to Connecticut to Hope Desmond's weekend retreat. Daniel's conducting career was slow in starting, but an agent he had retained managed to fill his time with solo piano engagements at colleges in the tri-state area. A few involved cancellations by well known pianists. The audiences were first upset that they were not going to hear someone famous, but some of these music lovers knew quality when they heard it, and many leaving the halls could be heard remarking on how fortuitous was the evening's discovery of this new talent. When they read the positive reviews a day or two later, they felt doubly rewarded. Thus Daniel's reputation as a pianist of the first rank was beginning to spread.

Hope had asked Daniel to begin the weekend with a Friday evening supper. She invited a lawyer and a banker and their wives. The lawyer was a member of the board of the community chamber orchestra that Hope was involved with and this alone, Daniel told himself, was sufficient reason to devote the weekend to this pursuit. The bank the other gentleman represented donated funds to the orchestra, so his participation was also of some importance for Daniel. Upon arriving, Daniel was shown to his room. Before he even put anything away, he asked to see the piano. Hope took him into the spacious living room that housed the piano Sergei Rachmaninov had himself played on. Daniel sat and immediately played the *Prelude in c sharp minor*, one of the composer's most popular works and one he had written at an age just a little younger than Daniel himself. After Daniel had dressed for the evening and the guests arrived, Hope suggested that if Daniel would honor them with his playing, they could have a mini concert before supper.

"Since Mrs. Desmond has informed me that this piano received a benediction from none other than Rachmnainov himself, I think it would be appropriate for me to play one of that composer's compositions. I'll begin with one of the composer's *Etudes*." Daniel sat and played the first of the *Etudes-Tableaux, Op. 33, No. 1 in F Minor*. He immediately followed with *No. 2 in C* and *No. 3 in c minor*. Exhilarated by the applause from his small audience and the sound from the magnificent instrument, Daniel went on to play five more of the eight *Etudes* that completed the set from *Opus 33*, the entire work filled with technical difficulties allied with poetic musings, studies in the same sense that Chopin wrote etudes, but combined with tableaux or paintings in sound. None of the five, hostess and guests sitting listening to Daniel knew the works he performed, but each could not help being enthralled by the beauty of the music and the sureness of the pianist's touch, so musical, shading the music's moods, now tender, now lyrical, now impassioned. Daniel thought of the Russian whose genius had created these resplendent sounds, and as he sat playing he imagined he was Rachmaninov himself, towering over the piano. When the piece ended, Daniel again sat still, oblivious to the enthusiastic applause. After nearly two minutes, he looked up and smiled.

At supper, Mrs. Jacobs, the wife of the banker asked Daniel about the composition, and as Daniel explained the type of work it was, she ventured her impressions of what the tableaux could represent.

"It's interesting that you should say that," Daniel said without the slightest trace of condescension, a trait that endeared him to friends and acquaintances.

"But Rachmaninov would never divulge his own thoughts on the extra musical meanings of this music. He wanted the public to decide for themselves what the music meant to them. So, you see, Mrs. Jacobs, your view is just as valid as anyone else's."

Daniel had done something to make the lady feel good without even realizing it. That night she told her husband that she was sure that this young man had extraordinary talent. He agreed with her assessment and assured her he would help Daniel in furthering his career.

After supper, a meal prepared by a fine local restaurant that serviced the Desmond residence whenever the need arose, and served by Mrs. Desmond's maid, the very same lady that had greeted Daniel when he visited Mrs. Desmond's Manhattan apartment, Daniel was again enjoined by Hope Desmond to play for her and for her guests. Appropriately for the late hour, Daniel played first a Nocturne by Rachmaninov, the one in F sharp minor, and concluded with Chopin's *Nocturne in c sharp minor*. After the guests left and Daniel thanked his hostess, he retired to his bedroom.

231

As he was about to turn off the light, he heard Hope's voice calling to him from down the hall.

"Daniel, please come here for a minute."

As he entered his hostess's bedroom, she was seated near the edge of a large king size four poster bed covered by a lace canopy, propped up by some oversized pillows.

"Daniel, would you do me a favor?"

"Yes, of course, what can I do?"

"My back is aching and I would really appreciate it if you would give me a massage. I know your strong pianist's hands will do wonders for me—just a little manipulation of my shoulders."

Daniel was somewhat embarrassed and didn't know if he should plead his inability for the task or if he should comply. His hesitation served to embolden the attractive widow. She had on a nightgown that partially revealed firm breasts that did not appear to sag under the silk material.

"I thought we could play tennis in the morning and a little massage can help me to sleep better and relax the muscles in my shoulders and arms. You do play?"

"Well, I do, but I haven't played in quite some time."

"Good, then perhaps I can beat you," and saying this she turned her back towards Daniel and lowered her gown down off her shoulders, leaving her breasts still covered but showing enough cleavage to prove, if such proof were needed, that her physical attributes belied her age. The fact was that Hope exercised regularly, played tennis, went swimming twice a week and boasted a body that a woman fifteen years younger than she would have been proud of. Daniel placed his hands on her shoulders and began kneading them. Each time he closed his hands over her skin, Hope murmured with obvious delight. After about seven minutes, she suddenly reached up behind her and pulled Daniel's hands down over her breasts, under the silk material. Impulsively, he pulled them away.

Mrs. Desmond, I don't think ...."

"Hope, call me Hope."

"Hope, I don't think I should be doing that."

"Why, Daniel, don't you find me attractive?"

"Yes, you are a very attractive woman, but that has nothing to do with it."

"Really? If that has nothing to do with it, what is it then? Don't tell me you're gay!" And turning around fully to face him, Hope waited for his confirmation or denial of her conjecture, smiling slightly, her eyes raised in anticipation.

"No, I'm not gay. But .... ." Daniel hesitated again, not wishing to say anything to offend her.

"You know, I'm Catholic."

"So, I'm Presbyterian. What has that got to do with it?"

Daniel suddenly felt ridiculous. How could he turn to his religion as a defense when he knew all too well that it did not deter him in the past? He felt dishonest, and he never wanted to be dishonest, not even in a situation like the present one.

"It's just that . . . ."

"Look, Daniel, I don't want to make you uncomfortable. We're both adults and we are both single. I'm a woman with needs and you also have certain needs, if you're normal, that is." She said this with a mixture of pleading and sarcasm.

"I just want you to know that I am not promiscuous, and I did not invite you to my home to get you to sleep with me. Honestly, that was not my intention. I liked you as a person immediately, and after your playing this evening I actually found that I became erotically stimulated by you, everything about you—your looks, your manner, your sensitivity. I want to kiss you, to hold you, yes, to make love to you. I know you must have many younger women after you too, but I can hold my own against women half my age. And I know I can be more passionate with the right man too. I am a woman with needs of my own that are hardly ever satisfied. You have to have some outlet yourself. I am not asking for commitment, just mutual pleasure."

Daniel was at a very real loss for words. Hope's candor, her open approach, the way she boldly sallied forth was something he found he liked and admired. It endeared her to him in a way, but it did not entice him entirely. For the brief seconds his hands had touched her breasts, he had felt an urge to abandon his demeanor and to throw caution aside, but there was something he could not quite explain to himself as to why he had no real desire for her. There was something off-putting about the very idea, something almost repulsive. But why? She was certainly not an unattractive woman. If one looked at her body without looking at her face, there was certainly enough sensual appeal there to draw in any young man with the usual urges and desires. Then what was it? She had a pretty face, but it was a face that was from another time, not his time. Many men would not think twice, but Daniel found himself utterly uninterested. He thought of Marilyn and Margareta, and the feeling was so different, even setting aside questions of romantic love. The thought of Marilyn gave him his escape route, a means of honestly voicing objections without hurting this obviously kind woman who sincerely appreciated his talent and even his character.

"Hope, there is a woman I am in love with. I cannot betray her."

Here, too, however, he felt a twinge of guilt, a manifestation within himself of dishonesty, for hadn't he overcome these feelings of disloyalty when he decided to make love to Margareta?

"Oh? Do you live together? Why haven't I met her?"

"She is a musician too. She is studying abroad, but we are very much in love with one another."

"How long is it that you have not seen one another."

This time Daniel could not help lying, a white lie, not harmful in any real sense.

"I haven't seen her for two years." It was actually four years.

"Two years? Daniel, do you mean to tell me that you are saving yourself for her? Do you think she has been as faithful to you?"

"Yes."

"Perhaps. But I know men and you can't honestly tell me that you have been celibate for two years while she has been abroad!"

"Well, I ...."

"Look, I'm sorry. I really have no right to drill you. Can I tell you something personal?" She laughed and her eyes glistened and there was something in her tone that made Daniel want to listen to her.

"Yes, of course."

"My husband David and I were married when I was twenty-three and he was thirty. If you think I am attractive now, you should have seen me then. I had many men after me. I had numerous proposals, not just from men I had dated, but also from family friends who had the perfect match for me. But although I was head over heels for Dave, I didn't want to marry him unless I could be sure he was *all* for me, absolutely and completely head over heels, you know what I mean. There were still old girlfriends calling. He had had a very active social life with lots of sexual activity. Little by little, he won me over. He promised that he would always be faithful to me. He had sown his wild oats, and he wanted only me. But then, after the first year, his penchant for novelty got the better of him. He was always coming home late. There was always an excuse, but I knew that the fire in him that had been reserved for me had cooled. He had a heart attack and died while having sex with a young associate in his office."

"I'm sorry."

Daniel's heart was opening to this woman with her sad tale. She was strong. Her words did not bring tears to her eyes as Daniel thought they would.

"No. I don't want you to feel sorry for me. That's not why I'm telling you this."

"There's nothing wrong with sharing your pain."

"Yes, that's true, but I'm telling you about my experience to bring home a point. No one was more attuned to the idea of romantic love than I was. I really believed in true love and in the inevitability of finding the one and only person meant for me. I thought Dave was that person, but I found to my everlasting dismay that the whole idea is a hoax."

"Yes, but what if I still believe in that inevitable culmination of one's hopes and dreams, of being together with the one woman that I still feel is meant for me, has been destined for me from all time?"

Hope smiled sardonically and took Daniel's two hands in hers.

"Then I would have to say that you still believe in fairy tales. That's beautiful in a way, but not exactly what one would expect from a sophisticated twenty-four year old man like you. Tell me, do you know anyone, any couple at all, I should say, whose love has stood the test of time, turmoil, discontent with one another, disillusionment with the other's faults, foibles, fancies. Excuse me, my poetic instinct is getting the better of me."

"You do have a fascinating and even beautiful way of expressing yourself."

By now, Daniel was seated next to Hope on the bed. She had swung around with her feet hanging from the left side of the bed and Daniel was to her left.

"Hope, to be honest with you," (Why was he saying that, he thought; he prided himself on always being honest) and Hope thought to herself, "Ah, now he will have to agree with me."

"Hope, yes, I do know such a couple. My mother and father."

"What's this?" Hope pondered. "This guy's really not as sophisticated as I thought he was. He still has his parents on a pedestal." She objected delicately,

"Children always think their parents are different, but I'm sure that if you ever had a serious discussion with your mother, you would find that your father did not always meet her expectations."

"No, really, my parents are even more in love today than when they first married." Daniel told Hope the story of how her mother's faith that his father was *the* one man for her had resulted in the death of another man. Hope found the story astonishing. It sounded like something out of a novel!

"My parents' love for one another is stronger today than ever. Perhaps it's because they have always done everything together, even in business, and always respected each other's ideas and feelings about everything."

"Come on Daniel, they never fought, never had disagreements?"

"Yes, they did."

"Aha!"

"But nothing significant, nothing that involved the two of them or their feelings towards one another. In fact, the only time I have ever heard or continue to hear them disagree on anything, and my father always gives in because he loves my mother so much and knows that it is part of her nature to be that way, is when it comes to my mother's charitable tendencies. She always gave away food to needy families. On Thanksgiving, for example, she learned of parents in our neighborhood who could not provide their children with the kind of dinner our family had, and she would arrange to send Turkeys and other food to them. She would very often not charge certain customers for things they wanted because she knew they were not well off. And this was her one argument with my father. He would say, 'Violetta, we are not the Red Cross. We are not a charity. We are a business.' But she would tell him how fortunate we were and convince him that they were doing the right thing."

"That's lovely." Hope now looked very sad. Daniel mused that perhaps he should not have told her about his parents. If she thinks that kind of love is impossible, she is saved from regrets about her own life. Hope looked very wistful. Daniel spontaneously put his arms around her. He felt such profound compassion for this woman, practically a stranger, but someone he thought he understood. With his arms around her, he felt like he needed to comfort her. He wanted to protect her from all those cold, uncaring feelings that permeated her world and swept her along in a senseless, unsympathetic and hostile whirlwind of emotions. She seemed so vulnerable to him and he wanted to make up in some way for the hurt she had suffered—at her husband's hands, at the sad turn of events that had left her alone and longing for love. These feelings were not enough to induce him to make love to her, but he could hold her, reassure her.

"Lie down here next to me," and Hope pulled back the covers for Daniel to get into bed next to her. He did as she commanded. She nestled her head against his shoulder and fell asleep. In the morning Hope awoke before her guest. After showering and dressing, she asked the maid to make breakfast for the two of them and had her bring Daniel's into the bedroom. Daniel felt self-conscious on being seen by the maid in Hope's bed, and insisted on getting up and having his breakfast in the dining area. His concerns were well founded, for some years later the story would get around that the fine conductor Daniel Lorelli had been intimate with Hope Desmond, and he would even have difficulty convincing the woman who would become his wife that the rumors were untrue.

Following a morning of tennis with his new friend and a restful day, Daniel again performed for a group of guests that Hope invited for drinks on Saturday evening. When Daniel left to return home on Sunday afternoon, he was certain that he had made important contacts that weekend, and Hope was now solidly aligned with him as a supporter and eventually even as a benefactor.

Thirty-Three

The months following were exciting and productive ones for Daniel. His engagements as a pianist multiplied. Harold Jacobs, the banker, told him that the conductor of the New York Musicians' Orchestra had accepted a European appointment and that they needed a new conductor, and he offered to help Daniel in obtaining the position.

"To be perfectly honest with you," Jacobs admitted, "I remembered you as a pianist. It was my wife who insisted that you were more interested in conducting, and that you had studied conducting, and she persuaded me to recommend you for the post. We both were totally impressed by your musical ability from the evening we spent listening to you at Hope Desmond's place. I called Sam Carter, the lawyer who is Chairman of the orchestra's board, and he suggested I invite you to apply."

Daniel applied and eventually got the job, but not without a fight, not so much on Daniel's part as among the members of the Board. One of these, Carlos Santiago, a Hispanic attorney, wanted to install his own man, a musician originally from Mexico. Edgardo Andres had had more experience as a conductor than Daniel did. He had conducted orchestras in his native country and directed some concerts in Texas before going to New York. Santiago, with the support of at least one other member of the Board, felt that the burgeoning Hispanic population in New York could be tapped as a potential additional audience if a conductor with a knowledge of orchestral works by composers like Revueltas and Chavez was on the podium. Santiago tried to badmouth Lorelli, but there was not much he could say besides pointing out that his man's opponent's experience as a conductor was limited to whatever he had done as a student and nothing more. Finally, each of the two candidates for the position was asked to come before the Board to explain his musical philosophy, what he hoped

238

to achieve with the orchestra and how he intended to maintain the present audience and expand its base. After the two presentations, Daniel was the unanimous choice. Daniel was fortunate in this instance. He was not political enough to have won in this particular contest if it depended entirely on his own initiative. This time talent won the day, but things would not always work out so easily and favorably for Maestro Lorelli.

Although the orchestra gave only six concerts a year, it was a visible and critically acclaimed ensemble, comprising some of the best independent musicians on the New York musical scene. They performed at Carnegie Hall and their performances were reviewed in the New York *Times.*

For his New York debut as a conductor, Daniel was given free rein, provided he could assure the Board that the selections would be pleasing to a somewhat conservative audience. The concert began with Prokofiev's *"Classical" Symphony.* This was followed by Mozart's *Piano Concerto No. 25* with Daniel as the soloist, conducting from the piano. After an intermission, the concert ended with Shostakovich's *Symphony No. 5.* This was a risky programming decision, for the Shostakovich was considered a specialty of Leonard Bernstein, and comparisons by the critics would be inevitable. In the event, Daniel's initiative was received with audience enthusiasm unparalleled in the orchestra's history and superior critical acclaim. The Times' critic wrote:

"Lorelli conducted the NYMO with rare skill and musical panache. It is obvious that this protégé of Carlo Maria Stagione, the noted Italian conducting teacher, has much to offer the New York musical scene. His Prokofiev was the very model of a symphony in true classical style. Hearing Lorelli conduct it, anyone unaware of the work's origin could be forgiven for attributing it to Mozart or Haydn. Mozart's *Concerto in C, K. 503* was both played and conducted by the enterprising Lorelli, a performance that was impressive for the seamless flow of the music. The last time New York heard a performance of this caliber was when Clifford Curzon performed the work with Szell and the Cleveland Orchestra. The real surprise of the evening, at least for this listener, came after the intermission. Lorelli conducted a performance of Shostakovich's monumental *Fifth Symphony* that brought out all the heroism and grandeur as well as the darker aspects of Shostakovich's life that inspired him to write this Symphony and that the work encompasses. It is safe to say that in this work Bernstein himself is faced with a worthy adversary."

Daniel was ecstatic. He sent a copy of the review to Stagione and the professor replied with a comment that meant more to Daniel than the review itself:

"Sono contento del tuo grande successo in questo concerto. Però, ti dico che sono stato sempre sicuro che tu sei una musicista impareggiabile."

During the course of the following year Daniel conducted a Christmas season concert that included Tchaikovsky's *Nutcracker Suite*, Bach's *Christmas Oratorio* and excerpts from the Christmas section of Handel's *Messiah*, the latter two works with impressive young soloists and a choral group that also performed regularly on the New York musical scene. Daniel's family attended all the concerts. Violetta and Vincenzo beamed with pride as their son took the podium. After the Christmas concert, when Daniel arrived for Sunday dinner, Violetta told her son that she was so proud of him.

"And Daniel," she added, "I can see from the way you conducted the religious compositions that your faith is still strong. You brought out all the beauty of the birth of our Redeemer in the music about him."

Daniel did not want to disagree with his mother, even though he was not sure that what she said was completely true.

"Well, I guess, Mamma, that one's background cannot be denied. For an artist, everything one has lived is part of the fabric that dresses his art."

"Yes, yes, I understand," Violetta agreed, smiling, certain that her dear son carried so much of her own temperament, her appreciation of beauty and her concern for others in his heart. Daniel would not tell his mother that he attended Mass only sporadically. He felt a certain guilt about this, since going to Mass, at least on Sundays, had been so ingrained in his psyche.

"Oh, Daniel, I almost forgot to tell you. A young lady telephoned earlier this week. She left a number for you to call."

"A young lady? Who is she?" For a moment Daniel thought it was Marilyn, but his mother knew Marilyn, so why would she refer to her as "a young lady."

"She said she knows you from Rome. Here, I wrote her name down."

Daniel took the slip of paper and read: "ANNEMARIE TAVIANI," followed by a local telephone number.

"Annemarie!" he exclaimed. "I didn't expect to hear from her again."

"Was she your girlfriend in Rome?" Violetta asked confident that her son would tell her if he had dated the young woman.

"No. She is a viola player and she was studying at l'Accademia. I think she's from Boston. I wonder what she's doing in New York."

The next day, Daniel telephoned Annemarie. Her voice sounded so much more buoyant than he remembered it. She told him that she had heard about his success as a conductor with the NYMO and wanted to congratulate him. Daniel learned that she was freelancing and suggested that there could be an opening for a violist in the orchestra. They agreed to meet for lunch in Manhattan.

On the way to meet Annemarie, Daniel thought about his mother's words. As he walked over to meet her, he had occasion to walk past St Francis' Church on 32nd Street between 7th and 8th Avenues. Confessions were heard by the Friars there throughout the day. Daniel entered the Church and chose a confessional. He spoke to the priest in a general manner since he had not confessed in such a long time. He found the priest to be congenial, non-judgmental and really kind. He left the Church feeling better. Perhaps he had kept himself away from Church for much too long.

Daniel looked around, trying to spot Annemarie when he felt a tap on his shoulder. As he turned, what he saw was not what he had expected. When he had last seen Annemarie in Rome, she was dressed casually and looked quite plain. Now she was stunning. Her hair had grown longer, now reaching shoulder length. She wore a blue skirt with a grey silk blouse, matching pumps, and makeup that was applied delicately with accents that enhanced her natural beauty. Her hair was very dark, nearly black, and her deep blue eyes once again evinced for Daniel a feeling that she was a woman well beyond the mundane. The special quality of her charm and personal warmth could not be gainsaid. Daniel recalled her self-assuredness and confidence from their meetings in Rome, but now he saw something else. Now he was quite aware that he was with a woman, a most attractive woman whose infectious smile made him feel comfortable. As she grasped his hand, as firmly as he remembered from their prior meetings, Daniel impulsively embraced her. She did not shrink back at all, meeting him with an equal degree of fervor.

The next two hours flew by. There was so much to talk about. They had so much in common. Annemarie was fluent in Italian, and in spite of her mixed parentage, she was more attuned to her Italian heritage. Daniel liked that about her and he liked other things about her too, facets of her personality that he had obviously overlooked in Rome. Those fascinating intangibles that he had sensed about her then were becoming distinguishable.

"A position with the orchestra cannot be your only activity, surely, but if you can work it into your schedule I would love to have you join us. And I think there will be an opening soon, since our principal violist may be moving to a major orchestra."

Annemarie smiled and assured Daniel that she would love to be a part of his music making.

"Right now I'm giving viola lessons. I have about twelve private students. I'm also a substitute for some of the orchestras of Broadway musicals, so I am kept fairly busy. But I would rather play classical music, and I would love it if we could work together."

She said this in a coquettish manner that surprised Daniel, but it made her even more attractive to him.

Annemarie joined the orchestra the following Spring. She and Daniel continued to meet for a lunch or a dinner from time to time. Annemarie shared her New York apartment with two other professional young women. The rent for the two bedroom flat was so expensive that they could only afford it together. On a few occasions when Daniel accompanied Annemarie home, she asked him to come up, but invariably one of her roommates was home so that the absence of opportunity for any degree of intimacy kept their relationship at the platonic level for some time.

In the Fall of the year Annemarie joined the orchestra, Daniel programmed Berlioz's *Harold In Italy*. Annemarie would play the solo viola part. It seemed like a wonderful idea since both Daniel and Annemarie had been, like Byron's Harold, outsiders in Italy, observers of all the wonders the country offered to its visitors. Unlike the soloist in the typical concerto, Berlioz's solo viola was integrated within the *Symphony*, not pitted against it. Nevertheless, it gave Annemaire the chance to shine on her own. This magnanimous gesture endeared Daniel to her more than ever. The New York press gave the concert high marks, singling out the violist and conductor for special praise.

Daniel thought about Annemarie more and more as a possible wife. Deep in his heart he still could not forget Marilyn, but he realized increasingly that his dream of their union was an impossible one. He did not want to give up. An incurable Romantic in temperament, Daniel needed to believe that their destinies would eventually bring them together. Annemarie was much more reserved than Marilyn. Although she and Daniel saw a good deal of each other, she would not touch the back of his head as Marilyn had done so often, or snuggle close to him, even in a darkened movie theater. She would hold his hand but thwart anything more intimate. A few weeks after the Berlioz concert, after having supper together one evening, Daniel suggested they go back to his apartment. Daniel had been living in a small single bedroom flat in Little Italy. He did not want to depend on his parents for money —they were always offering to help him financially—and he was not earning much as a part time conductor and sometime piano soloist, so he settled on living in a less expensive part of the City. Annemarie seemed eager to see Daniel's place. Daniel wondered as they made their way downtown whether or not he should make a move? Suggest that she spend the night? Physically, he found her very attractive. He knew he liked her very much, but he was not sure if he was in love with her. A small loveseat was all that fit in the extremely small living room area. Annemarie sat facing the tiny kitchen as Daniel gathered two glasses and a bottle of Merlot. He had grown very fond of her, but had never kissed her as lovers do. Glancing into a mirror over the sink, he could see her, but she could not see him looking at her. Her slender legs were slightly parted as she sat and as she crossed them and her skirt moved up revealing more of her thigh, Daniel suddenly felt an intense desire to hold her and to touch her skin, to explore areas as yet unknown to him. He sat next to her on the loveseat and poured the wine. They toasted their future success as musicians. Daniel moved closer and put his right arm around her shoulders. Annemarie looked at him lovingly, her sparkling blue eyes filled with anticipation. Slowly, gathering courage, Daniel moved his lips towards hers. Momentarily, he wondered about his own hesitation. It had something to do with his companion's reserve. There was something forbidding about getting too close to her, but here was his chance to see how she would react. She met his lips with fervor equal to his own. As his tongue slid between her teeth, there was a brief hesitation on her part, but she gave in to the moment and the intensity of their kisses grew more passionate moment by moment. Daniel felt her breasts through her blouse, firm and soft. Ever so slowly he unbuttoned her and placed his hand inside her bra. She did not resist. Annemarie's breathing became heaver. He parted her legs with his other hand and ran his fingers up her leg. Suddenly, she pulled away.

"Daniel, I can't do this."

"Do what?" he asked ingenuously.

"I can kiss you. I want to kiss you. But I cannot. . . I have to be careful." At once, she sounded so vulnerable, so unsophisticated, so innocent and so much more desirable.

"Why? Don't you like me?"

At this question, Annemarie began to weep, first quietly, then more and more intensely. Daniel took her into his arms and held her tightly, comforting her, soothing feelings he did not fully understand. She pulled away and looked into his eyes. Holding his temples between her small hands, Annemarie kissed Daniel again, holding the kiss for a long time. Then she let go of him and looked at him directly again.

"Daniel, I don't *like* you. I *love* you. I've loved you since I first met you in Rome. I've always thought about you even when I hadn't seen you for some time. It wasn't easy for me to try to contact you. I didn't know if you would want to have anything to do with me. I just cannot go all the way yet."

"I'm sorry. You sweet, dear girl. Why wouldn't I want to see you?"

Annemarie's revelation of her long standing love for him pleased Daniel and worried him too. What should he do now?

"But why won't you . . . go . . . all the way?" Daniel uttered the last three words with what sounded like trepidation, almost fearful that his repetition of her phrase came off as mockery.

"I take my Catholicism seriously too, but we're both responsible adults. If we are attracted to one another, what's wrong with expressing it in a physical manner?

"Do you love me, Daniel?"

Did he love her? He was not sure. He liked her looks, her personality, her sensitivity and skill as a musician. He found her physically attractive. Perhaps the way one loved was not always the same. His love for Marilyn was one kind of love. Wasn't his love for Margareta different still from his love for Marilyn? If he had matured as a person, couldn't his way of loving a woman change too? It may not be as overwhelmingly riveting as it was when he was younger, but couldn't this make it even more solid, more permanent?

"To be honest" and saying these words, he again thought of himself in a deprecatory manner. Why did he use the word "honest"? Wasn't he always honest?

"Well, I mean I have always been honest with you–with everyone, I think. I haven't thought very much about 'love' itself."

"See, that's what I mean," Annemarie replied in a tone that indicated to Daniel that she was so vulnerable, in spite of her self-assuredness. She continued, nearly on the brink of tears,

"You want me to give myself to you fully, totally. And I *do want to.*" She emphasized the three words almost as if she were pleading. "But am I to be just another woman you take to bed and then forget?"

Daniel was hurt by such an appraisal of his character, especially by Annemarie. After all, he had never just taken any woman to bed. He thought about the few possibilities he had had in his life to that point. He had turned down women he didn't love, hadn't he? And of the two women he loved, Marilyn and Margareta, the decision to "forget" had been theirs.

Daniel wanted to turn his thoughts into words, but he did not want to sound self-righteous. He knew Annemarie well enough by this time to know that she would not find his explanation salutary. He just said,

"I think you know me well enough to know that that is not my style. I do love you. Just how much I'm not sure. That's why we have to explore our love together, to see if we are meant to be together."

"Daniel, how can you call yourself a Catholic and say that?"

Immediately, Daniel was shocked into considering his motives. Once again he felt that old sense of guilt. Was he being selfish? Why should he want to compromise this honest young woman's moral standards? Why were these standards not his own?

"Daniel, this is hard for me to say, but you make it easy for me to be honest with you. I do feel like I can talk to you about anything and be completely open with you."

"Thank you. I'm . . . "

"No, don't say anything. I want you to know that I've never given myself to a man. I'm saving myself—oh, that sounds so trite in a way, but I want my husband to be the one. Maybe it's an old fashioned Romantic idea, but I do feel that way. It's true that my upbringing influenced the way I think, but truthfully, I've never wanted to make love to any man before you, and when I met you in Rome, I became determined that you would be the first man to make love to me. I've waited for you." Having said this, Annemarie kissed Daniel again and embraced him with a determination and ardor that made it all too obvious that she spoke truly and from the heart.

"Then, I think you have waited long enough. Stay here tonight."

"I really am tempted. But let's wait. I need to see if you love me enough."

Daniel felt a bit cornered. This meant she wanted to marry him, but did he want to marry her? He wasn't sure. Nevertheless, the idea that she was untouched appealed to him. It harkened back to something in his ancestry, perhaps in the genetic code transmitted down through the generations of men who prized this attribute, and who had insisted upon its absolute integrity in the woman they would or could marry. Hadn't Vincenzo told his son that he would never have married a woman who was "used"?

Annemarie had her arms around Daniel's neck. She looked at him with an expression of unbounded love and admiration. Daniel's eyes betrayed an attitude of uncertainty.

"There isn't someone else, is there?"

"No, not really."

"What do you mean 'not really'?"

Any other man in Daniel's place, any sensible man, would have dismissed the notion then and there, but Daniel's adherence to the concept of intact honesty, even when it could be unwise to be totally honest, as it certainly was in the present situation, led him into an area of discussion he had not been prepared for.

"I was very much in love with someone. I still cannot completely forget her. I really thought . . . never mind."

"No, what? You must tell me everything." (Even if I don't really want to hear it, she thought to herself).

"Was it that Polish soprano in Rome? I remember seeing you with her a lot, even on the streets away from the Academy. I was so jealous, wishing all the time that I was the one walking with you."

"No. We liked each other, but I was not really in love with her. Well, in a way I started to fall in love with her, but she convinced me that we had no future together."

"Then, who?"

Daniel told Annemarie about Marilyn. She certainly could not hold that against him, he thought, but Daniel really knew nothing about women, and he couldn't even imagine how something that had happened before he met Annemarie could disturb her so much. She didn't indicate as much then, but it would be a sore point in their relationship for years to come. Any time she felt insecure about his love for her, she would make mental comparisons between herself and this woman she had never met, and the "ghost" of Marilyn would be raised to Daniel's total incomprehension, the relevance of which would baffle him.

Calming herself, consciously damping her inner turmoil, Annemarie told Daniel that it didn't matter.

"I don't care about the past. The important thing for me is the future, our future, and when we are together completely, nothing and no one can come between us."

Her statement sounded ominous, but Daniel, ever eager to please, to keep things on a positive and happy tone, embraced her and they kissed with abandon for quite some time. Annemarie' skirt was up around her waist and her blouse unbuttoned, but as the heat between them rose to a point beyond which they almost could not possibly go back, Annemarie stood up, straightened her clothes and said with supreme assurance,

"We will bring this to its conclusion when the time is right."

Daniel pleaded with her to let him make love to her, but she was adamant in her refusal. After they parted Daniel remembered a poem he had loved ever since he first read it, Andrew Marvell's "To His Coy Mistress." The marvelous beginning,

"Had we but world enough and time,
This coyness lady were no crime.

Then the second stanza's metaphor that always came to mind when he felt that time was slipping through his fingers,

But at my back I always hear
Time's winged chariot hurrying near.

This represented for Daniel a truth that he never let go of, and which he applied practically in his everyday life. He realized that he would not always have the luxury of being able to see his mother and father, that the day would come when they would no longer be there. And so, he would make a point of stopping in to see them any time he was relatively close by. That inexorable march of time haunted him in his daily thoughts and even in his dreams. And, of course, there were the lines that Daniel always wondered about in terms of Marvell's mistress's coyness: was he expecting her to refuse forever?

Thy beauty shall no more be found,
Nor, in thy marble vault shall sound
My echoing song; then worms shall try
That long-preserved virginity,
And your quaint honour turn to dust,
And into ashes all my lust

No, absolutely not. With an appeal as beautiful, passionate and powerful as Marvell's was, no woman could possibly continue to refuse. Daniel was not quite the poet to appeal to Annemarie in that manner, but he would convince her, and, if not, they would have sufficient time after their wedding. Wedding? Did he say *wedding*, even in his unguarded thoughts?

The following day, Annemarie telephoned her mother.

"Mom, I think it's going to happen."

"What's going to happen?"

Annemarie's mother, Maureen Donovan, was a high school music teacher in Boston. She had studied the piano for twelve years when she decided to major in music in college. After her first year, she modified her course to include music education and was already teaching when she met Annemarie's father, Joseph Taviani. Maureen had just started to teach when she met her future husband at the wedding of mutual friends. He was in his last year of medical school and did not have time for dating, but he was immediately attracted by her dark red hair, blue eyes and slim but voluptuous figure. His parents owned a restaurant in Boston's Italian north end, a successful and highly regarded dining establishment that boasted a clientele of Boston's established gentry. Maureen and Joseph had three children, including two sons who both followed their father into medicine. Maureen started her daughter on piano lessons at the age of four.

"You know, Mom–the guy I told you about, the one I met in Rome."

"The pianist?"

"Yes, the conductor."

"What? Has he asked you to marry him?"

"Not yet, but it's going to happen. I'm sure of it. I know he loves me, and I love him too. He's the only man I've ever really loved, Mom."

Daniel and Annemarie were inseparable after that. He drove up to Boston with her to meet her family. She accompanied him each Sunday to have dinner with the Lorelli's. Violetta loved her. The fact that she spoke Italian and had lived in Italy made her even more special. Even Vincenzo, who usually did not express his opinion about his son's girlfriends, told Daniel how special he felt his young lady was.

"*Questa è la ragazza per te,*" Violetta told her son.

Daniel had thought about this important step in his life for many years. He always imagined that his marriage would be good. He would be devoted to his wife and there would never be any discord. Perhaps his naiveté here was a product of his own power of positive thinking, discounting or not even considering all the variables involved when another person, a completely different personality was an integral part of the equation. He had also had the distinct advantage of witnessing his own parents' remarkably smooth marriage, never a voice raised, never a discouraging word exchanged between the two of them. And Daniel, too, had a highly idealized view of marriage, and it was for this reason that he found it difficult, at first, to commit to Annemarie, since in his heart he had carved out this special place for his first real love, Marilyn. When his sensibilities about the subject and his rationality coalesced, it became possible for him create a new space in his heart, an area that would not obliterate the old, but relegate it to those realms of memory and emotion that remain with us always, capable of being recalled by the slightest provocation when subjected to conditions amenable to delicate stimulation.

Daniel was a true Romantic in the broader use of the term. Certain that Annemarie was the woman he was destined to be with, he now thought of all he could do to insure her happiness. First, he had to propose marriage officially. He wanted to come up with a unique and highly Romantic way of doing this. He thought of waiting until the next concert they would be performing at together and make an announcement at intermission. He would say that the viola player he would ask to stand was very special. She was a superb musician, but she was special to him for another reason, *that* being his love for her and his desire to be with her for the rest of his life, not only in the concert hall, but everywhere. Then, he decided that this would be too public, that Annemarie would feel uncomfortable, that she would like something more intimate for such a special occasion. Daniel's sensibilities turned to one of the most romantic occurrences in the history of music, Richard Wagner's presentation of a musical birthday gift for his wife Cosima's thirty-third birthday in 1870. Wagner had composed the *Siegfried Idyll* for the occasion and gathered thirteen musicians to perform it on the stairway outside her bedroom in their home on Lake Lucerne in Switzerland. It was played in the morning as Cosima was waking up. Daniel decided to recreate that event and then propose marriage to Annemarie. On a Sunday morning, he gathered thirteen musicians comprising two violins, a viola, a double bass, flute, bassoon, oboe and trumpet, two clarinets, and two horns, who were all quite happy to be a part of the undertaking, and assembled them outside Annemarie's apartment in the hallway at around 8:00 A.M. He knew that she would be sleeping late that morning since they had been out quite late the evening before. His plan was to begin by playing the *Siegfried Idyll,* and after Annemarie had awakened to the music and come to the door he would have the musicians accompany him in a work he had himself composed, "A Marriage Proposal in Music." Daniel had written the poem, which he then set to music. It was a romantic ballad in the style of Schubert. It made use of the same combination of thirteen instruments that played the Wagner work. It worked beautifully. Annemarie was at first taken aback, but she soon fell into the spirit of the occasion. At the conclusion of Daniel's "Marriage Proposal in Music," the couple kissed and Annemarie said,

"Now, let me die," Cosima's words to Richard after she heard the *Siegfried Idyll* for the first time that memorable morning. Daniel was overcome with emotion, thrilled that his savvy violist's knowledge of music history put the finishing touch on his carefully planned and somewhat unique initiative to ask her to marry him.

The entire Lorelli family went to Boston for the wedding, which took place in St. Rocco's Roman Catholic Church in Arlington, a suburb of Boston. Albert was Daniel's best man and the couple was married by Stephen Lorelli who had been ordained a Roman Catholic priest a year earlier.

Thirty-Four

Stephen Lorelli had been working in the family business since immediately after high school, but within a year he found that he was not cut out for that world. He, too, had inherited his mother's altruistic bent, and wanted to make a difference with his life, to help others. He enrolled in college as a history major and thought about eventually going into teaching. As a student at a Catholic university, he had many opportunities to go on spiritual retreats, and he eventually decided that his life should be dedicated to God. After graduation, he entered the seminary.

Seminary life shocked Stephen. While he found that, with minor exceptions, most of the priests instructing the novitiates were men of deep spirituality, totally dedicated to their Church and to their special mission in training future priests, some of the seminarians themselves were not there with the same measure of dedication and devotion to the true spirituality that Stephen felt was a presupposition for being there at all. Two seminarians in particular, Howard Driscoll and Jeremy Harvey were homosexuals who fully intended to live active sexual lives after ordination. Stephen overheard conversations between the two men describing the delights of anal intercourse. He didn't know what to do. At one point, in despair, he wanted to leave the seminary altogether. He spoke to his confessor within the secrecy of the confessional and explained that while he did not wish to be judgmental about others, he did not see how such men could become priests. Why, it went against the very strictures of the priestly calling! His confessor, Father Rocco Tornabene was a theologian, and a scholar who had written books on the Eucharist and on Mary's virginity. In the latter tome, he sought to separate the concept of the Blessed Mother's unique attribute in giving birth to a child, from the mundane concept of sexuality. Father Tornabene argued that the Church's teaching here was not the result of any abhorrence to sexual activity per se, and that this was not really why the virgin birth of Jesus was so important theologically. The important thing was not that Mary did not or could not have had sexual activity of any kind, but that God Himself was the direct creator of His Son, Jesus. In pursuing this position, the theological scholar sought to reply to those other scholars whose voices were becoming more and more dominant in the entire dialogue concerning Mary's virginity. Therefore, Father Tornabene dismissed as irrelevant the argument that Mary had had other children after Jesus and that, contrary to Church teaching, she could not have always been a virgin. Even if she did engage in sexual activity after Jesus was born, this did not nullify the fact that Jesus' birth was unique, and from this perspective Mary was forever a virgin, a conclusion based on an intellectual concept, having little or nothing to do with any physical reality that followed the divine intercession in the birth of the Son of God. This book was Father Tornabene's most controversial work, and even among Catholic theologians and clergy, one that did not achieve total approbation.

"Stephen, I have myself struggled with this problem many times, but *the secrecy of the confessional is sacrosanct.* I instruct those who confess to this failing that they must leave the seminary unless they honestly feel they can overcome these illicit desires. Of course, if they assure me that they will be faithful in the future, I have to accept them at their word. I am also sure that not all men in this category actually make it a matter for confession. God alone knows. But this should not deter you from becoming a priest. The Church is in urgent need, *urgent need*, my son, of young men like you who will maintain the foundation upon which our Faith is built."

Stephen's resolve was firmed up by Father Tornabene's words and he completed his training without further misgivings of any kind. Violetta was so proud to "give one of my sons to God," as she put it. Vincenzo, like many Italian men of his generation, was sorry to see his son "waste his life," as he confided to Daniel.

"Don't tell your mother what I said," he instructed his son. "She is happy and I am happy for that. Stephen seems to be happy too, but wouldn't it be so much better for him to marry and to have children of his own?"

Daniel did not know what to say to his father. In a way, he agreed with him, but in another way he still thought of the priesthood as having a mystique of its own. He recalled how he himself had found the concept attractive when he had been away on retreat as a teenager.

"Papà, as a priest Stephen can have a beneficial influence over so many people. As a husband and father his influence is much more limited. That is a consideration, isn't it?"

"Yes, I suppose it is," Vincenzo replied, sadly.

Stephen was assigned to St. Agnes Parish in Brooklyn, a neighborhood of old Italian families with an ever increasing Hispanic population. The pastor, Father O'Neill, a man in his early sixties, welcomed Stephen warmly. Another priest, Father Muldowney completed the regular parish staff of clerics, augmented on weekends by visiting priests needed to say some of the Masses. A number of lay people provided assistance in managing the parish. The rectory was very efficiently run by an Irish widow, Mrs. McAllister. She did some of the cooking herself, but she had the assistance of an Italian grandmother in preparing the larger meals. Mrs. McAllister adopted Father Lorelli as her very own charge. She saw that he was much too accommodating to everyone, and she was determined that no one would take undue advantage of his good nature.

"Now don't you worry," she told Violetta when Stephen's parents came to visit him at the rectory soon after his arrival there, "I will see that your son eats well and is not mistreated by anyone," a slight Irish brogue accenting her words.

"Oh, thank you, thank you, Mrs. McAllister," Violetta replied, smiling broadly, confident that her son was indeed in good hands.

The young women in the parish were beside themselves with glee at the arrival of this handsome young priest. Some wondered why such a man had to be sacrificed to the priesthood. Those of marrying age saw themselves with a man like Father Lorelli. Like the priest's father, they saw his vocation as a "waste" of manhood. There were so few good men to go around. Why was this one sacrificed *on the altar* when he should be at the altar getting married to one of them?

When Stephen told Father Muldowney, Father Tom as he was affectionately known to his parishioners, that he was getting a lot of invitations to dinner, the older priest suggested that he accept some of them.

"Everyone thinks that we priests are getting invited all the time, so no one invites us. You are new, so they figure you haven't been tapped yet. I would accept some invitations. Otherwise, you'll be eating in the rectory all the time."

But Mrs. McAllister had other ideas. When Stephen told her he would not be there for dinner on a Sunday after the Masses, she put her hands on her hips and demanded,

"Are you going to eat with your family, then?"

"No, I've been invited by one of the parishioners."

"And which one might that be?" Audrey McAllister insinuatingly inquired.

On hearing the woman's name who had extended the invitation, Mrs. McAllister, raising her voice somewhat, commented,

"That hussy!"

"Whatever do you mean?" Stephen asked incredulously.

"She is a woman who lives alone in her big house."

"But she's married. She told me about her husband."

"Yes, her husband, a husband who disappears for months at a time."

"Well, what if he has to travel in connection with his work?"

"Fine, but if he's traveling now, she should not invite you to dinner."

Stephen looked at his protector and smiled. Could he be that naïve he wondered?

"I think I'll telephone her and ask her who will be joining us."

"Yes, you do that," Mrs. McAllister said quickly, approvingly.

Stephen telephoned Mrs. Curtis and asked her about the time he needed to be there. She gave him leeway to arrive between 2:00 and 2:30, and Stephen then asked who would be joining them.

"It will be just the two of us. My husband is away on business. I thought this could be a good opportunity to discuss some questions I have."

Stephen's response came back swiftly with no hesitation or room for further discussion. He was not unkind, just firm and secure.

"I'm sorry to have to cancel on you like this, but I cannot dine with a woman of the parish alone. Mrs. Curtis, you realize that we have to beware of giving scandal. Such an encounter could seriously jeopardize the way in which my parishioners see me and consider my position as their spiritual advisor."

"I understand," Mrs. Curtis replied. "I meant no harm. I wanted you to see my collection of religious objects and books.

"Perhaps, when your husband is at home."

Mrs. McAllister, who had been listening from the adjoining room, smiled to herself. She liked this young priest. He could take advice and he could be strong too. She was content with the way she had handled his first crisis. After that, Stephen would check with Mrs. McAllister before agreeing to go to a parishioner's house for dinner.

The younger girls in the parish, like the older ones but for different reasons, loved the young priest. The girls in the Church school, especially the older eighth graders swooned over him whenever he came into the school building. Stephen made sure that he kept his distance from them, however, being kind, affable and entertaining by asking them about themselves, their families, their likes and dislikes, telling some good clean jokes and generally endearing himself to them, much as a kind and benevolent uncle would. As a priest, he was a great role model, and the young boys and girls, men and women he came into contact with would remember him as the perfect Catholic priest years later, especially at times when the priesthood would come under attack for failings that were all too human or so inhuman that it would be hard to understand them at all. But these things were unheard of in the experiences of those who had come under the sphere of a priest like Stephen Lorelli.

Father Lorelli found that his vow of chastity was one that was very difficult to maintain, but he was determined to do so. Father Tornabene often told him that God's grace was sufficient for all priests if they would just access it. They had to make the minimal effort and the strength they needed would permeate their beings in abundance. It was not easy, and no one should assume that a priest, like any normal man, was not subject to temptation all the time. When showering, it was difficult to avoid touching oneself, particularly as thoughts recurred of a young woman whose bodice was cut too low, or of another whose short skirt revealed more of a lovely leg than a priest like Stephen was prepared to deal with. But he was determined, and when thoughts that could compromise his vows tried to take hold of him, Stephen would quickly turn his thoughts to saints like Teresa of Avila or John of the Cross, saints whose love of God transcended everything else in life. Stephen was not as dogmatic in every minute detail of his faith as other priests he knew certainly were, but where real principles were concerned, he was as faithful as anyone, and truer to the highest ideals of Roman Catholicism than most.

Father Lorelli's line at confession became the longest of all the priests at St. Agnes. Most of the young people in the parish wanted to go to him as he quickly garnered a reputation for patience, understanding and fairness. Some of the older penitents were eager to extend their conversations with the priest so Stephen invited them to come to the rectory to talk about their problems, explaining that they could not take too much time in confession with all the other confessions waiting to be heard. A few quickly took advantage of this offer. Janet Bailey, a thirty-five year old housewife and mother of three children was very nervous as she sat before the priest who was her junior by ten years.

"Father, thank you for agreeing to speak with me."

"No thanks are necessary. It is my duty, my pleasure," Stephen assured her.

"I don't really know where to begin and I don't really know what my problem is, but as I was telling you at confession, I am guilty of the sin of envy."

"Please continue."

"I find that I have these feelings of jealousy of other women I come into contact with. My next door neighbor. She is always buying things I cannot afford–clothing, furnishings for her house. I think to myself, 'Why is she so fortunate while I have to struggle and count every penny.' Then there is my sister-in-law, my brother's wife. My brother does very well. He's a lawyer and they live in a beautiful house on Long Island. They go on vacation each year. He is my brother, but I, as his sister, have very little compared to him. It's not my brother I am jealous of. I love him and wish him the best. But his wife is no better than I am. Why is her life so much easier than mine? I know it's ridiculous in a way, but these feelings eat at my insides."

Stephen Lorelli was quickly learning that a priest had to fill the role of psychologist, and although he had had some training in dealing with people's personal problems, he found that he was really learning on the job.

"Janet," he said, consciously making the decision to address her by her first name even though this was the first time he was speaking to her outside Confession.

"Your feelings are not unusual. You are not the first person to be envious of others, nor will you be the last."

As Stephen said this he thought to himself how trite it sounded, how unoriginal. "The commendable thing about you is the fact that you are addressing this dilemma. So many of your fellow parishioners would never even admit to themselves that they are jealous of others they come into contact with."

Mrs. Bailey experienced a sudden surge of self-satisfaction. Yes, she was not such a bad person after all. She was doing something about her sin.

"Let me express it to you in this way." Stephen leaned forward and Janet Bailey sensed that she had the priest's complete confidence.

"Think of the bigger picture. There are many people in the world who are materially better off than you are, but there are probably even more who are worse off than you. Are your children healthy?"

"Yes."

"Does your husband have steady work?"

"Yes."

"Are most of your important needs provided for?"

255

"Yes."

"All right then. Think for awhile of how many in the world, in this very parish, do not have what you have of material goods and of the well being of their families. Is your husband abusive to you?"

"Oh no, Father, he is a good man."

"Well Janet, in the short time I have been here at St. Agnes, I have come across many women whose husbands are abusive to them in one way or another and who do not even provide for them in some instances."

"Really?" Janet Bailey wondered if she knew any of these people.

"There is something else I would like to point out. Forget about all the people who are worse off than you are. It's like the old story of a person in pain not feeling any better knowing that others have the same pain or worse pain than he has. Now think of the people you envy. All right. They may be better off than you are in some ways, but there are people throughout the world who are much better off than they are. You don't know them so you don't envy them. But just think about envying everyone who has a more glamorous life than yours, who has a nicer house, a much nicer house than even your brother's. People in California, in Texas, in Monaco, in Paris, in London, wherever. Why don't you feel envy of them too? Why limit your envy to those who live near you?"

Janet Bailey began to squirm in her seat. The possibility of her feeling envious of everyone, in all the places mentioned by the priest, was overwhelming. She would have time for nothing else. Somehow, the realization that the many others who were much better off than those she felt envious of had a chastening effect on her. Something inside her, popularly referred to as the "green eyed monster," had been subdued. After her meeting with Father Lorelli, she never found it necessary to confess to the sin of envy again.

A middle aged man made an appointment to see Stephen. His problem was not something connected to any sin he could think of. His was more of a philosophical predicament. Joseph Bilotta appeared to be very nervous as he entered the Rectory. He sat down and Stephen saw that the man was wringing his hands. Was this a bad habit, Stephen wondered, or just a reaction to the anxiety he felt in talking about his problem, whatever it was.

"Father, I hope you can give me an idea about why God is punishing me."

"You think God is punishing you?" Stephen replied, with obvious astonishment. "What makes you think God would single you out for punishment?"

"Well, when I was thirty years old I found out I had a tumor. It looked very bad and I was sure I was going to die. I felt as though I had not even begun to live yet. I made a Novena and prayed to God, asking Him to spare me. I asked for the chance to marry and raise a family."

"And God spared you?"

"Yes. The tumor was removed and it was benign. It was like a miracle. Then I met my wife and we married soon afterwards. We had four children, one after the other. I wanted to be a good Catholic and we did not practice birth control of any kind."

"It sounds as though God has blessed you, not punished you," Stephen said reassuringly, smiling broadly, trying to ease Mr. Bilotta's obvious discomfort.

"I know. He has blessed me in many ways, but I . . . ." The man's words trailed off. He lowered his head and shook it slightly.

"It's hard to explain."

"Please try. I will give you all the time you need."

"It's my wife. She is not nice to me. She belittles me all the time, even in front of the children. I try to talk to her when we are alone, to ask her why she is so hostile, but she just mocks me, tells me to grow up."

"I see." Stephen found himself wondering how he was going to handle this situation. "Why do you think this is God's punishment?"

"I asked God to spare me, to let me live to raise a family. Maybe God said, 'All right. I had other plans for you, but if this is what you want, you can live and have your family, but as part of the deal you must have a wife who is a shrew.' God is punishing me because I thought I knew better than He did about what was good for me. Sometimes I think I would have been better off dying then than living through this daily Hell."

Stephen now found himself in a quandary. Should he tell this man how ridiculous he thought the entire premise was? Should he agree that God had granted him his wish but also needed to exact something from him in exchange? Stephen did not speak at once, but sat there looking at Joseph Bilotta. He stood up and paced behind his desk, sat down again and spoke very softly.

"Joe, you came to me for advice."

"Yes. I did."

"You are looking to me as your spiritual advisor for a way of resolving your doubts, are you not?"

"Yes, exactly, Father."

"Very well. Then I will tell you exactly what I think. I think that your tumor was benign all the time. There was no miracle involved. If you were meant to die you would have died. What kind of God do you think would help you only to hurt you? I think you are attaching too much importance to events that are plainly a part of daily life, events that happen to all people, all the time. Some make good marriages, some do not. Before anyone could say anything on this matter, it would be necessary to hear your wife's side of the story. Remember: two sides to every story—right?"

Bilotta got up quickly. "I'm sorry I bothered you." He walked out without another word. Stephen was quickly learning that even as a priest he could not please everyone.

Counseling parishioners could be difficult, frustrating and even annoying, and Stephen had to guard against appearing less than extremely patient at all times, but the most difficult request for advice came from another priest. One day, Stephen got a call from a man he had met in the seminary. After ordination, Christopher Indelicato had been assigned to a parish in Queens, New York. He and Stephen had become friendly since both were from the same archdiocese and both would be assigned to parishes not too far from one another. They knew they would run into each other from time to time and had promised to keep in touch. They agreed to meet for pizza on the following Friday evening.

Christopher began tentatively,

"I asked you to meet me because I have a problem I would like to discuss with you."

That much was already evident and Stephen smiled, prepared to listen. Other customers in adjoining booths looked over at the two good looking priests, their white collars and black shirts giving them away. Two young women nearby bemoaned the loss of such manhood to them or to other lonely women.

"Before I decided to become a priest, "Christopher continued, "I was in love with a woman."

"Weren't we all?" Stephen asked rhetorically, adding,

"Except for the others who . . ." He broke off, not wanting to articulate the thought.

"Which others?" Christopher inquired?

"The ones in love but not with women."

"Oh, yeah." Christopher laughed.

"I'm sorry. Go ahead."

"Well, I was in love." Christopher lowered his head slightly and made an effort to lower his voice, even though he was already speaking so quietly that Stephen could barely hear him above the din of the crowd.

"Perhaps we should wait to discuss this until after we leave."

"Yes, yes," Christopher agreed.

Later, they sat in Stephen's car and Christopher began again.

"This woman I was in love with. . . . I would have married her if she would have had me."

"Are you saying that becoming a priest was something you decided on, on the rebound?"

"Yes and no. I had always thought about the priesthood, and when I knew I could not have Liz I made up my mind to enter the seminary. I've never had any regrets, either. Until last week."

"Last week?"

"Yes, last week I got a telephone call from Liz. She got my number from an old mutual friend. Apparently, he didn't tell her I'm now a priest. She just divorced her husband after a really tough marriage. For nearly the entire five years they were married, he beat and abused her. She eventually went to a shelter, got the support she needed and with the help of friends made it through this bitter divorce." Christopher hesitated.

"I'm waiting."

"I want to see her."

"As an old friend? As a spiritual advisor?" Christopher sat silently, so Stephen continued,

"Does she want you to help her with an annulment?"

"She doesn't know I'm a priest."

"Doesn't . . . know . . . you're . . . a . . . priest?"

Stephen spoke each word slowly, stopping as if for breath after each utterance.

"How is that possible if she called you at the rectory?"

"It seems that the guy who gave her my number just told her that this is the number where I can be reached, at work."

"Yes, but she had to know she reached a rectory?"

"She did, but when she asked me what I was doing there, I know it's crazy, but I told her I'm working on parish finances. She just said, 'Oh, you're an accountant.' And I let it go at that."

"Christopher," Stephen said in a tone of obvious annoyance, "What are you trying to do?"

Ignoring Stephen's sardonic tone, Christopher went on,

"She told me it was just like me to work in something Church related."

Christopher smiled with evident satisfaction, though Stephen could not quite fathom why he was so satisfied.

"She said, 'You always were such a good Catholic. You are the man I should have married.' She wants to see me."

"Good. Invite her to the rectory."

"I'm meeting her for dinner."

"To what purpose?" Stephen was thinking to himself that he had to show greater patience, but this did not have to include tolerance for foolishness by a fellow priest.

"Well, to eat together."

"Don't get funny. I repeat: to what purpose?"

"I don't really know . . . yet."

"You can't do this."

"I know."

"Well if you know, why are you doing it? You know it could be an occasion of sin."

"Exactly. That's why I asked you to meet me."

"What? Hoping I would encourage you to go ahead. Look, just because I was known in the seminary as the 'liberal' doesn't mean that I just accept everything and anything." Stephen's face reddened and it was obvious that he was annoyed.

"I wanted you to talk me out of it."

"Consider it done."

Christopher called Liz and told her he was a priest and that they could not see one another socially. She suggested that he see her, then, for spiritual guidance. He agreed if she would come to the rectory. Eventually, Christopher helped his friend to get a Church annulment of her marriage. After seeing so much of her, he realized he was in love with her and left the priesthood to marry.

Stephen's first years as a priest coincided with the Civil Rights Movement in the United States in the '60's. He found himself constantly engaged in discussions, disputes and arguments with some of his parishioners and even with some of the clergy he came into contact with over what was happening around them and across the country. There was one priest in particular, Father Cornelius Black, whose vituperative pronouncements shocked and dismayed Stephen. Father Black was one of the priests who came to help out with the Sunday Mass schedule, and the pastor always invited these priests to remain for Sunday dinner. Invariably, the discussion during dinner would turn to current events. One Sunday afternoon, after Stephen said that social justice demanded that legislation be passed to insure equality of opportunity for all Americans, regardless of color, religion or national origin, Father Black snapped back,

"What social justice? These Negroes have come a long way in this country. They have nothing to complain about! And let me tell you something else, young man, it's the Jews, it's these lousy Jews who are stirring everything up in this country!"

"Father," Stephen replied, trying to remain respectful in spite of his visually obvious agitation, "Do I have to remind you that you are a Roman Catholic priest? You, above all, should never speak disparagingly of an entire group of people. How can you say such things?"

"Because they're true," the older priest responded smugly. "You're too young and you haven't seen anything yet. Wait until you see how these Jews continue to spread their corruption, then you'll agree with me."

"I will never agree with you. Your words are a betrayal of our Lord's command to love one another. Don't tell me you have never heard of Jesus' praise for the Good Samaritan and all that it implies, and all that it demands of us."

"Ah, hogwash. Of course we have to love one another, but we do not have to love those who would destroy us. 'Love your neighbor' it says, not your enemy."

Much to Stephen's surprise, Father Black stood up, pounding his fist on the table as he arose. The visitor to St. Agnes was a man in his fifties, overweight by around forty pounds, balding, always very clean shaven with clear smooth skin.

"I repeat Father Lorelli, you have a lot to learn, and you will learn it sooner or later. How dare you question my wisdom?"

"It's not your wisdom I question," Stephen said with sadness and subdued anger, "I question your commitment to the priesthood and its ideals, to the basic tenets of our beautiful religion. As for your wisdom, I seriously doubt that you possess any at all after what you said here today."

"That's enough!" Father Black shouted back, walking out of the room.

Father O'Neill looked at Stephen and smiled,

"Stephen, you did not have to go *that* far."

"How could I listen to what he said and not reply?"

"Sometimes, Stephen, you have to know when to speak and when not to."

"But Father O'Neill. . . ." Stephen had instilled within himself a habit of deference to older figures of authority and continued to address the pastor formally even though O'Neill had asked him to address him by his first name.

"Father O'Neill, how can we accept that kind of talk within these walls?"

"Alas, there are those whom we cannot change no matter what we say or do. Cornelius is not as bad as he sounds. If a black member of the parish, if a Jew came to him with a problem and asked for his help, he would do everything he could to help them. It's just that he has these ideas about social classes and ethnic groups that have been stubbornly part of his makeup for most of his life."

"Oh, so he would help people he disparages, but he would do so condescendingly. No one wants to be looked down on even when they are getting a boost. I'm sure if he helps someone he doesn't really respect, it's out of pride. That, too, is sinful."

The Pastor smiled again. He was proud of his young assistant. He said things he himself should have said, and he knew that Stephen was right. On subsequent Sundays, Father Black would remain for dinner only if he was aware that Stephen would not be there. Stephen approached the bigot in an attempt to make peace with him on many occasions afterwards, but Father Black would just brush him aside. Years later, Stephen learned, Cornelius Black developed throat cancer and lost his voice altogether. The phrase "poetic justice" came to Stephen's mind, but he could not begin to believe that God would mete out such retribution.

Thirty-Five

In the year following their marriage, Daniel and Annemarie continued to work together in the New York Musicians' Orchestra, but six concerts a year hardly sufficed for either of them. Eventually, Daniel was appointed as the leading conductor of a small choral and instrumental ensemble in Boston. He and Annemarie commuted between the two cities, staying at her parents' home whenever they were in Boston and in their own apartment while in New York. With the Plymouth Choral Society, Daniel was able to explore and become familiar with another part of the classical repertory, that of the great choral works—masses, oratorios, cantatas. The group performed a major work every six weeks and gave four performances over the course of five days, Friday, Saturday and Tuesday evenings, and Sunday afternoons, the Friday and Tuesday evenings in the suburbs and the Saturday and Sunday concerts in downtown Boston. Before beginning his tenure with the group, Daniel threw himself into studying scores and listening to recordings of many of the works he hoped to perform with the organization, a professional body for sure, but one which needed polishing, and Daniel intended to accomplish this. He came to know the majestic power and beauty of Bach's *Mass in B minor*; the sublime inspiration of Beethoven's *Missa Solemnis* and the spirited variety of the same composer's *Mass in C* (thrilling indeed he found the wonderful "Gloria," with trumpets and kettledrums and the altogether sublime fugue at "cum sancto spirito" with multiple "Amens," so distinctively Beethovenian); the grandeur of Haydn's *Lord Nelson Mass*; the devotional fervor of Bruckner's *Third Mass*; and another *Mass* that surprised Daniel and gave him an entirely new outlook on a composer who wrote a most unusual *Mass* in the early Twentieth Century, shortly before his death, the *Glagolitic Mass* of Leos Janacek. Haydn's *Creation*, Handel's *Judas Maccabaeus* and Honegger's *King*

David also occupied Daniel. Among contemporary choral works, Daniel was quite enterprising in presenting one of the earliest U.S. performances of a work that was then being hailed by music lovers and critics alike as indicative of the direction classical music had to go—modern, yes, but with emotional viability and audience appeal. The work was the Polish composer, Krystzof Penderecki's *St. Luke Passion*. His performance of this piece helped to insure Daniel's reputation as a conductor who was both innovative and intelligent. He discovered more great works that he wanted to perform than any conductor could possibly find time for, unless he wanted to devote his entire life to the choral repertory. Daniel also received offers to conduct abroad. For the 50th anniversary of Gabriel Faure's death, commemorative presentations of the composer's *Requiem* were scheduled by a choral society in Paris, to be performed in Notre Dame Cathedral. A Monsignor on the Bishop's staff in Boston, a music lover who attended most of Daniel's performances, arranged for Daniel to conduct one of these performances, and the usually chauvinistic Parisian critical press acknowledged Daniel's conducting of the work as superior to any they had experienced in quite some time. Daniel loved the Faure *Requiem*. To him, it was the greatest *Missa Defunctorum* ever written because of its unquestioned beauty and the aura of serenity and supreme solace the music afforded a listener. On hearing it, one who mourned the loss of a loved one could easily identify with its message of consolation and hope.

After three years, Daniel received an invitation to audition for a position as artistic director and conductor of an opera company in Karlsruhe, a city of around 250,000 inhabitants on the Rhine in West Germany. The managing director of the opera company was an old friend of Daniel's mentor, Carlo Maria Stagione, and Stagione had urged his friend Thomas Guten to invite the young American to apply. Daniel flew over and conducted excerpts from three operas, Mozart's *Don Giovanni*, Verdi's *Il Trovatore* and Wagner's *Tannhauser*. The committee responsible for choosing the new director liked Daniel and felt that his ability to draw something significant from the singers and instrumentalists was extraordinary. However, as Daniel was to find, throughout his career, politics was a key factor in advancing in the music business and Daniel was not, never was and would find it difficult to ever become a political animal. The politics under discussion had nothing to do with any ideology connected with religion, nationalism or party affiliation. No, it was much more insidious since it was so difficult to identify. In the case of this position in Karlsruhe, it amounted to whom one knew, what one had done over a period of time for this or that person, the calling in of debts, real or imagined and a good deal less to do with talent, real or perceived.

A conductor from Austria who paid his dues over the years, a much older man than Daniel, was chosen for the position by the committee. Daniel returned to New York, disappointed, but appreciative of the opportunity to have had the experience to audition for such a job. To his great surprise, a week later Daniel received a telephone call from Guten asking him if he was still interested in the position.

"But what about the Austrian?" Daniel asked.

"Well, as you know, he was the committee's first choice, but you were high up there because of your obvious musical talent. But the poor man suffered a stroke, and it does not seem that he will ever conduct again."

Daniel did not like to profit at the expense of another person's suffering, and this sensitivity caused him to hesitate. He asked for a few days and Guten agreed, but warned him not to take too long. Daniel discussed it with his wife. Annemarie had urged Daniel to go for the audition. She was cosmopolitan enough to welcome the idea of living abroad. The couple now had a one year old daughter, Marta, and Annemarie thought it would be great for her daughter to learn German as a native.

"Don't be ridiculous!" she scoffed. "You had nothing to do with giving the man a stroke. If you don't take the position, someone else will." That was all Daniel needed. His wife's approbation had become the single most important factor in any decision he had to make whether it was personal or professional. At the age of thirty-five, Daniel Lorelli took the helm of the Karlsruhe Opera, a company that was well provided for as the result of an endowment it had been granted for a twenty-five year period by a consortium of some of the city's wealthiest manufacturing companies. The only requirement was that a new opera, preferably by a German composer, had to be presented each season in addition to works from the standard repertory. Daniel conducted passionate performances of a number of works familiar to his audience as well as new or recent operas by Werner Egk, Hans Werner Henze and Carl Orff among other German composers.

By the end of their first year in Germany, Annemarie gave birth to the couple's second child, a boy, Vincent, named after Daniel's father. Annemarie could have had a position in the opera orchestra, but she chose not to since it would have meant not spending enough time with her two children. She opted instead to give viola lessons, which she could accomplish in the house the couple had rented. Within a short time, she had twenty pupils ranging from beginners to quite accomplished players who had been studying the instrument for as long as 15 years. She hired a young woman to care for and entertain the children during the hours she needed for teaching.

In the fall of his second year in Karlhruhe, Daniel's New York agency, Simon Associates, contacted him about accepting guest conducting appearances within Europe. It was, the agent assigned to handle the conductor's engagements assured him, important for his career to be heard widely, to accept any and all appearances offered whenever possible. The particular agent who contacted Daniel, a young woman without much real experience in the business, had been convinced by one of the agency heads that without them or other top notch agencies an artist could go no place. There was some truth in this posture, but in Daniel's case almost every advance he had made in his career was the result of personal contacts, his own or those of friends. Daniel, however, trusting and credulous as always, believed that the agency handling him had actively been looking out for him, seeking dates and potentially worthwhile concerts for him to conduct. Of course, any engagements had to fit in with his demanding schedule at the Opera. The Opera's management liked him and assured him that he could accept such offers occasionally. The assistant conductor could fill in. Without Daniel's knowledge of the circumstances then connecting him to a particularly high profile appearance, it was a fact that the Israel Philharmonic, making an important European tour, found itself without its chief conductor, who had to return to Israel for his father's funeral. The orchestra had two concerts in nearby Stuttgart and its concert master had suggested that they try to get Maestro Lorelli to conduct since he was situated very close to where they would be playing. The orchestra manager made some inquiries, learned the name of Daniel's agency representing him, and contacted them in New York. With events set in motion in this way, Daniel received the invitation and agreed to go to Stuttgart. When he arrived for rehearsals, the orchestra manager assured him that his New York agent really had nothing to do with getting him this booking. It was the result of the orchestra's concert manager's strong recommendation. When the manager himself checked into the possibility of engaging the American conductor, he learned of the high esteem with which Daniel was regarded in Europe and in America. Daniel thanked the manager and assured him that he would personally thank the concert master as soon as he saw him. "Her," the manager corrected. "When you see *her*. We have a woman concert master." Even then, with his mind occupied with so many things, Daniel did not stop to think about who this concert master could be. At the first rehearsal, Daniel walked into the hall and immediately looked over to where the first violinist sat. Suddenly, he could feel his heart beating rapidly. Feelings that were buried in his subconscious for years were triggered by the appearance of this woman who had haunted his dreams on so many nights over a long period of time. He believed he had come to terms with everything connected with her, but did not imagine their paths would ever cross again. The feelings now welling up inside him did have a strange way of insinuating themselves. Daniel had come to believe that they were extinguished, but in truth they had only been dampened. As he approached, the concert master stood up and smiled.

"Daniel, it's so good to see you again. You look wonderful."

"Marilyn. Now I understand. You gave them my name. But how . . . ?" He found it difficult to complete the sentence.

"I have been following your career all along. I knew you were at the Opera in Karlsruhe, and when they needed a good conductor to replace our Music Director, I realized how close by you were. So, why not you?"

"Oh, thank you, Marilyn. You look wonderful too. You haven't changed at all. You are as . . . ." Daniel hesitated. He didn't know if what he wanted to say was inappropriate.

"As?" Marilyn asked.

"I was going to say, you are as beautiful as ever."

"You're too kind." Daniel had taken her hands in his and they were about to embrace but he hesitated.

"Perhaps we can catch up on each other after rehearsals?" Marilyn suggested.

"Yes, we should." Daniel thought it was good that Annemarie had not joined him for these few days in Stuttgart. It could have made things awkward for him. As quickly as that thought entered his mind, he wondered why it had even occurred to him. What possible difference could it make to Annemarie if he was working with an orchestra whose concert master was once his lover? Still, there was this nagging sense that Annemarie would make it the subject of a dispute between them in some way. There were things he still did not understand about his wife though he tried in every way he could to achieve the meeting of minds he had always craved with a thirst that desperately needed quenching at times.

During rehearsals, he did not feel he was performing in an entirely natural manner. He was somewhat self-conscious because of Marilyn, but once he got into the music, his usual instincts took over and he concentrated only on the music itself. The program was an interesting one with the theme of "Lieben in Orchester-musik" ("Love in Orchestral Music.") An important requirement was that Daniel would have to be willing to conduct the exact program devised by the Orchestra's Music Director, with no substitutions. It began with Tchaikovsky's *Fantasy Overture, Romeo and Juliet*, followed by the "Scene d'Amour" from Berlioz's dramatic symphony, *Roméo et Juliette*. After intermission, Schoenberg's *Pelleas et Melisande* would be heard and the program would conclude with Wagner's *Prelude and Liebestod* from the opera *Tristan und Isolde*. Daniel had gotten into the habit of thoroughly researching—at least to whatever extent was practically feasible—the life of any composer whose works he conducted. He wanted to identify with them, to see where they were in their lives when they composed the works under study. While preparing for this "Love" concert in Stuttgart, Daniel visited a local library and read as much as he could about Wagner's life at the time he composed *Tristan und Isolde*. The books were entirely in German, but he had developed a good reading knowledge of the language. He read Wagner's own comments about the music of the "Prelude and Liebestod." But fortuitously, in the course of his reading, Daniel came across a reference to Wagner's apparent belief in reincarnation. In a letter to Mathilde Wesendonck, the woman he dedicated his *Wesendonck Lieder* to, Wagner had written, "Only the profoundly conceived idea of reincarnation could give me any consolation, since that belief shows how all at last can reach complete redemption. Thus all the terrible tragedy of life is seen to be nothing but the sense of seperateness in Time and Space." Daniel was amazed that Wagner too had felt such great identification with this view of life after death, the exact concept that he himself had been intrigued with since early childhood and the belief that justice could only be possible if one *could* live again!

Late in the evening following rehearsals, Marilyn approached Daniel and asked if he would like to join her at a restaurant nearby for supper.

"There is so much we have to discuss," she said, smiling brightly and tossing her jet black hair to one side. Marilyn's hair was not as long as Daniel remembered, but its shoulder length and radiance framed a beautiful face that had grown even more striking with maturity. Daniel was hoping to have the opportunity to speak with her privately. He knew almost nothing about what had happened to her after their final communications and he was extremely curious to learn more.

"I know," he replied. "It's funny, you know all about what's been happening with me, but I know nothing about your life after you settled in Israel. You didn't let me know where you were." Daniel recalled the months when he had been trying to make any contact at all with Marilyn and had failed completely. His attempts to get an address or telephone number from her family were futile.

"You knew where I stood, Dan." Marilyn's tone became wistful. "But, sometimes . . ." she hesitated, "Sometimes I think that could have been a test of your love. If you really, really wanted me, you would have moved heaven and earth to find me and claim me."

"That's not fair. At a certain point, I loved you enough to let you have what you really wanted. That's how I saw it then, and I can't see how I could have acted differently."

Marilyn smiled, that smile Daniel remembered so well, the smile that told him all was settled. There was no need for further discussion on the subject. Later, however, lying in his bed that night, Daniel wondered if he should have done more to pursue the first real love of his life. He thought about his daughter and son and was confident that he had made the right choices. Then he questioned his own train of thought. Why did he think he had followed the right path because of his children? Shouldn't he be thinking that his wife was the initial right choice? Yes, yes, he reassured himself. Annemarie was his life's true love, his destiny. And yet, and yet, a nagging almost capricious tickle continued to flit inside his head.

They sat in a corner of the small and intimate restaurant and regarded one another with genuine affection.

"Before we get into the past, I would like to say something about the present. After seeing what you did with the orchestra today, I feel proud that I was responsible for getting you to conduct our orchestra during these concerts. This program of music about love was Mindy's idea." Mindy was the orchestra personnel's affectionate nickname for their conductor Mindru Abramowitz. When an orchestra truly loved their leader, it was not uncommon for them to refer to him in this fashion. The New York Philharmonic, for example, called Leonard Bernstein, "Lenny." But when a conductor was either held on a high pedestal or was regarded as a tyrant of sorts, the musicians would call him by his last name exclusively.

"Mindy had definite ideas about the music and about how the love theme should progress, culminating in Wagner's exquisite music. But I wonder how much he really knows about love—physical love, cerebral love, the ins and outs!" Marilyn laughed at her own unintended pun.

"Sorry, I didn't mean to be so graphic."

Daniel's expression, at first somewhat puzzled, broke into a broad smile when he caught the drift of her words.

"Yes, anyway, you made the music so much more meaningful. (I wouldn't want Mindy to hear me say this). Your instructions to the orchestra, to various instruments, proved that you understand the passion and, well, the heat in the music. After the rehearsal ended, I heard some of my colleagues discussing how you brought out things they did not know were even there."

"Really?" Daniel asked. His self-image was still that of one who knows he is good, but everything about himself and his abilities had always evolved so naturally that he never gave much thought as to why he excelled in the things he did.

"Well, thank you for telling me. It's especially gratifying to hear this from you."

"Yes . . . . " Marilyn mused and she appeared to have been transported miles, even ages away.

"Where are your thoughts taking you, Mar?"

"You called me 'Mar.' That's what you used to call me, remember?"

"Yes, of course. But it just came out without thought, spontaneously."

"I know. And I just spontaneously recalled the time we made love after we had that fight. Do you remember?"

Daniel felt the blood rush to his face. He wasn't ready for this. But it suddenly all came back to him too.

"The time when you wanted me to lie to your parents about being Jewish?"

"Yes, exactly. I think that night our lovemaking was the best we ever had. It was so deep, so intense, so communicative. We were almost as one. Dan, I have to admit I have never felt as one with anybody as I did that night with you."

Daniel could barely suppress sensations of love that sprang up within him, a choking sensation took hold, making the bittersweet revelation tangible in a disturbing way, but not without a provocative appeal.

"That feeling was rekindled in me when we played the "Prelude and Liebestod." The way you shaped the music was phenomenal. I have never heard the eroticism so highly charged in this music before. I shouldn't tell you this . . . ."

"What?" Daniel asked, fascinated by Marilyn's disclosures and anxious to hear everything.

"One of my violin colleagues, a young woman, told me she was totally wet after playing that and watching you conduct. It never happened to her with Mindy."

"Oh, come on?" But as soon as he uttered those words, he regretted them, for he knew quite well the power of that music to stir the soul, and the body.

"Well, it was either the music or you, but she's not the type to swoon over a man."

Feeling uncomfortable, Daniel disregarded her words and changed the subject.

"Now, how about telling me more about your life? Do you have any children?" Daniel asked.

"I had two miscarriages. After I was at the Institute for a year or so, Seymour, the director, and I were getting along quite well. He's fifteen years older than I and had never been married. He was always too involved with the violin—playing it, studying its history, teaching an entire generation of Israeli violinists, many of whom occupy key positions in the world's finest orchestras. Some are soloists that you know. Seymour is an excellent violinist himself, but he never wanted to pursue a solo career. He's a very self-effacing kind of guy. In some ways he reminds me of you, very humble. He never even had time for women. I knew he cared for me, but I think he was afraid of rejection. Once I made the first move, he followed naturally, obediently one might say. We married two years after I first met him. My family came to Tel Aviv for the wedding. First I worked with him in the Institute, but then he encouraged me to go out and develop my own career. As Seymour's wife, I had many doors opened to me, but I did not want to achieve anything on sheer nepotism. Anything I got, I had to earn by my talent—that's the only way I could operate. At first I was thinking of pursuing a solo career, but I really did not like the idea of constant travel, flying all over the world. Now I feel I have the best of both worlds. As concert master, I get to perform as violin soloist about three or four times a year. I've already played the Beethoven, Brahms, Berg, Stravinsky and Bloch Concertos. Next year I'll play the premiere of a new Concerto by one of Israel's most promising young composers."

"What about the miscarriages?"

"I couldn't carry the baby to term either time. Of course I was disappointed. I still miss not having a child of my own, but I try to spend time with the children of friends. I give violin lessons to the daughters of two of my good friends and to the son of another. I also see these children outside of the teacher-pupil framework, and my mothering instincts are somewhat fulfilled. Seymour was very disappointed, but he is an understanding man. Sad to say, he has always acted older than he really is, and at this point the difference in our ages tells more than at any time in our relationship. But I love him very much and we have the highest regard and esteem for one another."

After the light repast—actually neither Daniel nor Marilyn ate anything at all, leaving what had been served, for they both were tremendously wound up from seeing each other, recalling their time together and the excitement of making music together again—Marilyn suggested that she walk Daniel back to his hotel.

"Let me walk you to *your* hotel," he urged.

"No, let's go back to yours. Unless . . . "

"Unless what?" Daniel queried.

"Unless you walk me back to my hotel and I pack a bag for the night and come with you to yours."

"You mean stay in my room tonight?"

"Yes, exactly, sure, why not?"

"But Mar, you know I'm married. You haven't even asked me about my relationship with my wife."

"How is it?"

"Great!"

"Truthfully, really great?"

Daniel hesitated and was trying to decide as to just how honest he needed to be here.

"Well, you know. Or perhaps you don't. After a couple has had children, things kind of settle down into a routine."

"Sexually, too?" Marilyn inquired with a determination in her voice that surprised Daniel.

"Yes, of course. It's just more difficult to even find the time to work up the kind of intimacy that existed naturally before children. You know, Marilyn, I'm not sure we should even be having this conversation."

"Come on Dan, don't tell me you wouldn't like to make love to me tonight? The way you looked down at me from the podium during some of the most erotic passages, I knew you were thinking about it."

"That's not true. And even if I do . . . did have any such inclination, I'm not twenty-two anymore. I am a father. I have to exercise good judgment. I cannot jeopardize my family's welfare for momentary gratification."

"Is it still your Roman Catholicism?" Marilyn pronounced the two words as though they constituted a term of disparagement.

"Yes, that too, but something more fundamental."

"Really, what can be more fundamental to a Roman Catholic as a reason for not doing something he wants to do than the strictures of his religion?"

"What about your husband? Don't you feel any guilt at all about being unfaithful to him?"

"I told you. He understands me. He knows that he can't fulfill all my needs, so he . . . well, he looks the other way, as long as I don't embarrass him at home, in or around where we live. If an opportunity comes up, like tonight, I know he would not feel I have betrayed him. You don't have to worry about anything from my side. You just have to decide if you can act without guilt."

"Mar, we were having such a pleasant time. Why do we have to spoil it?"

"Dan," Marilyn laughed, starting quietly and then erupting into a good hearty laugh.

"What's so funny?" Daniel asked with obvious puzzlement.

"Dan, you are *still* a virgin. You are still the same as you were when you were twenty-two. For my part, I can tell you honestly that I never had any intention of becoming intimate with you again. But tonight, the emotions that flowed between us need release. It' like Wagner's music, don't you see? We *should* make love, relive that time."

"A one night stand," Daniel commented with obvious sarcasm.

"That's the beauty of it. When two mature adults can get together and do what they want to do, without anyone being hurt, why not? We can," Marilyn's eyes opened wide with mock astonishment. "We can relive one of the best times of our youth!"

"I can see that you've lost none of your pragmatism." Daniel felt morally superior to this beautiful woman he had loved so much, who still touched something deep within him that he could not himself uncover.

"And you? Wasn't expediency one of your favorite solutions?"

"That's totally unfair!"

"You're right. I apologize. My, we sound like no time has passed at all since we last met." They both laughed and Daniel embraced Marilyn with a fervor he had not expressed towards his own wife for some time. They had reached Daniel's hotel.

"Well?" Marilyn asked.

"Well, come up. There's a sitting room. We can order a nightcap and talk some more, but we do have early rehearsals, so we have to be prudent."

For a half hour or so, they sipped their drinks and talked mostly about music, contemporary composers and trends in classical music programming. Marilyn walked over to Daniel and squeezed next to him on the loveseat. She began to run her fingers through his hair. Their faces turned towards one another and slowly they drew closer together. Their lips met, their mouths opened and they kissed, deeply, fervently, with all the ardor that had been fermenting within each of them from the very first time they experienced their first sensations of love for each other. It was long and intense, blinding, almost stifling. After what seemed like a period of time suspended, Marilyn stood up. She began to unbutton her blouse and unzip her skirt. Daniel wanted to forget everything. He wanted her again. He needed to have this moment. Then just as quickly as he had determined that this needed to be done, the sight of his darling daughter flashed across his mind.

"Stop," he commanded.

"What?" Marilyn asked, with complete bewilderment.

"Let the kiss be all. I'm sorry. I really want to, but I just cannot give you more now." Marilyn smiled. She cupped Daniel's head in her hands and nodded gently.

"It's okay. I understand. I think I do. You always conceded when we were together. I won't push you on this. It's all right, dear."

"Marilyn." Daniel looked up. "You know that when I loved you I had never loved anyone as I loved you. And that's the way it was for a long, long time. When I fell in love with my wife, I did not stop loving you. I still love you, but my greatest love is for Annemarie, and for her alone. That love supersedes everything else. I cannot dishonor my family. We both made choices. We must now respect them."

"All right." She sat opposite him again, looked at him intensely for a long time, and waited, it seemed to her, until her entire body and soul had cooled down.

"Perhaps it is best. It could be foolish to try to recapture something that most people are fortunate to experience once in their lives." Marilyn stood up slowly.

"I'll see you tomorrow." She straightened her skirt, adjusted her hair, opened the door and walked out.

Later that night, lying in bed, Daniel thought about what had happened. At first he felt noble for having resisted, for having remained faithful to his wife. He wondered what Annemarie would think if she knew just how hard it had been to resist, if she would appreciate his resolve. But as he thought about it, his sense of guilt increased. That kiss! A kiss could be so much more intimate than the sexual act itself. Nobility? Be honest with yourself Daniel, he thought. You betrayed your wife.

During the rehearsals the next day, Daniel and Marilyn acted professionally. It was as though nothing had transpired between them the night before. That evening the audience was electrically charged. The local newspapers had written about the sudden change in conductors. Everyone wanted to know what was so special about this American with the Italian name. The articles had noted his training in Italy and this made him seem like someone a bit closer to home. Some of the attendees had heard Daniel conduct in Karlsruhe and spoke among their fellow subscribers about how Lorelli made everything he conducted sound extraordinary. At thirty-seven years of age, Daniel still cut a figure of comeliness and elegance. In a tuxedo, his five foot eleven stature appeared just about perfect, not too short or too tall. His full dark black wavy hair had a spring to it when he became involved in the music he conducted and moved about without becoming distracting, to himself or the audience.

When he walked out on stage, the applause started slowly and grew into a thunderous manifestation of approval, like the reception known and loved conductors get because of the audience's memory of past pleasures conferred, as well as respect for all the man had accomplished in his career. In Germany, audiences were much more generous to their artists than their counterparts in the United States. Daniel had noted how older singers at the Opera in Karlsruhe would always be accorded appreciative approval of their efforts, even when such efforts were below par. They were applauded as enthusiastically as the singer who truly excelled because of the memory of their past achievements. It was considered rude, unseemly and cruel to deny singers who had given so much pleasure earlier in their careers the accolades they deserved by virtue of splendors perhaps long gone, but unforgotten.

The Tchaikovsky set the mood for the concert—the trials and passion surrounding romantic love. The music depicts the feuding of the Capulet and Montague families as well as the expression of love between Romeo and Juliet. When the love theme is restated, culminating in one of the most beautiful climaxes in all of Tchaikovsky's or anyone else's music, a listener experiences one of those moments of overwhelming delight that truly great music can afford. This was music that Daniel was born to conduct and the audience sensed it.

Treating the same subject from Shakespeare, Berlioz's dramatic symphony, *Roméo et Juliette*, is a much longer work with vocal soloists and a panorama capturing a good deal more of the play's action. For this concert, however, only the love scene from Part Two was programmed. This is the sublime *Adagio,* lasting a quarter of an hour and expressing in Berlioz's unique sound world the physical, emotional and even spiritual union of the two lovers. The composer considered the *Adagio* to be his very greatest accomplishment in music composition. Berlioz explained in his Preface to the *Symphony* why he assigned the orchestra the job of conveying this most important aspect of what the main characters were living and dying for. Eschewing the use of voices to illustrate the all-encompassing passion of the lovers, Berlioz knew that instrumental music alone could encompass the sublimity and consuming rapture shared by the two lovers. The music of this *Adagio* flowed from the orchestra with a natural progression, beginning with the muted and divided lower strings and continuing with a radiance and intensity perhaps unequalled in all of music. The audience sat spellbound at the end of the Adagio, a full sixty seconds passing before the first sounds of applause could be heard. Daniel stood with his head bowed, and finally turned around to acknowledge the tribute.

275

At intermission Daniel's nervous excitement was so great he could speak to no one. The concert resumed with Arnold Schoenberg's *Pelleas and Melisande*, a symphonic poem based on Maurice Maeterlinck's drama of the same name. While Schoenberg's tone poem, scored for a large orchestra, is in four parts that depict the various aspects of the drama, it is the third part that was especially apposite to the theme of the evening's concert, for it is in this section that the composer presents an *adagio* representing the farewell and love scene between Pelleas and Melisande. The tension builds throughout the work, and is gradually released.

Wagner's *Prelude and Liebestod* followed within a few minutes after another round of ecstatic applause from the audience. Daniel's research at the library made him aware that Wagner himself had conducted the work in a concert in Paris in 1860. At the time, he wrote a program note that perhaps best describes the strange and powerful effect this music can have. After noting the transitory nature of almost everything in life, he commented:

"One thing only remains: longing, longing, insatiable longing, forever springing up anew, pining and thirsting. Death, which means passing away, perishing, never awakening, their only deliverance. . . . In one long succession of linked phrases [I have] let that insatiable longing swell from the first, timid avowal through anxious sighs, hopes and fears, laments and desires, bliss and torment, to the mightiest striving, the most powerful effect to break through, into the sea of love's endless delight."

Wagner then acknowledged that the effort is futile, and that only in dying can Tristan and Isolde achieve "the highest bliss." It is this "insatiable longing" that gives the music its unique and highly charged erotic sensibility. Lorelli possessed all of the panache necessary to give this music its fullest expression, to shape it in such a way that the audience could truly savor its power to approximate in sound the distinctive ardor of sexual longing. After the music's overwhelming climax, the audience was emotionally wrung out and it was some time before the applause began, slowly, slowly, swelling to a resounding wave of approval and appreciation for all that had been experienced that evening.

The reviews were ecstatic in their approval of Daniel's musicianship. Abramowitz was credited with having devised such an interesting program, but Lorelli was praised for having made it such an "event." Reading a review in Karlsruhe the next day, Annemarie was proud of her husband's achievement and translated the review into English, quickly mailing copies to her and to his families. When Daniel returned to Karlsruhe, she welcomed him in a manner he had missed for some time, embracing him, kissing him over and over and telling the children what a wonderful man and great conductor their father was. Vincent squealed with delight as Marta exclaimed over and over, "Daddy's great! Daddy's great!" The review Annemarie read described Daniel's uncanny skill in eliciting from the orchestra the strong sense of sexuality in the music. She winked at him saying,

"Well, you'll have to show me how you transmit that tonight, embracing him with evident approval of what he had achieved. This deepened Daniel's guilt and he worried about how to handle it. Falling back on his years of Catholic training, he thought it would be a good idea to go to confession, the only way he could think of to expiate this burden of guilt. He went to a priest who spoke English at the local Catholic church. He hadn't been to confession for years, since he and Annemarie practiced birth control. She was on the pill, and on the occasions she forgot to take it, he would provide the contraception himself.

"Bless me Father, for I have sinned. It's been a few years since my last confession.

"Why have you been away so long, my good man?"

"Actually, I shouldn't be here now, since I cannot possibly follow the church's teaching on birth control."

"You are married and practice artificial birth control?"

"Yes."

"Do you have children?"

"Yes, two. A girl and a boy. But we, my wife and I do not plan to have any more."

"I see. Well, it seems to me that you have followed church teaching in bringing two children into the world. You have done your share."

"Yes. And now you want to suggest that we practice the rhythm method of birth control advocated by the Church?"

"Well, yes, if you wanted to. However, if you chose not to, you could use any other form of contraception."

"But then I could not be a practicing Catholic?"

"Yes, you could. As I said, you have done your share. The world does not need to be peopled with multiple offspring from each and every married couple."

"Excuse me, but am I missing something? This is a Roman Catholic Church, isn't it?"

Father Gottinger laughed. The German priest was in his early thirties and had been in this particular parish since his ordination, five years before. He came late to the priesthood after studying for his doctorate in Eastern religions. Perhaps this was why he could afford to be so pragmatic in dealing with situations like Daniel's. Father Gottinger was one of the young priests in the forefront of a movement to reform Church teachings in matters where he and his colleagues felt there was room for compromise. In addition to his parish duties, he taught two courses at the University and thereby had the advantage of being open to new, if not to say radical ideas. He could, if he wanted to, devote himself entirely to teaching, but he had strong convictions that a priest who had no contact with the laity in a setting such as that involving parish life could not possibly be a viable clergyman.

"Yes," Gottinger allowed, "this is definitely a Roman Catholic Church, but you know that today there are positions that I and other Catholic confessors take that, well, deviates from traditional Catholic teaching."

Daniel could not believe what he was hearing. As a Catholic he had not truly followed theological or any other trends in the Church's public persona. Like so many other Catholics, what he had learned when he was young was the basis of his religious faith, except for things he, as in the cases of so many others, felt free to discard, keeping all the mystery, the mumbo jumbo, critics of the Church would say, and the pronouncements concerning Christ's divinity, the Trinity and everything else that did not interfere with a life of comforts and desires that could not, absolutely not be renounced. The Apostle's Creed, after all, did not say anything about birth control or premarital sex between two people who truly loved one another but could not approach the altar to marry at a given time for quite practical reasons.

"Are you saying that I can practice birth control and still receive the sacraments?"

"Exactly."

Daniel then explained the reasons that had brought him to Confession.

"On the contrary. I do not think you sinned in this situation. You strongly resisted sexual license with the woman."

"But, Father, I kissed her."

"You are a human being. You were tempted, but the fact that all that happened was a kiss is something I would consider, under the circumstances, commendable. Of course on the very strictest level of ethical behavior, you should not have kissed her. But you did and you are sorry for it. Anything else?"

"What? No, I . . . ." Daniel was at a loss for words.

"All right, then, say an Act of Contrition. For your penance, go home to your wife and extend some special kindness to her."

"What kind of penance is that?" Daniel asked with utter incredulity.

"Would you rather say three Rosaries?"

"No, no, I will do as you say."

Daniel thought about how Annemarie would never agree that what he had done was in any way commendable. Even though he had gone to Confession, he decided he would not go to Communion when they went to Sunday Mass. How could he possibly explain to Annemarie why he had not suggested that they go together? He wanted in some way to tell her that he had heard of a priest in their parish who would give absolution even if a couple practiced artificial birth control. He would have to lie to her and he didn't want to do that. He thought of himself as a hypocrite. What was a white lie after this first real deception in his marriage?

After Vincent's birth, the couple began to drift apart in ways that neither could have foreseen. Daniel was always close by, but basically away from the family. His involvement with the orchestra took a good amount of his time, and when he was at home in the mornings, Annemarie was usually teaching. He would join the young baby sitter, Sophie, to play with Marta and Vincent, and he tried to devote all his free time to his children. But there was not really much time available since he had to learn new scores, organize and direct rehearsals and attend public functions related to the orchestra in one way or another.

Each Sunday morning Daniel and Annemarie took the two children to Mass at the nearby Catholic Church where Daniel had his confession heard. As noted, they did not receive Communion since they were practicing artificial birth control. The decision was a mutual one. They had two children and were not sure if they wanted to have any more, but they certainly did not want another baby now. Daniel thought with self deprecatory amusement about how he had once believed that birth control was selfish and that the Church approved "rhythm" method could be used if a couple absolutely could not have another baby at a difficult time, but neither Daniel nor Annemarie wanted to take the chance. They had fallen into a routine, like so many other Catholics, of going to Church, loosely believing those parts of the Canon that they felt comfortable with, and basically disregarding anything that interfered with practicality and expediency.

Annemarie's and Daniel's relationship had also fallen into a pattern of taking one another for granted. Annemarie was very supportive of everything that was concerned with Daniel's career, and he was equally solicitous about her teaching, but the moments of true intimacy that had marked their first year together after their marriage—those times of tender exchanges were gone, taken over by diurnal concerns with work, the babies, the obligations of one kind or another that had to be met. When they did have a quiet moment together, Daniel often felt that Annemarie was holding back. He wasn't even sure what was being held back, but he did not feel as though he had her total devotion as he once did. Perhaps it was different for her now. She was a mother of two children, but did being maternal necessitate being matronly? Annemarie had always had her serious side, which could dominate her personality at times, and frivolity was not one of her distinguishing traits. Still, Daniel felt that his jocular initiatives should have been received a little more enthusiastically. For her part, Annemarie found those moments beside the point, irrelevant or misplaced, and while she did not want to hurt her husband by saying anything to him about them, she could not feign approbation regardless of how unimportant something was. Daniel sensed this reserve, this lack of candor on his wife's part. His idealized concept of marriage began to suffer. A small pin prick had inserted itself into the buoyancy of his belief about all that was possible in this union of bodies and souls, and the need for honest communication was met less and less. Daniel persisted and at times it seemed as though everything was perfect between them, but Annemarie could not be counted on for consistency. Daniel didn't know very much about women, about what made their moods swing from the totally upbeat to the depressing downturns. He wasn't even sure if any of this was typical of all women. He didn't know and when he tried to ask, the replies he received led him to question his own emotional barometer.

One Saturday evening after a relatively short performance, Daniel returned home to find Annemarie still awake, reading in bed. After showering and changing, he sat on the edge of the bed and spoke softly.

"Annemarie, can we talk?"

"Oh, Dan, can't you see I'm reading. I'm totally engrossed in this book."

"But Anne, we never really talk to each other anymore."

"What do you mean? We talk all the time."

"Yes, we talk–about the kids, the routines, the family back home, the bills, but we never talk about each other. We never share real intimacies."

Annemarie closed the book and leaned towards her husband. She put her arms around his neck and drew him to her, kissing him with more fervor than he had experienced in some time. This was good. Now he was glad he had initiated the discussion.

"Do you want to make love?" she asked without waiting for an answer, unbuttoning his pajama top.

"Yes, I do. I do very much, but first I want to talk."

"Oh, so you really don't want to make love!" She pulled herself back and picked up her book again.

"What are you doing?" Daniel asked, not understanding how she could switch from tenderness to tartness so quickly. "Can't you see that I need to talk to you?"

"I guess I'm too tired now," she brusquely replied and turned her back to him, switching off the light.

For a few days after that Annemarie was cool towards her husband. Gradually, she began to warm up again, but these cycles of coolness and affection were becoming more frequent, and whenever Daniel tried to discuss it in a serious way, Annemarie would shrug it off.

"Oh, you're just imagining things. I'm really not upset about anything," Annemarie said, but without real conviction.

"Then why will you suddenly cut off a conversation?"

"Don't you know that women are moody?" She said this with a mixture of sarcasm and humor. Daniel didn't know what to do to bring his relationship back to the point where it had been when they first decided to marry. There was a time then when everything was totally positive, a time when he truly believed that his marriage would be the kind of ideal marriage he had always hoped for and dreamed about in moments of utter desperation when he felt he would never find the wife who would be perfect for him. Marilyn had seemed like that person when they were together, but she couldn't be his ideal soul mate since there were too many differences between them, in spite of their mutually passionate feelings about each other. And now he realized more and more that she had been much wiser than he, that she knew that things would come up, develop from their differences that would eventually divide them in ways he could not then have imagined. But with his wife, with Annemarie, the things that could divide were not present in either of them. They had so much that they already shared—religious beliefs, family values, heritage, career aspirations—so that their marriage could be as perfect as possible. But one of the reasons why he could not quickly make the decision to seek her as his sole and solitary mate was his initial uncertainty about the nature and depth of his love for her. That changed and he was then certain in his heart that he loved her, and he was *in love too* with his dear, dear Annemarie.

Gradually, hints would come up that helped to explain why a barrier existed between them. Daniel felt kept out of his wife's most intimate thoughts, not thoughts about intimacy between two marriage partners, but mental notes that she could not even acknowledge if she wanted to. They consisted of thoughts fueled by emotions like those a child has when she sees a friend experiencing things, receiving benefits she feels she is so much better qualified to experience, or appreciate, or cherish. Annemarie enjoyed the teaching, but it was not nearly as satisfying as being a professional performer. If challenged to admit that she was envious of her husband, she would deny any such suggestion vehemently, but this unspoken desire to achieve what he was achieving, to receive the plaudits he was receiving, gave to their relationship a not inconsiderable measure of the bittersweet, which could become more bitter if not taken in check.

When Annemarie's mother came over to Germany to help her daughter after baby Vincent was born, she recognized the symptoms of her daughter's postpartum blues, but she was concerned about her Annemarie's total happiness. She stayed for two months and before leaving to return to the States, asked her daughter if everything was all right in her marriage.

"Yes, of course Mother," Annemarie replied with some degree of surprise in her voice. "Why do you ask?"

"Oh, I don't know. Call it a mother's intuition. You and Daniel almost seem to be like business partners rather than husband and wife."

"Mom, how can you say that? We love each other very much!"

"I'm sure you do, but do you take time for each other, exclusively?"

"We're both too busy. He's very involved with the Opera and I have the children and my teaching."

"Yes, dear. All couples, especially couples with children, find that they have less time for each other. But you need to make the time. Your relationship with your husband is paramount. It should not suffer, no matter what other interests you both have."

Annemarie thought about her mother's advice and for some time afterwards encouraged Daniel to talk to her. She tried to open up to him more than she had in the past—a somewhat difficult endeavor for her—and they enjoyed a period of a closeness that seemed to have disappeared in their lives. Daniel was so happy that this long desired *affiatamento* with his wife was developing, and his conducting even seemed to take on a more impassioned dimension than previously.

Daniel's name was becoming better known in European musical circles. He received invitations to guest conduct in cities throughout the continent. At the Karlsruhe Opera he became known as a Richard Strauss specialist. Each year he conducted another Strauss opera and by the time he had been there four years he had presented *Der Rosenkavalier, Arabella, Salome* and *Elektra*. His conducting of *Elektra* was especially successful. Although the singers' contributions were admired, it was Maestro Lorelli's conducting of this psychological drama, probably Strauss' most modern score that enthralled audiences and critics alike. His "Recognition Scene" carried such emotional weight that members of the audience were seen leaving the auditorium with tears in their eyes, unable to adequately express in words the experience they had just had. It was one of these performances, seen by a member of the Board of the Metropolitan Opera in New York that resulted in an invitation for Daniel to conduct five performances of *Elektra* the following season. Daniel juggled his schedule and had his assistant take over at Karlruhe when he was scheduled to appear in New York. Annemarie and the two children went to New York for the first performance and remained there for the two months during which the Strauss performances were being staged. Violetta and Vincenzo were no longer working in the business and spent their time in the expansive home they had built in Mount Kisco, New York. Violetta had an extensive garden and she loved to care for her flowers and vegetables. She and Vincenzo were thrilled to have the opportunity to have their daughter-in-law, son and grandchildren spend time with them.

Daniel's success at the Metropolitan Opera was truly sensational, considering that he was a conductor and not a singer. Mostly, singers received all the attention from the press, and conductors were acknowledged or not, but rarely made a fuss about. Daniel's star was rising.

The Lorelli's remained in Germany for another two years and returned to the U.S. when Daniel accepted a position as Associate Guest Conductor with the Boston Symphony, one of the country's finest orchestras. He made a number of recordings and was taking his place as one of America's most noted conductors. At the age of forty-three he was well on his way to an illustrious career in classical music. Call it fate or chance or what you will, or as some would have it, the gods smiling down on their chosen ones. If this be so, the gods had smiled down on Daniel Lorelli for some time, but things were about to change.

Thirty-Six

Silvana Manfredi was a gynecologist at New York Hospital in New York City. Eight years after she had started to practice in the United States, she committed herself to treating women with cancer and worked, too, at Memorial Hospital across York Avenue. She earned a reputation as one of the finest physicians dealing with this horrible disease. Unlike most of her male colleagues, Dr. Manfredi would recommend a hysterectomy only if she felt it was an absolute necessity. She was acutely aware that much of this type of surgery was unnecessary, and that less drastic measures could be applied to achieve salutary effects for many of the women who were referred to her. This departure from surgery at all costs endeared her to her many patients and her name became synonymous with compassion, sensitivity and skill to all those treated by her and to those who were seeking the best possible medical care for their individual problems. Silvana's husband Joseph had a very successful psychiatric practice, and became a well known personality on the talk show circuits because of his best-selling books, *Past Lives Explored; Regression: Discovering Previous Incarnations;* and *Did You Live Before?* As physicians, Silvana and Joseph never had the opportunity to work together, but their relationship was one that was admired by their family and friends and envied by all those unhappy couples who could not or did not want to believe that a totally happy married couple could even exist. They spent as much time together as their hectic and work-filled lives allowed them to. They planned their vacations and days off so that they would always be together with their one child, their son who was born four years after they became united in marriage. When they were seen together by neighbors around their home, by strangers in stores where they shopped together, or in restaurants where they dined, those observing them invariably got the impression that here was a couple newly in love. This was not due to anything demonstrative that they did, for it was not their style to kiss in public or to fondle one another in a crowd. Rather, it was the way they played off one other, the way she regarded him and he regarded her, looking at each other with such obvious warmth and depth of feeling. Their friends would often say, "Here was a marriage truly made in heaven!"

One evening Silvana struck Joseph as totally different from her usual self. He could sense that she was apprehensive about something. They usually had a late supper. Little Joseph had been fed earlier by his nanny. When Silvana and Joseph arrived home, they would play with Joey for an hour, read him a story and together put him to bed. As they sat down to a simple meal served by their Italian housekeeper, Silvana began haltingly,

"Joe, I need to discuss one of my patients with you."

"Really? What happened to our policy of never discussing work, especially at dinner?" he replied jokingly. In spite of his levity, Joseph was intrigued.

"I know. But this is different. I can wait until after dinner, but the fact is, I really can't wait. I'm just too excited about an idea that came to me today. I need your advice"

Joseph was thrilled that his wife wanted to discuss something professional with him. Since they practiced in such different fields, such discussions hardly ever came about. Oh, of course he would tell her about some situations in his practice and she would share her successes and her sorrows, too, when all of her efforts proved futile and she lost a patient, but they never actually asked one another's professional opinion, so this was a unique development.

"I would love to hear whatever you want to tell me. Hey, this sounds like it could be very interesting."

"It is. You're going to love it."

"Well," Joseph said with excitement, pushing his plate to the side, his appetite no longer of any concern to him, "Tell me, *tell* me!"

"A patient was referred to me privately, at my office. She had already been to half a dozen gynecologists and not one of them could find anything wrong with her. She brought me her test results—MRI's, blood tests, the works. Everything's normal."

"What's her complaint?"

"Pain. Vaginal pain, menstrual type cramps even when she is not menstruating, pain in her uterus, ovaries, all over."

"Does she mention each area specifically?"

"No, not at all. She doesn't even know where everything is, but she points and describes, and from the notes I read accompanying the test results, it appears that she has been experiencing this pain for many years now."

"Is she married?"

"Married twice."

"How old is she?"

"Twenty-seven."

"And?"

"At first she wouldn't discuss any of the really personal stuff, but then when I told her that I needed to know everything if I was going to help her, she reluctantly told me that she was a virgin in both marriages."

"Boy, you said this was going to be interesting, but I never expected anything bizarre!"

"The first marriage was annulled. Her second husband must be some kind of saint. Their marriage has never been consummated, as such, although she indicated that she brings him to orgasm, but without vaginal penetration. He is very patient and has been sending her for treatment to many fine doctors. They all tell him there is nothing wrong with her. She was twenty-two when she married the first time. On her wedding night, her husband could not penetrate her. Each time he tried, she would begin to scream."

"The poor guy must have thought she was having a premature orgasm."

"Yes, what else could he think? But after two weeks of trying and being frustrated, he asked her to consent to an annulment. She agreed. Three years later, she fell in love with her present husband, but did not tell him anything about her problem or her first marriage until he, too, failed to penetrate her barricade."

"I like that—'penetrate her barricade'—you're becoming poetic."

"Never mind! The thing that convinced me that some unorthodox treatment is called for was when I tried to examine her. As I started my *internal*, she began to moan in pain, and when I tried to proceed she screamed."

"It's obvious she needs therapy. Are you yourself convinced it's psychosomatic? Did you tell her you wanted to refer her to me?"

"Well, yes, but not for the usual therapy. And I don't think it's psychosomatic in the usual sense. Look, you have been so successful with your books and the cases you describe make such a strong case for past life regression. And we are both convinced that it is useful. As a respectable gynecologist, I risk being ridiculed if it gets out that I am advising a patient to find relief from pain through what many consider to be psychological nonsense. But, I am willing to consider the possibility that she had some severe trauma to her sexual organs as a child, which she has buried in her sub-conscious or perhaps—after all, I have an open mind—perhaps in a past life, and that is what is giving her the pain now."

"Did you already, then, suggest such a course of action?"

"No, not yet. I wanted to see how you feel first."

"How I feel? You know how I feel."

"I do. But I needed to discuss this with you first. In the meantime, I told her about your work without in any way suggesting she could benefit from it. I acted as though I was just making conversation. I told her I thought she may have seen you on TV. I gave her *Regressions* to read to see how she responds to your work."

"Fine."

It was agreed that Silvana would ask her patient to come for her subsequent appointment at Joseph's office where the two doctors would suggest a course of treatment they felt could be beneficial to her. The young woman was urged to read Dr. Manfredi's book in preparation for her next appointment.

When Marianne Wilson arrived at Dr. Manfredi's office, Joseph couldn't believe this was the same woman his wife had described. She was radiant, with an air of self-confidence, poise and as he was soon to see, natural charm. Her shoulder length red hair bounced as she walked, giving her an appearance of animated determination. Joseph was really expecting to see a woman with some of the more common signs of depression. Later, Silvana would tell him that she, too, was quite surprised by what she saw that day as her patient entered the room.

"I'm so happy to meet you Doctor Manfredi. You know, I read your book—I couldn't put it down once I started it—and I already feel better."

"You do?" Dr. Manfredi replied with obvious surprise. "Can you tell me what it was about reading the book that made you feel better?"

"For the first time in my life, I truly feel that I have a chance to find a real solution to my problem. I *want* to have a past life regression. It was so fascinating to read about what you accomplished with some of your patients who had conflicts throughout their lives. In the introduction, you tell how your asthmatic condition disappeared after your own past life regression."

Joseph smiled and asked Mrs. Wilson to sit. He did not want to disillusion her, but he had seen this type of enthusiasm turn to despondency when a particular session would turn up no relevant data to support the case for past life trauma transmitted to the subject's new incarnation.

"You know, Mrs. Wilson . . . "

"Marianne."

"You know Marianne that this procedure does not work for everyone. There is a good chance that we can indeed uncover something from a past life that has relevance to your current problems, but every subject does not achieve similar results. In my book, I did mention the failures I experienced, too, with some of my patients."

"Yes, I am well aware of that. But, well, the funny thing is that without actually giving it too much thought, probably because of my religious upbringing, I always had this underlying feeling that I was here before. I'll never forget the day I had my first period. My mother had discussed with me what was going to happen. My mother is a good and kind woman and she was very gentle with me. But when it happened and she told me that I could use either a tampon or a pad, showing me both, I remember instinctively pushing the tampon away with a sense of unexplainable horror, with a familiar fear of the very idea of insertion."

Silvana Manfredi was astonished at how freely her patient was now discussing these very private memories.

"Well," Joseph Manfredi commented, proud that his book had such a sanguine effect on this apparently, astonishingly articulate young woman,

"Dr. Manfredi has shown me the results of the various tests you've had performed in order to come up with a diagnosis. There is no evidence that there is anything physically the matter with you. You could begin therapy, but ..."

"Doctor, I have already had a number of therapy sessions with another psychiatrist. My husband loves me very much and he has the patience of a saint, so to speak, and has sent me wherever he could to try to get to the bottom of my problem. That's what brought me to Dr. Manfredi, to your wife. Believe me, I had a completely normal childhood. My parents are two of the most loving and dedicated parents anyone could wish to have. I have a sister and a brother, and we all get along quite well and always have."

"I understand. That's why I was about to say that you could have traditional therapy, but Silvana and I discussed your case at length, and we both feel that you are a good candidate for past life regression therapy. Everything else has failed. What do you have to lose at this point?"

"Exactly how I feel."

An appointment was made for the following week. That evening Silvana could not contain her enthusiasm.

"I saw that nothing was working for Marianne and I really hoped that you could do something to help her. But this is amazing. Just by reading your book she seems like a different person!"

"Well, she certainly seemed different from the way you described her."

"Different? It was as though another person entered your office. You know, I'm actually beginning to wonder if she could be schizophrenic."

"Well, let's not rule that out yet. We have to see what develops as a result of the regression therapy."

Silvana laughed and poked her husband gently in the ribs,

"You realize that if you're successful you'll have to publish your findings. I can see it now: new treatment for female disorders from a psychiatrist! I'm not sure I like your intrusion into my field. And if you succeed, I'll never hear the end of it."

They laughed heartily until Silvana suddenly got quite serious.

"What?"

"I was just thinking. If you succeed in helping her to discover a past life that is somehow connected with her problems today, the findings could be terrible, quite disturbing."

"We'll just have to see."

Dr. Manfredi's studio for regression therapy was beautifully appointed, conceived and decorated to insure a sense of comfort and security for those deemed eligible for such treatment. Unlike other past life regression therapists, Manfredi, a highly ethical psychiatrist, would not use the technique on anyone who requested it. One could not, for example, undergo a hypnotic regression merely out of idle curiosity as to the nature of one's previous lifetimes. There had to be a valid reason to pursue this therapy with a patient, and this usually involved some kind of trauma.

The environment was one of quiet dignity, and its stillness was not just a matter of the beholder's intuitive deduction based on the feel and appearance of the surroundings. In fact, a good deal of work had gone into making the entire area sound-proof, so that even the telephone ringing in the outer office could not be heard inside the main treatment area. If the doctor's secretary found it necessary to alert him to an important call or other matter that he needed to address immediately, a light would flash on and off. This was strategically placed so that the patient could not possibly see it or become distracted by it. The room was fairly large, two hundred and fifty square feet of space, arranged so that it seemed smaller. Ceiling to floor drapes in burgundy covered two sets of windows on adjoining sides of the room and were tied back, with opaque sheers covering the windows themselves to allow just the right amount of light to enter the room—not glaring or distracting in any manner at all. The oak hardware floors were partially covered by two complementary but distinctive oriental carpets. Decorative screens were positioned to give the treatment area an aura of security and privacy. Dr. Manfredi asked Marianne Wilson to sit on a plush upholstered upright chair that had various reclining positions. Before hypnosis began, the chair was adjusted to recline at a thirty degree angle. The doctor had carefully selected music that was conducive to hypnosis, usually Faure's *Pelleas Suite* or Satie arranged for small orchestra, all music that did not include any loud climaxes, but moved along slowly and quietly, and always played at a volume so low it could barely be heard. Sometimes the doctor would find it necessary to turn the music off altogether. Manfredi held a small light and flashed it in his patient's direction, asking her to look at it and suggesting that she focus on it. Through various suggestive phrases, Marianne Wilson slowly fell into a hypnotic trance.

"You are returning to the life you lived before. Do you see yourself there?"

"Yes."

"Who are you? Where are you living?"

"I'm living in a house in a small town. I am married but my husband is away. He is at war in France."

"Do you know what year it is?"

"Yes, it's 1919. America has gone to war. He is gone for more than a year. My family is not there. They live far from where I am. I am alone."

"Move forward. Does your husband return?"

"Yes. He comes back wounded, but he recovers. He is all right."

"How does he treat you?"

"He accuses me of being unfaithful. He tells me he knows I slept with a man who lives nearby."

"Did you sleep with this man?"

"No, no. He is a farmer. He used to bring me milk and eggs. He was good to me, but we never did anything wrong. I never betrayed my husband."

"O.K. Slowly now. Move ahead. Does your husband believe you?"

"No. No. He says I'm a liar. He is different, not as loving as before."

"How does he treat you? Is he doing anything to hurt you?"

"He's tying me to the bed. He's tearing at my clothes. He has a stick, a rifle. No! No!"

Marianne cries, slowly, then uncontrollably. Manfredi has to end the session since what she is seeing is too troublesome and she cannot even talk about it. Slowly, he leads her out of hypnosis. She sits there for some minutes without a word.

"Doctor, it was terrible. He was going to hurt me.

"Do you remember anything specific?"

"No. It was confusing."

"All right. Don't worry. We will continue in our next session. You were getting close. Perhaps next time it will be clearer."

Another session was scheduled for the following week. Once again Dr. Manfredi coaxed his patient back to the early twentieth century and it became evident that as Emily Burgess she had left her family in New York to marry a man from Ohio. After the wedding they went to Cleveland to live in a home he owned in a rural area. When the United States entered the war, he enlisted and left Emily alone in the house. After he returned from the war, some of his neighbors told him that his wife had been having an affair with the farmer who lived nearby, a married man with four children. He insisted that she confess, and if she did not he said he would punish her. She maintained her innocence all along, but he refused to believe her. He began to tie her to the bed, her arms extended above her head, her legs spread wide. Then he would taunt her, scream at her and say that if she was not satisfied with him, he could try other ways of pleasing her. He used the butt of a rifle, wooden rods and other large objects, forcing them into her vagina. After the last of these sadistic episodes, Emily suffered internal injuries, hemorrhaged and died.

Marianne Wilson came out of this session totally exhausted and debilitated, but she could now clearly understand her fears. Slowly, but fairly soon thereafter, she was able to enjoy normal sexual relations with her husband, became pregnant and had a baby. She named her son Joseph, after Dr. Manfredi.

Thirty-Seven

Back home in Massachsetts, Annemarie Lorelli had settled into a new routine. Marta and Vincent were now in school every day, leaving her time to schedule morning lessons at her home. The Lorelli's had purchased a comfortable old house in Arlington. She joined with three other women to form a string quartet. They practiced sometimes in the afternoon and sometimes in the evening, and eventually began to perform in and around Boston, gaining local recognition for their incisive and musical performances of works from the standard repertory as well as little known quartets by minor composers of the past, and contemporary composers too.

One morning while showering, Annemarie noticed a small lump on her left breast. She had never felt it before and was surprised. She thought about what this could be, but settled on thinking of it as some type of benign cyst. She thought it would disappear if she just forgot about it. But each time she showered, she would feel it again. One night, as Daniel began to make love to her, she asked him to stop.

"What's wrong, Annie?" "Annie" was his pet name for her that he preferred using to things like "Honey,""Sweetie" and the like.

"Put you finger here, on my breast."

Daniel felt the lump. It seemed to be hard, small but hard.

"How long have you had this?"

"I just noticed it about a week ago."

"I'm sure it's nothing serious, but you should see your gynecologist."

"Yes. I'll have to schedule an appointment."

Annemarie thought of all the reasons why this lump could not be anything dangerous. She recalled that her mother had once told her that no woman in their family had ever had any kind of breast problems and certainly no breast cancer had ever been detected. This had to be a good sign that her lump was benign. After all, she had read somewhere that breast cancer was hereditary. Her physician ordered ultrasound and Annemarie waited apprehensively for the results. She was so relieved when she learned that the lump was nothing to worry about. That evening she and Daniel celebrated the good news by going out to a small restaurant, the first time they had been out alone together in months. Everything was so romantic and perfect, and once back home they enjoyed ecstatic love making, the best physical and emotional encounter they had experienced in quite some time. Indeed, there was something about the prospect of danger that gave them a greater sense of closeness to one another. They loved each other dearly and lived their lives principally in terms of their relationship to one another and to their daughter and son. They had their careers, their individual interests, yes, but these were reflections of what they were together as a family, manifestations of who they were, but based upon their mutual needs. The burdens of daily living, however, could permit one to forget temporarily, to set aside the fact that everything they did was important only insofar as it contributed to the overall happiness they needed to share. Now this potentially ugly intrusion into their sense of well-being impelled them to focus again on what was truly important. They appreciated each other more than before, and they silently vowed to avoid finding themselves in a situation again where they would take one another for granted.

A few months later, Annemarie went to the doctor for a routine annual checkup. This time, her doctor, a woman who was not a gynecologist, but a general practitioner, discovered another lump, besides the one that Annemarie was already aware of. The results of another ultrasound were inconclusive, so she was sent for a mammogram and a needle biopsy. One of the lumps was cancerous. Daniel was with his wife when the doctor gave her the results. At first she was stunned by the news. She had developed a mind frame that would allow of no possibility that she could have cancer. During the ensuing conversation in the doctor's office, Annemarie sat silently, leaving Daniel to ask all the questions. Just once, in response to the doctor's assertion that early detection was the best defense against this disease, Annemarie asked if her cancer had been detected early enough. The doctor's reply was positive and encouraging. Inside the car on the way home, Annemarie began to weep, first silently, then uncontrollably. Daniel pulled the car over and took his wife into his arms.

"I don't want to die," she cried as the tears flowed freely and her shoulders moved in coordination with her sobs.

"You're not going to die, Annie. You caught it early. The doctor told you that. We're going to beat this.

"Who will take care of Marta and Vinnie?" she asked, with a tone so full of sorrow that Daniel's eyes began to water too, but he didn't want her to see this. He had to be strong, so he quickly wiped them away with his sleeve.

"You will take care of them. You will always be there for them . . . and for me."

"But I don't want to die, Dan, I don't."

"You won't. We'll get the best doctors, go to the best hospital in the country. We'll beat this."

When they arrived at home, Annemarie knew that she wanted to call her father before discussing her problem with anyone else. Joseph Taviani had built a successful family medicine practice and was at a stage in his own career where he could abbreviate his work schedule and devote more time to his family and personal interests—golf, model ship building, traveling. He was the senior partner in the professional organization he had established, with four younger associates covering most of the patients. One of these was his own son, Arthur Taviani, whose goal in life had always been to become a doctor like his father and to work with him in the same practice. Joseph retained as his own very private patients some of the older men and women he had treated for years.

Annemarie had always been very close to her father, but since she married and especially after moving abroad, she had spent little precious time with him. Nevertheless, the bond between them was strong and it was to him that she now wanted to speak, even more than to her mother. When she telephoned her father and told him the diagnosis, Joseph Taviani knew he could not discuss this by telephone.

"I'll be right over," he said. "And don't worry, dear, I'll take care of everything for you." Maureen was frantic, not knowing what was going on. She had answered the telephone, but Annemarie quickly told her to put her father on. Fortunately, it was a day when he did not have office appointments. When Maureen asked her daughter what was wrong, she heard only,

"I need to talk to Dad." After hanging up, Joseph looked at his wife dumbly and spoke to her haltingly, with an apprehensive demeanor she had never seen in him before.

"Annemarie's been diagnosed with breast cancer."

Maureen Taviani, a strong woman with a unique resilience for facing and dealing with almost any kind of problem, a daughter of Erin whose ancestors knew and understood sorrow better than most, and who had an almost genetic predisposition for dealing with tragedy, found herself now at a loss as to how to cope. Joseph saw the tears welling up in her eyes and the strange look of despair that had taken hold of her usually radiant countenance, and he implored her,

"Maureen, come now. You must be strong for Annemarie's sake. You cannot go there and show her you are upset."

"Yes, I know. Don't worry. I will be all right." Summoning up her courage and penchant for positivism, she joined her husband's determination to approach their daughter with affirmative moral support.

Dr. Taviani arranged consultations with two of the finest physicians known to him in the field, one from Brigham & Women's Hospital and one from Harvard Medical School. After reviewing her medical records and examining her, one doctor advised beginning the treatment with a lumpectomy while the other suggested a more radical treatment immediately. Daniel was not satisfied and wanted her to get other opinions. He had cancelled all his engagements and accompanied his wife to every appointment. He would not leave her side for a minute. The prospect of losing his wife affected Daniel profoundly. Suddenly, the only thing that mattered was defeating this dread disease and insuring her survival. For the first time in his life since he began studying the piano, music was secondary. It seemed so strange to him how he had completely eliminated the thought processes that normally propelled his activities when music was always on his mind. Now, it was as though he could not afford to stop long enough to think about conducting this or that piece, deciding questions of tempos, nuances, balances, hearing over and over again in his head how particular sections of the orchestra or the work itself should sound. While lying in bed one night, his arm over Annemarie's shoulder as she slept facing away from him, hearing her soft breathing, feeling the beat of her heart, the strains of Pachelbel's *Canon* began to play in his head, his wife's heartbeats providing the bass underpinning for the lovely, serene melody. Tears filled his eyes as he recalled the way she looked when she played her viola, intent on that and nothing else, moving with the music as though nothing else existed. He did not want that music to stop. He wanted to have the opportunity to play with her again—accompanying her on the piano in chamber music or directing the orchestra as she sat at his side and played the solo part in a concerto. This could happen again; it would be a significant part of their lives in the future.

Later the same night, Annemarie awoke. Daniel was now asleep and she could hear his heavy breathing, emitting sounds now and again, indicating that he was having a disturbing dream. She touched his right hand as he slept facing her, pondering the magic he could evince when raising it, wielding his baton over the orchestra, directing them in their exposition of the music's power to overwhelm or delight or transfix an audience. Thinking of his extraordinary talent and skill, she at once regretted having missed many of his concerts when she could have attended but chose not to, mostly for very good reasons, but now in the cold light of night she realized what she had missed. She touched her breast, felt the lump and again a shudder rippled through her body. These past days had been horrific for her. Her emotions ran the gamut from shock, to fear, to anger. How could this happen to her. She had loved living in Germany, but had looked forward to returning home. She wanted her children to have a good education at good American schools. She wanted to do all the things mothers did as their children negotiated the adventures of childhood, the perils of their teen years, the accomplishments that would make her and Daniel so proud of them. How could she not be there for all of this? She would fight! Yes, she would fight and overcome and be there for her children, for her husband. She touched Daniel's thick, dark hair. Her man! Hadn't she known from the very first day she saw him that he would be hers? How could she leave him now? No, she would not, could not allow this disease to ravish her. Her body could only be embraced by her lover, her husband.

Daniel had telephoned his mother to tell her about Annemarie's condition. Violetta and Vincenzo were now in their eighties. They were both still in fairly good health and still occasionally visited the flagship store of the Mamma's Kitchen chain. Violetta was distressed and told her son that she would pray for her daughter-in-law. Immediately after speaking with her son, she went to the small chapel that she had had built in her home, an extension of the family room, with statues of Mary and Joseph and a beautiful Byzantine style Crucifix over a small altar. She had decided on having this chapel soon after Joseph was ordained so that he could say Mass there for her and relatives on special occasions, or when he came home from time to time to stay for a few days. Violetta knelt before the altar and prayed with all the fervor she had always brought to each and every prayer she ever whispered as the sentiments emanated from deep within her heart. This time her prayer was especially ardent:

"Oh, Mother of God," she implored, "Help our Annemarie. You, who so loved your Son as he was growing, help her to live to guide her own children in all that is right."

Then a startling thought came to Violetta and she spoke it aloud,

"*Jesù, Dio, fammi morire invece di Annamaria. Ho vissuto, lei non ancora abbastanza. Vi prego, farla vivere!*"

"Jesus, God, take me. I have lived long enough. If someone has to die, let it be me. Spare Annemarie, I beg of you. Let me be the one to die."

Violetta's faith was never stronger than it was now. She had lived her entire life, steadfast in her beliefs, convinced that those who did God's will would prosper and be blessed. She believed in the power of prayer as she believed in almost nothing else. Hadn't God given her the four sons she so dearly loved, loved above all else on earth? Hadn't He given her these gifts in response to her prayers? She remembered that special Novena she had made so many years before, and she decided that she would make one now for Annemarie's recovery and cure. The next morning, she began nine days of Masses.

Daniel soon received telephone calls from each of his brothers as well as from his cousin Phillip. Father Joseph called to tell him that he would devote a series of Masses for Annemarie's intentions. Both John and Albert assured Daniel that he could count on them for anything. If he had to stop working to be with his wife, they would help him financially. John reminded Daniel that he still had his share in the family business, that Vincenzo and Violetta had already indicated in their will that all four of their sons would share in the part of the business owned by the parents. This represented about thirty per cent of the business since John, Albert and Cousin Philip owned seventy per cent outright, having helped Vincenzo and Violetta to develop it to where it then stood, worth an estimated one hundred million dollars.

A few days later, Violetta telephoned her son to check on Annemarie's condition and on what had been decided in terms of treatment. Daniel explained that it was difficult to know how to proceed since the doctors themselves were not in agreement. Just that past week, Violetta had seen Dr. Manfredi on a morning talk show. He was promoting his new book on past life regression and Violetta fondly recalled his visit with her some years before. During the interview, he mentioned that his wife was a specialist in cancer treatment for women at Memorial Hospital. Violetta and Vincenzo had met Silvana Manfredi when they went to Renato's funeral a year earlier. They had spoken in Italian and Silvana allowed how she wanted to visit *il paese* again, not having been there for some time. Violetta told Daniel what she had heard about Dr. Silvana Manfredi and the fact that she was established at the leading hospital in the country devoted to cancer treatment and research. She telephoned her old friend Paola and asked for Joseph's private number at home. She called later that evening to beseech him to ask his wife to get involved in Annemarie's case. Joseph was genuinely happy to hear Violetta's voice. He had never forgotten this kind woman, a person for whom the word *simpatica* must have been coined.

"I hope you don't mind. Your mother gave me your number."

"Mind? Of course not. I 'm so happy to hear from you. I should have called you. How are you?"

"Oh, I am fine. I saw you on television. You looked so good. Like an actor!"

"Oh, thank you. Yes, I am continuing with my work. You remember when we spoke about it."

"Yes. I know you are a good man. Perhaps I can ask for your help, something to do with your wife."

"Certainly! I hope you are not in need of her professionally?"

"I wish it could be me who needs her help."

"What do you mean?"

"I mean it would be so much better if I could be the one with the serious illness. But it is my daughter-in-law. You know my son Daniel, the conductor? It's his wife."

"Oh, I'm so sorry. I haven't seen your son since we were children. When I came to your home, he was away in Italy, I think."

"Yes, yes, he was." Thoughts of Daniel's meeting Annemarie in Rome flashed through her mind.

"We all want the very best care for Annemarie. Daniel's father-in-law is a physician in Boston and he is arranging for her to be treated there among doctors he knows. But we have heard that the hospital where your wife works is the best in the country."

"Mrs. Lorelli . . ."

"Violetta, please call me Violetta."

"Yes. Violetta, there are some excellent hospitals in Boston. What is the nature of Annemarie's condition?"

"She has been diagnosed with breast cancer."

"Well, Silvana can probably give you more information than I can, but I remember hearing that there is one Boston medical center that has earned a reputation for its treatment of women with breast cancer. But this is not to say your daughter-in-law should not come to New York. I know that Silvana will want to help in any way she can. She is very close with my mother and as you are my mother's old and dear friend, I am sure she will do everything possible for you or any member of your family. She is a great doctor if I say so myself, an oncologist, specializing in breast cancer, and that is the best doctor a woman can have if she has this disease, aside from the fact that Silvana is so personally involved with her patients and always goes to extraordinary lengths for them no matter who they are or where they come from. When it comes to *paesani*, she would move mountains if she could. *Figurati!*"

"Oh, thank you Joseph. Please give me your wife's office number so my son can call her."

Violetta knew that her daughter-in-law needed to go to this doctor. She had a feeling that Dr. Manfredi could and would help her to overcome this terrible turn of events in her life.

"Never mind the office. Please give Daniel this number and ask him to call me. I would like to speak with him and I will have him talk to Silvana too."

Violetta was quite taken with Joseph's kindness and concern. It brought back to her thoughts of the love she had shared with her townspeople through the years, how they had always had the highest regard for one another in the *paese*, those many years before, but in the new country too, whenever they could manage to be together.

Daniel spoke with his father-in-law and Dr. Taviani agreed that it could be best for Annemarie to go to New York. Memorial had, after all, a reputation as being the finest in its field.

Annemarie's determination to fight became offset by a torpor that left her sitting in the house for entire days, never venturing past the front door. Daniel tried to rouse her and sometimes succeeded in igniting a spark of light in her eyes, but only her two children could elicit a smile from her, and at such times Daniel could see the Annemarie he yearned to see completely again.

Silvana Manfredi set aside an entire morning to meet with Annemarie, examine her and study her file. It was a day when Silvana normally did not have office hours, so there would be no interruptions. During the meeting Silvana reverted to Italian at times, and this actually gave Annemarie a sense of comfort. Somehow, discussing her problem in the language she had learned so well at a much happier time in her life, blunted the impact of the words that, by their very nature had the power to strike fear. Dr. Manfredi was sure about what needed to be done, but she decided to discuss everything with two of her colleagues for whom she had the highest professional regard. They agreed with her evaluation. At the follow-up appointment, Dr. Manfredi very carefully, gently and thoroughly explained why a lumpectomy would be a waste of time and effort. A mastectomy was called for, and she was confident that with reconstructive surgery, Annemarie could soon return to a fully normal life. Dr. Manfredi was wary of radiation and chemotherapy since their effects only weakened the patient's immune system needed to protect a person from cancer in the first place. She saw the patient becoming more vulnerable to the formation of metastatic lesions in the body's organs that eventually brought about her death. Silvana was not herself a surgeon, but she would work hand in hand with the surgeon she herself trusted the most among her colleagues, and be with Annemarie throughout her ordeal, though Dr. Manfredi did not refer to what her patient had to go through in such terms. She chose to call it Annemarie's "necessary procedure," an expression that indicated the seriousness of the situation but did not pack quite the wallop that terms commonly used by less sensitive physicians could.

"We will do our own tests before the surgery, but from what I have seen on the reports you brought with you, there has been no metastasis. However, given the length of time you have had this tumor, we must be certain. We can take nothing for granted. I want to assure you that great strides have been made in the treatment of breast cancers, and I have every hope that you will have a complete recovery and return to a fully normal life within a short period of time." Silvana's words, spoken with obvious sincerity and compassion, gave Annemarie the first real hope she had had since she first learned the terrifying details of her condition. Silvana Manfredi was the same age as Annemarie. She was by no means an imposing woman in terms of physical appearance. Tall at five feet nine inches, but with a small body frame, she nevertheless was an imposing presence when one heard her speak because of her demonstrable self-confidence and poise.

After the surgery, Annemarie went home to recuperate. She would have to return to New York at regular intervals, but Silvana made it possible for her reconstructive plastic surgery to be undertaken in Boston. One of Silvana's colleagues, a man who had worked with her for four years at Memorial Hospital, had taken a position at Brigham and Women's Hospital.

Annemarie was doing well. She began to entertain the idea that she would be well again and that she would be around for her two children. Her dread of the disease, however, was replaced by another kind of apprehension. She dwelled on the idea that Daniel would no longer find her attractive, that it would be easy for him to accept the attention of other women. After all, hadn't he always told her that she had perfect breasts? He loved her breasts and always stimulated them when they made love. Now she was disfigured, and even if the surgeon could work miracles, it would never be the same again. She was afraid to approach him on the subject. Daniel's particular sensitivity, his ability to identify with women on various levels, however, made him cognizant of his wife's potentially destructive reactions to what she thought could be revulsion on her husband's part. He spoke to her about it calmly and gently.

"Annie, I know you must feel because of what has been done to you that things can change between us."

"How do you know how I feel?" Her tone was one of annoyance. How could he possibly know what she was feeling?

"I'm just saying that it would only be natural for you to question how your husband regards you in light of your surgery. And I want you to know that I absolutely think you are still the most beautiful woman in the world."

"What? Even with this disfigurement?"

"It doesn't matter to me one bit. The only thing that matters is that you are well. I will always love you no matter what happens, just as I am sure you will always love me, in spite of any physical changes that may come about."

Annemarie needed the reassurance and she saw, as she always had, just how much her husband loved her. She put her arms around him and held him so tightly, feeling his strong chest against her wound. He did truly love her. She could put her fears to rest. Or could she? The thought had an insidious way of recurring and infiltrating her thoughts and her dreams, even against her very strong will.

Weeks passed and Daniel refused to return to full activity, in spite of his wife's urging him to do so. The position at the BSO as associate guest conductor was withdrawn after Daniel cancelled six consecutive rehearsals and did not make himself available to conduct one concert in three months. The head of his agency in New York telephoned him.

"Daniel, taking yourself out of the loop can be disastrous for your career. You were just beginning to build some momentum, but now you are losing it."

Harvey Hammond had risen to the top position in Associated Artists after twenty-five years with the agency. He was an excellent manager and knew when and in which areas a particular pianist, violinist, cellist, singer or conductor needed to be inserted, so to speak, in order to capitalize on the all the possibilities. He himself had had very little to do with Associated's development of Daniel's agenda until he saw the excitement the young conductor could generate on an international scale. When he saw a photograph of Daniel, he became convinced that he had an artist with both talent and glamour.

"Harvey, I appreciate your advice, but my major concern right now is my wife, and until I feel she is well enough to be left alone, I will not leave her."

"All right. That is your decision, but you also have a responsibility to your audience and to those who have worked hard to place you where you are today, or where you were before you became unavailable, if I must be honest."

Daniel laughed inside himself, thinking that his agency only got interested in his career when he himself began to be offered important engagements. Then they saw that their fees could be substantial, and developed a keen interest in him. However, what Harvey said about his audience did impress him. He felt an obligation as an artist towards those who appreciated his art. And then he thought of Stagione. His old professor had always assured him he would one day be in the top echelon of conductors in the world. To Daniel, honoring a commitment to achieve was a moral duty, even if that pledge was one that had never been spelled out, and this did make sense to him. His responsibility to his wife and family was paramount, but perhaps things had improved enough to allow him to address himself to his other interests.

"Well, Annemarie has gotten better. Perhaps I can start to work again. Did you have something specific in mind?"

"That's good to hear. Yes. Although the position of Associate Guest Conductor has been withdrawn, it has not been given to anyone else. I think we can get it back for you if you resume a regular schedule. Uppermost in importance now, however, are the performances of Mahler's *"Resurrection" Symphony*. This is the concert that was to crown your association with the BSO. Because of your background in the choral repertory and your work with singers, and especially because the Mahler *Second* is the kind of thing you do so well, a work with drama and theatrical electricity, any other conductor who has been considered has been found wanting." Harvey had done his homework on this artist. He seemed to know all about his career and what Daniel had excelled in over the past years.

"Yes, I would love to do the *"Resurrection."*

"All right then. Can I start the ball rolling? You will need to be at all the rehearsals. You will conduct performances in Boston and then in New York."

"Just give me until tomorrow. I want to see if I can make arrangements so that my wife is never alone."

"I understand. But, Daniel . . ." Harvey was silent momentarily.

"Yes?"

"I want to stress that this could be *the* crucial opportunity to get your career back on track again."

"I do understand. Thank you Harvey."

Annemarie was totally supportive of Daniel's decision to resume conducting. She had overheard snippets of his conversation with his agency's head man, and his love and concern for her was just as apparent as it always was. But she was all right now. Her mother could stay if she needed help with the children. She was feeling stronger and she would be just fine, or so she thought.

Maestro Lorelli's interpretation of Mahler's *"Resurrection"* *Symphony* was a resounding success. The opening of the first movement had a particular urgency and drive that those who knew the *Symphony* had never experienced before. The finely honed details in the orchestration and the development of the massive funeral march in which Mahler's hero from his *First Symphony* is borne to the grave, prepared the audiences for a memorable musical experience which would culminate in the rapt finale. Daniel so strongly identified with the words Mahler set in the *Symphony's 5ᵗʰ Movement*, and this identification was so palpable, so intense and communicative, that listeners on those evenings in Boston and New York would never forget it. The words sung by the soprano and chorus—*"Auferstehn, ja auferstehn wirst du, Mein staub, nach kurzer Ruh! . . . Wieder aufzublühn, wirst du gesät! Der Herr der Ernst geht, Und sammelt Garben Uns ein, die starben!*–were so evidently, for Daniel, an affirmation of the concept of reincarnation, a belief which for him became ever more substantial and even desirable. The words then sung by the chorus and contralto, to music that is so exquisitely appropriate, stirred Daniel in the deepest fibers of his being: *"Was entstanden ist, das mussvergehen, was vergangen, auferstehen! Hör auf zu beben! Bereite dich zu leben!* And then, the choral finale, *"Auferstehn, ja auferstehn wirst du, Mein Herz, in einem Nu! Was du geschlagen, Zu Gott wird es dich tragen!"* As he conducted the finale, each and every time, in rehearsal or in full concert, Daniel felt deeply within himself that nothing could be so bad that it would not find resolution, resolution and renewal. He thought of Annemarie as he conducted. He thought that even if she died, he knew that her death would not be final. As the words in Mahler's *Symphony* promised, she would live again. These words, this music, music, too, that Lorelli was born to conduct, brought out all that made Daniel the great musician he was. He had an ability to distill from a composition the very essence of the composer's vision. And Mahler was a composer whose music he could become completely enveloped in.

In the following months, Daniel continued to gather laurels for his art. Articles were written about him in the Boston Globe and other New England publications. He was even cited in the New York *Times* in a Sunday "Arts and Leisure" article on aspiring young conductors who would eventually take over the top posts in the world's great orchestras. Maestro Lorelli's concerts were eagerly awaited by the cognoscenti who found his traversal of their favorite orchestral works refreshingly conceived, not so much for any new or daring insights he brought that they would probably disagree with, but for his adherence to the letter of the score and the spirit of the composer's creation. On one program Lorelli conducted Beethoven's *Seventh Symphony*. "The apotheosis of the dance," was Richard Wagner's singular characterization of the work, and this attribute of the *Seventh*, its ability to epitomize and celebrate the very essence of *dance,* and the conductor's ability to extract and convey the important rhythmic character of the work was what distinguished a performance of the Seventh or failing that, made it sound laborious and somewhat dull. A music critic writing about Lorelli's performance compared it to one he had heard under Leonard Bernstein in New York some months earlier. He noted that Bernsein, quite uncharacteristically since he was a man of the theater as well as a distinguished conductor of the classical repertory, had gotten the rhythms wrong, and as a result the *Symphony* plodded along ineffectually. The critic's analogy was to a finely tuned automobile. When it runs as it should, one can hear the motor's smooth transitions as the gears change and it accelerates. But imagine, he wrote, how disappointing it could be if the motor hesitated and fluttered. It was the same with Beethoven's *Seventh.* After the New York concert, a friend of the critic commented that the *Seventh* was not one of his favorite Beethoven *Symphonies.* He assured his companion that his thoughts along those lines were prompted by that unsuccessful performance, but if he heard it again in an idiomatic and rhythmically true reading of the work, he would know at once that this was one of Beethoven's finest *Symphonies,* and one of the most enjoyable too. Lorelli's conducting of the work in Boston was just such a performance. Beethoven was one of Daniel's first loves in classical music. He remembered when he first played the entire *Appassionata Sonata* for Vronitsky after studying it with his teacher for some weeks. The old teacher didn't stop Daniel once. When he came to the end of the "Allegro ma non troppo," with its repetitive scurryings and abrupt stands before scurrying off again, followed by the difficult fleet runs covering the entire keyboard and the final three chords, Vronitsky sat silently for about three minutes. Then he said something Daniel would never forget. It was a compliment unlike any other he would ever receive in his life.

"That was wonderful. I could not have played it better myself. I am certain that Beethoven himself would have enjoyed your playing of his *Sonata.*"

Daniel had been overwhelmed by his teacher's remarks and committed each word he spoke to his memory and never forgot even one of them. As he prepared the orchestra in rehearsal for the performance of the *Seventh Symphony,* Daniel silently repeated Vronitsky's words. This had been for Daniel one of the finest gifts his teacher had given him, for it secured his self-confidence and gave him the courage he needed to proceed on his musical voyage even when he was daunted by the magnitude of musical talent he saw all around him. If he could, at the age of sixteen, play the "Appassionata" as well as Vronitsky, by Vronitsky's own attestation, then he could do anything.

Things were settling back into a routine in the Lorelli household. Annemarie had begun to give lessons again at home and take the children to their after school activities, Marta to ballet classes, Vincent to soccer practice. And although Daniel was quite busy, he always found time to spend with his wife, quality time alone, when they would talk, hold hands and kiss, and make love on mornings when the children were in school. As the months passed, Daniel accepted engagements to conduct orchestras in Cincinnati, Baltimore, San Francisco and Seattle. As a conductor, he was more and more in demand. He conducted two operas at the Metropolitan in New York, Wagner's *Der Fliegende Hollander* and Puccini's *Turandot*. It seemed as though Maestro Lorelli could do no wrong. Even two of New York's nastiest critics who found fault with every performer and every performance came out strongly in favor of Daniel's direction of the singers, chorus and orchestra.

It was a good time for the Lorelli family. The children were happy, secure now that their mother was active again, smiling brightly much of the time as she had before her illness changed the way she appeared to them. Daniel's success renewed his spirit and Annemarie shared the joy and satisfaction of her husband's burgeoning career as never before. It was a good time for the Lorelli's. Then Annemarie discovered another lump on her other breast. It was sudden. She had actually stopped examining herself, perhaps because of an unacknowledged fear of a recurrence of the cancer. Her first reaction, before fear could descend on her like a bird of portentous doom, was one of anger. How could this happen again! How? Just now when everything had returned to normal, even if she did have a prosthesis—that was certainly not normal but she had accepted it, was living with it and coping—how could this happen to her again? She was afraid to tell Daniel. He was just getting back into the full swing of his career, blossoming again after a horrible time of abnegation with respect to his art. She noted afterwards that during her illness he had stopped playing the piano each day for the first time since they were married. He had been so concerned for her. How could she do this to him again! The time would come, when in the throes of self recrimination, she would admit to her husband that she had hesitated to tell him and to act because she refused to staunch again the odyssey of success upon which he was embarked. He would suffer too, his own culpability for not having sensed that something was amiss, attending his waking hours and disturbing his dreams for a long period afterwards. But it all meant nothing in practical terms, for some of the billions of cancer cells, malignant cells, had already metastasized and reached Annemarie's liver by the time she first noticed the new lump.

Dr. Manfredi saw this immediately and knew that her patient was one of the unfortunate ones, one of those for whom the new advancements in breast cancer treatment would not prove salutary. After examining Annemarie and seeing the test results she managed to speak to Daniel before confronting Annemarie with the unfortunate verdict.

"*Mi dispiace. Veramente.* I would do anything possible to help your wife, but I am afraid I can do nothing."

This was the hardest moment for a physician like Silvana. She was so thoroughly imbued with the idea that she had to save lives, that when she knew she could not, it was a kind of personal loss.

Daniel could not suppress his tears. As he stood there and sobbed, Silvana moved closer and embraced him. She patted his shoulders and then moved away, regarding him with a sadness so profound her own eyes moistened as she thought to herself that she should not be doing this, but by no means fearing that her professional demeanor was being compromised. She just felt that she was of no real use to anyone if she allowed her emotions to overtake her.

"How much time does she have?" Daniel asked with explicit trepidation.

"Not much, I'm afraid. When it reaches the liver as it has here, it moves very quickly. The only thing we can do is to try to make her comfortable."

Annemarie knew that she was going home to Boston to die. She clung to Daniel every moment after that. Driving back, she leaned towards him, holding his right arm as he steered with his left.

"You know you can find someone after I'm gone." Annemarie spoke firmly, without morbidity or the slightest hint of self-pity.

"Let's not talk about it," Daniel replied, barely able to finish the sentence. At the word "talk," he began to choke, recovering quickly, telling himself that he must be strong for her sake. But after that day Annemarie was the pillar of fortitude in the Lorelli and Taviani families. Unlike her first episode with cancer, when she needed to fight and was afraid she would not win the battle, when she feared death because the concept of it had stolen upon her and she was unable to confront it or even imagine not being there for her husband and children, she was now resigned to it. She found deep within herself the stamina and resolve to buttress her family, to lead them through the coming weeks of dissolution and despair, since she knew they were inadequate in the face of her own daunting destiny.

She had always been a very strong person, a young girl who followed her dreams with unflagging enthusiasm and engagement, a woman who demanded the most both from herself and from those she was responsible for, her students, her children and her husband. Who can truly say whence this strength came. Her Irish antecedents had known much suffering and deprivation. Perhaps the stoicism she was able to muster up was genetically transmitted through the ages. Whatever it was, she moved towards her own demise boldly.

Maureen and Violetta prayed. They prayed and got everyone around them to pray, to offer up petitions beseeching the Almighty, the saints, St. Jude, patron of impossible or lost causes, the Blessed Virgin, who could surely intervene to heal her child, anyone and all who could possibly come between her and this dreaded disease, stop it in its very path, to halt its decisive advance, turn it around, make it go away. A miracle! That is what was needed. A miracle for Annemarie. She was worthy of it. She was good, always had been. Why not, then?

But Annemarie prayed no more. She prepared herself for the inevitable and knew that she had to do the same for those she loved so dearly. She could not allow herself to think about it too much, especially not to think about what their lives would be like without her. If she did, it would cause her to deviate from the direction she knew she had to take. Of course she had to think about her children's future, her Daniel's future, but she just could not dwell on the picture she saw of them without her. She had to eliminate herself from that image, for surely she would not be there, so why imagine that she would. Marta was sixteen and Vincent was eleven. She knew they each had interests of their own, but she did not wish to impose upon them any formula as to the direction their lives should take. She remembered how when young her parents had had their own ideas about the careers she could pursue, but she herself had decided to make music her life. She wanted her children to use their own initiatives to decide their own futures, without interference from her from beyond the grave. It was up to her to reassure them now, to make it possible for them to remember all the positive things about their mother, to remember her as a living and vibrant woman, not as a dying and pathetic soul. She knew that they would need consolation. One day, a thought came to her and she called Daniel to listen to her idea. As soon as she mentioned the word "funeral," he became uncomfortable and asked her why they had to discuss that.

"We have to discuss it. I want you to know what I would like done with me. It is my life and it is also my death. Please listen. I do not want to have a prolonged wake, no open casket. You know how we both love Fauré's *Requiem* so much and how we both feel that it is one of the most consoling musical works ever written dealing with *death*?" She did not flinch at all in using the word, but said it firmly, without the slightest bit of morbidity, as if it were a family event that everyone was looking forward to with eager anticipation.

"Yes," Daniel replied, sadly, fighting back tears of anguish, tears of despair.

"That recording of the Faure, the one we both love more than any other—the Cluytens—I want that played the evening of my wake. One evening only. With a closed casket. No talking, just everyone sitting there listening to the music without interruption, no eulogies. That can be held for the church, for the Mass the next morning."

Daniel could only hold her, bury his face in her bosom, this part of her body where the destructive processes had begun. He loved her so much, didn't want to be without her. Nothing and no one could console him.

A week before she died, Daniel was sitting at Annemarie's bedside. He was there every waking moment it was possible for him to be there. She had insisted on being taken home from the hospital. She wanted to die in familiar surroundings, in the presence of those she loved. A nurse was on duty throughout the day and Daniel slept beside Annemarie at night. Dr. Taviani looked in on his daughter every day, ascertaining that she had enough of the pain killer she needed to be comfortable, administering the morphine, instructing the nurse as to the type and quantity of intravenous medication needed. He, too, knew that he had to be strong for the sake of his daughter, his wife, his grandchildren and yes, even for his dear son-in-law, a man he had come to love as much as his own children. But each day as he left her room, Annemarie's father, a man who had witnessed death countless times, had seen firsthand the ravage this disease could wreak, each day he would collapse in the seat of his car and weep bitter tears. It was hard indeed for a father to see his daughter die. He thought of her through each moment of her childhood he could recall, of her growing into young womanhood, as an adult. He remembered her recitals and how she looked as she held the viola, so serious and intent on the music that was coming forth from her instrument, and of the time when she was soloist with the orchestra in William Walton's *Viola Concerto*. He had held Maureen's hand and squeezed it when their daughter took her bows and the audience applauded vociferously. They had both been so proud. They loved her so much. He thought of her as a mother, of the time he and Maureen had visited her in Germany after Vincent was born. He had been filled with pride and admiration for her, for the way she nourished and reacted to everything her children did. A father should not see his daughter die. Such a thing was inconsistent with the regularities of life.

And so it was that after Dr. Taviani departed one day, kissing his daughter's forehead and caressing her hand, she spoke to Daniel, feebly, but steadily.

"I know the time is coming when I will not be with you anymore. It will not be long now." Daniel drew in his breath, trying with all his strength to suppress the sobs he could feel arising within him.

"I know you will take good care of Marta and Vincent. Talk to them about me whenever you can. Tell them that their mother loved them with all her heart. Tell them about me, about my viola." Daniel could but say, "Yes, yes," as he listened to her. If he tried to say more, he knew he would break down.

"And Dan, we will be together again. You *are* my true soul-mate. I always knew you were, from the first time I saw you in Rome." Daniel was astonished. This was the first time Annemarie had ever used the word "soul-mate." He had spoken to her many times of his thoughts about reincarnation and of how we meet souls we have known in prior lifetimes, but Annemarie had always brushed these avowals aside, preferring the tenets of the faith she had been raised in.

"Yes, I know now that I will see you again and I will see Marta and Vincent too, so I am not afraid to die anymore because I know I will be with you all again."

She had said so much that all the strength she summoned up was dissipated and she could say no more. Daniel nodded his head, "Yes, we will, my sweet, we will, we will."

Everything went according to Annemarie's directions. Family and friends listened to *her* Faure *Requiem* and did find consolation in listening to it, reading the Latin words and a translation in a commemoratory folder that was provided them, especially the section "In Paradisum." At the words closing Faure's masterly affirmation of faith in the face of death, the promise of continuance in the hereafter, "*Chorus angelorum te suscipat, et cum Lazaro quondam paupere aeternam habeas requiem,*" not one eye in the room remained dry. At the Mass the following day, a Requiem Mass celebrated by Father Stephen Lorelli, the church could not accommodate all those who had come to bid farewell to the dearly loved woman whose life—cut too short—had touched them all in one way or another. After the Mass, at the cemetery, as his brother said the final prayers at the coffin, Daniel, strangely, as he was to think of it later, did not think of Mahler's *Resurrection Symphony*, a work that it would have seemed fitting to think of then, especially since he had conducted it so recently, but no, instead, he heard other music, also by Mahler. It was a section of the Third Movement from the *Fourth Symphony*, the "Adagio." Mahler, himself, was active as a conductor when he wrote the work. This "adagio" that played in Daniel's inner ear had been inspired by a vision the composer had of a tombstone on which an image of the departed, with arms folded in eternal sleep, had been carved. The bittersweet strains had the power to move one any time it was heard, but for Daniel at that moment the music with its insistent but delicate urgings tore at his heart and punctuated the sense of loss and sorrow that so forcefully enveloped his entire being. For Daniel, as always in his life, music had the power to define a particular moment.

Thirty-Eight

After the funeral Daniel could not find himself. His outlook was bleak. He could not stop thinking about Annemarie. Every single event connected with her, not just the singular ones, filtered through his mind. He remembered everything about her, the way she looked, dressed, undressed, dressed up, dressed down. He remembered the way she held her viola and heard the sounds that poured forth from her and her instrument, even her low but audible breathing as she strenuously practiced, particularly in the *allegros* and the *vivace* passages of some of her favorite compositions. He saw in his mind's eye each encounter he had had with her over the years, the happiest times and the saddest. He could not get over her, and his loss had penetrated a part of him deep inside, where it had implanted a knot that could never be untangled. He had his two children to look after and they certainly gave him the courage and the fortitude to get up in the morning and to try to be somewhat productive. He had to console them, for they were totally bewildered and disoriented by the loss of their mother. But they, too, gave him the consolation he needed to get through this most difficult period of his entire life. Music, which had always been a support mechanism for him, did not help him at first. He found he did not want to even touch the piano. His reaction surprised him, for he had always been able to turn to music to give him strength and reassurance in times of doubt, dismay, and, yes, occasionally, despair. But this despair was different. It reminded him of something his mother had once told him about how her people mourned the death of a loved one where she came from. There would be no music, no entertainment of any kind for a long, long time. Some of Violetta's *paesani*, she had told her son, would not even smile for years, until something happened to break the spell, as when a relative married and a wedding celebration took place. The women would

311

never remove their black attire after the death of a husband or a child. Daniel had seen them when he visited his mother's town, Longobardi, those women in church, a massive block of black kneeling together at the front, close to the altar. Yes, he could understand them now. The death of one you love cannot be dismissed, set aside quickly as when one gets over a minor disappointment. Gradually, however, music came back. He could not live without it. Without his music, he would surely die. Annemarie had warned him of this. She had told him to sit down at his piano immediately after her passing and to play his heart out.

"Let your music be a catharsis for you," she had said, for she knew how much he loved her. She had seen it manifested through everything he did during the months of her illness, every glance, every prolonged gaze as their eyes met and held on to one another, every delicate touch as his fingers caressed her brow, stroked her hair, intertwined with hers. When he began to play again, he thought of her. And even Marta, who never commented on her father's playing, would come over as a piece ended and say,

"Dad, that was so beautiful. I don't think I have ever heard you play so beautifully before."

Daniel thought this unusual, but attributed it to her own burgeoning interest in ballet. She had taken dance lessons for years and was a very talented dancer, but only in the last year or two did she evince the kind of interest she now had in classical ballet, expressing a strong desire to pursue it as a career.

During Annemarie's illness, Daniel Lorelli had once again put his career aside. He had turned down each and every offer he had received to conduct, both at home and abroad. After nearly ten months, he was no longer being asked for his services, except for a few cases of non-consequential conducting of minor ensembles, dates that some of his dear friends arranged to try to buoy him up. His agent informed him dryly that he had kept himself away too long, that he had done this more than once and that there was no sympathy among impresarios and booking agents for artists who cancelled once too often, no matter what the reason was. Daniel now had to depend on the possibility of other conductors canceling so that he could be called upon to fill in for them. In this way he conducted the Boston Symphony again and directed a performance of *Il Trovatore* at the Metropolitan Opera. In Boston the program included a performance of Jean Sibelius' *Second Symphony*. The apotheosis in the final movement was delivered with such exuberance and panache that Daniel was cited by critics and audience members alike for his ability to inspire an orchestra to play their hearts out, and to extract the very essence of a composer's vision and transmit it to his listeners. This was especially noteworthy in a town like Boston that had its own Sibelius tradition, beginning with Serge Koussevitzky. One critic referred to Daniel as "the elusive conductor from whom we would all like to hear much more."

As always, however, Daniel's commitment to his family came first. Marta and Vincent had to be cared for and he would not leave them alone while he traveled to distant cities for days at a time to conduct orchestras, whether they involved major ensembles or not. After some months of living at the house he and Annemarie had purchased outside of Boston, Daniel decided to move back to New York. He rented a small house not too far from his parents' home and settled down there with his two children. He came up with the idea of starting his own ensemble, to be made up of the finest free lance musicians in the area and to concentrate on good contemporary music for chamber ensemble, with occasional backward glances to include seminal works that had had unique importance when they were first introduced. He asked his brothers if they would sponsor him, assuring them that it would be prestigious for the company and that it would eventually be possible to sustain itself and he could then pay them back for whatever they invested. Mamma's Kitchen had continued to thrive, growing into a family owned chain of some forty stores and eateries throughout the country. They did not spend much money on advertising, preferring to have their message of quality Italian food at reasonable prices spread by word of mouth. John and Albert Lorelli were only too happy to help their brother and to connect their company with a cultural enterprise. They did have one request, that Daniel program Italian music from time to time. Daniel had no problem with this since Italy boasted a number of composers who had within recent years written important music, such as the late Gian Francesco Malipiero, and others continuing to write fine music, composers whose work was already known on an international scale, such as Luciano Berio, Franco Donatoni and Salvatore Sciarrino. Of course, once the Lorelli brothers had the opportunity to hear some of the Italian works programmed, they would wonder why they had requested such music at all. The dissonances and difficulties would cause them and their wives to writhe in their seats, applauding at the conclusion of each piece as vigorously as the other members of the enthusiastic audiences that came to hear the Lorelli Chamber Group, perhaps from sheer relief that the music had ended, but also because they knew they had to appear to be supportive since Daniel would call on them to take a bow in recognition of their sponsorship of the series.

The Lorelli Chamber Group played their concerts in various halls around the city: Cooper Union, Merkin, Hall, Alice Tully Hall, Hunter

College Auditorium, The 92nd St. Y, Walt Whitman Hall at Brooklyn College, Queens College in Flushing, the Frick Museum and the Metropolitan Museum of Art. Gradually their reputation grew and their support base of patrons and subscribers increased. They were becoming a staple in the city's musical life, at least as far as concert music was concerned. One of the reasons for the success of the Lorelli Chamber Group was the way in which Daniel interacted with the musicians. Contrary to the popular belief that a conductor had to be a martinet to get good results, Daniel treated each member of his ensemble with respect and consideration. As a result, the musicians loved him and would do anything he asked of them, even offering to extend practice without additional pay. The twenty musicians were unanimous in their feelings of warmth for their conductor, from the sixty year old cellist to the twenty-three year old oboist.

One of the younger members of the ensemble, a very talented violinist learned that Daniel's birthday was the day of their next rehearsal. She asked the members of the group to each contribute something to buy a cake and a gift for their conductor. Daniel was completely surprised by the candle-lit cake that was brought to the stage after rehearsals ended. The gift was a new baton which Daniel would use and cherish for many years afterwards. Daniel spoke to the young violinist and suggested that they have a little celebration each time it was one of the musicians' birthdays. And thus it became a regular event and a way for the colleagues to socialize briefly from time to time. Daniel soon noticed, however, that one of the musicians, his clarinetist, Gary Stoneham, never participated in these celebrations, either leaving as soon as they started or sitting them out in the dressing room. One evening after rehearsals, Daniel stopped Gary and asked him why he was boycotting their little parties,

"I'm a Jehovah's Witness. We don't believe in celebrating birthdays."

Daniel was surprised. "You don't? What could possibly be wrong with sharing a little good cheer in commemorating the birthday of a friend?"

"We live by the true word of the Bible, Jehovah's word, and the only reference in the Bible to a birthday is when Herod uses his own birthday celebration for evil purposes."

Daniel had spoken to Jehovah's Witnesses before, patiently hearing them out when they knocked at his door when he was a teenager living in Brooklyn, and again while he lived in Boston and once even in Germany. He thought that those he had spoken too were not very articulate. Never in his experience with them were they able to adequately reply to questions he asked. They were definitely anti-Catholic and spoke with deprecation of his religion, but he never heard one satisfactory explanation from any of them as to why they believed that their interpretations were correct and those of the Church were in error. Whenever the questions he asked became too difficult for them to adequately encompass in their stock replies, as Daniel thought of their apparently rehearsed speeches, they would give him a copy of *Watchtower* and encourage him to read it for a clearer idea of their position. These unexpected visitors with their peremptory pronouncements could be annoying, but they were always respectful, always well dressed and courteous. Nevertheless, one was always left with the impression that they were brainwashed victims of a fraudulent enterprise. This was why Daniel was so confounded as to why a man with Gary Stoneham's apparent intelligence and talent as a musician could have been taken in by this "sect"? Was it even a sect, or was it a cult? Daniel wasn't sure.

Over the following months, Daniel had a number of conversations with Gary and it soon became apparent to him that the young musician was trying to convert him. Unlike Daniel, Gary had been raised in a home where religion had had no real importance. His mother and father were Presbyterians in name only—at least that is what they would reply if asked about their religion—but they never attended church or took their son there, and they did not have the habit of saying prayers at home, whether before meals or at bedtime. Gary had been searching for something fundamental, for something to believe in. He had studied different religions on his own. Eventually he accepted the offer of Bible study with a group of Jehovah's Witnesses and found their interpretation of the Bible unique. They rejected many of the traditional beliefs held by most Christians and offered what to Gary was not only a reasonable alternative, but the only proper way to live as a Christian. They did believe that Christ's death was a ransom for mankind, that Jesus died to redeem all men for what had been lost by Adam's disobedience. They rejected the concept of the Trinity, the immortality of the human soul and the idea of eternal torment in hell. When Daniel countered that Roman Catholicism was the one true faith because it had been established by Jesus himself, Gary argued that Catholics had misinterpreted what Jesus had said, that Peter was not the rock upon which Christ would establish his Church, but that Jesus himself was the cornerstone of the faith. He quoted St. Paul, stating without the need to even refer to a text, "And you have been built up upon the foundation of the apostles and prophets, while Christ Jesus himself is the foundation cornerstone." Daniel was impressed. Here was a Jehovah's Witness unlike any he had ever met before, a man who could take on questions and answer them, if not to Daniel's complete satisfaction, at least with some measure of intelligence and logic. Gary explained to Daniel that the early church became corrupted, deviating from the teachings of Jesus. Catholicism

315

had taken over religious customs that had been common in pagan Rome. Examples were the stole and vestments of pagan priests, the burning of candles before the altar, the acceptance of Roman law as the basis for canon law. Gary scoffed at the institution of the priesthood, calling it an abdication of the absolute necessity and obligation for true followers of Jehovah, and Jesus to be personally involved in the general ministry of all Christians as Jesus himself had taught.

"Why don't you look into the history of the Papacy?" Gary challenged. "During the first two centuries, there was not even any mention of a Pope. It is fairly evident that the title 'Pope' was used for the first time in the 3rd century and by the 5th century it merely meant the Bishop of Rome."

He further demonstrated his impressive knowledge by discussing the importance for the Catholic Church of Constantine's conversion, with the adoption of the Nicene Creed and its stress on acceptance of the Trinity as a basic tenet of the Faith, and of Pope Leo I's crowning of Charlemagne as Emperor of the Holy Roman Empire.

Gary invited Daniel to accompany him to a meeting at the Kingdom Hall he attended. Daniel just knew that he could never be a Jehovah's Witness himself. There were simply too many things about their beliefs that he found weird. And besides, how could this sect that had been founded by a man, one Charles Taze Russell, who had lived from 1852 to 1916, possibly have the authority accorded to religions that had been in existence for centuries? Yes, he knew that the organization claimed to have members present even during the lifetime of Jesus, but this to Daniel was just grasping at straws. But he went to the meeting with Gary out of curiosity. The Hall was filled. Everyone was well dressed, the men in suits and ties, the women in conservative dresses, not even one of them wearing pants, all looking as though they were attending a wedding or some other formal celebration. Daniel pondered how this contrasted with the appearance of parishioners at Sunday Mass, many of the men in blue jeans, the women with tight fitting garments.

The group sang scripture related songs and read selections from their Bibles. Daniel was given a personal welcome by the congregation. Afterwards, a number of Witnesses approached him to tell him how happy they were that he had decided to join their meeting and that they hoped to see him at future meetings. "Not likely," Daniel thought, but he did attend one or two additional meetings and was then paired off with one of the elders who agreed to try to resolve some of the questions Daniel had about the organization and their beliefs. Daniel met him at the Kingdom Hall on an evening when it was unoccupied and brought up matters such as the Witnesses' refusal of blood transfusions, their prediction of the end of the world and Armageddon on at least two dates, which had passed without incident, their adherence to the concept of a heavenly Kingdom class of 144,000 people who would rule with Christ from the heavens, while the remaining millions of the faithful would live on earth in eternal bliss, free from care, exempt from illness and any other kind of human discomfort. All the rest, those who had rejected their salvation would die forever. When Daniel tried to reason that so many of their beliefs were based on inaccurate or even fanciful interpretations of scripture, things they adhered to because there was either a reference or no reference to them in the Bible, the elder could not provide what Daniel would have considered an adequate response.

On many occasions after that, Daniel would see these Witnesses, going from door to door, standing on street corners in busy areas in New York City, in piazzas in Rome, once even during a short stay in Calabria, where the local pastor of the Catholic parish in the town there told him that the Jehovah's Witnesses were stealing away his parishioners. Daniel saw them as devoted participants in an exercise in futility. He felt sorry for them in a way, for he was so sure they were wrong. But what if they were wrong? They seemed to be happy. They had found something in life that many were still searching for, a confidence that they were acting according to the way Jehovah wanted them to act. Yes, they were happy, but did that justify them going through all these useless and meaningless motions? To them it did, but to Daniel looking at them objectively, as he was certain was the way he did look at them, they were wasting so much time for something that had no real basis in reality and, when studied and examined, no validity even in terms of the spiritual status that the great religions had achieved. He had made the point with Gary that even if Catholicism was imperfect in ways, the Church had still done a great deal of good and continued to do so. Think of the Catholic hospitals, orphanages, think of members of the Church like Sister Teresa who dedicated their lives to helping the poor and the sick. Where was any of this kind of charity evident among the Jehovah's Witnesses? Was there even one charity associated with them that did anything to help people? Did they even help their own members when in need? Gary had dismissed that as not important in the larger scheme. What happened here in this life was not important. It was going to soon be over anyway, so all the efforts to cure people and to treat victims of AIDS was not significant. What was significant was returning to God's Kingdom as the only hope for mankind. Daniel could only smile and think to himself how gullible his young friend was. Still, each time he saw them in the streets, the women with their long dresses, the men in suits and ties, carrying a briefcase, he could not but feel a deep sympathy for them. One thing did come out of this experience with the Jehovah's Witnesses: it stimulated his interest to learn more about Christianity, and particularly about his own Roman Catholic faith.

One evening Gary did not appear for the rehearsal, but did come in to see Daniel after it ended.

"Daniel, I'm afraid I will have to resign my position here."

"Resign? But why, Gary?"

Daniel was visibly upset at hearing this news from a man and a musician he had come to like.

"Well, after you attended our meetings, I was asked by some of the Elders about the organization. They thought highly of you and hope that you will join our community as a permanent member."

"Yes, what does this have to do with your leaving?"

"They asked me about the other members of the ensemble and I had to be honest."

"Honest? Yes, but I still don't understand."

"You must be aware, as I am, that some of the musicians are homosexuals. It's not hard to figure out since some of them actually flaunt their immoral life styles."

"To be honest, Gary, I didn't notice. I don't think what the musicians do in their private lives is my business."

"That's how I used to think too. But the Elders showed me how mistaken I was. What they do, the way they live, their sexual practices—why it's all an abomination in the eyes of God! It's right there in the *Bible*, Leviticus, Chapter 18, 22."

"But why should that prevent you from playing in an orchestra with them? As long as they don't discuss their practices with you, why should it bother you?"

"The Elders pointed out to me that as a Witness, I cannot be associated with a group that condones such behavior. They asked me if I can find other work as a musician and I told them that I can, so there is no reason to for me to retain this job. And besides, they have offered me work at Bethel, at headquarters, and that can be much more fulfilling for me than playing in an orchestra."

"Gary, be reasonable. We neither condone it nor do we condemn it. We are neutral, so to speak, at least in terms of our stance before the public."

"I'm sorry, Maestro." Gary suddenly turned very formal and it was obvious he did not wish to discuss it any further. "I have enjoyed working with you and I appreciate your superior musicianship, but I cannot stay."

"But Gary," Daniel pleaded in a tone that demonstrated his sincere friendship for the younger man,

"Gary, I cannot believe that working in this organization can possibly be more fulfilling for you than performing music. You are a musician. You have music in your heart and in your soul. Don't you see that they are controlling you? If religion is true, it does not need to control its members."

"They are not controlling me. It is my decision. And, Daniel . . ."

"Yes, Gary?"

"I want you to know that I have not given up on you—as far as Jehovah is concerned, I mean."

With that pronouncement, Gary smiled a smile that could have been taken as sardonic if Daniel did not know better, turned around and walked out.

Some of the other members of the group asked Daniel why Gary had left and Daniel merely told them that he had other obligations. But one evening, another young man whom Daniel had grown fond of, Jack Morelli, a superior violist whose playing sometimes reminded him of Annemarie's, stopped to speak with the conductor. He was a very friendly young man, was gay, and found Daniel very attractive. He looked at Daniel the same way a man would look at a very beautiful woman that he knew he had no possible chance with. It was admiration from a distance. Jack knew about Daniel's history, his wife's death, his two children and just how devoted he was to them. Still, he derived a kind of satisfaction from talking to him. Daniel always retained that quality of making the person he was speaking with feel that nothing or no one was as important as he or she was at that particular moment. Jack, too, eventually got around to asking Daniel about Gary's departure. Daniel smiled to himself, thinking how ironic it seemed just then, that this fine, sincere, capable and sensitive man and musician was the reason, along with perhaps four other members of the group, for Gary's departure.

"Why are you smiling?" Jack asked, himself smiling broadly now.

"Jack, please keep this between us."

"Certainly." Jack felt privileged that Daniel wanted to share something with him that he obviously would not share with the others.

"Gary left because of you and a few of your colleagues."

"What? I never even had an extended conversation with him. Why would he leave because of me?'

"You are aware that he is a member of the Jehovah's Witnesses?"

"Yes, I heard that is why he did not come to the parties, some crazy restriction they hold to."

"I don't know how much you know about Jehovah's Witnesses, but they are under the control of the Elders in their group. If they do something wrong, or even if they think they are doing something wrong, they must discuss it with the Elders and are then given instructions as to how to deal with it."

"That's absurd!"

"Perhaps for you and me, but not for a believer like Gary. He told the Elders in his Kingdom Hall that he played in a group that had a number of gays in it and they decided he had to leave, fearing you and the others would corrupt him, or, at least, compromise his principles."

"But we don't go around trying to convert anyone to our way of life!"

"I know, I know, but that's the way they think."

This led to a conversation that brought back to Daniel memories of his classmate at Curtis, Sam Halstead. Just as with Sam, Daniel listened to Jack's contention that he had no choice in his sexual orientation. Like Daniel, he came from an Italian-American family. His parents had been born in America, but his grandparents on his mother's and father's side came from Italy. His parents had four children, two girls and two boys. His sisters were married with families of their own, as was his brother. Jack was the youngest and the only member of the family to display homosexual tendencies, from quite an early age.

"Daniel, I can assure you that my earliest memories were of being attracted to my own sex. I never looked at girls the way my classmates did, not when I was ten, or fifteen, or twenty. It was really not my decision. I was just born the way I am. You might say that God made me this way. It was His choice, not mine. If only all these so-called Christians would learn to be a bit more Christian towards everyone, as Jesus himself was."

Daniel thought about how a similar conversation with Sam Halstead had ended so uncomfortably for him, and he felt a little ashamed of his behavior at that time. There was much about himself that had changed over the years. He was able to accept things he could not when he was younger, capable of greater tolerance for ways of thinking different from his own. There was still so much more he needed to investigate. One thing was obvious to Daniel: after living for more than half a century, he still had a great deal to learn. He just could not stand still like so many of his friends and relatives.

After his discussions with the Jehovah's Witnesses, Daniel's appetite had been whetted. At first, he just wanted to find information about Catholicism that he could use to refute statements that Gary had made to him. But soon, this turned into a much larger quest. He wanted, needed, more information about his own religion, about Christianity and about

Jesus. He began doing research on these topics with the enthusiasm that he had always brought to researching composers, musical styles, and musical scores. He went to Barnes and Noble in Manhattan on 18th St and Fifth Avenue, to the Strand Book store at 12th Street and Broadway, to the main branch of the New York Public Library at 42nd Street and Fifth Avenue. He bought and borrowed books, old titles and new ones that he would then devour with an insatiable appetite for information about a man his Church called "the Son of God," and about the Church itself; how its beliefs had developed over the centuries and what it had done to maintain its authority and its rule over the laity. He read and marveled at writings on the subject of the historical Jesus by Albert Schweitzer, Rudolf Bultmann, James M. Robinson and others. He learned of the existence of other Gospels associated with Jesus besides the canonical Gospels, like the *Gospel of Thomas*, a collection of 114 sayings of Jesus. Daniel became aware of a massive body of scholarship that had been developed by Biblical scholars and theologians, men and women who were not trying to ridicule and debase religion, or Christianity, or Jesus himself. No, they were working towards a better understanding of who Jesus really was, why he was important, and why the accretions that had grown up over the centuries about the man and his life encompassed so much that was fanciful, questionable and unreliable. Why was none of this ever discussed in the circle of Catholic believers that he was a part of? Even among friends of his who had attended Catholic Universities and had taken courses in theology and Thomistic philosophy, there was no one he knew of who had ever questioned whether the Church's teachings on Jesus, on his life and assumed resurrection were accurate and valid. All the Catholics he knew believed what they believed because this is what they had been taught since early childhood, had had these beliefs reinforced by sheer force of habit—the celebration of feasts like Christmas and Easter, the repetitive confirmation of these "truths" during celebrations of the sacraments like Baptism, First Communion, Confirmation, and Marriage—so that their beliefs remained grounded and unchallenged throughout their entire lives. Yes, this is what we believe, what our parents and grandparents believed. Why should we not believe? And besides, we can basically do whatever we want to do. No one is stopping us. We can ignore Church rules we don't like, those rules that interfere with our perceived quality of life, and just practice the parts that we are comfortable with. Daniel thought of the German priest who told him that he could receive Communion and still practice artificial birth control. There was division in the Church. Daniel had read about Bishops who deviated from official Church teaching and were severely reprimanded. But even in such cases, the ordinary Catholic merely assumed that the differences involved some abstract theological concept that didn't really matter so much at all. There was never any indication that anyone in the Church questioned the divinity of Jesus or whether he had truly risen from the dead.

Daniel read widely. He discovered the writings of Arthur Schopenhauer and read the essay, "Religion: a Dialogue," with especial interest. In this imaginary dialogue between Demopheles, a defender of religion and Philalethes, a philosopher who seeks the truth that he feels religion lacks, Daniel better understood the rationale that had developed, at least among some who knew better, about leaving the masses in ignorance about religious truths or falsities. Demopheles argues, "Religion is the metaphysics of the masses; by all means let them keep it: let it therefore command external respect, for to discredit it is to take it away.... for mankind absolutely needs *an interpretation of life*; and this, again, must be suited to popular comprehension. Consequently, this interpretation is always an allegorical investiture of the truth: and in practical life and in its effects on the feelings . . . as a rule of action and as a comfort and consolation in suffering and death, it accomplishes just as much as the truth itself could achieve if we possessed it . . . . The various religions are only various forms in which the truth, which taken by itself, is above their comprehension, is grasped and realized by the masses; and truth becomes inseparable from these forms."

Amazing, Daniel thought, that this had been written some one hundred and fifty years earlier. Certainly there could be some justification for leaving people in ignorance if nothing better could be offered them. But Daniel was intrigued by the reply from Philalethes in the same "Dialogue." Philalethes argues that it is "shallow and unjust to demand that there be no other system of metaphysics but this one, cut out as it is to suit the requirements and comprehension of the masses; that its doctrine shall be the limit of human speculation, the standard of all thought. . . that the highest powers of human intelligence shall remain unused and undeveloped. . . . Isn't it a little too much to have tolerance and delicate forbearance preached by what is intolerance and cruelty itself? Think of the heretical tribunals, inquisitions, religious wars, crusades . . . is this today quite a thing of the past? How can genuine philosophical effort, sincere search after truth, the noblest calling of the noblest men, be let and hindered more completely than by a conventional system of metaphysics . . . the principles of which are impressed into every head in earliest youth, so earnestly, so deeply, and so firmly, that, unless the mind is miraculously elastic, they remain indelible. In this way the groundwork of all healthy reason is once for all deranged . . . the capacity for original thought and unbiased judgment . . . is . . . forever paralyzed and ruined."

Yes, Daniel thought. This is what happened to me and to my ancestors before me. We were indoctrinated at an early age, discouraged from investigating anything concerning religion on our own, and left to just believe all that had been fed to us. Oh, yes, Daniel and friends of his used to discuss aspects of religion. They would argue about this or that, and some would even become apostates. But so many, like Daniel himself, would continue to adhere to doctrines they had been indoctrinated with, even if their convictions did not carry the kind of weight such convictions should if they were to be a part of one's system of essential beliefs. Daniel had always had his doubts, but he never had the time to devote to resolving them one way or another. But now, now he felt an intense obligation to follow this path he had embarked upon, no matter where it would lead him. Since Schopenhauer had written his essay, religion had not improved mankind any more than it had in the hundreds of years before. Since the philosopher penned his objections, intolerance fueled by religion had resulted in the deaths of millions of innocent people in the Second World War, and the same kind of intolerance had a disastrous effect on relations between peoples throughout the world. And what of the so-called "Holy Land?" What was so holy about it? Down through the centuries blood had been shed there in the name of God, and it continued, on and on and on. Daniel saw day by day how so-called Christians, "the Christian right" they were called, devoted their energies to destroying anyone and anything that did not meet with their concept of "the truth". Theirs was a system of exclusion. Anyone who could not subscribe to their beliefs was anathema. If only, Daniel thought, if only they could truly follow the philosophy of the Jesus they claimed to love and to have in their hearts! If only they could adhere to the most important part of his philosophy, that of non-exclusion, acceptance of everyone, even if they differed markedly from you in their beliefs or way of living.

Thirty-Nine

Two years after her mother's death, Marta Lorelli graduated from high school with honors and was admitted to the Dance Program at New York University's Tisch School of the Arts. She planned a career in ballet. Vincent was just entering high school, but he already had definite ideas about following his maternal grandfather and becoming a physician. He was interested in working in cancer research, stimulated by a desire to combat the disease that had taken his mother's life. Daniel was busy with the Lorelli Chamber Group and devoted whatever time he could to reading about religion, pursuing his interest in this area with an unflagging desire to make amends for his ignorance on the subject for most of his life He still attended Sunday Mass, but mostly because of a promise he had made to Annemarie that he would see to it that their children continued to practice their faith until they were adults. She had been aware of Daniel's ambivalent thoughts about Catholicism, many of which she shared, but she considered it important for young people to have their own religious foundation and to have it intact until they were old enough and mature enough to make any decisions about their own relationship to God, and whether or not their Church would continue to occupy an important place in their hearts and in their lives. For Daniel, attending Mass was no longer spiritually satisfying. The sense of mystery he remembered from childhood was missing. The sermons were mostly irrelevant and prosaic. He still considered himself a Roman Catholic, but perhaps in name only. Whenever he thought of leaving the Catholic Church, of becoming an apostate himself, he never thought of the possibility of joining another church. James Joyce's quip came to mind about abandoning a logical absurdity for an illogical one. Even here, though, Daniel's studies had shown him that logic in Catholicism was a contradiction in terms.

Soon after Marta entered New York University, Vincenzo died. He had lived to the age of eighty-seven and had been in excellent health for most of his life. His death had been sudden, following a brief illness. Violetta, always the woman of strong faith, was sure she would see him again before too long in the afterlife. Theirs had been an ideal marriage. Their success as a married couple was due to several factors, including mutual respect and interests, a deep and abiding love for one another, and their ability to dissipate tensions that arose from time to time by talking openly with one another and never, ever holding a grudge over anything whatsoever, settling any differences that arose during the day before they retired for the night. Violetta still had her sister Rosina living in the same house with her, in her own apartment as she had for many years, and although both women needed a good deal of assistance, they could still exercise a degree of independence. Sophia had truly become for Violetta the daughter she never had. They had worked together in the business and loved one another very much. Sophia went by the house each day and took care of any needs Violetta had. When her health began to deteriorate, Sophia took her to doctors, to laboratories for tests, and saw to it that she was always comfortable.

Daniel's aunt Rosina had kept in touch with her husband's family in Falconara for many years. She had even gone back once or twice to visit them. One of her husband's cousins had a distant relative who had managed to emigrate to Italy from Albania with his wife after the downfall of the Communists, following forty-four years of ironclad control of the populace in that country. Eventually, the couple wanted to come to the United States to seek a better life. Rosina asked her nephews to give the young man work in their company, and they were only too happy to do so, finding a job for him handling stock. Daniel's cousin Philip Sandreva called to ask if he could use a woman to do household work one or two days each week. He and Daniel's two brothers had agreed to hire her for three days, and since she really wanted to at least work a five day week, they thought that Daniel could possibly use her services. Daniel had had women coming in to clean the house during Annemarie's illness and afterwards, and he quickly agreed to the proposal.

Mira Nucullaj was born in Shkodra, the city in Albania with the closest ties to the Catholic Church. In Albania only 30 per cent of the population is Christian, and only ten percent are Roman Catholics. During Albania's official period of atheism, the famous Franciscan Church in Shkodra had been converted into an auditorium. Mira's parents were not religious at all, but her maternal grandmother had instilled in her some basic concepts of what it meant to be a Roman Catholic. Her grandmother would quietly celebrate the important feast days in her home and Mira and her sister and brother enjoyed these times and looked forward to their grandmother's festivities. They represented a dramatic and pleasant departure from the stark monotony of the Communist landscape they were subjected to on a daily basis in school, on television, indeed everywhere they turned. Shkodra is in northeastern Albania, not very far from Montenegro and Yugoslavia. At the age of eighteen Mira went to the capital of Albania, Tirana in central Albania, to attend the University there. While studying Economics, she met her husband, Anton. His family lived in Tirana and they too had been practicing Catholics before the Second World War, but in Anton's family as in Mira's, only the older generation of grandparents had any real affinity for Roman Catholic practices or tradition. Mira and Anton lived together for two years before deciding to marry. After the wedding in Shkodra, a non-religious ceremony, the couple settled in Tirana. Soon afterwards, Mira and Anton decided to make their way to Italy, settling for a brief period in Rome, and then seeking a visa to visit the United States. It was in Rome that Anton met his father's cousin who was born in Falconara and often returned there for visits to see his family. This man was also a cousin of Rosina Sandreva's long deceased husband, and when Anton asked about work in the United States, he mentioned his cousin's family's business and agreed to contact them on Anton's behalf.

Mira came to Daniel's home accompanied by Philip's wife Vivica. She introduced them and they set up a schedule for Mira to work in the house, doing general cleaning and housework on Tuesdays and Thursdays. Mira spoke English fairly well, with an accent that Daniel found attractive. The very first time he saw her, Daniel was struck by her quiet beauty. She was dressed in a pastel colored two piece skirt and jacket for her "interview," and appeared to be quite reserved, even a bit shy, turning her head as she spoke, looking away quickly when her eyes met Daniel's, but looking back again as if in apology for having averted her glance. Mira was of medium height with a slender body. She had long, straight dark brown hair that hung loosely onto her shoulders. Her eyes were dark brown, and when she looked at Daniel he saw a woman both reserved and sensual. She was not just another person passing through, someone you looked at, settled matters with and moved on from. There was about her a quality that Daniel did not even know he was making mental notes about, something that told him she was a person he could communicate with and that suggested a possible connection. At that point, it had nothing to do with the two of them as man and woman. That thought did not enter Daniel's mind and it would not, not of his own conscious volition. Mira was close in age to his own daughter, and appeared to be a happily married young woman. No, it was more in the nature of a father and daughter affiliation that his amorphous thoughts gravitated towards. He sensed that this lovely person could use a friend in this new world she found herself thrust into.

While Vivica spoke to Vincent, Daniel took Mira through the house and explained what needed to be done. With some of the terminology Daniel used, when Mira did not seem to understand, seeking to find a way to explain, Daniel asked if Mira understood German. No, she didn't. What about Italian? Yes, she did speak some Italian, having lived in Rome briefly and having learned it as one of the languages she studied at school in Albania. After that, Daniel and Mira communicated in English and in Italian. Daniel explained that he would probably not be home whenever she arrived to do her work, so he gave her a key to the house. They agreed that he would leave notes and she could, in turn, write any concerns she had to him on a pad he would leave for that purpose, or she could telephone in the evening as well.

The routine began a few days later. Daniel was amazed at how clean the house now appeared. He found his clothes and Vincent's washed, shirts pressed and everything in order. He quickly felt guilty about all the work the young woman was doing and after only a month, left her more money than they had agreed upon in the usual envelope with her salary. Occasionally over the following weeks and months, Daniel would still be at home when Mira arrived or return before she had completed the housework. At such times, Daniel's solicitude towards the young woman became more and more evident. He made it clear to her that he was willing to assist her and her husband in any way he could. Their conversations took place at the kitchen table with young Vincent often nearby. Mira told Daniel about her life in Albania, the way her family lived from day to day under the Communists, the less than full accord between her father and her mother and how that situation influenced her decision to leave home to attend the University, how she had met her husband and everything that led to their decision to seek a better life in America. She knew about Daniel's loss of Annemarie and let him know that she was aware that he had loved his wife every much. Even the way that she broached that subject told Daniel something about her, about how sensitive she was, sensitive and intelligent, independent and assured, yet still vulnerable in a way that Daniel could not quite understand, not just then, at that point in their relationship. Actually, Daniel didn't even think of his conversations with Mira as a "relationship." He was just trying to be helpful. It was that trait he had inherited from his mother, a compassion for individuals that translated itself into more than most of those who lacked such feelings could comprehend. One day Daniel arrived home and Mira was just getting ready to leave. After thanking Daniel for some new blouses and pants that he gave her, clothing that belonged to Annemarie which she never got to use, Mira stood at the front door. She opened the door and then closed it. She looked at Daniel directly and said,

"I have never met a man like you. You are a wonderful man." Daniel felt uncomfortable.

"Oh come on. I'm just like any other man."

"No. You are different. I feel as though I know you. In fact, I am sure that I have known you before."

"Before? But you are only in this country for a short time. And I have never been to Albania."

"I know. I know," Mira said, smiling with a look that bespoke a wisdom that someone her age could not be capable of.

"I feel I know you from another life."

"Another life? Do you believe in reincarnation?"

"Yes. I do. I am sure I have been here before, and now I am sure that I knew you before too."

"Wait a minute," Daniel said with an enthusiastic smile that Mira had not seen before. "Do you have a few minutes to talk about this? I am so fascinated by the concept of reincarnation. I would like to talk to you about it."

"I have to get home to prepare my husband's supper, but I can spare a few minutes I guess. I, too, am very interested in this topic."

Mira told Daniel how she and her husband had read about reincarnation while they were still at the university, but that there was precious little material about it. She had thought about the idea as a young girl, but had not been aware that others believed in such possibilities. Daniel told her about the doctor who had treated his wife and about her husband whose family came from the same town his family was from in Calabria.

After Annemarie's death, Joseph Manfredi telephoned Daniel and invited him to come for dinner one evening. The psychiatrist knew from Violetta about Daniel's interest in past lives and had long wanted to get together with him. Daniel heard about Joseph's experience in Longobardi and how he had met his wife. He found intriguing the stories about past life regressions the doctor had guided patients through. Both Mira and Daniel were excited to learn that they had this mutual interest.

Some days later, Mira arrived mid-morning as Daniel was preparing to leave for the day.

"You know," she said. "More and more I am certain that I knew you before, that we were together in a life before this one."

Daniel was pleased to hear this, but he didn't understand exactly what Mira was trying to convey. She, herself, was unsure as to whether she could say what she wanted to say, but she felt confident with this unusual man she had met. After all, he loved her, as a friend of course. What did she have to be afraid of? She could be open with him.

"Perhaps you are right. Maybe I was you father, or even your brother in a prior life."

"No, no. It was more than that. We were even closer. I know it."

Daniel was at a loss as to what to say in response to this somewhat startling revelation. No rejoinder was forthcoming. As he stood looking at Mira, searching her eyes, apprehensive about what they offered in explication of her remarks, he blurted out,

"We'll have to discuss this some more. Right now I'm running late for an appointment."

When the subject came up again days later, Mira simply told Daniel that she just knew that they had been very close. Afterwards, their conversations became more and more familiar without being intimate in any way. During a school break, Marta had come home for a few days and met Mira. After overhearing her father's conversation with the young immigrant one afternoon, Marta told him that she found it inappropriate.

"Inappropriate? What do you mean? We're just talking about common interests."

"Common interests? Your common interests should just concern her work in this house and nothing more."

"How can you say that? She is a human being and has needs too."

"Yes, but her needs don't really concern you, do they Dad?"

"I think you are being too harsh. Here is a young woman, basically alone in this country with her husband, with a desire to learn more about life here. I have made it clear to her that she can come to me with any questions she has, and if those questions extend to her interest in my musical career or anything else, why shouldn't I be nice to her and entertain her questions."

"That's the trouble. You're always trying to be too nice."

"And what's wrong with that? Haven't you learned anything from your grandmother?"

Daniel was frustrated by his daughter's lack of empathy. Was being educated at a large urban university depriving her somehow of the humanistic element that he had raised his children to value? He wondered.

"Oh, fine Dad. Do what you want to do. Forget that I said anything."

Marta thought to herself that perhaps she was being too harsh on her father. In a moment of self-reproach, she considered the possibility that she was envious of another young woman's reception of the attention she was missing from her father since she was no longer at home day after day.

The next time Daniel and Mira had a chance for a conversation, he wanted to ask her opinion about his daughter's view of his relationship with others, particularly anyone who was not a family member. He felt a unique confidence with the young housekeeper. "Housekeeper," his daughter had called her. She didn't seem like a housekeeper to him. She seemed more like a good friend, despite the big difference in their ages.

As Mira sat folding a wash she had just done, Daniel sat opposite her and asked,

"Mira, do you think I am too friendly? How shall I say this—too familiar?"

"No, Daniel, that is what I like about you so much. Don't ever change. I think you are perfect just the way you are."

"You do? Well, Marta thinks I am too friendly with people outside the family."

"With me? She thinks you are too friendly with me?"

"No, not with you," Daniel lied. He did not want to upset her.

"Let me give you an example." He thought of a young woman in his ensemble, a violinist who always stopped to talk to him after rehearsals. Once or twice, she asked him if he would go to a coffee shop for a cup of coffee after their practice sessions. He agreed to go and they had some friendly conversations that soon verged on the dangerously intimate. She invited Daniel back to her apartment a few times, but he always made excuses.

"Look, Mira, I'm a widower and she is single. But we work together and I don't think I should get involved with someone I am working with, particularly since I am the conductor. Then, too, while it's very flattering, she is so much younger than I. I mean, she's only a little older than you!"

Mira smiled, knowingly, suggestively, mysteriously. She looked at Daniel squarely in the eyes, looked down, blushing ever so slightly, then looked at him again.

"You know, Daniel, you do have something that younger woman find attractive."

"What do you mean? Attractive in what way? How do you know that?"

"Well, Daniel, I, too, find you attractive. You are a very handsome man. I have felt this way about you for some time, and I would never have told you, but since you brought it up, I have to be honest and tell you that I do have feelings for you."

"But, Mira, you are married. You love your husband, don't you?"

"Yes, of course. I love my husband very much. And I am not saying I want to act on my feelings. I am only telling you this since I feel it is important for me to be honest with you. I want us always to be honest with one another. You have been so good and so kind to me. There is no one who treats me the way you do"

Daniel was truly astounded. Never could he have imagined such a thing. How could she feel that way? He was old enough to be her father. True, he was not a bad looking man for his age, tall, not overweight at all, a full head of black hair with gray streaks that he was told made him look distinguished, and, of course, his lucent blue eyes that always generated compliments from women. And yet, the thought that Mira found him attractive pleased him. He was flattered, but it went beyond flattery. This boost to his male ego exhilarated him. First, the young woman in his ensemble! He was really not attracted to her in any way, or perhaps something might have developed in spite of his reservations about work-social relationships. But this was different. All at once, he had to admit to himself that his presumed fatherly interest was more than that. He had looked at her in a different way at times. He recalled the day he came home and she was bending slightly, vacuuming the carpets. He viewed her from behind and admired the form of her derriere in her tight fitting slacks. The shape of her legs whether seen hugging the legs of the jeans she was wearing or, occasionally their very silky whiteness when she wore a dress and he quite naturally looked to see how the curves behind her knees gracefully met the lower part of her slender thighs. Was it lust he now wondered? No. He never fantasized about her sexually. It was simply male appreciation of the female form.

It was some minutes before he could reply.

"Yes, exactly. I want us to be honest too. But how could you have those feelings for me if you really love your husband?"

"I'm not sure. I want you to know that I do love my husband. He is a good man and I want to do all that I can to make him happy. But I can tell you this much: if I were not married to my husband, I would marry you in a minute. I would not hesitate."

"How can you say that with such assurance? You don't even really know me that well, if you think about it."

Mira looked at Daniel with that loving glance that he had come to know, without realizing just how much it portended. Her dark eyes penetrated into his own and made a contact that he felt was tangible. Upon reflection later that evening, it reminded him of his mother's description of *malocchio,* and of how some believed that when certain individuals looked at you, there was a force in their eyes that they could not even control, a force that was capable of smiting the recipient without the person's realization of what was happening. That was a force for evil or to do harm to its recipient, but Mira's eyes sent out a force of beauty, a lance of love-filled energy.

"I know everything I need to know about you. I know your goodness and your love. For me, you are everything a man should be. I only hope you will wait for me in the next life."

Here now was something to consider! Daniel had thought about a life after the present one, about having been on earth before, but he never actually thought about the possibility of actually making plans for it in the here and now. And if he did in any way, it was to meet his beloved Annemarie again. He didn't know what to think about this. He just smiled at Mira and nodded his head. Following that day, there was an awkwardness between the two of them. Daniel tried to keep the subject on the mundane, the diurnal activities for which Mira had come to his home. Then one day as Daniel arrived at home and Mira was leaving, she told him she had left a note under his pillow.

"A note? About what?"

"You will see when you read it."

"Are you quitting?" he asked. Mira laughed, throwing her head to the side and looking at him with an expression of satisfaction and approval.

"You will see," she repeated and walked out. He ran upstairs, his heart beating faster in anticipation of uncovering something either very disturbing or very enjoyable, but if enjoyable, disturbing nonetheless, if in a different way. He sat at the edge of the bed and pulled out the note, written on a sheet of white paper and folded twice.

"Dear Daniel:

I am so happy we talk other day. You know now how I feel. It is o.k. you don't feel same way. It is enough you know how I feel. I want no thing from you. Already, you give me enough. I love you.

Mira"

Conflicting emotions welled up as Daniel tried to understand his own reaction to the note. He was happy, yes, but should he be? Was she really just interested in a kind of detached admiration and nothing more, or did she secretly hope that he would act decisively, without regard to the consequences for either of them? Oh, how he wished he could understand a woman better than he did! He thought of the times that his frustration had overwhelmed him when he didn't know why Annemarie reacted to things he did in ways he could not understand. Whenever he had tried to pin her down about these conflicts, minor but still disturbing to him, she had laughed and dismissed his apprehensive inquiries with clichés (he hadn't thought of them as clichés then, but thinking about it now he concluded thusly) such as, "Oh you know, Venus and Mars," or "The eternal battle of the sexes: what more is there to understand?" What was bothering Daniel more at this point was his own ambivalence about how he should behave under the circumstances. For at least a year after Annemarie died, his grief was so deep, so all-encompassing that he never thought about another woman and never even considered the possibility that he would ever be with another woman again. Then, gradually, he began to think about his future and about whether he would ever fall in love again. The idea had a certain appeal. He remembered particularly the times he had "fallen in love" as a teenager, those crushes on girls that kept him thinking about them during every waking moment. He knew now that what he had experienced was not real love, but only that adolescent frenzy, that lunacy when one throws oneself headlong into a dependence on a favorable outcome of an initiative towards the object of one's hysterical adulation. But there was also the real falling in love, the surrender to a more mature and solicitous adoration, the kind of love that had developed when he and Marilyn came together and especially when he and Annemarie had pledged themselves to one another. That brought a rare happiness that was both joyful and serene. Would he ever be able to experience that again? Did he even want to? He wondered. It did have a certain appeal.

During the following weeks, Daniel and Mira quite spontaneously implemented a system of note giving, always placing the missive under the pillow on Daniel's bed. Mira's messages generally expressed gratitude for something Daniel had given, or informed him about things she had done in the evening or over the weekend. One evening Daniel opened a note to read, "Dear Soulmate." This was new and different. What did she mean by it? In replying, he thanked her for the new greeting and asked her to explain why they were soul-mates. Mira arrived early one morning, knowing that Daniel would still be at home. She rang the bell instead of using her key.

"Oh, you're here early today."

"Yes, I wanted to talk to you."

Images of lovemaking filled Daniel's head, but he dismissed them as quickly as they had manifested themselves. They sat at the kitchen table where Daniel was just finishing some coffee.

333

"I didn't know how to write this, so I thought I would explain it. I am not even sure I know how to explain it, but you asked me why I am calling you 'soulmate.' "

"Yes, I was wondering . . . no, I mean I am not displeased by it, quite the contrary. I like it. It means that you feel we have a connection. I was just wondering how intimate this connection is."

"Daniel, look. I told you I cannot be intimate in the way I am with my husband. As much as I think I would like that at times, I know it cannot be. But I feel you are my soulmate, that we are soulmates. I feel like you understand me in a way that no one else understands me, and I feel I know you, too, the real you, not just the great conductor, the wonderful musician and father, and brother and son that you are, but the you who is you, the person inside that makes you so wonderful in all these ways. And I feel certain that you understand the real me. I know I am not a beautiful woman." Daniel interrupted,

"But you are a beautiful woman, a very beautiful woman."

"Yes, to you I am, but there are many women who are really beautiful. I do not have what they have in physical beauty, but when I am with you I feel beautiful, like the most beautiful woman in the world. And it is not because I look in the mirror and see this. No, it is because I see this beauty reflected in your eyes when you look at me. It is what you see in me, how you understand me, the things you say that tell me you understand who I really am. This is why we are soulmates."

Without even thinking about it, Daniel always made Mira feel special whenever they had a chance to talk. He told her about his life, how he had started to play the piano, his years at Curtis, in Rome, in Germany. She asked him to play the piano for her and he did, playing lovely short works like Anton Rubinstein's *Romance*, or Chopin's *"Raindrop" Prelude*. One day a melody came into his head. He couldn't place it. It was lovely. It had to be from a piece he had performed at some point, but which he had forgotten. For some reason, he associated the melody with Mira. He sat at the piano and developed it into a composition. It dawned on him that this was no tune from an existing work, but something he had spontaneously put together in his head. After he had worked it out, Daniel wrote it down on music paper. An infectious melody, adorned with seductive harmonies gave the piece a tonal allure that Daniel knew was good, one of the finest of the few pieces he had ever composed. The next time he had a chance to speak to Mira, he told her about the piece he had written for her. Her reaction was one of incredulity.

"For me? But why for me?"

"It just came to me. Come over to the piano and I will play it for you."

Daniel sat at the piano, looked at her and said, "I call this 'Mira's Song.'"

Mira stood quietly and listened, feeling each note as little emblems of love that entered the chamber of her heart and would remain there forever. When the music stopped, Mira stood with her hands clasped in front of her. Her head was bowed and tears were falling from her glistening eyes.

"Do you like it?"

"I love it, Daniel. It is so beautiful. Thank you for this gift. I will never forget this melody."

"To make it easier for you to remember, I recorded it on a cassette for you." Daniel handed her the tape. As they stood next to the piano looking at one another, spontaneously, without any forethought by either one of them, their lips met. Their mouths opened and their tongues touched. Mira stepped back and smiled. Slightly flushed, she walked into the kitchen. That evening when Daniel returned home, he sensed that there would be a note from Mira. Under his pillow he found it and read,

"Dear Soulmate:

That kiss today was so unexpected, but very beautiful. It was so natural, as I always imagined it would be. Thank you again for the very beautiful work you composed for me. I only ask you for one thing. Don't kiss me again when you see me.

I love you,
Mira"

"Don't kiss me again?" Why would she say that if she acknowledged that she enjoyed the kiss? Once again, Daniel was confused, but he was certain about one thing: he loved her and he wanted to make love to her. He thought about this desire and realized that he wanted to make love to a married woman. Adultery! Why didn't he feel guilty about this? Was this retreat from religion making him an immoral person? No, he could not think of himself as immoral. In this situation, he was amoral! That was it: morality was not even a factor here. But he could not convince himself that this was the entire truth. He just did not want to think about the question of right or wrong. He felt as though he was entitled to this. He wasn't looking for it. It just came his way and it was honest and wholesome—nothing tawdry about it at all, he thought—and it was a union that transcended time. Didn't he believe that they had known one another? Mira believed that, and it was enough for him. And if that was true, it really did not make a difference if she was now married to someone else. Oh, come on, Daniel, he thought to himself. Don't take something that you believe in and debase

335

it for your momentary pleasure. True to himself, Daniel could not lie, not even to himself. Still, he needed this.

Daniel dreamed of making love to Mira. He wouldn't attempt anything in his home. He still had the same bed that he and Annemarie had slept in. Most of the furniture was the same. He still had all of Annemarie's clothing, no longer hanging in the bedroom closet, but in boxes nearby. Making love to another woman here still had the taint of betrayal about it. It was foolish, but he would have to go someplace else if he were ever to fulfill his fantasies with Mira. He determined that he would not make a move to convince her to do anything against her will. Love meant responsibility and to Daniel it had always meant placing the interests of the one he loved above his own. If she told him again that she wanted him, he would act. The notes under the pillow continued sporadically over the next weeks and months, some beginning with intimate greetings such as "My love," and signed similarly, while others were written as a simple note from one friend to another. One day when Daniel arrived home, Mira was lying on the sofa, obviously in a great deal of pain. When Daniel offered to take her to a doctor, she obstinately refused, assuring him that she would soon be fine. As she tried to stand, she fell back onto the sofa.

"I'm taking you to see a doctor," Daniel insisted. "Come on, I will carry you if you can't walk." Daniel carried Mira out to the car and took her to see a doctor nearby who was a friend of his, actually an amateur musician. Mira occasionally suffered pain during her periods, and she had thought that this was just such an occurrence. But on this occasion she had a pelvic infection that caused pain she had never experienced before. After the visit to the doctor, Daniel drove her back to her apartment and assured her that he was available for anything she needed. Within a few days, she was fine and returned to work. The evening of her first day back, Daniel found a note under his pillow that made him feel compelled to act decisively. He read:

"Hi, my love,

Thank you for everything you did for me when I was sick and in pain. I don't know how tell you what this mean for me. The way you carry me, the way you look at me with love in your eyes. Now I feel I want to make love to you. I feel it inside me. Down below the desire is strong to have you. I know it cannot be, but I want it a lot. I love you so much it hurts.

Mira"

Daniel felt he could no longer ignore her true wishes. What kind of fool was he to remain impassive? What other man would hold back as he had done. This was a signal, no it was more than a signal, it was a bold clear, crystal clear request for him to make love to her. He thought of how her body felt as he carried her out to the car, soft and lithe, supple and sensual. He fantasized slowly undressing her and covering her body with kisses, from her forehead, to her neck, down to her breasts, her stomach, covering her thighs and calves with his burning lips and finding the spot "down below," as she had described it, where all his pent up desires would find their release. It was so long since he had made love to a woman, and she was not just any woman, but a woman he loved. The morning of her next workday, Daniel waited at home for her. She was surprised to see him there as she unlocked the door. She smiled at him that smile that had so endeared her to him. It was a smile of affection, of approval, of understanding and what was so obvious, of happiness at seeing him. Daniel walked towards her and they embraced. He bent to kiss her lips, but she turned her head so that he could kiss only her cheek. Daniel looked at her and spoke slowly, deliberately,

"Mira, your note . . . . "

"Yes, I know, it was too much?"

"No. It was perfect. But now, I can no longer just stand by and make believe I did not read what I read. It is obvious that we both want the same thing. I didn't want to make love to you here in the house because of memories of my wife, but I have waited long enough. I want to make love to you, and I don't care where it is."

"No, Daniel, I don't think we should here in your house. Your first feelings are right. You have to respect your wife's memory. I could not make love to you where I sleep with my husband either."

"Then, let's go to a hotel."

"No, Daniel. The idea of a hotel sounds cheap to me. I could not, not there."

"Then, where?"

"Daniel, I don't know, I don't know. I told you, I cannot betray my husband. He is a good man and I love him too much!"

"But you love me too, Mira!"

"Yes, it is true. And if I were free, I would be with you in a second; I would marry you without another word if you would have me."

"Then why did you write what you wrote in your last note?"

"I meant it, but I meant it the way I explained to you. Please forgive me. I know it looks like I am playing with your emotions, but I am not. We said we would always be totally honest with each other, so I have to tell you how I feel even if I cannot act the way I would like to. I'm sorry, Daniel. You have been so good to me. You deserve better. I am so sorry."

Daniel embraced Mira again.

"I understand," he said with a mixture of sadness and compassion. "At least I think I do." After another firm embrace, and kisses on Mira's forehead and cheeks, Daniel gathered his things for his day's activities and left. As he drove to the City, Daniel pondered all that had happened since he had met Mira. On the one hand a great deal had happened; on the other hand, nothing much at all had come to pass. Once again he wondered how other men would have handled such a situation. Was he just a fool of sorts? But slowly, slowly, he came to believe that perhaps it was better that his relationship with Mira had gone so far and no further. What would have happened? Would she have left her husband for him? How would his family react to this? His children? What would Marta think? Would she lose respect for her father for having a woman nearly the same age as she was for a lover? Yes, one had to be realistic. Oftentimes in life, what seems so promising, so wonderful because of the novelty involved, the mystery, the mystique, turns out in the end to be a matter for serious regret.

Things remained cordial between Daniel and Mira over the next few weeks. Then, one day she gave him the news that she would no longer be able to work for him.

"But, why?" Daniel asked, with evident misgivings and regret.

"It has nothing to do with you Daniel," she replied. "Well, it does have to do with you, but I mean not so much, so directly. Do you know what I mean?"

"No. I don't. You can continue to work here. You have seen that I have respected your wishes. I have not done anything to try to compromise you or your feelings in any way."

"Yes, I know that. That is another reason why I love you."

Daniel shook his head, almost as if to say that she should stop making statements that could not fade like the morning mist under the heat of the sun.

"I know you may find it hard to believe me, but it is true. But the reason I cannot work anymore is that we are moving. My husband has been thinking that we should try to see other parts of the United States. And my husband's cousin in Rome told him about some mutual cousins in California, in Fresno who are willing to put us up and help us to find work if we want to go there. There are Albanians living there for a long time, and they are happy to have members of our generation from the home country join them. And you know, Daniel, I think this is best for us too. I don't think I could continue being near you all the time and nothing happening. Sooner or later, we would have to do it, and then what? So it is best this way. But don't think I am sorry about anything that happened between us. I am happy for the love we share. I am happy to have you as my friend, to have you in my life, even from far away."

Daniel's thoughts wandered. What did happen, really? At the least, if he did anything for this young woman, anything at all to help her feel more confident, more self assured, then it was worth it. What about himself? She, too, had given him something, something intangible perhaps but there nonetheless, a sense that his age was not an impediment at all, in any way. This realization gave him the impetus to firmly believe that his career could still rise to new heights, and perhaps more importantly, that he could love again. After Annemarie's death, he thought it would never happen, but it did. Coming as if from a distance, he heard Mira's voice again,

"Daniel, you seem to be, how do you say it? Off somewhere?"

"In a trance?"

"Yes."

"Yes, I was just thinking of everything. Thank you Mira. Thank you very much."

"For what? I am the one who needs to thank you."

"Perhaps, but I too need to thank you. You have given me very, very much."

"Not as much as you have given me. But I am happy I could be *something* for you."

"Yes, me too."

"So, Daniel, I will be leaving. I will miss you."

"I will miss you too Mira. I wish both you and your husband well. I will miss you very much."

"Me too, me too. But just remember that we will always be close friends. Anytime you think of me, I will be here with you, and when I think about you, I know I will have you next to me. And don't forget, I want you to wait for me in your next life. Then we will have everything, together."

"Yes, everything," Daniel repeated, not really certain if he believed that their paths would ever cross again. He did believe in the concept of reincarnation. He was sure he would return to earth after his present life was over, but he did not have that assuredness that characterized Mira's beliefs on the subject. Perhaps she was more advanced spiritually than he was.

When Marta came home for Thanksgiving for a few days, she told her father about some volunteer work she was doing with the Gay Men's Health Crisis.

"What?" Daniel asked, surprised by this revelation.

"Well, Dad, as you know, being involved in the music world, one meets many gays who are involved in the arts, and especially in dance."

"Yes? And how does that involve you?

"Don't worry, Dad, I'm not a lesbian."

"I should hope not." Daniel replied with a mixture of sarcasm and relief.

"And what if I were a lesbian? What then, Dad?"

Marta loved her father dearly, admired him and would never forget the courage and self-sacrifice he had shown in dealing with her mother's terminal illness. And yet, as a daughter she felt as though she had a proprietary right to question her father's attitudes and values, yes, even his values. Like many intelligent young people growing up in a rapidly changing world, she felt the need to discard and retain, abandon and retrieve ideas and positions and postures that were open to question in the light of new discoveries and new things learned, whether they were new for everyone or just for her.

Daniel smiled at his daughter and thought to himself that he had better make the most of this challenge.

"I would love you just the same as I do now, the same if you are or if you are not."

"Well, I'm not."

"I know that."

"But if I were you would love me exactly the same, and accept me and accept my lover if she were a woman?"

"Yes, of course I would. Why shouldn't I?'

Daniel told his daughter about his experiences with homosexual friends, about how he had as a youngster felt that it was a sinful way of life because of how he was brought up as a Catholic. He told her about his conversations, and how he came to realize that these men had no real choice in their sexual orientation just as he had no choice in being attracted to women. It was inborn; a part of one's makeup, an element of one's being that one had no power to change.

"Dad. I am very proud of you. I really didn't think you would look at it that way."

"Well, Marta, I guess I wouldn't be looking at it that way if I didn't have the personal experiences that showed me differently. And, of course, one always has to have an open mind if one is to learn the truth about anything."

"But Dad, most Catholics don't accept homosexuality as a valid alternative to heterosexuality. I cherish my religion, but on this question I find myself at odds with it. And not only with this, but with questions involving artificial birth control and abortion too. How are you able to reconcile your differences with your basic beliefs?"

"Well, honey, frankly, I cannot. In fact, there are many things, many beliefs of the Church that I don't give credence to myself. And now that you have brought it up, I should tell you that I am finding myself more and more at odds with the Church and its canon."

"But Dad, you don't intend to join another church do you?"

"No. I don't think any other church, Christian or not, has anything more to offer me than the Catholic Church does."

"What does that mean? Are you becoming an atheist?"

"No. I do believe in a Supreme Being. I'm just not sure if He is as the Church envisions Him. I think I am a very spiritual person. I have always been fascinated by the spiritual side of myself and also of others." Daniel thought it best not to go into the subject of reincarnation just then.

"But, Dad, as I started to tell you, I am doing volunteer work for the GMHC, and the reason I got involved is that one of my fellow students in the dance program, a very talented young man, became so ill he could not return to school. It turned out that he is afflicted with AIDS, he is HIV positive. I began by going to visit him, and then I was asked by some members of GMHC if I would be interested in volunteer work. Once I saw all the suffering and the anguish, I knew I had to do what little I could."

"Your grandmother would be proud of you. In fact, if you don't mind, I would like to tell her what you are doing."

"Of course, Dad. In fact, that was the thing that spurred me on. I remembered the stories I heard all my life about Nonna and how she always helped everyone. I thought, if I can do something to help, why shouldn't I?"

"Yes, I agree that you should."

And, you know, Dad, even though the Church is against homosexuality, they probably do more to help the victims of AIDS than any other religious organization. We can be proud of that I think. St. Clare's Hospital in Manhattan has one of the most extensive programs to aid sufferers of HIV anyplace in the country. That is where I visit my classmate and help out."

"I know that the Church does a great many good things. I would never deny that. I think the Church makes a positive contribution to society in many ways."

"Then why are you against it?"

"I'm not against it. I just find that I cannot believe all or most of its theology. As far as charitable works are concerned, I am all for that."

"Dad, that brings me to the other question I wanted to ask you."

"Go ahead, ask."

"Well, Dad, you grew up in the Sixties. I mean, you were in your twenties in the Sixties, a student during a part of those years,"

"Yes, that's true."

Daniel was puzzled and intrigued to hear what this line of questioning was leading to.

"Were you active during the civil rights demonstrations? Did you participate in any of the boycotts, the March on Washington, any of that at the time? Please tell me you did."

"I did not."

"But Dad, knowing who you are, the kind of person you are, the man of integrity you are, I was sure that you would have been actively engaged in fighting racism in the sixties. A young woman in my program told me how her father nearly got killed while working in voter registration drives for blacks in Alabama. I wanted to say that my father was also involved, but I wasn't sure."

"If I had been killed then, you wouldn't be here now, would you?"

"Dad, this is no time for levity."

"You're right. Look, honey, our family was never involved in direct political protest."

"Why not?"

"It's hard to say. My parents never did anything to hurt anyone, no matter who they were, what color or religion, that didn't matter to them. They treated everyone with respect."

"That's not enough, Dad. In a time like the Sixties, to be silent was like condoning racism."

"We were not silent. There were times when things came up, when we had to take a stand and we did. My father rented one of the apartments above the store to a black family. He was criticized and pressured by the neighbors. In fact, I remember that a number of customers told him that if he didn't get those people out of their neighborhood, they would stop patronizing his store. My father told them that this is a free country. I am free to rent my apartment to whomever I choose to, and you are free to shop elsewhere."

"What happened?"

"They lost customers, of course, but your grandfather stood his ground."

Daniel told his daughter about other events, about her grandmother's example of inclusion in helping and loving others, even when they had done things that others would have found unforgivable. He told her about her Uncle John's wanting to fire Sophia for seeing a black man socially.

"Fire Aunt Sophia? I thought she was involved in building the business?"

"She was, but this was before that time when she was just working for your grandfather and uncle. I will never forget how Nonna told him that what she did with her life, who she chose to be with was no concern of his, that she had every right to be with any person she wanted to be with, as long as he was not a bad person. In those days, that was a remarkable thing for a white person to say, especially a person who always lived only among whites."

"Still, Dad," Marta persisted, didn't you have the desire to become active in a movement that was so important in the history of this country? Especially considering the family you came from—not a family of bigots like so many others at the time, from what I have heard, didn't you feel the need to get involved."

"Marta, when you put it that way, I know it seems that I failed in some way. I can see that I failed in your eyes, in retrospect. The only way I can explain this is to try to make you understand the type of family I grew up in. We never discussed politics. For my parents and so many other Italian immigrants, America was the land of opportunity, the land where anyone who wanted to work could succeed. And as long as they worked, they were so busy that they had no time to get involved in politics, to go to meetings of political clubs. Their business took up all of their time."

"But Dad, forget your parents. You were a student. You went to American schools, colleges. You were exposed to things your parents were not exposed to."

"Yes, that's true. But what can I say. I was involved with my studies, with my music. Looking back, there wasn't time for anything but the things I was involved in."

Marta looked at her father with an expression that conveyed both annoyance and love. Who was she to criticize a man who had accomplished so much in his life, who had done so much good for others? She felt ashamed and contrite.

"I'm sorry Dad. I have no right to grill you on this. It's just that it came up, and when the mother of that sick man thanked me the other night for being there to help, she asked me what it was that made a young woman like myself want to be of service while most people my age were too selfish to consider anyone's needs but their own."

"How did you reply?"

"I told her that helping others runs in my family, on my mother's and father's sides. I told her how Grandpa Joe had started the family clinic in Boston to serve the poor who could not afford medical care, how Nonna

343

gave food to poor families during the holidays, all that. Afterwards, I thought about you and Mom and the fact that you lived during one of the most exciting times in this country's history, and I wondered."

Honestly, honey, I have had misgivings myself, regrets that I didn't get involved in those activities. It's true that some of the time I was away, studying in Italy, but there were other times when I could have done more. Still, what's done is done. The important thing is that you are living according to your conscience and taking a stand on an issue that is very important today. I am very proud of you. And you are carrying on a family tradition of concern for others, even if you have shown me that I have not always done so myself."

"Oh, Dad. I didn't mean it that way. I'm sorry, but I am disappointed to know that you didn't stand to be counted at a time when it would have meant so much."

"I know. You're right, but one doesn't have to be an activist to contribute in a positive manner to society. The important lesson here, for you as well as for me, is that we must be totally honest with ourselves and live according to our beliefs, and what we know to be right. We must grasp what is essential in our lives and run with it, no matter who disapproves or to what degree we are criticized by others."

Saying that, Daniel embraced his daughter and kissed her forehead. He held her before him and saw the little girl, the toddler, the youngster, the teenager, saw her through the years as she had grown, beautifully, wholesomely, into this extraordinary young woman she had become. He looked into her eyes and saw Annemarie, and himself too. She and Vincent were the true treasures of his life, and whatever else he accomplished or would accomplish could never have the importance for him that they did.

Fourty

Three years after her husband's death, Violetta, at the age of eighty-eight, succumbed too. Father John Lorelli said the funeral Mass for his mother as he had for his father. Daniel had never told his mother about his doubts concerning their Faith, but Violetta was a wise woman and she knew her son much better than he himself ever realized. She was well aware of Daniel's ideas concerning reincarnation. She knew that he lacked the overriding faith that she herself had, but her benevolent nature made it possible for her to accept others without regard to the degree to which they adhered to her own beliefs, and she had the unique perspicacity for a person so religious as she was to allow that the beliefs of others could be as valid as her own, that one's spirituality was not limited by one's adherence to a particular dogma. She saw everyone as children of God, and she felt that everyone's journey to God could be realized, could be accomplished on a different pathway. Daniel went up to receive Communion at his mother's funeral Mass. It was strange. In the past, as a child, as a young adult, even as a mature adult, he would never receive Communion unless he was in a state of grace. To him this meant that he had to be free from sin, even if he did not feel he had sinned. As long as the Church considered something sinful, he would not show disrespect by receiving Holy Communion, something believers truly considered the body and blood of Jesus Christ. That was why he never received Communion while he and Anne Marie practiced birth control. In no way had he believed that what they were doing was sinful, but if the Church that administered the sacrament of Holy Communion insisted that it was alien to their requirement for a full confession of faith, then Daniel could never be a participant, partaking of a ritual that was sacrosanct to others when he could not accept all the conditions they required for Communion. For his mother's funeral, he felt he had to be pragmatic. The entire family would be receiving Communion, including his own two children, and his abstinence would be noticed, raising unnecessary concerns. At this point, what did it matter? He knew the wafer of bread was merely symbolic. He no longer had delusions about its transubstantiation.

His mother's death, so soon after the loss of his father, left Daniel with a feeling of aloneness in the world. He was not really alone, and he knew this. Above all, he had his children, and then he had his brothers and their families. But still, the two people in his life to whom he knew he could go for anything, besides his dear wife, those two were gone forever, or at least until he met up with them again in a new and possibly different relationship at some future time. It was his mother's death that left him devastated, much more so than his father's. At first, he accepted it, realizing that she had reached an advanced age and that death was inevitable sooner or later. But this initial stage, this seeming lack of deep feelings about the event, did not last. After the funeral, after the first week of "official" mourning when friends called or came to visit him to offer their condolences, after the period of numbness had worn away, Daniel was left with the realization that his present life would be devoid of that very special bond he had always had with his mother. There was never a time in his life when he had felt his mother was anything but the dearest, most understanding, kindest person he had ever known. It was she who had encouraged him to study the piano, to pursue a career in music, even when his father gently prodded him to join the business, to work with his brothers in a unity that Vincenzo found especially satisfying as the father of four sons who would take over the business he had built. Not so Violetta. She knew that Daniel was very different from his brothers. She loved them all equally and appreciated the unique qualities each of her sons possessed, but she knew that Daniel's vision went beyond the ordinary aspirations of most young men his age. To Violetta, God had given her son a talent, singular and splendid, that needed to be embraced fervently, nurtured and developed to its full potential. For that reason she insisted that he remain at home to practice when his brothers were busy working in the store. For that too she had encouraged him to go to the summer camp, to take the offer for study abroad, even when she knew in her heart that she would greatly, greatly miss him. Daniel had always known this and had always tried to show his mother the appreciation he knew he owed her, but now he knew it more forcefully, more painfully than ever before. How could he do without her? Relatives and friends had tried to console him by saying that she was in Heaven. He didn't believe that at all. He knew her soul had not died, but that knowledge, though beneficial, could not assuage the pain of his great loss. At such a time, others would find solace in their religion. More and more, Daniel's solace came from distancing himself from anything connected with religious faith, replacing it with a deeper spirituality. He liked to think of the Native Americans who sought communion with the Great Spirit or the Master Spirit. The American Indians did not regard their own beliefs as a religion. Rather, these beliefs were an integral part of each person, something that one did not just take to church, but which derived from the very essence of all that the person did throughout each and every day and which informed every action taken by him or by her—a communion with the Unknown One who could, however, be known through all of His creation.   And music, yes music too could express the spiritual so much better than words alone could. Daniel thought about the great Austrian symphonist, Anton Bruckner. It was true that Bruckner himself saw his compositions as a reflection of his beliefs as a Roman Catholic. But there was in his massive symphonies, works that had been compared to majestic cathedrals—cathedrals in sound—a grandeur that embodied the essence of the divine, insofar as any human being could achieve such a synthesis of spirituality and humanity. Indeed, Bruckner had dedicated his last symphony to "Dem lieben Gott" ("Dear God"), and it was this love and awe of the Creator, Giver of humanity, in all its manifold beauty and mystery, that gave the Austrian's music the dimension of spiritual engagement that Daniel found so revelatory and appealing, so otherworldly and overpowering. Bruckner was a composer that he wanted to dedicate himself to when his career got back on track.

Daniel continued to search for meaning beyond the boundaries of understanding that had been imposed on him, and on so many others like him, by virtue of their acceptance of all those basic tenets that were not really open to question by "true believers." His appetite for alternate viewpoints became voracious, reading, evaluating, discarding or retaining with intellectual probity as much as he possibly could.   Daniel learned that he, like Charles Darwin, did not lose his faith suddenly. Rather it was a gradual unfolding, a slowly developing disinclination to accept ideas and beliefs that had been taken for granted as being true, perhaps not absolutely in a totally literal sense, but true nonetheless, generally speaking. Darwin had been a mature person, well on in years, when he really began to seriously question, doubt and ultimately disbelieve. Indeed, Daniel felt a kinship with Darwin as he read the scientist's description of his own ascent into disbelief. He read the scientist's words with the recognition of one who had traveled down that same path and who now fully comprehended the cathartic nature of renunciation.

"By further reflecting that the clearest evidence would be requisite to make any sane man believe in the miracles by which Christianity is supported,— and that the more we know of the fixed laws of nature the more incredible do miracles become,—that the men at that time were ignorant and credulous to a degree almost incomprehensible by us—that the Gospels cannot be proved to have been written simultaneously with the events,—that they differ in many important details, far too important, as it seemed to me, to be admitted as the usual inaccuracies of eye-witnesses;—by such reflections as these, which I give not as having the least novelty or value, but as they influenced me, I gradually came to disbelieve in Christianity as a divine revelation."

"But I was very unwilling to give up my belief; I feel sure of this . . . . But I found it more and more difficult, with free scope given to my imagination, to invent evidence which would suffice to convince me."

And *these* words were particularly cogent in connection with his own experience: *"But I found it more and more difficult, with free scope given to my imagination, to invent evidence which would suffice to convince me. Thus disbelief crept over me at a very slow rate, but was at least complete."* It was an amazing discovery, like so many others that came to Daniel by reading, studying and exploring, to find that one of the arch enemies of doctrinal believers of Christianity was not at all as he had been portrayed in the mindless tradition of denigration of the man and his ideas. Darwin never thought of himself as an atheist, but consistently referred to his position as one of agnosticism. When Daniel spoke to friends who had never believed, or whose religious beliefs were curtailed by events or persons that influenced them at an early age and left them impervious to the demands *inflicted*—yes, exactly that, not just *imposed*, since that word carries too little weight for what is a burden that its bearer carries unmindful of its crushing effect—when he spoke to those of his acquaintances who never experienced the grace, the luminosity and sublimity afforded by the acceptance and acknowledgment of divine faith, to all those Daniel Lorelli's dilemma, his arduous mental and emotional journey to truly comprehend, and then to set aside cherished doctrine, all this appeared as so much ado about nothing at all.

The pragmatists would ask him, "Who cares?" The secularists would express surprise that he still thought of all that as important. The believers— to the believers he would not speak, not yet, still fearful of offending people he loved.

And so it came about that Daniel Lorelli, credulous First Communicant at the age of seven, strict Confirmand of his Faith at the age of eleven, devout Roman Catholic throughout his youth, paternal transmitter of all accepted beliefs to his own children, was finding it more and more difficult to adhere to the articles of faith that had been so ingrained within him and that had dominated his thought processes for most of his adult life. He would have gone along, like all the others, the Sunday Catholics, the Palm Sunday Catholics, the Christmas Midnight Mass Catholics, and even the daily Mass Catholics, participating at will, often or sporadically, in what their Church had to offer them as individuals. From the cradle to the grave, accepting, rejecting some things, but not the essence, not what his forebears gave tribute to, fervent when it suited them, lukewarm when it did not. But the time had come for Daniel, the time for honesty, at least to himself. He had to question and he had to learn.

One day while browsing through the Religion section of the Barnes and Noble store on Fifth Avenue and 18th street in Manhattan, Daniel came across various publications of the Jesus Symposium, a group of scholars of religion and clergymen from various Protestant denominations, Roman Catholicism and Judaism. These men and women met regularly to discuss Jesus and the New Testament. Concerned with religious literacy, with learning who Jesus really was and what his mission had been, they were determined to publish the results of their convocations, and they were then in the process of doing so. By carefully evaluating the evidence, including the provenance of the accepted Gospels, alternate Gospel sources, and extensive documentation bearing on the transmittal of information down through time, the Symposium concluded that actually very little of what had been attributed to Jesus had been said by him. Perhaps no more than thirty per cent of the words spoken by Jesus in the New Testament was accurate. And the words that were accurate had a great deal to do with one's personal relationship to the Kingdom of God. It was not difficult for one who had an open, inquisitive mind, an intelligence willing to see, to conclude that Jesus never thought of himself as a Messiah, never expected to be resurrected after death, and never thought for one moment that God's Kingdom was a far-off event that would come about in the by-and-by. No. By uncovering and studying multifarious sources, it could be demonstrated that Jesus himself was making the point that God's Kingdom is within each of us, here already, present in Jesus' time as it is now. As such, there was no need for any intermediaries in a personal relationship with God, no saints, no priests, and certainly no need for Jesus himself as a personal savior. And the truly surprising thing for Daniel was that much of this was already known to members of the clergy. They had heard and learned about these "revolutionary" thoughts in their seminaries, but they could not bring themselves to inform their congregations about any of it, they could not, absolutely not, rock the boat. But there were those who could and did uncover and unravel, the accretion of mythology—for that was what it surely was— the mythology that had evolved over the centuries into an orthodoxy that had become so powerful that it could no longer be encountered with any degree of speculation by its loyal adherents.

A year after Violetta's death, Father Stephen Lorelli invited family and friends of his beloved mother to a memorial Mass that he himself would celebrate. For all in attendance, it was a beautiful experience. In addition to the religious manifestation of love for "the dearly departed," individuals were invited to speak about their relationship with the deceased, about their memories of her and of how she had influenced or helped them. It was a truly wonderful event. So many wanted to speak, even some who were totally unknown to the members of the Lorelli family. Men and women told of how this kind woman had befriended them, had given them food or clothing, money or even time, time to listen to their problems and to give advice which had always proven beneficial. Father Stephen was delighted. He couldn't have asked for a better outcome of his memorial to his mother, to the memory of dear Violetta. In his heart Stephen knew that his mother was a saint. Surely she would never be canonized by the Church, but he knew that she was right up there with all the other saints, known and unknown, enjoying the beatific vision of their Creator. Stephen was very happy about everything, everything except for one thing. As he administered Holy Communion, he could not help noticing that his brother Daniel did not come up to the Communion rail to receive. Daniel's two children came up, his other brothers and their wives and children came up, yes even his cousin Philip and his wife Vivica received, but not Daniel. Stephen thought about this for days. His brother was an adult, even older than he, and he had a right to his privacy. But the fact that he did not receive Holy Communion at a memorial Mass for his beloved mother had to be addressed. Stephen knew how much Daniel loved his mother and how deeply he cherished her memory. Daniel had told his brother that he found it difficult to talk about her. He could so easily be overcome by his emotions. Instead of getting up to talk about some memories of her as others would, he composed a "Largo" for organ in her memory, which he played when it was his turn to get up before the assembly of friends. Before playing it he simply said, "My mother was the kindest, most understanding and most beautiful person I have ever known and ever hope to know. The music I composed for this occasion expresses my feelings about her much better than I can express them in words." Essentially slow, the "Largo" nevertheless comprised moods of joy and sorrow. Daniel made full use of the organ's potential for evoking the sense of light coming forth from darkness, beauty overpowering the tawdry, goodness and decency triumphing over the mediocre and the banal. The piece lasted about fifteen minutes, and even those who were not attuned to the idiom favored by Daniel, found the music meaningful.

Father Stephen convinced himself that it was his obligation to confront his brother. Perhaps he was in a state of serious sin. It was his duty as a priest and as a brother to help a family member. He telephoned Daniel and asked if they could get together to discuss a matter of importance to both of them. Daniel offered to go over to his Rectory, but Stephen thought it better if they met at Daniel's home to avoid interruptions. Daniel surmised that his brother wanted to discuss some aspect of their inheritance, their parents' share of the business which had been left to all four sons. But he was a bit put off by his brother's sudden interrogation.

"Why didn't you come up to Communion at Mom's memorial Mass?"

"What? I thought such questions were reserved to the confessional."

"Look, we are brothers. You know how important going to Communion was for our mother. The fact that at a memorial Mass for her, you don't go to Communion, this is cause for concern for me. If you were anyone but my brother, I would wait for you to come to consult with me. Imagine my going to parishioners to ask why they did not come up to Communion!"

Daniel's initial surprise and momentary annoyance at the question quickly gave way to gladness and an almost welcome sense of relief that he could discuss his own transformation with a family member, and best of all, with a priest.

"Why, do you think I have gone to Communion throughout my life?"

"I would think so. What has kept you away, if you don't mind discussing it with me? I am only concerned with your spiritual welfare because you are my brother and I love you."

"Well, you might imagine that during our marriage, Annemarie and I never went to Communion because we practiced birth control."

"I can appreciate that. But you are no longer a married man. You are a widower. If you are sexually active with a woman now and that is keeping you from going to Communion, I can appreciate that too. I guess what I wanted to see you about concerns your spiritual welfare. I know you have suffered a great deal in the past few years. You lost three of the people most dear to you. Are you all right?"

"Steve, I'm glad you asked. I am fine. In fact, I'm better than I have been in a long time."

"I'm glad to hear that. Is it a woman you're involved with?"

"No. It's not a woman at all. I'm not against that possibility, but there's nothing like that right now."

"I have the feeling you want to tell me something else, something I may not enjoy hearing?"

"You're very perceptive. Yes, I think you should know that I am no longer a practicing Catholic."

There! He had said it, but he knew as soon as he came out with the pronouncement that he was still holding back. Why? Why couldn't he have left out the adverbial modifier?

"Aha! I thought it was something like that. We all go through periods of doubt, Daniel, but our Faith is something wonderful. It's like an organism that can be cut into pieces, but the main piece always continues to thrive and to reconstitute itself, and becomes stronger and stronger all the time. It just needs some nurturing. Now what is driving you away from practicing your Faith? You haven't joined another church, have you?"

Daniel wanted to go into the matter with his brother, but he did not want to astonish him too quickly. He thought the jocular approach would be best, but for no especially valid reason, he told himself.

"Well, I have attended some meetings of the Jehovah's Witnesses."

"What? Jehovah's Witnesses! Those kooks. How could you possibly find anything of value in what they have to offer? You haven't become a member, have you?"

"No, no, I would never even consider it. But I can tell you that I found them to be much more devoted to their beliefs than most Catholics are to theirs."

"That's not fair, Daniel. You may not have the opportunity to see them, but I see many Catholics every day, parishioners in my parish who are alive in their faith, in both the spirit and the letter of the law. Good people, people who practice their Faith as your own mother did."

"I'm glad to hear that. Are they tolerant of others too?"

"I think so. But Jehovah's Witnesses are certainly not tolerant of others."

"Yes. I'm very well aware of that." Daniel told his brother about Gary Stoneham, the extremely talented young musician who was jeopardizing his career by refusing to play with avowed homosexuals

"See. I think Catholics have a greater sense of charity towards others, even towards those with whom they do not agree. If you're not a practicing Catholic, what are you practicing?"

Just then, Vincent came home and greeted his uncle. Vincent was preparing to graduate from high school and the conversation turned to the young man's choice of a college and what his long range plans were. Soon, Stephen had to get back to the rectory. He asked Daniel if they could continue their conversation at another time. They agreed to meet a week later, and these meetings were to continue for some time as the two brothers discussed Daniel's "apostasy" as Stephen characterized it. At first

Daniel was reluctant to speak to his brother with complete candor. He didn't harbor any anxiety concerning their dialog. It was just that he didn't wish to offend.

"You were saying last time Dan . . ." Among themselves the four brothers shortened their names when speaking with one another—Joe, Al, Dan, Steve. "You said you did not practice Catholicism any longer and that you have not joined another church. What is it then? Are you an atheist? I cannot fathom that you no longer believe in God!"

"No, Steve. I am not an atheist. I am truly a very spiritual person. You must know that I have been a believer in life after death for quite a long time."

"Yes, but we all believe in life after death. How does that jibe with your abandonment of the Faith of your fathers?"

"I mean that I do not believe in the Catholic concept of heaven and hell."

"Dan. Even the Church has changed its position on those concepts."

"It has?"

"Yes, of course. Catholic theologians are constantly studying, re-evaluating, re-considering all kinds of things. Why even the Pope comes out with statements now that shows that the Church is open to change."

"Really? At what point do they make the faithful aware of these changes, these new looks at old concepts?"

Daniel knew he sounded sarcastic, but he could not resist posing the question since he had been thinking about it for some time, the practice of secrecy in the Church, secrecy about so many things, as if the people were too stupid to deal with the truth.

"Things like this take time. People are steeped in their beliefs. Many cannot handle change. They need the security of knowing they belong to a Church that has not changed, a Church that has carried forth the banner of truth over the centuries since Jesus' own time, since he founded that Church and gave the keys of the kingdom to St. Peter. What other Church can boast an unchanging tradition down through twenty centuries?" Daniel was now squirming in his seat.

"Just as I thought."

"What? What is just as you thought?" Stephen saw the frown on his brother's face and saw that he had to proceed with more patience. He had felt himself becoming annoyed and he knew he would make no progress by adhering to a confrontational approach.

"The clergy knows that many of the things people believe are absolute rubbish, but they allow them to continue in these beliefs for fear they will lose their faith if they tell them the truth."

"There is that possibility. Most people are not strong enough to accept sudden change. They wouldn't know how to deal with it."

Daniel found himself thinking back to the time when he was studying in Rome, when he decided to take a trip down to his parent's home town, a weekend to visit some cousins. He was smiling as the thoughts filtered back to him.

"What's so amusing?" Stephen inquired.

"I was just thinking about the time I was in Longobardi and I went to Sunday Mass in the Church with the body of the saint under the altar."

"La Chiesa di San Francesco?"

"Yes, exactly. You've been there. You remember how the townspeople, at least *i credenti*, which I guess included almost all the *paesani* there, how they worshipped that corpse under the altar, Santa Innocenza?"

"Yes. I remember it well. I was even there once during her feast day when they marched with the statue through the town in procession."

"Well, this one time I asked the *parroco*, Don Alfonso, when their saint had been canonized, since I had never heard of her apart from the connection with Longobardi and with Beato Nicola, who was a Longobardi native who had been beatified."

"Yes. I know. There is still a movement to try to get him canonized. They have evidence of one or two miracles attributed to his intercession."

"Yes, well, that's another story, but when I asked Don Alfonso about the saint, knowing that I was a university student, he probably felt he could speak to me openly and honestly about what really was a fraud."

"How? What do you mean?" Stephen was becoming agitated in spite of his best efforts at being patient.

"He told me that she was not really a saint, that the people believed her to be a saint, and the Church knew that they needed this belief to bolster their faith. 'It is something the people need, so we let them have it.' That's how he explained it."

"Well, what's wrong with that? Simple people. They need something to believe in. Why should the Church try to disavow them of their need to pray to a saint that is their saint? What real harm does it do?"

Daniel wondered why the treachery of such deception was so obvious to him, while his brother could not even grasp it, or perhaps just refused to do so.

"Stephen . . . " Daniel measured his words, distending each word, each syllable in an attempt to convey the weight of his conviction about what he was saying.

" . . . I thought the Church was all about the Truth, with a capital 'T.' 'Know the truth and it will make you free.' Perhaps I paraphrase, but isn't that the essence of what we were brought up to believe? That the truth was of paramount importance in our religion? Uh, I mean your religion?"

"See, Dan, you can't get away from it. In your heart of hearts, you still know it's your religion, your Faith, the One True Faith of all those that exist in the world."

No, in my heart of hearts I know otherwise. It's true that we were brought up with all of this being so much a part of us, of our everyday thoughts, the motivation behind our actions, yes the impetus for us to do good, I admit that. That's why it took me so long to seriously question so many things about what we believe, are supposed to believe and how to relate it all to daily relationships. You know that I was in love with a woman once, but because she was not of my religion, I did not marry her."

"You mean the Jewish girl you met while studying in Philadelphia?"

"You mean you remember that?"

"Of course. Mom was quite concerned about your relationship with her."

"I knew she was against my seeing her in principle, but she never tried to influence me to break off with her." Daniel's thoughts drifted back to his last meeting with Marilyn in Stuttgart. A twinge of nostalgia, a nostalgia for something evanescent that he knew could never materialize again, filled him with familiar but forgotten longings. It was not Stuttgart, however, but Philadelphia, the last time he saw her in that city of first love, for him real love, that brought forth in him evocations of youthful delight, the thrill of being alive and loving each moment of new discovery, surging emotions, rampant *joie de vivre*.

"Well, what are you saying? That was our mother. She would never have tried to stop you as so many other mothers would. She loved you enough to let you follow your own path in life. But she knew, somehow, that you would do the right thing for your life, just as I know you will do the right thing in your life now."

"I can't deny that," Daniel replied, knowing all too well that he meant something completely different from what his brother intended by his words.

"But to get back to my point, I met Marilyn years later in Germany. She was playing first violin in an orchestra I was conducting. Even though I was reluctant to even bring it up, I found myself asking her why she never maintained contact with me, why she had rebuffed my attempts to find her. Do you know what she told me? She said that if I had really wanted her, I would have found her and made it my business to be with her, one way or another. First, I honestly believed that we could not be together because of her family. She had made it clear to me from the outset that in spite of how much she loved me, she could never marry me. And I believed that. It took me some time to realize, many years were to pass, in fact, before I could acknowledge to myself that what she said was right. I didn't fight for her, didn't go to the ends of the earth for her, because of my upbringing, because of my overriding desire to carry out the life plan that intuitively was part and parcel of my very being."

"Come on Dan," Stephen insisted, "There are countless cases of Roman Catholics marrying Jews. Some still bring their children up as Catholics. She saw it as it was. You just didn't love her enough or you would have married her."

"No, no, no, no no!" Now Daniel's frustration at getting his brother to see something that appeared so simple to him was causing his usually calm demeanor to break apart.

"I did love her. In some ways I loved her more than any other woman in my life."

"Not more than Annemarie. Come on Dan! I saw the love you had for your wife. Only a man who was totally devoted to and completely in love with his wife could have acted the way you did all through her illness. I could see that you suffered with her, shared her pain day after day."

Daniel began to choke up. The sorrow that it had taken him so long to become reconciled to, that had finally died down to embers without ever being extinguished, was flaring up once more.

"Of course I loved her. She was the one true love of my life. I'm just saying that this other woman . . ." He hesitated to speak her name again without knowing exactly why.

"I learned something about myself. At the time, I was a dyed-in-the-wool true believer. But because I loved her so much, my first real love affair, I went about assuming that it was all right for me to talk to her about marriage, to even plan when we would be married. But she let me off the hook. She gave me my 'out,' so to speak, and I did not pursue her as I would have if she had been . . ."

"Been what?" Stephen asked impatiently.

"If she had been a Roman Catholic. Look, I'm trying to show you how deeply ingrained these beliefs are for so many of us, so ingrained that even if we have doubts, we never acknowledge them."

"I see." Stephen agreed, but Daniel was not sure if his brother really did see.

In those first meetings with Stephen Lorelli, Monsignor Lorelli now, for he had been elevated to that position after being made pastor of his own parish, Daniel continued to experience a certain trepidation in confronting this brother, this priest who was both familiar and obscure. Or was it he himself who was being confronted? It was curious, but he wasn't sure why he even continued to meet with this upholder of all that he had come to abjure. Part of it was his sense of loyalty to family, and another part his own desire to divest himself of any false attachments. To achieve the latter, it became incumbent upon him to encompass the origin of all he had renounced, to disengage himself from that aspect of it that he could no longer honor. Total honesty demanded this of him. His discussions with his brother were "safe." The Monsignor was not especially worried, for he had counseled many others who had similar doubts, and they eventually returned to the fold with their faith stronger than ever before. Growing up, Stephen Lorelli was of a less mystical bent that Daniel himself was. He went through the motions and never allowed serious questions about their religion to "faze" him, as he used to tell Daniel whenever his older brother wanted to discuss a particular practice or tradition, even some minor religious representation. There was the time when Stephen was studying to make his confirmation and Daniel was helping him with some questions. Daniel noted that the book they were studying maintained that Confirmation made one "a perfect Christian," but Daniel couldn't understand how this could be so. "If that is true, then why do we still have to go to confession after Confirmation?" he had asked. Stephen just brushed the whole matter aside, saying simply, "I guess confessing makes us even more perfect." Stephen never even went on a retreat, refusing to join Daniel on the few occasions that he decided to go to a spiritual house or a retreat house from a Thursday evening through a Sunday morning. Stephen even missed Sunday Mass on occasion, whereas Daniel never did. Still, Stephen would strongly denounce any of his friends who spoke critically of the Church, whether they were Catholics or not. Daniel was actually surprised when he first learned that his brother was entering the seminary. He never thought of Stephen as one who would ever take a vow of chastity. He was a man, quiet yes, but strong in his love of women. He had been dating the same girl since sophomore year in high school and everyone thought they were going to be married. Stephen loved Amy, but this did not stop him from flashing his winning smile at any attractive young woman he encountered. It all appeared to be innocent flirting, but Daniel was never sure. Then, one year during Lent he began attending daily Mass, hoping to complete the full forty days. After Easter, he continued, going to an early Mass before arriving for work at the family business. Eventually, he told his mother that he had had a vision and had an overpowering feeling that he was being called to serve God. Violetta was overjoyed and agreed that he should attend college and enter the seminary.

Stephen could be a very serious young man. The youngest of Violetta's and Vincenzo's four sons, he was also the quietest and the most pensive, save when a pretty face appeared before him. He was more like Daniel than he was like either John or Albert, but Daniel was more open, not to say personable, and much more willing to talk to just about anyone, regardless of how attractive or interesting the person was. Stephen only engaged in long conversations after he had become a priest, and only then when it was necessary to fulfill his duties in espousing, explaining or promulgating matters involving faith or morals. When he took it upon himself to try to save his brother's immortal soul, Stephen dedicated himself to the task with all the vigor and enthusiasm he could muster.

To the best of his ability, Stephen had responded to statements Daniel made about the early church, the origin of the Gospels, the various important Councils, the contributions (dubious to Daniel) of St. Augustine and Thomas Aquinas and a good deal more, but to Daniel all of it was just the reiteration of concepts that no longer provided assurance or comfort or any measure of veracity. The time had come for him to be brutally honest, forthright and bold. Daniel knew his brother loved him and that he would not judge him. This assurance gave him the comfort he needed. The next time they met Stephen embraced Daniel and smiled broadly. Their last conversation had almost turned to acrimony, and Stephen promised himself that he would be kind, considerate and above all, patient. He thought of some of his favorite saints as models of patience and he would emulate them, follow their examples. There was Saint Therese of Lisieux, "the Little Flower," whose piety inspired millions. She had to learn patience the hard way, overcoming emotional outbursts. But trusting in the Lord, she persevered and lived a life of quiet dignity, fortified by prayer. And St. Francis of Assisi! Stephen had visited the town where he was born and had felt so close to him, reconstructing in his mind the saint's year long imprisonment in a dark dungeon. Imagine the patience of such a man! After such a severe trial, he was still able to smile, to show the world his love of everything and all around him. And St. Monica, mother of St. Augustine! If patience is a virtue, and indeed, indeed it is, Stephen assured himself, no other saint could possibly match St. Monica. She had converted her husband and mother-in-law through strenuous endeavor, and then patiently, steadfastly, worked and prayed to bring her son Augustine into the arms of Holy Mother Church. Yes, Stephen knew that he had good models. He had immersed himself in the literature of the lives of the saints. There were so many, martyrs, doctors of the Church, miracle workers themselves before and after their death on earth.

Daniel returned his brother's embrace with equal fervor. Stephen held his brother's hand in his own and took a positive tone,

"You know, Daniel, I have been praying for you. Every day, at every Mass I celebrate."

"Thank you." Daniel did not want to hurt his brother, but he no longer wanted to disillusion him by his silence.

"Thank you, Steve. If that helps you, it's fine."

"If it *helps me?*" The Monsignor sensed anger in his own tone, and spoke more moderately. "I am praying to help *you*, Daniel."

"Steve, listen. We are brothers. You know that I love you."

"And I, you."

"Yes. Then don't you think we must place honesty with one another above everything?"

"Yes, but I thought that was what we were doing."

"Well, you have been honest with me, but I have not been totally honest with you."

What could this mean, Stephen thought to himself. Had his brother, then, already joined another church, converted to a non-Christian religion perhaps?

"I'm sorry, Daniel, I don't understand."

"I will explain. If it makes you happy to pray for me, do so. If it does you some good, continue. But I can assure you that your prayers will do nothing to change the way I feel, or to change my beliefs, or maybe I should say absence of belief in all you would want me to believe."

"How do you know that? Surely you are aware of the power of prayer? 'More things are wrought by prayer than the world dreams of,' as the saying goes."

"Tennyson, I believe."

"I'm not certain, but it's true."

"Another English writer, Samuel Butler, pointed out that Tennyson wisely refrained from saying whether the things wrought by prayer were good things or bad."

"That's ridiculous!"

"Ah, Stephen, there is so much about prayer that is so complicated."

"Complicated? Prayer is one of the simplest things we know."

"Really? I'm reminded of something Gandhi said. I don't remember the exact words, but he pointed out with true wisdom that in praying it is better to have a heart without words than words without a heart."

"True prayer includes both, I think."

"Yes. That is my point. I am not saying that prayer is useless. It can do wonders for the person praying. It can give him solace, renewed determination to do good, comfort in times of distress. But it cannot change something external to the person praying. You may pray for me, and it can make you feel better, but it will do nothing for me. There is no divine intervention. Do you understand what I am saying?"

Monsignor Lorelli again felt the blood rising within him, but he tried to maintain his composure. His body stiffened. Although younger than Daniel, despite having lived a less stressful life overall than his brother, the lines the passing years had etched upon his face gave him an older appearance, and when he tensed up as he was at that moment, he appeared even older. He shook his head in the manner of one who is sorry but at the same time contemptuous about what he was hearing.

"The son of Violetta Lorelli! How can the son of a woman like your mother reach such conclusions? You know how much your mother valued prayer, how she prayed day after day. Don't you remember that she always had a rosary in her hands, and died with the beads wrapped around her fingers?"

"Yes, I do, of course I do. And this brings my point home."

"How? I have to hear this. How can you think of your mother's praying as anything but the most honest and effective communication with God?"

"Honest it surely was. Effective? Look, when Annemarie was dying, no one prayed more than Mamma did. She even prayed that God substitute her life for Annemarie's. I remember her saying to me, 'I pray to God that he spare Annemarie. Let Him take me in her place. I have lived my life. She needs to live now.' I remember her anguish growing out of her great love for all of us. And you know that neither you nor I have ever known a truly better person that she. Why didn't God answer her prayer then? Not to take her life, I mean, but to spare Annemarie. That prayer could not have come from a more devout or devoted supplicant."

"It is not for us to question God's will in these matters. Mamma prayed, but she ultimately put herself in God's hands. 'His will be done,' she said. Remember, '*Sua volontà sia fatto*,' she would say." Stephen made his point with evident self-satisfaction. He was satisfied with the conclusion, so everyone else should be accepting of it too. Daniel thought of the irony in the present situation: two sons brought up by the same parents, raised with the same beliefs, and yet the divergence of their views was remarkable. One son was a staunch upholder and defender of the creed they were brought up to live by, while the other no longer felt even the slightest identification with it (the other two brothers most likely fit in somewhere in-between). Daniel didn't know if he really wanted to continue the dialogue. After all, he wasn't out to change anyone's mind about religious beliefs. He just wanted to be able to live his own life openly and honestly, to be allowed to acknowledge his disbelief within his own circle of family and friends, especially among them since they would be looking to him to participate in activities that precluded an avowal of that faith they held so sacred. His brother, Monsignor Lorelli, represented more than anyone or anything else, the part of his life he needed to disassociate himself from. He wanted a relationship with this bastion of tradition and stability, with the one person among all those he loved so dearly whose understanding—a certain recognition of honest intentions at the very least, if not total acceptance—of his reasons for wanting to discard this heritage of generations reaching back hundreds of years, could bring him a measure of gratification. It wasn't something he needed absolutely, but his need for approval, the kind of approval from his family that his mother had made to appear as his birthright, he instinctively sought.

"It's very convenient, isn't it?"

"What's convenient?"

"Anytime anything doesn't work out, anytime a prayer goes unanswered, whenever an injustice is unresolved, all one has to do is refer to 'God's will.' If it's God's will, whether we understand it or not, especially if we don't understand it, there's nothing to do but accept. Accept, accept, accept!"

"Yes, of course. What other choice do we have in the face of . . . .?" Daniel waited for the right word, but Stephen did not complete the sentence. Daniel suggested,

"The unknown?"

"Yes. The unknown if you would put it that way. There is so much we do not know about God and His ways. Man is continually trying to know God better. At least, men who want to know Him always do."

"But He has revealed Himself to us through Holy Scripture?"

"Yes. He has told us by His inspired words, as set down in the Bible, what we must do to live good lives. Do you doubt that too?"

"Well, Steve. . ." Daniel was about to say "Father," for he suddenly had the sensation that he was in the confessional. The familiar feeling when one has been instantly transported back to a recognizable situation or experience gave him pause, unsure as he had been and was now as to how much he could safely disclose.

"Stephen, I do not wish to offend you by my remarks. Perhaps they are better left unsaid." But I need to say them, Daniel thought, quickly recovering his determination to effectuate his own liberation with total truth. "You should know that anything I say is not intended to test or to challenge your own faith."

"Daniel, don't worry. You can tell me nothing that would cause me to compromise my beliefs. My faith is much too strong."

Even if God came before you and told you otherwise, Daniel pondered, not maliciously, but with some sarcasm, imagining a situation like the one in the George Burns movie.

"Good. Then I can feel comfortable in proceeding. The Bible, the Old and New Testaments both, were written by a number of different writers, with various objectives."

"Everyone knows that, Dan."

"Yes, but many of the writings were intended for the people at the time. They were meant as examples, even as a guide for good living, but they were not meant to be taken literally."

"How do you know that?"

"At one time, it was not possible for human beings to know it. But with the development of science, it became more and more obvious that many of the things presented in Biblical accounts could have no basis in reality."

"That doesn't matter. Whether God created the earth in seven days, and whether the seven days were seven days as we know them or otherwise is quite beside the point."

"Agreed! But what is the point then?"

"That a loving Creator made the world for all of us; that He gave us the opportunity for happiness, but that man is imperfect. The Bible is the history of God's place in men's lives and man's compliance or failure to comply with God's laws. Even though you can say that individual parts of Scripture are open to interpretation or even to question, the overall unity of the Bible, the Old and New Testaments' logical progression is really quite remarkable and could never have come about without God's direct intervention, especially when you consider how these writings were put down in ancient times without any of the benefits of communication or transmittal of knowledge that we take for granted today."

"I'm sorry, but to me the basic premise is preposterous."

"How?" Stephen's tone, the way he looked at his brother expressed beneficent pity. Daniel knew it. He forged on.

"Let's think about this. An omniscient, omnipotent Deity creates man and tells him that he can be happy if he follows the rules. The Deity knows that man will not follow because He knows everything beforehand, but he creates man and gives him the opportunity to prove that he cannot obey his God. As a result of man's failure, the so-called 'original sin' is committed and man is doomed to live with pain and suffering. But God is good, so he gives man the chance for redemption. This will come about when God sends the Redeemer who will save man."

"You're forgetting about 'free will,' Dan!" The Monsignor now spoke like one who was trying to make a child aware of the error of his ways, exhorting and chastising, but carefully, so as not to cause the child to cry.

"Yes," Stephen continued, confident that he was making progress in his argument.

"God knew man would fall, but he created man with the means to make the choice himself. It's so simple that some people just can't get it."

"It's so simple that it's a myth. There is no literal truth in the story, and even metaphorically it's invalid. The surprising thing is that it has been handed down through centuries with people believing in the validity of this mythology even today. People generally are so gullible and do not think critically, rationally. They *want* to be told what to believe. Apparently, Jesus understood this and tried to get the people of his time to see through all the nonsense. But instead of listening to what he was actually saying, they developed a whole new mythology out of his life. The man's personality and message were truly remarkable, but because the Romans considered him temporally dangerous and executed him, his followers wove an entirely new story from the bare events, tying them to prophecies in the Old Testament. And these were not even the early followers of Jesus, for they had beliefs that differed markedly from what was to develop in the first few centuries, not to speak of what would materialize later on. And to what purpose? To bring about religious wars, persecution of non-believers, the incurable scourge of anti-Semitism that resulted in the state sponsored annihilation of millions in our own century. Think of the absurdity of all these Christians believing in Jesus, having Jesus in their hearts, yet hating the group he was so much a part of. I remember rebuking a woman for an anti-Semitic remark once, telling her that Jesus was a Jew. Do you know what she said?" Daniel did not wait for a response. He wanted to get into his argument as much as he could while his daring was in full motion.

"She said, 'Yes, I know. I only learned that recently and I was really surprised. But Jesus knew his own people were in error and that is why he started Christianity.'"

"No," Stephen laughed. "Did she really say that? I guess I shouldn't be surprised. I've heard as much or worse in and out of the confessional."

"Exactly. And the Virgin birth, the Resurrection. These were things that later writers made up. It's well known that Jesus had brothers and sisters, and that even his mother and father and family thought he was mad at times. The whole cult around Mary, the way Catholics have made a god of Mary, elevating her to a supreme position in the heavens, even while denigrating women throughout the centuries and making them second class citizens within the Church. Have you read the book by that German woman Catholic theologian? She shows how the Church has glorified Mary's virginity while making all normal sexual activity and childbirth appear to be defiled."

"Oh, come on Daniel. You know that's not true. The Church regards childbirth as the one thing that makes man most like God."

As if not hearing what his brother said, Daniel went on.

"And do you know what they did to her for her attempts to shed some light on a history of abuse and misuse by the clergy? They prohibited her from teaching theology at the Catholic University where she was working. That's the Church's way. Silence anyone who finds fault. Excommunicate. It's true of all religions. Bridge no dissent."

"All right Daniel, let's say that you are right about some of your grievances. Terrible things have happened when bad people directed good beliefs to evil purposes. But just imagine what the world would be like without religion! Without religion the world would be a total disaster! Without the good the Catholic Church has done and continues to do, where would we be?"

Daniel smiled, reminded of something he had read.

"I rather agree with the writer who said that religion for him was always the wound rather than the bandage. Yes, the Church does a great deal of good. I don't know if I told you that your niece is doing volunteer work with AIDS patients at St. Clare's Hospital. Certainly one cannot deny that the Christian impulse for charity is a wonderful thing. But good deeds should not be dictated by or because of one's affiliation with a Church. I have seen this borne out in reality too. I know many who perform good deeds all the time who are not religious in the traditional sense at all."

"I never said that good deeds are the exclusive practice of Catholics, but just think about it. In this country alone, what religion that you know of has more hospitals, orphanages, homes for the elderly? I won't even mention schools and universities since you would probably just consider them repositories of the Church's propaganda."

"I agree with you. I think that some very good Catholics have done some very good things, and that they continue to provide compassion and relief for the sick and the suffering."

"Then, what is your problem?" Stephen's frustration, now palpable, curtailed his desire for patience with this errant brother. "*You* can deny the positive influence of the Church in all of our lives because you have been out of touch with the wonderful way it touches people, how it enriches their lives."

"I don't doubt that for a minute."

"You should meet some of my parishioners, wonderful, productive people. They raise wonderful children and their families, generation after generation are productive and useful citizens. Just yesterday, a man with a large family was telling me how happy he was with his life, with his children, wife and extended family, with their economic well being. He said, 'Monsignor, we have been truly blessed by God!'"

Daniel thought about this, and could not help thinking about all those who were not so fortunate, all those who suffered from illness, misfortune, those who had been born blind or ill, and those who through no fault of their own suffered day after day, throughout their lives, even when they placed all their faith in God. He asked Stephen about these poor souls.

"Why weren't they blessed? Why are some of your parishioners so blessed while others, no matter what they do, are doomed to lives of pain and distress?"

Stephen looked at his brother and saw the compassion in his eyes. Truly, this was something he had wondered about many times, too, but he always had to fall back on the answer that his ancestors had always resigned themselves to in the face of uncertainty about life's mysteries, "*La volontà di Dio*," God's will.

"Well, do you have an answer to that dilemma, Dan?" the Monsignor asked in a now subdued, almost apologetic manner.

"Well, yes, in a way I do."

"And what is it?"

"It goes back to my belief that we have many lives, and that before entering the world again we make choices about the kind of life we will have in the next incarnation."

Stephen looked at his brother as if he were talking to a fool.

"That is so absurd! Why would anyone choose a difficult life, a life of suffering when they could choose one that's comfortable instead?"

"It depends on what that soul wants to achieve in the next life. Perhaps a life of suffering will bring the soul closer to its ultimate goal."

"Which is what?"

"Unification with what you call God, but which could be the universal life force from which we all came initially. When we are perfect, or as perfect as can be, we can finally return to our real home."

"Back to God, huh?"

"Yes, in a way."

"That doesn't sound so different from what I have been trying to tell you." The Monsignor sat back with a smug air, as if he had checkmated his opponent in a game of chess.

"No, it doesn't, does it?" Daniel replied sadly.

"You know, Steve, if you really look into it, you'll find that early Christians believed in reincarnation."

"And where did you find this information?" Stephen's visage took on an appearance that Daniel found somewhat repulsive. It was a look that said, "You know nothing! How dare you try to instruct me?"

"I've done a good deal of research, and I looked into numbers of sources for information about this subject. For example, can you accurately show me where the Bible—the New Testament—repudiates the concept of reincarnation? In Matthew's Gospel, Jesus identifies John the Baptist as the reincarnation of Elijah." Daniel smiled sardonically.

"I know the passage you're referring to, but that is just a fanciful thought, as when people say a young child reminds them of their grandfather."

"Steve, I'm sure you've studied all about the origin of the Church in your years in the seminary." Saying this, Daniel tried not to sound patronizing. "You must remember how for the first few hundred years after Jesus' death, as Christian ideas spread throughout the Roman Empire, different groups of Christians held to various concepts about their basically new religion."

"Of course," Stephen replied smugly, "Peter and Paul were not in total agreement about everything."

"And," Daniel continued with emphasis on each word, "Some of the groups believed in reincarnation while others did not. When Constantine, out of what were likely selfish motives, decided to accommodate Christians, and convened the Council of Nicea, new doctrines became the foundation of the official Church. But it's also clear that a belief in reincarnation did not disappear and, in fact, continued to dominate the thinking of Christian sects for centuries."

"I'm very impressed by the amount of research you've undertaken, Dan. Where did you fid the time with all the work you put into your music career?"

"Funny you should ask that," Daniel said, smiling broadly. "When something interests me—just as when I discover a new composer—I become absolutely compulsive about gathering all the information I can find."

"Meaning that you read all you could find against the Church?" Stephen's interjection was conveyed with a tone of excessive sarcasm. "Have you done any reading at all among the great classics that support the Church's validity?"

"Steve, I've read books from both sides, but after freeing my mind from the restrictions that membership in a church seems to impose on all of its members, I found the arguments against Catholicism much more convincing that arguments in its favor. But to get back to reincarnation, I think it is a salient point that the concept of reincarnation among certain Christians was still quite strong by the 13th century. Then the Pope struck out against the Cathars, a Christian sect in Italy and Southern France that still held fast to the concept of reincarnation, and totally destroyed them. Ethnic cleansing has a history within your own Church, you know.

"I'm sorry. I can't continue our discussion now." Stephen said. He really had no answer for his brother and didn't feel confident enough at that moment to continue the conversation. "I have to get back to my duties at the church, but I am not giving up on you."

The brothers embraced and each went away assuming the other was totally unreasonable. A week later Stephen telephoned and asked Daniel to come to the rectory. He wanted to continue their discussion. As they settled into the Monsignor's sitting room, Stephen admitted that after their last discussion, he didn't even know if he wanted to continue their dialogue.

"Then I thought of Mom. I knew she would want me to try to get you back." Stephen loosened his clerical collar and removed it.

"It won't happen Steve. I have been reading up on and researching all that we have touched on. I am more convinced than ever that all that Catholicism stands for is untrue. No, wait, I shouldn't say all, but the basic premise on which it is founded is flawed."

"Then you see some truth after all?"

Daniel looked at his brother and felt sorry for what he was doing to him. He seemed to be trying to salvage something from all that his sibling had once been.

"What I mean is that everything about the religion is not untrue. There are many wonderful things that have developed from it and the happiness it brings to many people cannot be gainsaid. And the spirit behind it—the spirit that honest devoted believers feel in their hearts—the idea of personal goodness is a wonderful and holy thing. I am not out to change the hearts and minds of others, of those who like you, still believe with fervid affirmation. I know it makes you happy. I just want to be able to believe as I see fit, without interference or pressure from others. I want to be able to say among my family and friends that no, I am not a Roman Catholic! I am spiritual, but I have my own ideas about what spirituality, true spirituality is. Respect me for that and for what I stand for.

"But what do you mean when you say the basic premise of our Faith is flawed?"

It was as if they had discussed nothing over the weeks they had met. Daniel saw that his brother was as steeped in his righteous certitude as ever. The priest just could not suffer any viewpoint contrary to his own.

"Your religion is founded on scripture, and that scripture, the Hebrew Bible as well as the Gospels, is made up of stories that were written to induce belief in anyone who would be inclined to believe. But even if some were not inclined, they were coerced so that they came around one way or another. Once the foundation was laid, the rest followed naturally, or not so naturally. For every once in a while, dissension had to be dealt with. We, you and I and all our relatives, we are all products of the program that set it all in motion." Daniel saw his brother wince when he spoke the words, "your religion."

"Whatever are you talking about?" Stephen asked, feeling that he hardly understood Daniel's words any longer.

"I told you: I have to be true to myself. For me, that means that I can no longer harbor or pretend to put my faith in fairy tales. It was nice to believe in the tooth fairy, in Santa Claus, but now I have come of age. I cannot permit the fact that I was indoctrinated into these things continue to rule my life. For me, it is not enough to passively accept what is given, without thought or rebuke. I cannot. Jesus was a man who lived and died just as all other men do. There was no virgin birth, no resurrection, no ascension and certainly no founding of a church by him. It's incredible to me that so many people actually still believe this! It's as though a part of humanity is still stuck in the Dark Ages, as though they are incapable of moving ahead in spite of all that man had learned and established since then. When I hear someone say that he has accepted Jesus in his heart, that he is alive in Jesus, I'm sorry, but I am filled with revulsion at times, revulsion at the total ignorance of what they are themselves experiencing." Daniel knew that what he had just said would not be understood by Monsignor Lorelli.

"But I thought you told me that you don't care what others believe as long as you are left to believe what you want to?"

"Yes, and I mean that."

"It doesn't sound to me as though you mean it. Now you are judging those who say they have Jesus in their hearts. Come on Daniel!"

"You misunderstand me. I would not say anything to such a person. I am just telling you that what they say sometimes disturbs me."

"Why should it?"

"I told you. I think they are taken in by the mystique of it. The human mind is remarkable, and with effective direction, we can convince ourselves of almost anything."

"Ah, Daniel, Daniel." The Monsignor's voice took on a tone of condescension.

"This is what I wanted to talk to you about today. I think you are forgetting one important factor."

"Which is?"

"The Devil!"

"The devil? Come on Stephen, let's be serious."

"I am entirely serious, Daniel. Even if you don't believe that Jesus is the Son of God, the Redeemer of mankind, you have to acknowledge that there exist in the world forces of both good and evil."

"Yes, forces, but let's define these forces." Daniel thought about good and evil and the words of Marc Anthony came to mind. "The evil that men do lives after them; the good is oft interred with their bones." Shakespeare was right in a way, but wrong too. Evil continues to manifest itself, but it cannot dominate for too long. Good—Daniel was convinced of this— ultimately triumphs over evil, and this is because of the nature of man, perhaps the part of man that is connected to what religious people think of as God. If this were not true, civilization would never have advanced. Just then the intercom rang and Stephen had to attend to an urgent visit from a parishioner. Daniel was left alone in the room to ponder the subject his brother had briefly touched upon. Daniel abhorred evil, cruelty, the mistreatment of anyone who did not deserve it and even those who did. Images came to his mind. He recalled incidents he had only read about and others he had witnessed himself. There were the atrocities committed by the Nazis. A piercing sensation jolted him as he recalled tales of soldiers throwing babies into the air and impaling them with their bayonets as their mothers watched with unspeakable horror and an anguish so intense there are just no words to describe it. Was it the Devil who induced these men to perform such acts? Was man incapable of such evil without the prodding of demonic forces?

He remembered a beautiful day in Longobardi. He had gone to greet a distant cousin of his father, simply because someone told him that the man was somehow related. Knocking on the door, he was admitted. The family was having dinner. The wife invited him to join them. He sat down and accepted a glass of wine. As Daniel discussed the circumstances of his visit, the wife appeared to enjoy listening to him. Three young children sat around the table, in addition to the husband's parents and younger sister. It all came back to Daniel as he shuddered to even think about it. The husband told his wife to get up and get his sister something else from the kitchen. She had wanted to listen as Daniel spoke and told her husband that the young woman could get it herself. Spontaneously, he struck her across the face, once with the front of his hand and again with the backside. The wife jumped up and began to run up the stairs. Running after her, her husband pulled her down the stairs by her long hair, hanging down over her shoulders. The three small children began to cry. It was obvious that this scene was familiar. The man's mother tried to reason with him as her own husband insisted that his son was justified. The poor wife was so embarrassed that she again ran up the stairs, but this time her brutish husband looked at Daniel, smiled as if proud of himself and said, "She'll be all right. In fact, she'll thank me later on." Daniel remembered telling the man that his actions were unjustified and vile, to which the aggressor answered angrily, *"Fai i cazzi tuoi, vatene!"* Daniel felt that he had to do something. The pastor! He would talk to the pastor. Certainly a priest in that town wielded a good deal of power. He could, he would talk to the man, try to reform him. After Daniel told the priest his story, the cleric simply said, "The man does not come to Church. And while I cannot divulge the secrets of the Confessional, I will tell you that the woman accepts her lot, even thinks she deserves it, and offers her sufferings up for the sins of others. You see, young man, some good comes of everything when one places oneself in God's hands."

Daniel had seen that further discussion was futile. How sad, he had thought, that one's perception of abuse could be so distorted as to make a victim feel she was the culprit. Still young at the time, and a believer, this incident planted a seed in Daniel's consciousness that would grow with time. A picture eventually developed with clear details of how the Church continually exploited women in order to advance and maintain its abominable agenda.

Yes, there were many degrees of evil, but it was all intolerable. Daniel's heart went out to victims of mistreatment of any kind and he felt the hurt that others felt, even with ordinary occurrences that others would not have given a second thought to. He thought about the day he had stopped his car to buy a cup of Italian ices. As he stood there enjoying the lemon refreshment, an obese and unattractive teenage girl counted out her coins to purchase a piece of pizza. Apparently she just had enough money to complete the purchase and looked up with evident satisfaction as the server handed her a slice. As she walked out of the store, just as she reached for her prize with her right hand, the pizza slid out of the paper plate and fell to the ground, top side down. With an expression of bewildered hopelessness, the young girl stood there. Daniel watched as tears flowed down her cheeks. No one noticed her. Daniel walked over to her and offered to buy her another slice. Startled, she scurried off, too embarrassed to even face her would-be benefactor. A simple occurrence like this, something that many would dismiss as utterly devoid of any need for compassion moved Daniel, made him want to embrace and protect the person who suffered even minor slights, or what appeared to others as minor, but which he knew could sear one's soul and wound one's heart.

There was something ineffably sad about the way people were knocked down, insulted, defeated, destroyed day by day, whether by others who should have known better, or by circumstances they either could handle but did not understand how to or that were beyond their control, or by what is commonly known as *fate* or *destiny*. He would look at someone with an ailment, a cripple, a blind person, a shabbily dressed hobo, and his heart would go out to them. He could never pass anyone by who had his hand out asking for money. Daniel thought of it rather as *karma*, and his belief that karma was involved in such happenings made it intellectually and even emotionally palatable to his peculiar sensibilities. In his own way, Daniel had always tried to show consideration and respect for everyone whose path crossed his. There was something that Annemarie had told him as she lay dying, something he could never forget, words that gave him the fortitude to withstand any negative impulses that assailed him.

"Daniel," she had said, speaking softly with barely enough energy to get the words out,

"I may have complained about things every now and then. Maybe I gave you the idea that I did not think you were all you could be as a husband. I realize that now. That's why I want you to know, before it's too late, that you were the best husband a woman could hope for, that I could ever have hoped for. You were always kind and understanding. You gave me fulfillment." The last word came apart and Annemarie needed fifteen seconds to get out its three syllables as her voice weakened and broke, her strength dissipated by the sheer effort needed to speak as much as she did.

Stephen returned to tell Daniel that he had to cut their session short. A woman parishioner had come to see him, distraught over the news that her brother had been arrested for abusing his wife and three children. He is a church-going, God-fearing man, she told her pastor. How could he do such things?

"You see, Daniel, "the Monsignor announced solemnly, "I was just telling you about the forces of evil in the world, of how the Devil constantly roams the earth, seeking to influence those who are weak to do evil things."

"Steve, can't you, even you, see that this is total nonsense, superstition left over from a time of ignorance. How easy it is to blame something, an unknown spirit, for the bad that we do. We have to accept the fact that we are all responsible ourselves for our own actions. And society is responsible and culpable when it perpetuates these myths about devils and dark forces that cause us to sin. People need understanding, not blame."

"But this is very interesting. I always knew you were more like Mamma than any of the rest of us."

"That's a real compliment, but I don't know if I deserve it and I'm not even sure it's true."

"It is true." The Monsignor spoke as he did then whenever he wanted to establish his authority or re-assert it among his parishioners.

"But it's not as much of a compliment as you may think."

"Why?" Daniel asked with feigned incredulity. He could not see how anything connected with their mother could possibly have a down side.

"It's just that like her, you think everyone is good. You look for the redeeming qualities in people even when it's clear that they do not have such qualities. Some people cannot be redeemed without Divine help. That's why they need religion. That's why God sent His Son as the Redeemer of mankind since man cannot do it on his own. Even if you don't want to accept the accounts of how man fell, it's obvious that man is not perfect and some men are far more imperfect than others, but we all need to be redeemed and we cannot do it on our own. At least Mamma knew this even if she looked for the good in others that often was not there. People need to have some structure. They need to have something to fear, yes, even if what they fear may seem silly to you. But it helps them to get through the days and the dark nights."

"I rather think it makes them more open to dark nights and dark days as well." Daniel looked at his brother with an expression the other saw as sincere.

"I don't agree with you Daniel." The sadness in the Monsignor's eyes as he looked at his brother was evident. In all their discussions, Daniel had never heard his brother speak in such an impassioned manner. Over the weeks their talks had touched upon the early days of Christianity; the contributions of St. Peter and Saint Paul; the life and death of Jesus and his relationship to his disciples and to his family; the Emperor Constantine; the various councils that brought about so many of the doctrines held sacred by Roman Catholics and the *raison d'etre* for practices that Daniel tried to show were basically meaningless. Daniel had poured out all his objections, all he had learned about why so much of what was believed by Christians and Catholics specifically could not be seriously entertained by a person with a mind open to other possibilities and, for Daniel, realities. But as he listened to his brother then, the full impact of one basic truth hit home. Stephen's faith was too strong to be shaken by anything. The years, decades, centuries of practice that had permeated the living cells of Stephen and others like him could not be broken down and were not subject to further analysis as far as they themselves were concerned. No, the practice of faith that derived from his parents, grandparents and beyond was thoroughly ingrained and so mightily buttressed against the onslaught of *error* as some would see it, *reason* as Daniel would have it, that there was no room for consideration of contrary thought.

"Yes, you are so much like her, but at least she had her faith to sustain her. That's what worries me about you. What will sustain you?"

"I am sorry, but I don't agree with you, Stephen. I am sustained by my own intelligence and determination to learn, to separate what is false from what I know to be true."

Daniel knew he was hurting his brother and this was the one thing he feared most about these discussions, but striving for truth was not an easy task.

"Then you see no value in religion? What is your solution for the troubles of the world? Don't you think that without religion we would have total chaos?"

"I have no solution."

"Aha! Just as I thought. You can sit there and criticize, question and condemn, but you have nothing better to offer."

Daniel knew that this was the low point in his relationship with his brother. He could only hope that Stephen's compassion and intelligence would give him a better understanding, and if not understanding, at least tolerance for his brother's position.

"Look Steve, for me religion is something that divides people. We agreed at the beginning of our discussions that much good derives from religion and that perhaps people need something like what religion offers to identify with, to bring a measure of understanding in a world of confusion and turmoil."

"So?"

"Yes, but that is just a stopgap. Religion, as we have seen in our own lifetime, as we have learned from history . . . religion brings greater harm than any benefits that can possibly accrue. It sets one group of people against another. It makes people feel superior to those who do not share their beliefs and this destroys peace and unity. I don't know how it can be achieved, but eventually enlightened man must assert a new doctrine and it must be accepted universally."

"This sounds like a new kind of dictatorship!" The Monsignor evidently felt that he had trapped his brother and uncovered a serious flaw in his argument.

"I said that I don't know how this can be implemented. I am not suggesting that anyone be forced to accept this. I am just hopeful that this new doctrine, not really new at all, but one that has been seeking recognition among men of intelligence and good will for centuries, that this will come to be the dominant means by which men will live. I am referring to the concept of humanism. This concerns a way of life that centers on human interests and proclaims the dignity and the value of man. It embraces strongly the idea that man has a capacity for self fulfillment and the realization of all that is best in life, and this is achieved through reason at its highest level." Daniel finished the sentence, rushing ahead at the conclusion with increasing volume.

"And of course this doctrine traditionally discards God altogether!" Stephen spoke even louder than Daniel had, almost but not quite sounding angry.

"No, that's not true at all. Man, through his reason is free to acknowledge a force greater than himself, call it God, the supernatural, or whatever one chooses. Each man must find within himself the object toward which he directs his spiritual energies, but no man would force anyone else to accept his conclusions about the unknown, even if he feels it is abundantly well known to himself. The possibilities for good are endless."

"Dan, I must go. I have to find a way to give comfort to the woman I told you about. We are always brothers and I will always love you. Take care, and if you ever have need for anything from me, spiritual advice or anything else, remember that I am always here for you."

"Thank you Steve. I love you too, and I am always here for you too. And don't worry about me. I will be all right. You see, I finally understand myself and can be true to myself."

The brothers embraced and left one another with renewed admiration and respect for both what they had in common and what they did not.

Some weeks after Daniel's final discussion with Stephen, the entire family gathered at John and Sophia's home to celebrate Christine's graduation from college. Christine was the third of John and Sophia's children. The oldest, Vincent (another grandson named after the paternal grandfather according to Southern Italian custom—there could be ten grandsons from ten children and they would all carry the grandfather's name), had received his M.B.A. from Columbia Business School, and the second son, Peter, named after Sophia' father, earned his law degree at the New York University School of Law. Both young men entered the family business after graduation and worked with their father, mother and Uncle Albert at the corporate offices in Stamford, Connecticut. It was a short commute for John and Sophia from their lavishly appointed twelve room home in Greenwich.

Later in the day, John winked at Daniel and suggested they go for a walk.

"Come on, we'll take Rusty out for his constitutional." Rusty was an Irish Setter that the Lorelli's had purchased when the children were younger. The family pet was now advanced in years, but still in good health. One reason for this was the regular habit of exercise that the family had trained their dog to practice. John, Sophia or one of the children had always taken the dog out for a brisk walk on a daily basis, and there was never a question of whose job it was, since they considered walking with Rusty a privilege.

As John and Daniel walked, John looked at his younger brother, smiled broadly and asked, "Is it true what Steve tells me?"

"What does he tell you?" Daniel's reticence was an act. He just wanted to draw out from John what he already knew his brother was well aware of, but he thought he would enjoy hearing how John would characterize it."

"Well, he says that you've lost the Faith."

"That's true."

"But why? You always seemed to be most like Mamma when it came to religion, until Steve became a priest, at least."

"I was always very curious about all the things we believed as Catholics. For a long time, I just went along, believing, not believing, selecting this or that as worthy of belief. Eventually, I had to learn more and I began to study the background of the New Testament, the Old Testament, the practices that Catholics take for granted as being valid. I came to the conclusion that so much of it is based on misconceptions, wrong information, erroneous thinking. I had to find myself in all of this, not to continue to pay tribute to something handed down from generation to generation without any real thought going into our acceptance of so much of it."

"Like what? What do you find hard to believe?"

"That Jesus was anything but a man, an extraordinary man to be sure, but a product of his time. He was no more the son of God than you are or I am. There was no resurrection. The entire story was made up. That and so much more."

"That's why you're no longer a Catholic?"

"Exactly!"

"What are you then?"

"I don't adhere to any organized religious faith."

"Then why leave Catholicism?" John's tone sounded like that of a person pleading with a totally unreasonable adversary.

"Why should I continue to pledge fidelity to something I know in my heart is false?"

"Dan, come on! Do you think I believe everything that the Catholic Church teaches? I'm not even sure I believe that Jesus is God. I mean, this is something we were brought up to believe, a part of our heritage. It's like a social contract. We all need something, a religion, a culture to belong to. Let me ask you this: would you say you no longer considered yourself an Italian? Look, we are children of Italian parents, but we were born in America. Does that mean we should say honesty demands that we acknowledge and state to all that we are Americans, first, foremost, no, not even foremost, but exclusively? We're proud of our Italian heritage. Why should we deny it?"

"I would never deny my pride in being born of Italian parents, but that is something entirely different."

"Different? How is it different?" John's face took on an expression of annoyance combined with pity, a look Daniel well remembered from his father when Vincenzo was beginning to feel frustrated in trying to convince one of his sons that a particular thing had to be done.

"The fact that we are Italian, that our parents came from a place called Italy and that we were brought up to appreciate certain customs that have become part of our lives—there is nothing false about any of that, but there is a good deal of untruth in what we have learned through the religion we were brought up to believe."

"Oh, Dan! I'm not trying to tell you what to do, believe what you like, but why change? When your daughter gets married, don't you want to walk her down the aisle?"

Of course I do, but Marta is still a practicing Catholic. I am not trying to change others. I told you, I am just trying to be at peace with my own conscience."

"I really don't see what the big deal is. I just explained to you, I don't believe most of the things either, but you go along, you just go along. It's easier that way."

"Don't rock the boat. Is that it?"

"Of course! Why rock the boat when things are going smoothly. You live, you have an affiliation. Can you imagine any Jew saying he is not a Jew?"

"I know many Jews who are not believers in the religious sense."

"Yeah, but they will never say they are not Jews!"

"Of course not, just as we will never say we're not Italians. It's a cultural thing."

"Don't you see how foolish you're being? There are things in life when you need this connection. Birth, baptism, marriage. There are times when you need the comfort that religion affords. Then when you die, you have a funeral Mass. It's comforting for your family. When you die, God forbid, they won't even give you a Catholic burial if you continue like this."

"That's fine with me. I don't want one." Daniel had never even thought along those lines, but he felt a bit sad about renouncing the kind of service he had arranged for Annemarie. His imagination flittered about, covering the possibilities of what could happen after his demise. He rather liked the idea of the Fauré *Requiem* being played at his funeral, but it could be in a room that had no connection with a church.

"Why do you have to be different? It must be the artist in you. You artists are always eccentric in your own ways. My advice to you ..."

"Yes?" Daniel waited for words of wisdom from the man who after the death of their father became the symbolic head of the extended Lorelli family."

"My advice to you is, forget all this nonsense." John had never looked so much like their father as he did at that moment. Vincenzo's words to Daniel came back with a rush. When Daniel wanted to follow music as a career, his father had used the exact same words, "Forget all this nonsense," followed by, "You have a secure place in our business. Why throw that away for something as uncertain as music."

"Forget all this nonsense," Daniel repeated.

"Yeah, forget it. Just go along. Things can be much easier if you just go along."

Daniel spontaneously embraced John who thought he had had a positive effect on the errant brother.

For days Daniel would think about their conversation and smile to himself. John didn't know it, but Daniel had indeed forgotten all the nonsense. As for going along, he had to laugh to think that something so important for him could be so simple for others. He could never again just go along.

Fourty-One

Maestro Lorelli's career began to blossom once again. The director of an enterprising Swedish recording company that specialized in contemporary Scandinavian music knew Daniel's reputation and had learned of his affinity for the Twentieth Century Swedish Composer, Allan Pettersson. Following a series of discussions by telephone, Daniel was invited to visit Stockholm to discuss a project to record all of Petterson's fourteen symphonies. By the time Daniel's recordings of five of the symphonies had been released to worldwide critical acclaim, he was being noticed in circles where his name had never been at all familiar. The prestigious *Gramophone* noted that "for the first time, these gems of late 20th century symphonic craft are being heard as their composer envisioned them." The review continued, "Lorelli is a first rate Mahler conductor and Pettersson's craft owes a good deal to the Mahlerian prototype, even if his works are distinctive and uniquely his own, but Lorelli's affinity for Mahler's sound world makes him the right conductor for the Swedish symphonist's tragic and complex works, and he delivers extremely sensitive and resilient readings of Pettersson's masterpieces." Although Daniel was basically a very optimistic person with a perennially sanguine outlook on life, there was, as noted, another side to his personality. His sensitivity to the pain and suffering of others, this singular empathetic quality, enabled him to understand and interpret musical works like Pettersson's, works that had been inspired by the relentless currents of human misery occasionally made bearable by flashes of radiance and beauty, carried onwards, above the waves of sadness and despair, composed as expressions of comprehension and compassion for emotions so deep and mysterious that only music among all the arts could nearly perfectly encompass them. Allan Pettersson had suffered extreme physical pain and had written extensively about his ordeal. Daniel identified with him on various levels. Pettersson's symphonies demanded a conductor who could organize them and sustain the momentum over movements that lasted longer than entire symphonies by other composers. The undulating forward motion, the torrents of sound, the shrieking winds and slashing chords of the strings were in themselves quite daunting, but Daniel enjoyed the challenge and succeeded in capturing the spirit of the music at the highest possible level. And the fact that the composer had been a violist when he performed in a Stockholm orchestra before beginning to compose, somehow endeared him to Daniel even more. Daniel didn't know exactly what it was, but to his way of thinking, a person who chose the viola as his or her instrument possessed extraordinary moral attributes. The viola didn't have the flamboyance of either the violin or the cello. The person playing it could be thought of as being reticent by anyone who considered the matter in a cursory manner, but Daniel knew differently. Annemarie certainly never called attention to herself as a musician, except for the times when she played as soloist, but the viola had expressed her personality perfectly. Like her preferred instrument she had been serious, bold when called on to be bold, unobtrusive but integrally connected with all around her, continually making a contribution that was essential, and without which the composition's concept or the personal influence would be markedly different. Dependability, discipline and an exhaustive desire to excel were characteristics of his late wife as they were in another sense of the exquisitely lovely viola. Daniel often thought of the works that Annemarie loved to play whenever she had been able to settle down and play her instrument, not for an audience, but just for herself. He recalled how she would get into Max Reger's *G minor Suite for Viola.* The *Vivace* and *Molto Vivace* 2nd and 4th movements brought her to life and he lovingly recalled how her body's motion would match the energy inherent in the music. But the 1st movement's *Molto sostenuto* and the 3rd movement's *Andante sostenuto* seemed to give her the opportunity to uncover through the music inner feelings so deep and personal that a sensitive listener like Daniel could feel at one with her. He remembered how he had sat listening to her on evenings when the children, still quite young, were fast asleep. She also loved Paul Hindemith's *Op. 25/1 Viola Sonata,* and again the *Sehr lagsam* and *Langsam, mit viel Ausdruck* 3rd and 5th movements engaged her so much more intensively than did the faster movements of the work. As he watched her playing those sections, Daniel knew that if anyone could disclose her innermost passions through music, she was certainly doing so on those rare occasions, and this explained why he could recall them with such heart-rending intensity. Every now and then they had gotten together to play Brahms' *Opus 120 Viola Sonatas,* two works that they had performed together in public soon after they first met in Rome   Afterwards, after those evenings at home when they played together or Annemarie played solo, or whenever she would ask Daniel for some of her favorite piano works like Schubert's *Moments Musicaux,* they would make love, and the tenderness or the fervor that the music had generated inside each of them would make it better than at other times and more memorable for both of them..

Soon after the release of the Pettersson recordings, Daniel's agent got inquiries about the availability of the conductor for guest engagements. A number of American orchestras were looking for high profile American conductors to lead concerts during the temporary absence of their music directors.   Once Daniel's publicity file was seen with his impressive curriculum vitae and the new color photograph that gave evidence of a man handsome, mature and distinguished, with hair graying at the temples, black and full otherwise, long but not excessively so, orchestra managers knew they could have someone who would be a real audience pleaser. Soon Daniel was conducting the basic repertory and contemporary works as well all over the country. Over a period of two years he had engagements with the symphony orchestras of Milwaukee, New Jersey, Tulsa, Virginia, Seattle, Rochester, Buffalo, Oregon, Tallahassee, and Indianapolis.   Prior to his appearance to conduct the Houston Symphony, Maestro Lorelli was interviewed by *Parade Magazine.* The publication is widely circulated throughout the country, accompanying the Sunday newspapers of dozens of communities. Daniel was asked questions about his background, his experience as a pianist and conductor, his family and, ultimately, about his religion.   Daniel's disclosure that he confessed to no organized religious faith piqued the interviewer's curiosity. The young woman journalist saw this as an opportunity to make her interview more sensational than she had thought possible when she was first given the assignment to meet with the conductor.   Since he had a strong Italian heritage, she wondered how it was possible that he was not a Roman Catholic. Lorelli admitted that he had been a Roman Catholic for most of his life, but his beliefs had changed. This, of course, led to additional questions about what he did and didn't believe.   His description of his thoughts concerning Jesus the man became the focus of the printed interview and it appeared with the headline, "Conductor who loves sacred music denies the divinity of Jesus." One week before Daniel was to conduct the Houston Symphony for the first time, a group of students from nearby Baptist universities began to picket outside of Jones Hall. A controversy erupted and the incident was widely covered by the media.   Daniel was concerned.   He had not been looking for this kind of attention, but his agent told him he couldn't have gotten better publicity if he had invested a fortune trying to buy it. The agent was right. The management of the Houston orchestra nearly capitulated, but in the end upheld the right of a conductor's freedom of speech, even if the Texas Baptists abhorred his philosophy. This brought about a groundswell of support for Maestro Lorelli and soon the managements of some of the finest orchestras in more liberal cities invited him to conduct. Engagements followed with the orchestras of San Francisco, Los Angeles, Atlanta, Baltimore, Detroit and Saint Louis.

When a well known guest conductor had to cancel his New York appearances with the Cleveland Orchestra at Carnegie Hall, Daniel was asked to take his place for a single concert. The program consisted of works by one composer, the Russian Serge Prokofiev. Prokofiev was a composer Daniel favored over most other Twentieth Century creative musicians. Indeed, he was convinced that Prokofiev was one of the century's greatest musical geniuses and was often surprised that he was left out of discussions or off of lists of the greatest composers of the age. Daniel had studied and performed many of Prokofiev's works for solo piano, including the ten *Sonatas.* He was familiar with the five *Piano Concertos* and had performed the *First* and *Third* in concert. The Carnegie Hall program was made up of the *Classical Symphony*, a *Suite* from the ballet *Cinderella*, the *Third Piano Concerto* and the *Fifth Symphony*. The day before the concert was to take place, the pianist, a young American who had won a prize in the Van Cliburn competition, had to cancel for personal reasons. The orchestra's tour manager was beside himself. It wasn't hard to find a pianist willing to perform, but he needed to get the right pianist. He didn't want to settle for just anyone who happened to be available. Then Daniel offered to play the *Concerto* and conduct from the keyboard. Such a feat was common with, say, a Mozart Concerto, but to play Prokofiev's *Third* and conduct it too seemed too much to ask of one artist. Nevertheless, the idea fascinated the manager and he agreed to have Daniel tackle it. The concert was a huge success and contributed in no small way to a surge in new proposals for Daniel to conduct guest engagements. Soon, too, stirrings were heard of offers for permanent appointments to the music directorships of important orchestras.

After the concert, Maestro Lorelli had a crowd waiting to greet him in the green room. He was thrilled to accept the good wishes of fans, and old friends with connections to him from the world of music. But he was especially happy to see the familiar faces of Joseph and Silvana Manfredi. Daniel never forgot how Silvana had cared for Annemarie and he had invited her and Joseph to dinner on a few occasions. As he embraced Joseph and Silvana, he espied a beautiful young woman standing behind them. He didn't realize at first that she was with the couple and was nearly spellbound by the way her striking deep green eyes seemed to penetrate him, disarming him to the point that Silvana noted his attention to the mysterious stranger and turned quickly to introduce her younger colleague.

"Oh, Daniel, this is Carolyn Cheruel, Doctor Cheruel, a friend."

Daniel took her sleek, delicate hand in his and had the urge to kiss it in the European manner, but this was a gesture he was not accustomed to and he felt it would appear to be superficial.

"I loved the concert," Carolyn enthused. "Especially your performance of the *Concerto!*" Daniel laughed and commented jokingly that he knew he shouldn't have played the piano since it encouraged the public to think of him as a pianist instead of as a conductor.

"Oh, no, not at all," Carolyn's rejoinder assured him, "Your conducting was superb too, but having studied the piano myself for some years, I naturally paid special attention to that."

"Can you join us for a drink, a late snack?" Joseph Manfredi asked.

"I'd be delighted." Actually, Daniel had wanted nothing more than to get right home to get some much needed sleep after the grueling days he had spent preparing for and executing the concert. But this young woman, not so young that he would have to worry about his daughter's disapproval (or would he?) had captured his fancy in short order and he wanted to see more of her, learn more about her. Looking at Carolyn, Daniel had the distinct feeling that they had met before, but he knew this could not be. He recalled once traveling on a train in France and seeing a young woman in a seat diagonally across from him. She had looked at him with the same penetrating gaze that emanated from Carolyn's eyes as she looked at him with a mixture of admiration and interest. The girl on the train—she couldn't have been more than seventeen or eighteen at the time—looked across at him boldly, uncharacteristically so he had thought, for a young woman traveling alone. In his experience they would usually avert their eyes from glancing back at men who sought to engage them in conversation. He had exchanged a few words with her when, just as he was thinking of asking her where she was going and suggesting an innocent rendezvous when they reached Paris, she stood up, bid him a wistful adieu and got off the train at a suburb some eighty kilometers outside that city of romance, the Paris that was for Daniel rife with the promise of sensual love. Each time he thought back to that evening, he would think of the girl and wonder about what he had missed. It was a "what if" that provided fantasies that danced around in his head, changing in some details, but always involving lovemaking of rare delight, consummate pleasure and never to be matched fulfillment. But that is the way with fantasy, isn't it? The unattainable always appears most desirable. Carolyn was certainly not that girl from the train, even if Daniel thought of the possibility with a certain delectable relish. The ages just would not match up.

Carolyn Cheruel was the daughter of a French father and an Italian mother whose parents were in the diplomatic service of their respective countries when they met, fell in love and married. Carolyn was born in Rome but had lived in Washington for most of her life. Both parents had worked at their countries' embassies in that city. Carolyn spoke French and Italian fluently, had received her medical degree from Johns Hopkins and had been doing her residency at Memorial where she met Silvana Manfredi. She remained on staff as a research assistant to a coterie of physicians who were making significant advances in cancer research. The two women quickly became friends, enjoying their lunchtime conversations in Italian, baffling the other doctors around them who wondered if they were being talked about. Silvana had told Carolyn about the concert and the fact that an old friend was the conductor, inviting her to join them. Silvana, Joseph and Carolyn waited as Daniel greeted everyone else who had stopped in the Green Room. Carolyn noted with admiration how Daniel spoke to each and every person with a warm, personal and unique greeting. She could see that he wasn't just going through the motions. He was old enough to be her father, and she had never really been interested in older men as some women are, but there was something about him that defied any such categorization, one way or another. The truth was that Carolyn found Daniel to be extremely attractive, and she admitted as much to herself when she was lying in bed that night after having spent two hours with him. She wanted to see more of him and was determined to enlist Silvana's aid in getting it to happen.

During the following weeks, Daniel was conducting concerts on the West coast, but he thought more and more about this . . . new woman in his life? What was he thinking? She was not really in his life at all, but he was determined to learn more about her. Sometimes he would shake the thought, trying to convince himself that she could possibly have no interest in him. Their careers, too, made demands on each of them and the possibility of spending time together seemed remote. Still, Daniel could not get her off his mind and remembered her gaze, that look that told him that somehow, she and he had a connection that could not and, hopefully, would not be denied. He wondered if she had any thoughts at all about him. She did. She dreamed about him and remembered at least three dreams in which Daniel figured significantly. In one dream he was the doctor in charge of an important research project to find a genetic link that would provide a cure for certain types of cancer. She was his assistant and when another physician tried to denigrate Carolyn's achievements, Daniel stepped forward to proclaim before the entire staff that Carolyn had single-handedly accomplished more than anyone else involved in the project. In another dream Daniel was making love to her and the sensation was so intense that she awoke feeling certain that he was there in bed with her.

When Daniel returned home, he found four messages on his answering machine from Silvana, asking him to please call as soon as he could. Daniel called quickly, hoping to hear that Silvana wanted to invite him to their home and that Carolyn would be there too. He was not disappointed.

"Daniel, please excuse me if I am bringing up something that is really not my business, but, well I know how devoted you were to Annemarie, how much you loved her, and I don't know if you have any interest at all in other women at this point in your life."

"I . . ." Daniel barely had time to say a word when Silvana interrupted and continued,

"Of course you must have interest in women. You're a man and still a young man after all, but you may already be seeing someone. You may even be planning to re-marry for all I know."

"Silvana."

"Yes"

"May I get a word in before you cover every possibility?"

"Of course. I'm sorry. It's just that I am a bit nervous."

"Nervous? Nervous about what?" Just then a dangerous thought accosted Daniel. What if Silvana herself was suggesting that the two of them have a tryst? He thought that perhaps women her age found themselves in a rut, particularly intelligent women who did not necessarily see monogamy as the panacea for every woman's inclinations, desires and designs. It could be that after the concert she had found something about him that she wanted a part of. Wasn't it possible that Carolyn had spoken to her about him and that the power of suggestion was manifesting a plan for the two of them to share the kind of intimacy . . . . Oh, what was he thinking! No, that couldn't be. She had begun by saying it was not her business, so it must have something to do with someone else, with Carolyn?

"I'm nervous because I am about to make a suggestion that I have never made in my life before now." What was this? It was true then. Silvana was going to talk about the two of them, not about him and Carolyn.

"Are you absolutely sure you want to make the suggestion then?"

"Sure? I think so. Why, don't you think I should?"

"I don't know. I have no idea what you are about to suggest. I mean I can guess."

"Guess? " Silvana started to laugh. "Joe, I think he knows," she said not entirely out of Daniel's range of hearing.

Joe? She is talking to me with her husband in the room, so of course it has to concern someone else, Daniel quickly concluded.

"Oh, go ahead. I am not going to guess. What do you want to suggest?"

"Daniel, you remember Carolyn?"

"Of course. How could I ever forget such a beautiful woman?" Daniel again recalled her deep green eyes, her dark brown hair cut to fall slightly over her shoulders. But most of all he continued to be haunted by the way she had looked at him, without constraint, without any hint at all of reserve, confident, secure, it almost seemed, in the apprehension of his secret soul.

"Daniel, Carolyn would like to see you again."

"Well, I would love to see her again too."

"Great! Then let me give you her number. Or, if you like I can give her your number. She's a modern woman. She has no qualms about initiating, making the first call."

Daniel liked that, even if it did go against the grain. After all, in his day the man always called the girl.

"Silvana, whatever you prefer. Give me her number and give her mine."

"Oh, Daniel. That's wonderful. As I was trying to tell you, I have never been involved in matchmaking before, and I worry about whether it will work out or not. And you are both friends and I don't want to do anything to alienate either one of you."

"Don't worry. You won't."

"How can you be so sure?"

"I don't know. It's just that there was something about her that told me that I had to meet her and . . . ." Daniel hesitated, wanting to say that he needed to spend time with Carolyn, but it seemed somehow presumptuous. Instead, he offered the notion that perhaps they had met before.

"Are you serious?"

"Very serious. Just ask your husband. He's the expert when it comes to past life and this life, soul mates and all that."

"You mean you think that the two of you . . ." Silvana could not finish the sentence.

"Yes. That's exactly what I mean."

"Oh, all right. Whatever works for you," Silvana laughed. Daniel thought of her patient, the one whose problems Joseph Manfredi had resolved through past life regression. Joseph had once told Daniel about the case, but Daniel thought it best not to bring it up.

Over the next two weeks Daniel was busy with concerts. He thought about Carolyn, but didn't want to call her unless he could invite her to join him for dinner or a drink so he could have an opportunity to get to know her better. But she called him first and her voice on the telephone sounded different from what he was expecting. She sounded business-like. Perhaps it was her telephone voice. Some people had one that did not match what one heard in the course of a casual conversation. After all, she was probably on the telephone throughout the day, talking to patients, other doctors, and hospital administrators. Then, too, curiously, he expected her to say, "This is Doctor Cheruel," but she said quite naturally,

"Hi, Daniel, this is Carolyn. Silvana gave me your number. How are you?"

After the customary amenities and before Daniel himself saw fit to suggest they get together, Carolyn made clear the reason for her call.

"I would very much like to see you again."

"I would like to see you, too, Carolyn." Daniel's heartbeat accelerated. The prospect of something happening with this beautiful and intelligent woman, anything really, excited him with a sense of anticipation he had not felt since he was a young man. No, he thought, he had sensed it not that long ago, when he was fantasizing about making love to Mira and it seemed that she was about to accede to his desire. But this seemed so much more probable. Carolyn was not married, and he was a widower, and he thought, trying to justify himself, that Annemarie would want him to pursue this attraction.

They did not become intimate until they had been out together on eight occasions, but when the time came for them to sleep together they didn't sleep very much. The sex they shared was animal-like in its total disregard for anything but pleasure. The fact that they were both falling in love made it meaningful to both, but tenderness and delicate stimulation would have to wait for their next encounter. Carolyn hadn't been with a man for nearly two years, and before that the men she had agreed to sleep with had disappointed her. They were totally committed to their own egos and she resented them for that, proudly, totally. Two men, physicians themselves, had wanted to marry her, but she saw through them. She would be another object to place beside their medical degrees, their honors and the distinction that others would find in them. Here she would be, the wife of the doctor who herself was a respected doctor, beautiful, intelligent, worthy to give life to the offspring of this man of high esteem and integrity. When Carolyn tried to explain this to her mother, the diplomat, a woman who was ahead of her time in breaking out of the mold that Italian womanhood had been poured into, she could not understand her daughter. The suitors seemed so well positioned to give her daughter the life that a mother—a mother such as she, at least—hoped for fervently and felt intuitively was her daughter's birthright. No, Carolyn's mother could not understand. Even if she was an independent woman, she had no idea how totally apart her daughter was from any need whatsoever to fulfill herself through a man, especially if he took it for granted that her needs were best realized in union with him. Carolyn, rather, preferred to be alone. She didn't want that, but if the man she could respect as well as love did not come into her life, she would settle for solitude.

The first time Carolyn saw Daniel after the concert, she felt that familiar if elusive desire, sensual, insistent and hard to disregard. Each time she saw him after that, it intensified. Daniel's did too, but he was at a different place in life and would have succumbed sooner if his feelings for Carolyn did not go beyond the merely physical. For her part, the still young doctor recognized in the musician a quality that she had been searching for in a man ever since she first began to consider the possibility of caring for someone else above virtually everything else, the only rationale possible for those who truly love and love altogether truly. Carolyn knew that Daniel found her physically attractive. She was much too intelligent to deceive herself by believing that her intellect alone would bring the right man to her. But there was so much more *to* him. His sensitivity to her feelings, his ability to anticipate whatever it was that she was herself expecting, the ability he had to make her feel much more beautiful than she actually felt she was—these qualities she had never experienced while being with a man, then, invigorated her sexual drive and made her impatient to consummate her intense desires and her desire for him, for him particularly. Daniel hoped for the same consummation, but he needed to go more slowly, for he found himself going down the path he never expected to traverse in the years left to him, to be totally in love again. He had thought, oh how many times had he thought of that sensation he had first known in his youth, the intemperate temper that went beyond infatuation, that all-encompassing, totally engrossing regard for the object of one's deepest and most arduous ardor. Now that the evanescent promise seemed to reappear, he didn't want to lose it altogether in a night of delectable but empty passion. And so it was that on their fourth evening out together, Carolyn was ready to give herself with complete abandon, more ready still by the fifth evening and the sixth and seventh. When Daniel got inside the door of her apartment on that eighth night, their touches and kisses intensified and control was no longer an option for either of them. Daniel covered Carolyn's mouth with his. She pulled away slightly and extended her tongue, inserting it into his mouth and as he responded, their tongues intertwining, darting about within, Daniel's breath was taken away by his young enticer's impetus towards him. Some of his old reservations about the woman acting as seducer were penetrating his thoughts, but he dismissed them as he had dismissed all the wrong-headed inhibitions that religion had unreasonably imposed on him, and he was certain that this new found freedom could make him the lover he had always wanted to be. With Carolyn it was happening. They undressed each other quickly and did not even wait to reach the bedroom, falling to the floor and pulling at one another, caresses of whiplash like intensity, their legs flailing and encircling each other's torsos. By the time each had reached an intense orgasmic culmination to the frenzy they had mutually unleashed, they lay exhausted, smiling at one another.

Two nights later, they *made love* for the first time. It was slow, and gentle and even more sexually exciting in its own quiet way than their night of uninhibited sexual play. Carolyn had put a CD into the player— Elgar's *Cello Concerto,* Jacqueline Du Pre's performance of the classic work. Carolyn had always fantasized about making love to this music. Slowly she would caress her lover as the cello made its deliberate entrance. They would kiss and he would enter her as the cello took up the theme, one and two and one and two, one and two again. Slowly at first, she would rock with her lover up and down, she on top, controlling the motion. Delicate but determined, they would move in unison until some six minutes into the first movement, and then when the orchestra enters with the one and two, one and two, their movements would intensify. After that, they would be on their own with the music merely background. Daniel kneeled behind her and lifted her loose dress, a lovely red organdy fabric. He moved his hand over her buttocks. Carolyn was wearing a thong, the underwear of the modern woman, Daniel thought to himself. He could never have imagined Annemarie wearing anything like it, but the sight of Carolyn's delicate skin as it blossomed out from the recessed edges of the tight fitted undergarment excited him with a mixture of lust and love. As Carolyn sat over her lover, she used the remote to begin the recording. Daniel was surprised but delighted at her choice of music. Pushed to a choice himself, he would have selected Rachmaninov's *Piano Concerto No. 2 in c minor,* a work he had performed a few times during his career as a concert pianist.

"I have been waiting for the right man to make love to with this music. You are that man," Carolyn whispered.

Afterwards Carolyn said, "I want to marry you."

Daniel was inclined to tell her that he was too old for her, old enough really to be her father, but he felt so young at that moment, so young that he knew that was not really the case.

"Are you sure about that?"

"Daniel, I have never been so sure of anything before. I think the first time I saw you I knew."

Daniel mused on Carolyn's words and seemed to her to be far off somewhere else.

"Where is your mind wandering, Daniel?" she asked.

"I was just thinking that I must have known, too, the first time I saw you."

"Must have? You're not sure?"

"Perhaps I'm not as sure as you are, but I knew there was something special about you. I immediately felt as though I knew you or that I had known you . . . from another time and place."

"You share Dr. Manfredi's philosophy about reincarnation?"

"Most definitely. Do you?"

"I've had discussions with Silvana about it. She told me about one of her patients who was apparently cured of an ailment as a result of her husband's past life regression therapy."

"Yes, I'm aware of that too."

"I don't know. As a student of science, I think I am more skeptical. I don't think Silvana is in complete accord with her husband's theories."

"Has she ever told you that?"

"Not exactly, but she never seems very eager to discuss it."

"She's probably concerned about compromising her position as a prominent physician, but I'm sure that she believes in past lives and reincarnation as much as or even more than I do."

"How can you be so sure? Has she told you?"

Daniel recounted the story of how Joseph and Silvana had met in Longobardi and Joseph's subsequent regression to learn that they had loved one another before. Carolyn was impressed by the story and allowed that it could be possible that she and Daniel had known one another before too.

"It's funny, but I couldn't understand why I was so certain about you when I had never felt so secure in my feelings about a man before. Perhaps there is something to it."

But as soon as she said it, Carolyn's intellectual probity gave her pause in embracing the idea wholeheartedly.

As the weeks passed Carolyn and Daniel were together as much as their individual schedules would allow them to be. Carolyn did not bring up the subject of marriage again. She was waiting for Daniel to continue the dialogue. Her fiercely independent spirit would not allow her to place herself in a position of subjugation and this was exactly where she felt she would be if she broached the subject again. She was completely confident that Daniel would ask her to marry him. If he was the man she knew him to be, it would happen. If not . . . but that was not possible. He was not one of those men who are afraid of commitment. His entire life, she quickly learned, had been one in which he was totally involved in whatever he was doing, with whomever he was with. Of course her instincts were correct, if they could be called instincts at all since her confidence in her lover precluded any possible doubt.

One morning as they sat enjoying coffee together, Daniel asked the question Carolyn had been waiting to hear.

"Carolyn, I know I am a lot older than you, but I love you and want you be my wife. Will you?"

Carolyn took his hands in hers, gazed into his eyes as she had the first time he saw her and nodded her head in silent affirmation. After a few moments, she spoke, "There is nothing I want more. I love you as I have never loved anyone before."

Daniel wanted to say as much to her, but he thought of how he had loved Marilyn, and Annemarie especially, and, yes, Mira too, even if they had never brought their desires and passion for one another to physical fulfillment (that was for another time).

"I love you very, very much. There is nothing that would make me happier than to spend the rest of my life with you."

Carolyn understood. Silvana had told her of his deep and abiding love for Annemarie, but in spite of this, Carolyn didn't feel like second best. She knew that she was firmly positioned deep in his heart.

"About the wedding?"

Daniel was compelled to make it clear that he could not marry her in a Catholic Church ceremony. Up until this point they had only discussed religion superficially. Carolyn had been baptized in the Catholic Church in Rome, principally at the request of her maternal grandparents. Her mother and father were not practicing Catholics, and never even arranged for her to make her First Communion or Confirmation. They never took her to Mass on Sundays, so it was more a loose feeling of affiliation than any real attachment to the Church that characterized her religious thinking. She never had a crisis of faith such as Daniel's, since she had never experienced or lived the life of faith that he had either. She had never given much thought to where her marriage would take place when the time came for her wedding, and a Church wedding was not something she had ever counted on. Daniel had told her that he was brought up in a strong Catholic environment and that one of his brothers was a Catholic priest, but when he said he was no longer a Catholic, she assumed he meant he was no longer a practicing Catholic. This was the time for Daniel to tell Carolyn all about his apostasy and his complete disillusionment with organized religion.

"You mean you don't believe in Jesus' divinity?" Carolyn asked, not judgmentally or with any sense of surprise, but matter-of-factly.

"No, I don't. Why do you?"

"Truthfully, I never gave it much thought. I just know that these are the beliefs of the religion I was baptized into when I was a baby, but they have never had any real influence on my life, except perhaps as a kind of moral barometer, you know, feeling connected to the basic beliefs: love for your fellow man, forgiveness, charity, all those things. But I never had any significant religious training, so these beliefs remained on the periphery of my life, important in theory, but not consequential. But I was not aware that Christian scholars were leaning in that direction." Daniel had been showing Carolyn some of the writings from the Jesus Symposium.

Daniel smiled, thinking how less complicated his own life would have been if he had been brought up as Carolyn had. And yet, in a way, he would not have exchanged his experience for anyone's. There was something to be said for that aura of religiosity that had pervaded his entire existence from a very early age. Were these foolish thoughts? Was the comfort he sometimes felt because of his beliefs worth the emotional turmoil that it also engendered? Was it better to have believed and learned the hard way, or would it have been better if he had never believed at all? In order to live life fully, one must be subjected to trials, and experience as many possibilities as one can. If not, how could one come to value truth sought with intellectual probity and humility? Ultimately, he concluded that Carolyn's upbringing was more desirable, if only because so many who had lived as he had would *never* be delivered from foolish credulity. Daniel found himself becoming more and more impatient with those who would explain every development in their lives as a consequence of divine intervention, whether through the intercession of a particular saint, Jesus' mother Mary, the Holy Spirit or whatever came to their minds to help assuage the turmoil of any and all diurnal afflictions, whether minor or major in the impact these matters had on their lives. He found himself mentally cringing when an acquaintance or a complete stranger would tell him that he or she had prayed to the Lord for guidance and the Lord had helped to resolve the dilemma. He knew that people needed this type of reassurance and he did not wish to be judgmental, but still, he couldn't help feeling annoyed at what he simply had to conclude was their stupidity. He valued the wisdom in the aphorism "Live and let live," but he knew that it could never be truly lived out in actuality as long as organized religion continued to exert its tremendous influence on the lives of so many of the world's people. They, indeed, wanted to live as they saw fit, but they would not allow others to live according to their own choices if those choices could not be reconciled with theirs. He would hear them say things like "God talks to me," or "I have a personal relationship with Jesus," and Daniel would not answer for he knew the futility of trying to dissuade those who had made up their minds and would heed no contrary views whatsoever. He wanted to be tolerant of others, to avoid placing himself in the kind of position he so abhorred in those who could not see beyond their defined limitations, and it was a matter of principle with him to respect others' beliefs, and say nothing to contradict them unless he was asked a direct question.

Carolyn was receptive to Daniel's ideas and agreeable to a civil ceremony when they married. He found that he could talk to her so much more freely about his crisis of faith, as he himself would sometimes think of it, than he had ever been able to with anyone else. Certainly with Stephen he had opened up, but it always felt like a battle was being waged. Even with his daughter, he had to tread carefully. Marta just could not understand how and why her father had changed his ideas about religion so drastically. In Carolyn he had found, yes, he was certain of it, another true soul mate. She understood him, intellectually, emotionally, and in spite of her superior intelligence, she was willing to learn from him. He spoke confidently to his lover and her approbation encouraged him to be himself, unreservedly and unafraid, certain that his words were being understood and not taken as the rantings of someone who had lost his mind.

"I hear it over and over again, this personal relationship with Jesus. Born again Christians! There is no doubt that Jesus was an extraordinary man, but he was a man trying to get his fellow Jews to understand that most of the things they did that were directed towards God were totally meaningless. He tried to tell them that they had to change. They were waiting for something that he assured them was there for them already. The Kingdom of God was there, not coming at some future time. They needed to grasp it. He rejected many of the rules and regulations that their religion imposed on them. His message was misunderstood. To the Romans, he was a trouble maker. I'm convinced that it was just an accident of circumstances that he was crucified, not the result of a prophecy fulfilled as we grew up believing. All these events resulted in initiatives on the part of some of his followers, but even there, as a study of the early church reveals, there were conflicting ideas as to who Jesus actually was. There were those who could not believe that a messiah could have been crucified. But man is ingenious in devising and fabricating stories. The problem is that the stories are then taken as truth, when all they really are, are stories, myths, fairy tales. Just examine the history of the Catholic Church down through the ages. If it were really true that Jesus was a ransom for mankind, why have so many people had to die across the centuries to bolster it? Who knows how many, countless lives were sacrificed because of this insanity, especially in that geographic area where it all started! In God's name the killing goes on and on and on. And it is accepted, and they each, each group, justify themselves and their atrocious actions. Is this the legacy of religion? Death and destruction? Is that what God wants from man? It is as though what is preached is forgotten as soon as the faithful encounter opposition to their ideas. And still it goes on."

Carolyn saw how emotionally charged Daniel's words were. He had given her articles to read that she found intellectually challenging. She had some doubts at first about some of the statements he made, but she was glad that he had made her aware of the new scholarship that was transforming the thinking in academic theological circles. The discovery of new ways of thinking about traditionally held beliefs would never transform her life as it had his. For Carolyn, it had never really mattered that much. But he had taken on the burden, for himself if for no one else, of dissolving all the lies, inexactitudes and hypocrisies that had kept his family and his ancestors for centuries before in a bondage they were not even aware they had been coerced into embracing. The fervor with which he spoke to Carolyn caused her to admire and respect him even more.

"It's also evident that Jesus preached that man did not need an intermediary between himself and God. He was actually denigrating the priestly class, but instead, the total opposite of what he talked about was adopted by the Church. And any true history of the Church shows clearly just how abusive the clergy has been throughout the centuries."

Daniel remembered his brother's arguments about the need for a priest in order to administer the sacraments and the importance of the sacraments to help man get closer to God. But even though Stephen had spoken passionately on these subjects, Daniel could only see it as an argument directed to those who already believed. To them it strengthens their faith. For them it makes real sense, just as it makes sense to believe that if you accept Jesus in your heart, he will be with you and comfort you and make you whole. Once this premise is accepted, everything flows from there and the believer gets more and more deeply involved in everything directed towards a position of acceptance, and the least possible questioning. The tactics were the same with every religion. A true believer had to agree to acknowledge and uphold. No deviation is permitted, period! Daniel had been through all this, and he was certain he understood why believers delude themselves into a conviction that they have a relationship with a spiritual being who is not God, but who is needed to get to God because this is what they were taught.

Daniel told Carolyn that he considered devotion to Jesus' mother Mary one of the more preposterous things practiced by Roman Catholics and other Christians as well. This was a belief he found much more difficult to denigrate because of his memories of his mother with her Rosary beads, saying the *Hail Mary's* over and over again. But how many Catholics have any idea at all that Mary was seriously concerned about her son's actions and couldn't understand why he was going about stirring up so much trouble? And then, too, were Catholics ever trusted to be told that Mary had other children besides Jesus, and the idea of a virgin birth itself was something adopted from earlier religions, as so many aspects of Christianity were too?

Over the following weeks and months, Daniel's and Carolyn's mutual love and understanding reached a level unusual for two who had known one another for such a brief period of time. She could very well understand his theory that the creative artist especially—the sculptor, painter, architect, poet or composer—was much closer to God, the creative Spirit, than many who devote themselves exclusively to religion. The re-creative artist, too, the musician, the actor, shared this unique attribute of creative artists in revealing through their art man's ineffable assimilation of the divine that he finds all around and within himself, and of making it tangible for others in a way that no sermon, short of one so poetically conceived as the Sermon on the Mount, ever could.

Fourty-Two

Carolyn Cheruel and Daniel Lorelli were married one year to the day on which they first met. Carolyn wanted a child, and although Daniel was in his mid-fifties, he relished the thought of becoming a father again. Daniel saw how his two children had become totally independent of him. Oh, they respected him, tried to spend time with him now and then, sought advice from him which he gave with reluctance and which they never followed, and made a sincere effort to keep their Dad abreast of their activities. But they were much too involved with their own lives now. They didn't *need* him, and he knew that this was as it should be. And yet, that preoccupation with being needed, of seeing one's children *interested* in every move one makes, this was something he could have a second chance at if he had a child with Carolyn. For Daniel, fathering a child at his age would be a validation of his self-perception as a man who was young *and* virile.

Both Marta and Vincent liked Carolyn and were happy that their father had found someone he could love and have that love returned in kind. Vincent actually saw more of Daniel and Carolyn after their marriage. He was very excited about being able to talk to one who knew so much about medical research, and Carolyn, for her part, hoped to have him join her on the research team she was part of when the time came for Vincent to intern.

Daniel Lorelli had traveled far on his many journeys. He was looking forward to a future filled with exciting and rewarding happenings. His spiritual journey had helped him to resolve his doubts concerning what and what not to believe in. He didn't have all the answers, and he knew he never would, but he felt more secure in his doubt than he had ever felt as a believer. He could no longer be content, confused and docile. To be alive was to explore, to learn new things day after day, to seek knowledge and find truth in places that he had never imagined possible before.

"Carolyn," he told his new bride, "I think I am as happy as a man can possibly be. I am really free now. I no longer feel confined. My thought processes are my own. Even if I thought I was free before, I always had this burden of my past, my family's past, this wonderful but ultimately damaging heritage to keep me from opening myself up to all that I can be, to achieve all that I can achieve and to love without reserve. Please understand when I say this that in no way do I regret or minimize the great and wonderful heritage that is mine. There are so many aspects of my cultural and, yes, even religious background that makes me the person I am, for better or worse."

Carolyn embraced Daniel and looked into his eyes. The magic of her gaze had not changed for him. Their hearts were united as were their souls.

"I know, dear. I understand you. Even if the things that make such a difference to you never affected me in the same way, I'm glad that you showed me all that you've shown me, and made it possible for me to appreciate life in a totally new way."

Daniel's musical journey, too, had brought him great satisfaction. He had achieved much in his career. His talent at the piano had given joy to himself and to many others. He had conducted a number of the world's finest orchestras, achieving results that stood out even amongst the great names of his time. Now the Vienna Philharmonic was beckoning! This would be truly special, conducting the orchestra he had always dreamed of standing before, the orchestra of Hans Richter, Felix von Weingartner, Clemens Krauss and Gustav Mahler. The Vienna Philharmonic, the orchestra of *the city of music*! It had been conducted by Furtwangler and Toscanini. The *Second* and *Third Symphonies* by Johannes Brahms and the *Eighth Symphony* of Anton Bruckner had had their premieres with the ensemble. Then, too, an important appointment was in the offing, and hopefully, before too long, Daniel would have his first truly important permanent position as director of a first rate orchestra of international standing. He also never forgot the promise he had made to himself to compose a work based on the terrible experiences of his great aunt, Maria Saggio. Yes, he could still make his mark as a composer of note.

Daniel's journey on the long arduous pathway of love had found fulfillment too. He had loved and been loved in return. His relationships had been marked by an extraordinary degree of caring and commitment. He saw that it was possible to love, to love again, and still again.

A new century was looming, and perhaps men and women would finally come together and find that their common humanity was so much more important than all the foolish differences that had divided them for centuries. This outlook would insure that man and his basic goodness would, indeed, prevail.

In Carolyn, Daniel had rediscovered a soul-mate, but this did not mean that the others who had touched his heart and stirred his soul were forever gone. Naturally, he didn't know what the future would bring, but in his heart he was sure that he and Annemarie would meet again. And not only Annemarie. Yes, he would connect once more with Marilyn and Carolyn, and he would see Mira; she would be with him once again too. Of course he could not know what the circumstances would be, but he felt certain he would see them again, as well as Violetta and Vincenzo, his beloved parents.

And Daniel *was a believer* after all, even if he did believe differently from others he was close to in his life. As long as love is the criterion, he felt, all beliefs are compatible. He would never adopt a position of infallibility about the possibility of living again, even if he himself was convinced it could be the only way of believing about life after death that made sense rationally. He realized that other humanists considered that belief as absurd as a belief in heaven and hell, but he had a profound conviction about it based on a strong intuitive sense that sparked his spirit. Thus, Daniel continued to be driven by and to take comfort from those very familiar words at the end of the *Resurrection Symphony*:

"O believe my heart, believe, nothing of you will be lost! What you longed for is yours, what you loved and strived for is yours. You will rise, yes, you will live again."

About The Author

Roméo Mannarino was born in Brooklyn, New York of Italian immigrant parents. He attended New York City public schools, going on to earn graduate degrees at New York University and the City University of New York. Working first as a teacher and then as a classical distribution company executive, Mr. Mannarino gained valuable experience in both fields. He established Roméo Records in 1999, thus far issuing 28 releases of primarily classical music. He has written poetry and songs, some of which have been published. This is his first novel. Mr. Mannarino has traveled extensively and continually over the years in the United States and Europe. He is married and has two daughters, a son and seven grandchildren. Mr. Mannarino lives with his wife, Rita in New York and spends summers in Calabria

Printed in the United States
24213LVS00002B/208-219